THE DRAGON SISTERS

by

Virginia Fox

Dragonbooks

About the author

From an early age, Virginia Fox, born in 1978, has been fascinated with written texts in any shape or form. After soaking up countless books and writing various essays and short stories, she has now embarked on her biggest project yet: The Dragon Sisters Trilogy, a set of real life stories from Switzerland (with the addition of some not-so-real characters).

Virginia lives together with her daughter, an Australian Cattle Dog and a moody tomcat in Zurich. Whenever she is not writing her books, she is busy living her second passion: training horses.

THE DRAGON SISTERS

by

Virginia Fox

Translated from the German edition by Holger Laux.

Book 1

Dragonbooks

For Fey Raven Angelina, you made this book possible…

1

"Go, go, go! Don't let me down, you old banger!" Kaja was swearing and gave the throttle a desperate push. But with one last groan, her little grey Peugeot came to a halt and went completely silent. Zorro, Kaja's three-year-old husky-Alsatian cross, was yapping excitedly.

"Zorro, be quiet! I don't need you making a racket as well. Can't you see I'm at the end of my tether?" Kaja was losing her nerves. 'What's wrong with Zorro?' she thought, suddenly realising that the dog had not calmed down since their hasty departure. He had been yelping excitedly all through their journey. It didn't make any sense to Kaja. Of course she was stressed and exhausted, but Zorro had always been by her side and should be used to her chaotic lifestyle - this was not likely to be the reason. She slumped back into the seat and used her hands to rub the tension from her face. Zorro took the opportunity to push his wet nose into her ear to get Kaja's attention. "What's up, big boy? Do you want some of my cereal bar?" Automatically, she had grabbed her emergency food, a chocolate cereal bar - it was her strong conviction that chocolate was less unhealthy if consumed together with cereals - and devoured a large bite of it while also offering some to her pet companion. But to her surprise, the dog ignored the delicacy he normally couldn't resist. Instead, he started to whimper again. Kaja watched Zorro with increasing concern, suspecting that something might be wrong with him, but she had no idea what it might be. Then she suddenly remembered her current situation and got distracted.

"No need to get upset, my furry little friend. She can't see me, although I hope that's going to change soon."

These words did little to calm Zorro down and he snarled: "What do you mean, she cannot see you? She can see me, can't she? And she can understand me, at least most of the time."

"But she is not listening to you right now. Her head is full of other things and she is not ready to pay attention." The dragon seemed to fill the whole interior of the car. Zorro howled again at Kaja in a desperate attempt to make her aware of the monster but then curled up as close as possible to the door and as far away as possible from those shiny blue scales.

In the meantime, Kaja tried to calm down. She knew she had to assess her situation rationally, otherwise she would have started to scream her head off. Here she was, in the middle of nowhere in southern France, left with only three cereal bars and a dog that had obviously gone mad. The good news was that her grandma's village was only 3 miles ahead. The bad news was that she did not feel fit enough for a long walk after a sleepless night and a long drive. To add to her misery, a fine drizzle had started falling out of the grey clouds that are so common for that part of the country. But she had no choice. Sitting here in the car was no real alternative. Kaja stuffed the last of her emergency food into the baggy holdall she had packed hastily that morning. She had no idea whether it contained any protective clothing against the rain, but she had a feeling this was one of the things she had left behind. She only knew for certain that Zorro's food, bowl and blanket were among the items she had packed. It brought a smile to her face: "At least the dog is well looked after." She pulled her hoodie up and put another jacket on. Taking a deep breath, she opened the door and pulled the holdall from the passenger seat. Zorro shot across the centre console and out of the open door. Kaja, venting her anger at the tatty Peugeot, slammed the door shut.

"Ouch!"

Kaja's head whipped round: "What was that? Zorro, are you OK?" The dog started to jump up on her, excited and convinced that she would finally see their stowaway - but he was wrong. Kaja just ruffled his ear and said: "I must be tired. I really thought I heard you talk just now." Absent-minded, she put the holdall on the car bonnet and started searching for some rain protection.

The dragon flashed a mischievous grin at Zorro who angrily returned the look. "I told you, Cutie, she'll take her time to recognise me."

Zorro snapped: "Don't call me Cutie. And besides, what are you shouting 'Ouch!' for if you know she can't hear you?"

"She caught my tail in the door, remember? Even we dragons appreciate some courtesy now and then." the dragon protested.

"What's the point?" the dog replied, "You got out anyway."

"Right, I am a higher form of energy and don't need any doors - but they are quite a convenient invention. And once I am prepared to use one, it is rather uncomfortable getting it slammed in my face." the dragon kept complaining and put on a moody look. Zorro had now definitely enough of having a silly conversation with this shiny blue creature. He decided to follow Kaja's example and ignore the dragon for now.

In the meantime, Kaja had finished searching her bag, with unsatisfactory results. The rain was getting heavier and all she could do was to zip her jacket up right to her chin and remember the old adage that rain makes you beautiful. "Whoever came up with that nonsense must have been one of those obnoxious eternal optimists." she moaned to herself. "I'd rather be ugly and dry right now." But despite feeling miserable, she suddenly had to grin. Come to think of it, she was much better off now than during all those weeks back in Zurich. Nobody was putting her under pressure, telling her to hurry up and mind the next deadline. The air was full of moisture, the smell of humid soil, wet grass and fresh summer herbs and Zorro seemed to have calmed down. Her mood improved considerably. She threw the heavy, old bag onto her shoulder and whistled for Zorro who hadn't wasted a second following a scent and digging for one of the numerous wood mice living in the grass verge by the roadside.

"Come on, Zorro, let's go to Mémé. She's got lots of mice for you in her garden." Kaja was walking along the road. She had started calling her grandma Mémé when she was a little girl. 'Grandmère' had just been too difficult for her to pronounce and so she had stuck with Mémé to this day. Zorro took a last, wistful look at his current mouse hole and then hurried up to his mistress. On the way, he did find enough time to growl again at the hated dragon who was also getting ready to follow them. Apparently, they would have to put up with that monster for a little while longer.

2

Kaja and Zorro had barely walked a few yards, when an old Renault came round a bend half a mile ahead. For a moment, Kaja wondered whether she should flag it down and ask for help, but then decided against it. Now on her way, she was looking forward to the little walk. She was scanning the horizon, trying to remember how far it was until she reached the start of the footpath across the fields. The Renault had already gone past them, but then slowed down and went into reverse to catch up with them again.

A window was wound down and a deep voice said incredulously: "Kaja, is that really you?"

Surprised to hear her name, Kaja stopped and turned towards the car. She had to use one hand to restrain Zorro by his collar, preventing him from running across the road. "Do we know each other?" Kaja said in French and used her other hand to wipe the rain from her face to get a better view. The man in the car was tall and had dark hair and yellow eyes. Somehow, he appeared too big for the little Renault.

With a beaming face, he waved her over, saying in a broad Thurgau dialect: "Of course I know you, Ragamuffin. Have you forgotten about me?"

Hearing her old nickname, Kaja's face lit up: "Tim! What are you doing here?"

As a teenager, she had spent all her holidays with Mémé, glad to escape the boarding school routine in Davos and just as glad to enjoy a home that her parents apparently never missed. Being in the diplomatic service, they had been - and still were - constantly on the move, either on business or on holiday. A daughter was not really part of their career plan. However, thanks to Mémé, Kaja still had an enjoyable childhood. She grew up believing that this was normal. And Tim, originally from Lake Constance in Switzerland, had always spent his long summer holidays together with his parents and his three older sisters at their holiday home, which was just a stone's throw away from Mémé's house. She had teamed up with Tim for numerous adventures and mischief that usually drove his older sisters mad. Kaja, often dirty and dripping wet, did not behave at all like a nice little girl should, which earned her the nickname "Ragamuffin".

"I'm just looking after our old house. We haven't been here for a long time and the last time we came, it was only for a few days. The garden and the vineyard are a mess and, well, the internal walls can do with a lick of paint, too. The whole place needs a makeover. Last week, I already did some repairs to the roof." Tim said. "But why have you suddenly turned up here? This morning, picking up some fresh eggs, I spoke to Mémé. She didn't say anything about you coming." he asked. Tim used to feel just as comfortable with Mémé as she did with his family. He also got used to calling her Mémé instead of Josephine, which was her real name. Kaja was not surprised that he was still in touch with her. - At least that seemed to be the case when he was here in France.

"She doesn't know I am coming. It was quite a... shall we say: spontaneous decision." Kaja suddenly seemed evasive and tight-lipped.

Tim noticed and decided not to press her any further for now. Instead, he made a friendly offer: "Shall I give you a lift? I am just on my way to Luc and could tell him to tow your car away. I presume it's not by choice that you are braving the rain?" Luc ran the only garage in the area and was a real character, with long grey hair and a thick beard. There was nothing he could not fix, no matter whether it was a tractor, an electric cooker or, as happened regularly in their childhood, a bicycle - you could trust Luc to get it going again. And now Kaja remembered that the old codger also had an open ear for human problems. He never said much, but those one or two sentences he eventually mumbled were enough to make you think. They helped to put problems into perspective, turning them into less insurmountable obstacles. 'Of course,' Kaja thought, 'I forgot about Luc. Why not have a whiskey with Luc one day? But first I want to see Mémé.'

"Ground Control to Kaja." she heard Tim say.

"Sorry, Tim. My thoughts were somewhere else." Kaja apologised.

"So I gathered." Tim grinned. "What's up? Do you want that lift?"

"Thanks, that's very kind of you, but I think I can do with a walk right now. And Zorro - you haven't met him yet - will be more than happy to stretch his legs after the long drive and scare the local mouse population on the way. But it'd be great if Luc could pick up my car. I'll pop round to his garage tomorrow and ask him what can be done to cure the old banger." she explained.

"OK, no problem. I am sure we'll see each other over the next few days. We could meet up for a beer, if you like. By the way, you look just like in the old days, dripping wet as you are, Ragamuffin!" Tim joked, "Ciao!"

Kaja could not help a grin: "That's booked. Looking forward to it. See you then." She watched him starting his engine and driving off. "Exciting" Kaja said to herself. "It must be ages since I last thought of Tim. And now he is in front of me and it feels just as if we had seen each other yesterday. I had almost forgotten that people can be so easy-going and helpful, eh Zorro?" She turned round and whistled for Zorro who had occupied himself again with digging.

Against his usual habit, he stopped immediately and ran up to her, although not without barking at the thin air. "You're acting weird. There's nothing wrong here, is there? Come on, let's visit Mémé." Kaja said to Zorro.

Zorro was barking back: "You call that giant blue monster nothing? I give up - you really don't seem to see it!"

"Stop it, Zorro! Be quiet now." his mistress was losing her temper. Frustrated, Zorro turned ahead and immediately picked up the scent of a hare by the wayside.

The dragon followed this banter between Kaja and her four-legged friend with amusement. It looked like Kaja would take some time before she was ready to pay attention to all the things around her. Never mind, time was not of the essence.

He followed them with big strides and decided to wait and see what would happen next.

3

Kaja stopped on top of the hill and looked down towards her grandma's house. It nestled between a small vineyard and a stream. Smoke was rising from the chimney stack and was immediately blown into all directions by the wind. The rain had eased off a bit. She took in a deep breath of humid air, closed her eyes and turned her face into the cool wind. Lost in thought, she scanned the width of the small valley and thought: 'This is such a nice place - I had almost forgotten about it.'

Over the past few months, she had postponed the visit to Mémé several times. Why? Somehow she had been caught up in an urban career treadmill, living with the illusion that her presence was indispensable to the current project. Kaja fell into a bitter laugh: She had learned the hard way what it meant to be indispensable. And all this only because she had been stupid enough to trust Frédéric. In frustration, she tightened the grip on her bag and banished any thoughts of that cheat from her mind.

"Zorro, come here. It's not much further now. I am sure Mémé has got some goodies for you." she called for her dog. Zorro emerged from between the grapevines. He was covered in mud from the rain-soaked ground. "Oh dear! What happened to you? You look like you need a dipping in the stream." Kaja laughed, "Come on, let's go."

The small group moved on, Zorro happily wagging his tail next to Kaja and, unnoticed by the young woman, the dragon trotting behind.

When they reached the house, Kaja put down her holdall on the old wooden bench next to the door and tried to carry out her threat of dragging the dog down to the stream. "Zorro, don't make such a fuss. Get in here." She gave him a hefty push into the water and, holding his collar with one hand, used her other to wash the sand and clay from his coat and paws. Finally she was satisfied with the result and released the struggling dog. It took him just one leap to get out of the water before running towards the house. There, he got up on his hind legs, pushed the door handle down with his paws and squeezed inside.

Kaja followed him into the house and immediately felt at home again. Mémé came out of the kitchen and welcomed her: "There you are at last. I've been waiting for you. What is this? You brought two extra visitors?"

"Salut Mémé. Why? It's only me and my little rascal here." she answered and gave the lady an affectionate hug "I met Tim on his way to the village. He and Luc will pick up my car later. What do you mean: You have been waiting for me?" she wondered.

Mémé hesitated for a moment before realising that Kaja did not have a clue about the dragon being with her. She subtly shook her head. Kaja had always been a fairly rational girl, rushing through her life and never wanting to know anything about intuition. Very well then, she did not intend to alert her to something she was apparently not prepared to see.

"Just behave yourself." she hissed at the dragon, "I'll put a bowl of milk for you in the window. Be content with that for now."

"Mémé, what are you doing? Talking to your resident spirits again, are you?" her granddaughter teased her.

"Mind your language, young lady. You are still my little granddaughter and it is up to you whether to believe in ghosts or not. But this is my domain and you'd better talk about them respectfully. I can't have them being upset and getting into mischief. Is that clear?"

"OK, understood." Kaja laughed the lecture off and raised her hands in surrender. She knew how sensitive Mémé was about her rituals. Her grandmother was considered a wise woman in the village and far beyond and her healing powers were much appreciated. In addition, she made the best scented candles in the area and sold them at the village market every Friday. They were popular as tourist souvenirs but also appreciated by the locals who knew the beneficial effects of the pure essential oils she used as ingredients. As a child, Kaja had watched Mémé making them for hours on end. And when she got older, she had spent many a rainy afternoon preparing herbs in order to extract precious oils, mix wax from paraffin and stearin and mould the candles. During Christmas time, they also made soft smelling candles from beeswax, working together in intimate silence or listening to Mémé's voice telling old fairy tales. But she used to keep her distance from everything else her grandmother did. It was bad enough being called "the witch's daughter" at boarding school. Looking back now, she was not even sure what made the other kids call her that. Perhaps she had just mentioned something in passing about her summer holidays. Anyway, it had taught her to be more careful and only to tell innocuous stories from then on. And she also decided she would no longer talk to Mémé about anything you cannot see or touch.

"So, how did you know I was coming? I only knew once I was sitting in my car." Kaja insisted. Although she could not care less about such things for herself, she was always surprised at Mémé's sixth sense.

"You do know that we have a strong telepathic link, don't you. If only you switched on your antennae now and then..." She did not finish the sentence, knowing that her granddaughter was not prepared to listen. On the other hand, the dragon appeared to be here because of Kaja. "Lots of fun ahead." she said quietly to herself. But to Kaja, she said aloud: "Time for a proper welcome. I made your favourite cake and the kettle should be boiling by now."

She led the way into the kitchen and Kaja followed her. They both had to duck to avoid the drying herbs, strung in sorted bundles from a wooden beam in the ceiling. The kitchen was the focal point of the small farm house. The floor was made of carved granite slabs which created a

17

nice visual contrast to the wooden furniture. In the centre, there was an ancient wooden table scarred all over by many years of use. Various nicks and pale stains were reminders of Kaja's artistic inspirations and her first attempts to slice bread using a big knife. The evening sun, now daring to show itself again, sent its last rays through the old double-hinged window with its wooden glazing bars, painting glowing patterns onto the walls. The small CD player in the corner was softly playing some classical music. Kaja suspected it was a piece by Mozart but was not sure. She liked listening to classical music but was rarely able to identify it. Zorro had already curled up in front of the open fireplace.

She took a place at the kitchen table and started to stroke Ria, Mémé's snow-white cat who squinted majestically down at the dog. Ria had replaced a tabby tomcat called Fighter who had ruled and terrorised the whole farm with his rowdy behaviour. When Kaja was little, he used to follow her like a shadow. He accompanied her on her tours of exploration round the farmyard and slept in her bed at night. Unfortunately, he lost a fight with a stray dog that he was adamant should not be tolerated in the old barn. Kaja had been inconsolable. For a long time, she did not want to hear anything about a new cat. Until one day during her summer holidays she stumbled across a small, white, lonely ball of fur. Mémé helped her nurse the little kitten back to health. However, Ria seemed to be more fond of Mémé and was most certainly her cat. 'There's nothing you can do about it.' Kaja thought, 'Cats choose their masters and that's that. Perhaps it's better for her anyway. I haven't been around much over the past few years.'

"What kind of tea would you like?" her grandmother's voice came from a cupboard above the kitchen sink.

"Perhaps orange blossom. It'll calm my nerves." Kaja replied without thinking twice.

Pleasantly surprised, Mémé turned towards her and said: "Oh, you do remember a few things I told you about herbs."

In mock desperation, Kaja replied: "It's not my fault my brain memorises everything I hear." and then she went into a giggle.

At least, this ability had helped her to get through school and university with minimal effort. But once she was thinking about her studies, she soon remembered the job she had taken on afterwards and the problems it had caused her. Immediately, her mood turned. Nervously, she drummed her fingers on the table top sending the CD player into a spatter before it stopped playing altogether. Mémé, who had just poured hot water over the herbs and was about to put the steaming teapot on the table to brew, looked up, her eyes wandering from Kaja's grim face to the electronic device and back.

"What's the matter, my dear? Who made you so angry?" she wanted to know from her granddaughter.

"Nobody, why are you asking?" Kaja answered evasively, "Oh, thanks for the lovely tea."

"Don't you avoid me, young lady. Stay on the subject and at the table." Mémé said as Kaja was about to get up to fetch the tea cups. "Seeing your face and watching my brand-new CD player die - don't even try to convince me everything is OK." She turned round to get two cups from the cupboard.

Kaja tried to calm her features and put on an innocent face but failed miserably. So she buried her head in her hands and took a deep breath: "Yes, Mémé, you're right. Nothing is OK and I'm going to tell you everything. But, if you don't mind, I don't want to do that right now. For the moment, I would just like to enjoy your company and your cake, if that's possible."

Shocked by the desperate tone in Kaja's voice, Mémé went over and ran her fingers through the girl's hair. "Yes, of course it is. Take a rest. Here, have a piece of poppy seed cake. We can talk about it tomorrow." and after a while she said teasingly: "I do live in hope you may be around for a few days."

Kaja was grateful for the piece of cake offered to her and took a big bite. She suddenly realised that she had only been living on cereal bars all day. No wonder her stomach was rumbling. Finally, her tension subsided. The hot infusion worked its calming effects and she leaned back on the chair in order to stretch her long legs under the table.

19

Mémé was the first to break the silence: "You mentioned Tim earlier on. Where did you meet him? And what's wrong with your car that Luc needs to have a look at?"

"Oh, my car." Kaja sighed. "If only I knew. It just stopped. Luckily, we didn't have very far to go. It happened just before the last big bend in the road coming from the east. Tim came past by chance and instantly recognised me. So he stopped and offered to help."

She had to smile thinking back to their brief encounter. How long was it since they had last seen each other? Was it eight or nine years? It didn't matter.

But aloud she said: "Anyway, it is a nice co-incidence that he is here as well right now. He said he was going to ask Luc if he can tow my car away. I think I'll go round to his place tomorrow to see what he says." she finished her report.

"While you are at it, you might as well take the CD player you broke. Perhaps he can fix it, too." Mémé responded.

Kaja grimaced. Oh my, not this again? In her teenage years, lots of electronic devices had fallen victim to her tantrums. Light bulbs had exploded and other things broken down, at least temporarily. Later, she had learned to control herself, but more recently she felt increasingly like a pressure cooker ready to explode. This was also the reason why she hated mobile phones. These things were guaranteed to fail when you needed them.

She got up to fetch her bag which was still sitting on the bench outside. "I'll just go and feed my little monster." she said to Mémé. Zorro knew exactly what she meant, jumped up and followed her keenly into the hallway, to the outside and back into the kitchen. Kaja laughed: "You old scallywag. Don't miss a trick, do you." She filled one bowl with water, another one with dry food and put them both on the floor next to his usual place.

Mémé had to smile watching the two. Communication between humans and animals could be so easy, as long as the humans were prepared

20

to watch and listen. But no, the human mind is much more complicated than that. An animal is not allowed to be an animal any more. A dog has to be a person and supposedly needs an expensive psychologist or other kind of "whisperer" in order to interact successfully with its desperate master.

Kaja turned to Mémé and said: "I'll go upstairs and have a shower now. Do you need any help with preparing dinner later on?"

"That would be nice. If you take care of the food, I can finish the candles I started making this morning."

"OK, let's do that. I'd better leave Zorro downstairs. He likes to be with you in the workshop anyway."

A few years ago, Mémé had converted the old lean-to shed into a workshop. It used to be a simple wooden shelter to store hay and wood in, but she had it re-built in bright, natural wood cladding that was just starting to weather slightly. The south-westerly aspect included a large set of windows that made the room feel light and airy. If the sun shone too hot in the summer, awnings could be extended to provide shade. Mémé stored her wax and the finished candles underneath in a vaulted cellar. This allowed her to carry on working whenever she wanted to, without the need to clear everything away at night in order to make room, like she used to in the kitchen, in the old days.

Feeling refreshed from her shower, Kaja came downstairs half an hour later and inspected the fridge. She found dried meat and locally produced ham, as well as some crème fraîche, three unpeeled potatoes and a few eggs. These seemed to be the perfect ingredients for a large omelette. To her right-hand side, there was a door leading to the larder where she managed to find carrots and onions.

While chopping the onions, she melted some butter in a pan. Once finished, she added the onions and sautéed them on low heat. In the meantime, grabbing a pair of scissors, she went outside. In a small patch to the south of the house, Mémé grew herbs for cooking. This was convenient because she always had fresh ingredients available. Kaja was looking for thyme, oregano and a bunch of chives, cut off as much as she needed and, heeding her grandmother's advice, briefly said thanks to the spirits of nature.

Back in the kitchen, she chopped the herbs and added them to the onions to braise them slightly. In the meantime, she peeled the potatoes and diced them into small cubes. "Why didn't I do this first?" Kaja grumbled to herself, "Now I'm running out of time." She quickly sliced the ham into thin strips and whisked the eggs. Altogether, she tipped the mixture into the pan and kept stirring while she peeled and grated the carrots.

Zorro suddenly stormed into the kitchen and tried to steal a surplus piece of ham from the table. Kaja did not think twice and threw the wooden spoon she had in her hand in the dog's direction. Zorro, already used to the routine, managed to snatch the meat and hide under the table just in time for the spoon to miss him.

"I see you still haven't got your little rascal under control." Mémé's voice came from the hallway.

"I don't know what to do - I can hardly ask him politely to stop it, can I? In fact, I tried to and he took no notice." she answered slightly irritated. "While you are laying the table, I'll do the dressing for the carrot salad. Do you have mustard in the kitchen? I couldn't find any." Kaja asked.

"I'll get it for you. It's in the earthenware pot next to the tinned food." Mémé placed the pot with the coarse mustard next to her granddaughter and laid the table. While Kaja was preparing the salad, she dished out the scrambled egg onto two plates. Kaja decorated the salad bowl, placing the dried meat and the crème fraîche in the centre, and sat down next to her grandma at the table.

"This is absolutely delicious." Mémé complimented her.

These were the last words to be heard for some time. Together, they ate in companionable silence, enjoying a simple, healthy meal. After they finished, Mémé brought Kaja up to speed with the latest village gossip that had happened over the past year. In the meantime, Kaja cleared the table and put the plates into the kitchen sink.

"Leave them there." Mémé said in between her stories, "I'll do the washing up later, since you did the cooking."

"Fair enough." Kaja said and helped herself to another slice of cake, "Do you want a piece as well?" she asked Mémé while making fresh tea.

"No thanks, but a cup of tea would be nice."

Kaja poured two cups of the aromatic brew and put them on the table. After fetching the teapot and her piece of cake, she dropped back onto the chair. Making herself comfortable, she sighed: "Ah, I needed that. I do like cooking and eating but it's no fun doing it all by myself. Anyway, usually I'm so busy that the only time I can enjoy a meal is when I'm eating out, and that's not the same." Zorro came over from the fireplace and sat down by her feet. In fact, he sat on her feet. Automatically, Kaja started to ruffle his ears, which he obviously enjoyed. When she stopped, he nudged her impatiently with his nose, telling her to carry on.

"OK, kid, I know." and, turning to Mémé, she joked, "He's turned into a right little tyrannosaurus rex. I think I must have spoilt him too much. Perhaps I'll take him for a walk to the old mill. That'll give him some exercise and he can do his business." She got up and grabbed the leash. It was unlikely she would need it but better to be safe than sorry. She gave Mémé a hug - just like in the old days: "We'll talk tomorrow. Tonight, when I'm back, I'll go straight to bed, OK?"

"Of course. Sleep well and sweet dreams."

"Same to you." Kaja followed Zorro, who was keen to get out, to the front door and soon they disappeared into the darkness.

"So." the old lady said after a moment of silence. "Nice to see you can keep quiet and behave yourself. Now tell me: What do you want from my granddaughter? And don't even dare lying to me. Let me get you a drink first."

She got up, filled a glass with milk and added a generous shot of elderberry brandy. Holding the glass in her hand, she sat back down at the table and waited. Suddenly, the room was illuminated by a flickering blue light from which the dragon slowly emerged. With elegant movements, he sat down on the opposite chair and said with a rebellious grin on his face: "Hola Josephine, long time no see..."

4

The next morning, Kaja woke up early. Although the clock had not turned seven yet, she felt more refreshed than she had for many weeks. On the other hand, she had not gone to bed before midnight for many weeks either. And getting away from her daily routine may have been partly responsible as well. For a moment, she considered curling up in her duvet again but then changed her mind. She quickly jumped out of bed, almost tripping over Zorro who was lying on the floor next to her bed still fast asleep. "Come on, get up, lazybones. You can carry on sleeping later." She disappeared into the small en suite bathroom to splash her face with cold water, brush her teeth and tie up her straight dark hair into a loose ponytail. Back in the room, she dug into her holdall for a track suit. After putting it on, she whistled softly to tell Zorro to follow her. While she was sitting on the staircase tying the laces of her trainers, she suddenly remembered that she had heard grandmother talking in the kitchen as she had returned from her evening walk. Did she have some late visitors? Surely she would have told her? 'Well maybe I was just imagining it.' she thought, skipping down the stairs with the dog following her. Outside, she switched on her iPod, put her earphones in and cheerfully fell into a jog.

Just over than an hour later, she returned to the house. She brushed a few stray strands of sweaty hair from her red face and did some stretching to the music of Ulalena, a Hawaiian musical. She had her eyes closed and was so immersed in the music and her exercises that she did not notice somebody approaching from behind. Suddenly, she felt a hand on her shoulder, whipped round and clenched her fist, ready to strike. At the very last moment, she stopped her punch.

Well, at least she tried to.

"Wow, Tim, what are you doing here. - You gave me a shock." she shouted and rushed towards Tim, who was sitting on the ground grimacing with pain and holding his chin.

"Your right hook could win you a title." he groaned.

"It was my left one." Kaja corrected him casually, "But it was your own fault. Why did you have to sneak up on me like that?"

"I didn't sneak up on you." He was pointing to the earphones which were now dangling from her neck, still emitting the sound of music. "I called you three times and thought you must have heard me by then. How was I to know you were suffering from blocked ears?"

"Oh, it can't be that bad if you are well enough to joke again." She reached out and pulled him up from the ground. Once he was standing there and had let go of her hand, her palms started tingling. 'What's the matter with me?' Kaja thought. 'This is only Tim, the Tim I have known for such a long time and who still calls me Ragamuffin.' She suddenly became aware of her appearance and her face turned a tinge redder than it had been already. 'I wish I didn't look as if I'd come out of a puddle each time I meet this man. - This man? Goodness, I really need a cold shower if I suddenly think of little Tim from next door as a man!'

Tim, on the other hand, had taken a quiet look at Kaja and was rather impressed with what he saw. In that track suit bottom and the sweaty long-sleeved t-shirt you could make out a figure that was undoubtedly feminine but nevertheless sporty. Ragamuffin had grown up, it seemed.

Kaja's voice interrupted his highly agreeable thoughts. "Did you want anything in particular or was your highness just trying to scare innocent damsels?" she asked, deliberately leading the conversation to a more harmless subject by referring to their childhood games of Knights and Maidens.

"Uh." Tim needed a moment to compose himself. "I wanted to collect some eggs like I usually do in the morning. Luckily, I didn't have them with me when I bumped into you." he grinned. "It would've been quite a mess. - I wanted to ask you if you feel like coming for a drink with me tonight?" Kaja had to laugh at the expectant look in his face.

"Yes, of course. But first I'll have to go round to Luc's and see what's up with my car."

"Good, so we have a date. I'll pick you up at five."

"OK. I'll get your eggs." Kaja said and disappeared round the corner into the chicken-coop. When she came back, she had three eggs in her hand. "Are three enough for you? I don't know all the hens any more, so I only took the ones from Gris-Gris, Alma and Elsa."

Once, she had tried to take eggs from hens she did not know: Just once and never again! The scratches on her hands had taught her a rather bloody lesson. Ever since, she preferred to ask Mémé to introduce her to any new hens first and to explain their habits. This worked very well, even if she was not around as often as she used to be. She had no idea how other people's chicken-coops worked, but she suspected that only Mémé kept such little divas in hers.

"Yes, thanks. More than enough. See you tonight."

"Ciao." Tim turned and left.

Kaja watched him for a moment, lost in thought. She then whistled for Zorro, who had made himself comfortable in the shade of a tree. She went upstairs, took a shower and changed. When she came out of the bathroom, she saw Zorro snarling at her pillow. "Zorro, you stupid dog. That's only my pillow!" She took her duvet and pillow and shook them vigorously out of the window. The dog jumped up at the window and barked triumphantly at something he apparently saw outside. "That's enough now! If you have too much energy, you might as well go outside."

Resolutely, she grabbed the dog by his collar, led him downstairs and sent him outside. Still barking, he disappeared round the corner. Kaja shook her head and went back inside.

"I've won. I've won." Zorro barked excitedly and circled the dragon who grumpily climbed out of the nettles growing underneath Kaja's window.

"Yeah, yeah." he grumbled. "But you are banned from her room as well, if I am not mistaken. Otherwise you wouldn't be out here. And I am better off because I won't need anyone to open the door to let me back in. Hehe!"

"Neither do I." Zorro protested. "Opening doors is child's play for me. Only Kaja gets a bit upset when I do it."

"Well, tough luck for you. I'm off now." The dragon shrugged his shoulders and disappeared through the wall into the house. Puzzled, Zorro stared at the spot where the dragon had sat a moment ago. Where had he gone? Anxiously, he started to sniff about. But luckily he got distracted by the fresh scent of a vole, otherwise he would have kept on racking his brains.

In the meantime, Kaja returned to her room. Just as she was tidying up her bed, she found her mobile phone lying right in the middle of it. 'That's strange.' she thought. 'I am sure I put it on the bedside table.' She picked it up and saw the display flashing: Five missed calls and four messages. At first, she did not want to know. Wasn't this why she had switched it off yesterday? She played with the phone in her hands, trying to decide what to do. Finally, curiosity got the better of her. Now the phone was switched on, alerting her to the messages, she might as well listen to them. She keyed in her mailbox number and her thumb was already hovering over the enter key when she hesitated. Then she changed her mind and decided not to let it spoil her buoyant mood. She flipped the phone shut and switched it off completely before casually dropping it onto the bedside table. Then she went downstairs.

5

Kaja found her grandmother in the workshop, where she was assembling gift sets. Her gift sets came in three versions. The most basic one consisted of three different-sized candles in three different scents. The second set only contained one candle, but also a small flask with the same pure essential oil that was used in making the candle and a small earthenware oil-burner with a tea light holder at the bottom. The third set contained a scented candle as well as some bath essence and body lotion in the same fragrance. The wooden boxes were decorated internally with a photo collage showing the various plants needed to produce the relevant oil. This decoration could be retrieved and made into a large postcard. All the sets were complemented with dried original flowers and herbs.

"Good morning, Mémé." Kaja exclaimed cheerfully.

"Morning Kaja. You're up early."

"I've already been for a jog. It's such a nice morning. I was even able to watch the little family of foxes in the forest clearing."

"Oh, they are back then. I haven't seen them yet this year. Can you give me a hand and put the finished parcels into my car? I want to do a delivery run later on. Actually, you can come with me, if you want to. We can buy pains au chocolat and orange juice at the bakery because I've run out of food for breakfast."

"Yes, sounds good. It'll give me the chance to see where you sell your goods. And, I haven't had real French pains au chocolat for a long time." Kaja answered.

She made piles of three gift boxes each, took them to the car and loaded them into the boot. Her grandmother came with the last three she had just finished. "Can Zorro come along?" Kaja asked. "As soon as he realises I'm going somewhere, he's like a shadow. He doesn't want to miss a thing!"

"Of course he can. You get the dog and I'll quickly get changed."

Fifteen minutes later, they left the farmyard and turned onto the main road into the village. Zorro, sitting on the back seat, pushed his wet nose into Kaja's face every few minutes. She had to giggle.

"Stop it, you brat, it tickles!" She pushed the dog back and said to Mémé: "He's been acting strangely ever since we left Zurich yesterday. It's almost as if he's trying to tell me something urgent."

'Well, fancy that.' Mémé thought to herself. 'It seems she's slowly realising something has changed. Maybe the dog will get her up to speed.' And to Kaja, she said: "That's quite possible. You know animals have better senses than us humans."

Kaja was surprised that Mémé stopped after this short statement and did not use the opportunity to add one of her famous speeches about "Recognising the signs in your life and interpreting them" or some such. She shrugged and turned her attention back to the landscape outside. It was not long before the first houses of Aujargues came into sight.

"Do you remember Madame Bouvar? She used to run that grubby little tobacconist in Lunel, together with her husband."

Kaja nodded and she continued: "Well we weren't surprised to hear that he died of a heart attack last winter. Shortly after, his widow closed the tabac and had the windows boarded up. Everyone thought she'd sell the shop and join her sister in Paris, when in fact she was single-handedly refurbishing the place in secret, without anyone noticing. In April she turned up at my house, a completely changed woman, well dressed and wearing make-up, telling me she was going to re-open the shop and that she wanted to include my hand-made candles and soap bars in her range of goods. I was quite surprised. Her shop is one of the nicest and best-stocked in the region and needless to say she has become one of my best customers."

"What's the secret to her success, I wonder? And what else is she selling?" Kaja, who had listened with much interest, wanted to know.

"You'll see in a minute. We're almost there."

They got out of the car and released Zorro from his back seat. The September sun was shining unusually hot out of a cloudless sky. It would have been too hot for him to stay in the car. Mémé asked Kaja to take two of the parcels into the shop and carried another two herself. 'Café des Arts' was written in curved letters above the entrance. They both entered by a glass door. Kaja did not have time to look at the shop windows. But now, being inside, her jaw dropped and she was simply overwhelmed. Madame Bouvar certainly did not do things by halves! The shop windows were in fact empty, allowing passers-by an unhindered view of the shop interior. "Shop" was perhaps not even the correct word for what was more like a gallery. Elaborate paintings in Indian ink and water colour were hung on the walls, separated by yellow and orange lengths of fabric. A clever, indirect lighting system gave the room a bright and airy feel. A large glacier boulder was placed in one corner with one single candle alight at the top, which Kaja recognised as one of Mémé's. The candle emitted the typical local fragrance of lavender and rosemary without being overpowering. Even as a child, Kaja was fascinated by Mémé's candles. Gently and sub-consciously, their scents managed to put you into different moods that made you feel as if you were on holiday. Diagonally opposite the entrance, an archway led into a smaller room, tightly filled with wooden shelf units full of handicraft and other specialities from the region. There was also a small glass counter offering fresh salads, tapas and delicious cakes. Hungry visitors could either buy them to take away or enjoy them in the courtyard under one of the tall sycamore trees.

30

Kaja went up to the pictures to take a closer look. "Mémé" she exclaimed, "These are all motifs from our area. This one here is the old mill by the stream where I went yesterday. And there's the famous cathedral in Uzès. And Luc's garage... Wow, and those over there look like a whole collection of famous sites from all over France. That's amazing!"

"Glad you like my pictures." a voice said behind her. "Madame Bouvar! You didn't paint them yourself, did you? They are absolutely beautiful, so full of detail and yet with a feel of airiness."

"You can call me Alice." she offered Kaja. "Yes, these are my pictures. You didn't expect me to be a painter, did you? No wonder. I used to be a completely different woman when my husband was alive." she sighed recalling her memories. And you could clearly see the relief in her face that times had changed for the better. "Come outside in the garden, I'll make us some coffee."

"How did you get the idea to open a 'Café des Arts'" Kaja asked curiously.

"I'd had the idea for a long time. I started painting when I was much younger and was fascinated by places, buildings and squares, their stories and the people who had shaped them." She hesitated to collect her thoughts. "Well, soon after I got married, I realised that my husband Paul wasn't impressed with my 'paint splashing' as he used to call it. And he was too attached to his tatty old shop to allow me to renovate it. I never even mentioned the idea of incorporating a small gallery. It wouldn't have got me anywhere. For all those years, I kept painting in secret which is why I had to stick mainly to local objects and places. After he died last winter and once I got over the first shock about the huge changes that lay ahead of me, I decided to take the plunge and realise my big dream." Alice continued.

"Mémé says your venture has become a huge success. - What's your secret?" Kaja enquired further.

"I think it comes down to several factors. Firstly, people here have known me for a long time. Some of the older folks found it outrageous at first, me giving the old tabac a complete revamp. But most of them have got used to it by now."

"Weren't you worried they might boycott your new enterprise?"

"I simply ignored them. They were mainly our few regulars who used to chat with Paul while drinking beer all day or playing the slot machines. They couldn't earn us a living anyway back then, so I needed a new clientèle. And my secret recipe", she smiled, "is the fact that I managed to create an attraction for tourists and locals alike. Because my pictures show many buildings and places from our area, the locals can make a connection. Many discover their own home or another place they like in one of my pictures and therefore decide to buy it. Holiday-makers, on the other hand, have a choice between motifs showing famous landmarks or regional landscapes. And I give a discount of ten percent to the locals on everything they buy, including food and drinks. That makes me less dependent on the holiday season and my shop is always packed at lunchtime. Passers-by get curious when they see such a crowd inside. I am planning on closing the shop for two months in the winter and I would like to use the break to travel, relax and continue painting."

For a moment, all three of them went silent enjoying the shadow of those wonderful trees. Each of the women was immersed in her own thoughts and Zorro was sleeping under the table. His coat twitched occasionally when flies pestered him too much.

"That's wonderful!" Kaja sighed. "I admire people who dare to live their dream."

"My dear, you sound frustrated? What are your dreams? You just need a bit of courage and stamina and most of all you must believe in your dreams." Alice said.

"If it were that easy. At the moment, I am not even sure what my dreams were or are..." Kaja fell silent.

Mémé, who noticed that Kaja had perhaps already revealed more of herself than she meant to, got up and said: "We have to be on our way. This was just the start of my delivery round. Many thanks for sharing your story and the coffee."

"Oh yes, thanks." Kaja said with a grateful look towards Mémé.

"I am sure we'll be back sometime, while I'm here."

"You are welcome. It was nice of you to come and to catch up. It's been a long time since we last met."

They stocked up on breakfast supplies and left the shop with two cans of orange juice, a large bottle of water and a bag full of fresh pains au chocolat. Their tour took them to various surrounding villages where, without exception, shop owners seemed to be extremely satisfied with the service. Many of them used the opportunity to place new orders, including several special requests from regular customers. These regulars were mostly local residents, but they also included visitors who spent their holidays here every year and had come to appreciate Josephine's products.

When they left the last shop, Kaja admitted her surprise: "I'd never thought the gift set idea would catch on like this."

Mémé parked her car in the shade of a few trees by the bank of the river Vidourle. They had finished their tour in Sommières, where Josephine used the well-known herb market to stock up on herbs which she either had run out of or did not grow herself. She was well known with the herb dealers and they gave her a warm welcome. Everyone wanted to know how long her granddaughter was going to stay. Although it was a nice feeling to be welcomed in a community, it was quite exhausting as well. Kaja felt as if she had completed a marathon.

"Let's have something to eat here. I'm starving." Mémé suggested. They found a spot that was sheltered from the blazing sun and sat down on a large rock, close enough to the bank to dip their feet into the refreshing water. "That's right." her grandma picked up the conversation, after they had settled down. "It really has become a big success. If business didn't slow down in the winter, I'd hardly have time to keep up with my production. And as I mainly use local fragrances and grow them myself, I can keep my costs down and make a tidy profit. I am not only selling from my home and at the market, but I have a real distribution network. This means I can reach many more people."

"I'm impressed." Kaja admitted. "And I am glad you finally found work to earn yourself a good, secure income."

This had not always been the case. Kaja remembered how hard Mémé used to work in the past. Often she gave advice to local people for free. The market sales had always been rather lucrative, but there were only three local market days in a week and her catchment area was relatively small. Kaja's parents regularly sent cheques in the post to cover their daughter's expenses. But it did not escape Kaja's attention that her grandmother was constantly concerned whether there would be enough money. Unexpected events were especially worrying, such as the storm that had ripped off half of their roof. In such cases, they quickly reached their financial limits. Kaja had always tried to support her grandmother as best as she could, for instance by earning her own pocket money. After completing her education, she regularly bought things she knew Mémé needed or wanted but would never have spent her own money on.

"Yes that's true. With all the orders coming in, I can now plan up to six months ahead. But there's something else I wanted to discuss with you: This whole gift set business was originally your idea. You made the first set for me and a customer discovered it in my workshop. From there, it gained its own momentum. Suddenly my phone wouldn't stop. Everyone wanted to have the sets or even keep some items in stock. This is why I put ten percent of my net profits into your old children's savings account, right from the start."

"What did you do that for? Mémé, you shouldn't have!" Kaja exclaimed. "Everything I know I learned from you and you did all the work. It has nothing to do with me!"

"Of course it has. Without you, I wouldn't have started it. It is your fair share. I always wanted to you to have it." Mémé insisted.

"I have enough money. I don't need yours." Kaja said.

Josephine sensed she would not be able to change Kaja's mind right now, so she replied: "Let's do it this way: We leave the savings account as it is. I'll keep paying you your ten percent and if you ever need any money, you know where it is. If not, at least it will provide you with a good pension." her grandmother joked. "With all the bad news about Swiss pension funds, you might need it one day."

"OK, but you must promise me to use it yourself if you are short of money." Kaja tried to insist.

"I think you still haven't grasped how successful your idea is. If I carry on like this, I will soon need to employ more helpers."

"Oh." Kaja went silent.

Suddenly, they were interrupted by Zorro's angry barking. One moment he was playfully trying to pick up pebbles from the river bed, the next he was darting around in circles as if the devil was chasing him. Josephine had to laugh. The dragon must have got bored and had apparently started to tease Zorro. Of course, the dog fell for the trap and tried to catch him, jumping around in big leaps. Kaja was still trying to figure out what Mémé found so funny when the dragon led the dog to the shore and towards the stone where the two women were sitting next to each other. Zorro was fixated on the dragon who had no trouble slipping away between the two. Josephine moved sideways in anticipation but Kaja was knocked over by the boisterous ball of fur and splashed head first into the water. Gasping and swearing, she appeared back on the surface.

"Zorro, you stupid dog." she shouted. "Where are your eyes and brains?"

In the meantime, the dragon had literally disappeared into thin air and Zorro, dripping wet, with his hanging tail and ears made such a sorry picture that Kaja's anger evaporated immediately. She started laughing and said: "I'm so glad Tim can't see me like this. Yet again I'm living up to my nickname."

Mémé was still sitting on the rock and could hardly breathe for laughing. Kaja splashed her before pulling herself up on dry land. "Come on, let's go." Mémé said. "Luckily this is a warm day and you're not likely to catch a cold."

6

In the afternoon, Kaja groomed her - by now dried-off - dog. He was starting to moult again, a sure sign of autumn approaching. It must be nature's way of preparing him for the polar winter, Kaja had to smile. There was nothing you could do about it, it was the husky genes in his blood. Finally, she was satisfied with the result and released Zorro from the brushing procedure with a gentle slap on the back of his head. Relieved, he jumped a few steps sideways before rolling in the dust with gusto.

"Right, and now give it a good shake." Kaja shouted. As if he had received an order, the dog shook the dust off and then lay down in a shady place as far away as possible from his mistress, just in case she had silly ideas and wanted to continue with her grooming.

Kaja took the dog's brush and comb back to the tool shed. They belonged here. She had deliberately bought a second set so that she didn't have to carry it with her each time they came for a visit. Then she went to her grandmother who was busy in a vegetable patch.

"I am cooking a vegetable lasagne today. Is that OK with you?" Mémé asked when she saw Kaja.

"Yum yum, yes please! But I am meeting Tim at five and might come home very late. I'll just warm some up for myself later."

"Yes, you do that." Mémé answered and was about to continue with her garden work.

"I was wondering if you want to join me for a cup of tea, so we'll have some time for a chat?"

Although Kaja had made the suggestion quite casually, Mémé immediately realised this was important to Kaja. "I'll be with you in a bit. Just getting the veg for our dinner."

"Perfect. I'll put the kettle on." Kaja said and made her way to the house.

By the time Mémé came from the garden, she had already laid the table under the pergola with some left-over cake from yesterday and a refreshing infusion of dried peppermint leaves with a dash of lemon. "I am quickly going to wash my hands." Mémé said showing her soiled fingers. "I'll be with you in a sec."

"Take your time." Kaja responded, passing her time trying to solve a sudoku puzzle.

"So, here I am, finally." Mémé said, sitting down next to Kaja and taking a large sip of tea. They kept chatting about unimportant things for a while until her grandmother asked straight out: "Now come on. What is wrong? What's bothering you?

Kaja took a deep breath and started to talk: "You know, after I finished my course in computer sciences, I started at this software development firm called PC Lux Solutions. I have been there for three years now. At first, I was happy at the company, getting more and more involved in creative Web design. It suited me because I enjoy it much better than strictly implementing other people's programming ideas. However, about six months ago, my company merged with another one called Qubus and this led to some rapid changes."

"Kaja, you didn't get the sack, did you?" Mémé asked anxiously.

"No, I didn't." Kaja tried to calm her down. "Not yet, at least." she added with a bitter laugh. "But let me start at the beginning. What changed most was our working culture. Before the merger, the emphasis was on delivering good results. They had to be excellent, and they certainly were. In return, we enjoyed quite a few privileges as employees. Nobody checked when and where we did our work, there were relaxation rooms on the premises and we had a large degree of input about the way orders were processed. Now they keep us under tight control. You have to do your eight and a half hours - at least, often ten without any extra pay. Management gives us unrealistic deadlines that are impossible to meet, if you want to take a product through sensible and thorough testing procedures as normally required. Every day, they come up with new modifications that often make the previous day's work obsolete."

"I can imagine that must be frustrating." Mémé expressed her understanding. "How do you look after Zorro? I remember you used to work from home a lot."

"I had to make a stand on that one. I told my old boss: Either I was allowed to bring my dog in and take a two hour lunch break to exercise him or I'd quit. My ultimatum worked. One of the reasons was perhaps that I am responsible for a whole area and they couldn't find a good replacement at short notice. He must have put in a good word for me with his superior from Qubus and convinced him that it would work. I have to give him credit for that, but my ultimatum is not likely to help me for much longer, what with all the high-flying new colleagues we now have. We're supposed to show team spirit. Haha, very funny."

Kaja took a sip from her tea and collected her thoughts. "So, where was I?"

"You were talking about your new colleagues." Mémé helped her.

"Right. Everyone was assigned a so-called team buddy, even those of us who had been solely responsible for their own projects up to that point, like me. Well, at first, I wasn't too unhappy. You see, I was paired up with Frédéric, whom I fancied at first sight. In fact, I was stupid enough to fall in love with him, would you believe it?" Kaja sighed.

"There's nothing bad in that. I should be happy for you."

"Hold it right there, my story doesn't have a happy ending. Shortly before Frédéric and I were paired up, an in-house competition was announced. The task was to design a new piece of software for our finance department. It was supposed to be location-independent, obviously with the intention of marketing it externally later on. Normally, I am not into number-crunching and book-keeping, but the system was meant to be Web-based and I had a few great ideas - you might even call them revolutionary - with regards to user friendliness and interface design. So I put my name forward."

Throughout her studies, Kaja had kept her grandmother up to date. She had bought her a computer and introduced her to the internet. This meant she was familiar with all those technical terms and was able to follow Kaja's explanations without problems.

"Soon after, Frédéric and I started dating." Kaja continued. "He was very charming and attentive. But one thing that should have made me suspicious was the fact that he only used to have time for me late in the evenings. I didn't catch on. On the contrary, I was happy that this gave me enough time to finish my work and to look after my dog. He also insisted on keeping our relationship a secret in the company. His reasoning was that they might split us up and assign us to different buddies. And it would have been a pity if we were no longer able to work together, wouldn't it! I agreed to play the game. You know I am not a clingy person who always wants to hold hands, so I didn't have a problem with that. To cut a long story short: After a few weeks, I thought I was in seventh heaven, which is a nice way to describe the female ostrich tactic when it comes to men." Kaja snorted sarcastically. "But it wasn't long before I came down to earth with a bump. The first thing I noticed was that he was constantly asking me to do small, time-consuming jobs for him. His excuse was that he still had to catch up on things from his previous assignment. Being a good girl, I did as I was asked until my boss enquired when Frédéric's documentation on the new desk solution was due. It hit me like a ton of bricks. I didn't even know the project had already started. Apparently, charming Frédéric had told our boss he didn't want to bother me with such a trifle as I was rather busy anyway. This was true in a sense, but it was due to the extra work I was doing for him. As a result, I had missed the most important meetings and was excluded from the most interesting parts of the project. At least, the shock woke me from my sweet dreams and I started to scrutinise our so-called partnership - professionally as well as privately - in more detail. It led me to intensify my efforts for the competition project and I cooled down my relationship with Frédéric. I just managed to finish my entry in time for the submission date. On the evening before I was due to hand it in, Frédéric suddenly turned up on my doorstep, rather late as always, and tried to apologise for his unprofessional behaviour over the past few weeks with a large bouquet of flowers."

"I hope you took the flowers and sent him packing." Mémé commented.

"That's what I should have done." Kaja responded ruefully. "But I was a stupid cow. I felt flattered and didn't want to be seen as a vengeful bitch, so I asked him to come in. We had a few glasses of wine and ended up in bed. So, and now I'm coming to the truly ugly part: When I woke up the next morning, Frédéric had already left and taken with him, as I soon found out, my competition entry. At first I thought my computer had lost the data in a crash, but then I realised that the files had not only disappeared from the pc, my USB stick had also gone walkies. Frédéric not only stole my project, he also destroyed all my documentation." Kaja took a deep breath to calm herself down.

'Luckily I don't keep electrical appliances in the garden.' Mémé thought and asked: "So what did you do? Did you take him to task?"

"Wait, it gets worse. I was furious and stormed into the office to find the bastard. But he wasn't there and his desk looked strangely empty. So I started to work, or at least I pretended to, because I was actually too upset to concentrate. At some point, our section leader called me into his office to inform me that Mr. Scherrer had asked to be assigned to a different team because he was no longer able to work with me. I was shocked. It took me a moment to find enough composure to ask what exactly the problem was? My section leader appeared rather uncomfortable. Nervously, he shifted in his chair before finally answering that Frédéric felt I was stalking him, kept calling him, asking him for a date. Frédéric apparently said he himself could have handled it, but his wife was rather upset. 'It was for your mutual benefit that we decided to disband your team.' he said. 'Me? Stalking him? His wife?' I parroted, desperately trying to make sense of it all."

"Let me tell you, Mémé,..." Kaja's fingers were drumming nervously on the table top. "I felt like I was in the wrong movie or as if I had taken a wrong turn somewhere on my way to work. I was unable to gather any clear thought and only have a hazy recollection how my section leader explained to me which responsibilities I still had. I wasn't prepared to listen. Mechanically, I said goodbye, left his office, collected the most important things from my desk and took Zorro home. All this happened yesterday morning. I came straight to you, just wanted to leave that mess behind." Kaja finished her report.

"That's terrible." Mémé said. Normally, she was never lost for words, but now she did not know what to say. This story was just unbelievable.

"Telling you my story, I now realise that it sounds like an intrigue, like someone - perhaps Frédéric - had planned it well in advance. But how can that be? We'd never met before."

"Hm, you mean you had never met him before. If I understand it correctly, he came with your new partner company? You are right, it sounds very much like a case of industrial espionage or something like that. Most certainly. But on the other hand, perhaps he was just an opportunist. Having got to know you and your good work, he may just have decided to take advantage."

"That's possible as well, but I can't imagine how he would have got all the details so quickly. Anyway, I think I have to stay here for a few days. Perhaps it'll give me an idea what to do next."

"I'll think about it as well." Mémé said. "If not, we can always use a voodoo doll." she joked.

"You know, I had similar thoughts already. As long as it really hurts him... But enough of that. I have to get prepared for my date with Tim.

Just for once I want to look respectable for him." Kaja said.

'Now look at that.' Mémé thought. 'Do I detect a romantic interest in Tim? All the better, as long as she has an enjoyable evening that takes her mind off her worries.' she kept musing. Kaja got up, stacked the plates and took them, together with the cake, back to the kitchen. For now, she left the teapot and cups outside on the table.

7

At exactly 5 o'clock, Tim's car pulled into the farmyard. In the meantime, Kaja had taken a shower and got changed. She quickly ran a brush through her thick, dark hair and took a last look in the mirror. She felt she scrubbed up reasonably well today. Her light brown eyes sparkled under a dark fringe. She had put quite a lot of effort into her make-up. Satisfied with her appearance, she took the jacket from the back of a chair and went downstairs. Zorro had already noticed the visitor and jumped up on him, wagging his tail.

She went over to them and said cheerfully: "I see you two made friends already."

Tim had not seen her coming and turned round when he heard her voice, almost tripping backwards over Zorro: "Wow... I mean... hey." he stammered.

"What's the matter?" Kaja asked surprised.

"Nothing, nothing really, only... well... you look... amazing." he hastened to add while his face slowly took on a blush.

Kaja had to suppress a smile. 'Serves him right.' she thought. 'It's time he realises I am not the little Ragamuffin any more. He looks cute when he blushes.' she thought slightly amused. 'Isn't it amazing what some pretty clothes and a little make-up can do?'

"Thanks." she acknowledged the compliment calmly. "You don't look so bad yourself." Being honest to herself, this was an understatement. Wearing a pair of casual workman's jeans, a striped shirt and Timberland boots, he looked quite attractive. His brown, medium-length hair was combed straight back, except for a few unruly curls that fell cheekily across his forehead. Kaja could hardly stop herself from brushing them off his face. 'What's happening to me?' she wondered. 'Firstly, I should be fed up with men, for the next three hundred years at least. And secondly, this is only Tim, my old childhood buddy Tim. Hello, wake up!' she tried to remind herself.

"I hope you don't mind me bringing Zorro." Kaja said. "It's just that I don't go anywhere without him."

"Do I have a choice, then?" Tim joked. "Hop in, big boy." he said to Zorro, folding a seat forward so that the dog could jump into the rear of the Renault. Zorro happily obeyed and settled down on the back seat.

Shortly after, they reached Luc's garage. "That's the best thing about Luc and his garage: You can always rely on him. No matter whether the world is all changing or coming to an end, this place will stay the same." Kaja remarked with satisfaction.

"Yes, that's true." Tim agreed. "But you have to give it to him: He is always up-to-date with his technology."

The three of them entered the old building and crossed the workshop area. It took a moment for their eyes to adapt to the gloom before they recognised Luc's legs sticking out from under a car. Kaja could never understand how he was able to work in these lighting conditions.

"Hey Luc. I have a visitor for you." Tim shouted.

At first, they only heard him grumbling, but then the man belonging to the legs emerged from under the car and got up with some trouble. "I'm definitely too old to be crawling on the floor." he complained. "But my car lift is on the blink again. Ah, Kaja, nice to see you!" He put his huge arms around her and gave her such a big hug that she had trouble breathing. Then he held her at arm's length and gave her an inquisitive look. "Hm, you look like you've taken the wrong turn, my girl." he said cryptically. "Never mind. If it means you ended up in our parts, it can't have been that wrong." He turned round and shouted over his shoulder: "Come over to the office. I've just made some fresh coffee."

Without another word and without looking back to see whether they would follow him, he disappeared into his jam-packed office. Kaja was perplexed and followed him mechanically. Was it that obvious?

Tim asked: "What did he mean? Do you know what he's on about?"

"Mmh." Kaja replied vaguely.

Luc poured them some coffee, an original Italian espresso which smelled delicious. In certain things, Luc was very particular. Original Italian coffee, authentic American motorcycles, real Irish whiskey, Swiss chocolate... 'Damn.' Kaja thought. 'I forgot to bring some chocolate for him.'

"I've just remembered, I forgot your usual treat of Swiss chocolate." Kaja apologised.

"Hm." the old man mumbled into his beard. "I'll have to take your wheels hostage then." he joked.

"How is my car anyway?"

"Oh, it's up and running again. It just needed a new fan belt and an overdue..." he looked at her seriously. "Listen to me: an overdue oil change. All done. You really should take better care of your car." He clicked his tongue with disapproval.

"Oh, I see." Kaja said sheepishly. "I always forget." She felt like a little schoolgirl being told off by her headmaster. But apparently she was not the only person Luc had this effect on. "How much do I owe you?" she asked.

Tim followed the conversation with much interest while Luc watched

Zorro sniffing about in the office, painstakingly inspecting the chaos.

At first, it appeared as if Luc had missed the question, but then he suddenly said: "I would like to have a candle. Not one of Josephine's, I want you to make one for me." Then he turned to Tim. "Make one for him as well and we can call it quits."

"But I can't. I'm not half as good at it as Mémé!"

"Nonsense!" Luc dismissed her objections. "You've helped her often enough to know what to do."

Kaja tried to say something else but then decided against it. Once Luc had made up his mind, you could not convince him otherwise. "OK, your wish is my command. But don't complain if you don't like it."

"Good." he nodded. "And don't forget the candle for Tim."

"Of course I won't."

"So, that's business done. Now let's come to the fun part." He reached into a cupboard and brought out three clean glasses plus a bottle of old Irish whiskey. "Fancy a drink?" filling their glasses without waiting for a response.

'The last thing I need.' Tim thought. He had not eaten much all day. Kaja looked at him with a knowing grin. They had both been talking in the car about how hungry they were.

"Here we go: Santé!" they clinked their glasses.

Two whiskeys later they were finally on their way to the bar to get some food. Kaja had told Luc she would pick up her car the next morning. They found a bench in a corner and told Zorro to lie down underneath. As Kaja looked at the simple menu, Tim suddenly said: "You do know you don't have to make a candle for me. I have no idea what's got into Luc."

She had no idea either, but one thing was certain: Luc always knew why he preferred something to be done in a particular way. He must have had his reasons. That was why she answered casually: "It's no bother, I don't mind making one for you. While I'm doing one for him, I might as well make two. And if you don't like yours, you'll have a present for your mother."

"No no, I didn't mean it like that. If you make one for me, of course I'll be happy to use it myself."

"I know what you meant." Kaja said and smiled at him. "But now we'd better place an order before that whiskey on an empty stomach knocks me out completely."

They ordered a large salade niçoise and a coke each. Kaja wouldn't have minded a cider but decided to have a non-alcoholic drink in sympathy with Tim who had to drive them both home later on. After they finished eating, Kaja enquired: "Now come on, tell me. What have you been doing? We last met... when was it? Eight years ago? That's ages! I only remember that you had just bought your new photography kit and couldn't wait to get started. Has it been a success?"

"Yep, you could say that. I'm living my dream."

He stopped because Kaja suddenly mumbled gloomily: "Another dream fulfilled, this is becoming an epidemic."

Tim did not understand and could not make sense of the look in her face. "What did you say?"

"Nothing. It's not important. Sorry, I didn't mean to interrupt you. Carry on."

"Well, thanks to one of my father's friends, I was able to join a project about Swedish elks as an unpaid volunteer. It was a lucky break because it was my introduction to wildlife research. But they didn't take me on because of my photography skills, of which I was so proud..."

"They didn't?! But you've always had a good instinct behind the camera. I do enjoy your pictures."

"Thank you very much." he said with a mock bow. "I'm glad you like them. But in the end, it was my degree in biology that secured the job for me. They had lost a member of their team and I suddenly found myself responsible for all the statistical data about the elk population in central Sweden. Today I'm glad it all worked out like that. Photography is only a sideline to my research which helps me to decide where and when I might get the best pictures. Without my work, I'd probably never find the right locations. So I can combine both passions. What more do I want?"

"So you are busy hunting elks with your camera?"

"No, that was only at the beginning. I am now part of a team of scientists that is often consulted if someone wants to set up a nature reserve or reservation anywhere in the world. We establish which species live there, what the population density is and how local people can be included and involved in the plans. It is especially important to make sure that the locals benefit from a nature reserve, profit from it economically. Only if this aspect is covered, will the project be viable and has a realistic chance of protecting the flora and fauna."

"That sounds very exciting and immensely varied. What has been your favourite project so far?" Kaja asked impressed.

"I am particularly interested in the rainforest area of south-western Canada, It has only recently been given nature reserve status. Spirit Bear Island is part of it."

"A spirit bear? I thought you were dealing with live animals?" Kaja chipped in with a puzzled look.

Tim had to laugh: "You heard me correctly. The island was named after the white bears that live there. The natives gave them the name spirit bears because of their colour."

"White bears? Aren't they simply called polar bears?" Kaja enquired.

"No, white spirit bears belong to the family of brown bears. The only difference is that their genetic make-up contains a mutation that gives them a white coat."

"At the risk of repeating myself: I find your work unbelievably fascinating and exciting." Kaja said.

"Most of the time it is, but it can also be extremely exhausting and frustrating if we can't get a project off the ground. Luckily, our team does not have to deal directly with the relevant authorities and politicians, but our work depends on their goodwill."

"I see." Kaja said, pondering. "But you still have your photography to fall back on, haven't you? Or did you put it on the back-burner in favour of biology?"

"No no, of course not. I just integrate it into my research work. It is often an advantage because it livens up our published reports and makes them interesting to a lot more people, even non-scientists. An article is much more likely to be read if it is supported by powerful pictures."

"That's true. It looks like you've found an ideal combination." Kaja agreed. "Do you have any pictures of the spirit bears?"

"Yes, do you want to see them?"

"Of course. I'd like to know much more about your work." she said with genuine interest.

"Unfortunately I don't have any pictures with me, but I'm showing some at an exhibition in Bern at the moment. Why don't you pay our beautiful capital a visit? We could meet and go to the place together. - Well, what do you say?"

Kaja hesitated for a moment. Tim felt slightly disappointed but said casually: "Of course, you can go there on your own. You'll be more flexible about your time and everything."

"Oh, I would like to see them, and preferably with you, of course. You'd be able to tell me all about them." Kaja interrupted him. Staring absent-mindedly at the table top, she missed the relief in Tim's face.

"It's only that my life is in turmoil at the moment and I don't have a clue what's going to happen over the next few weeks. But I'm sure I can spare a weekend. Why don't we fix a date here and now? That'll remind me to keep the day free for you." She took an old-fashioned diary from a pocket in her jacket and looked at him expectantly.

"Well, uhm, I'm not as organised as you are. In fact, I deliberately leave my organiser at home when I come over here so that I can fully enjoy my holidays. Let's do it like this: I'll give you a call as soon as I'm back in Switzerland, OK?"

"Yes, of course, no problem." she agreed and put the diary back in her pocket.

"That's decidedly low-tech." Tim pointed at the diary in her jacket. "I thought you had a degree in IT and you nerds can't live without a PDA, can you?"

Kaja laughed and shook her head. "Do you remember that electronic devices often don't agree with me? My mobile regularly packs up, so at least I want my diary to be safe."

"Since you mention your mobile: Can I have your number, please? Otherwise I'd find it difficult to call you..." he asked.

"Oh - seven - nine..." Kaja started.

"Stop, my... er... as I said I'm on holiday and left my mobile at home, so I can't save your number."

Kaja grinned, pulled out the diary again and scribbled her number on a page which she ripped out and pushed it across the table. "Low-tech still works best." she teased him.

"How do you cope at work? Do you write your programs on a piece of paper by hand? And don't the computers go haywire when you touch them?"

"I do work on a computer, but I frequently run into problems. I've had to make special arrangements with our support team. Normally, I would have to report each problem using a 'ticket' as they call it. This must include meticulous details about the type of service interruption, how long it lasted and, if known, its cause and repair costs. If I had to do that each time something went wrong, I'd have lost my job long ago, for over-stretching the cost centre for our support department."

"So you have special arrangements with them? How did you manage that?" Tim laughed.

"I happen to know that our support boys have a weakness for Appenzell Full Moon Beer. A free crate every month does the trick. - Did... most likely..." Her face had taken on a melancholic expression when she said these words.

"What's the matter with you, Ragamuffin?" Tim wanted to know but only earned an angry look from Kaja. "OK, OK." he raised his hands in surrender but could not help a little grin. "I know, the nickname does not suit you as well as it used to. Especially not today. But I've told you already."

"What have you told me?" Kaja said in her sweetest voice. 'Let him stew a bit. Serves him right for teasing me all the time.'

He cleared his throat. Was Kaja flirting? Damn, he already felt this give-away blush creeping up his neck again. But he couldn't help it. He found her prettier each time they met. Well, if this was a game, he could play it as well, provided it still was a game. "That you look fantastic, not only tonight, but also in your sweaty t-shirt after a jog." His eyes met hers but then slowly wandered down her neckline until they rested on her cleavage where her blouse revealed soft curves. Now it was Kaja's turn to blush. But before she could think of a snappy response, he looked into her eyes seriously again and said: "Don't stray from the subject, Kaja. Please tell me what's wrong with you. You've dropped a few cryptic hints already. I really want to know."

So she told him the whole story, albeit in an abridged version and without mentioning her amorous liaison with Frédéric. It would have been inappropriate, especially since she was starting to feel rather fond of Tim. Sometimes, it was better to omit certain details, you never knew where things were going...

"That's incredible." he said after she had finished. "What are you going to do? I mean, you can't just leave it at that and let this Frédéric get away with it!" he was getting upset for her.

She shrugged her shoulders helplessly: "What am I supposed to do? I don't even know if I still have a job after running away in such a mad rush without telling anyone."

"Hm, in any case, let me know if I can help. I'll be in Switzerland for the next three months. Afterwards, I'm going to Brazil."

"Thank you, I may pick you up on it. What's the time anyway?"

"Almost eleven. Shall we make a move?"

"Good idea, time to go home."

On their short journey, both of them were lost in their own thoughts and neither spoke a word. Soon they reached Mémé's farm. Kaja got out of the car and let Zorro jump out. Then she bent down through the open window to give Tim three goodbye pecks on his cheeks. But at the third one, he could not resist. He gently held her face in front of his and pressed a quick kiss on her mouth. Bewildered, Kaja stared at him, moistening her lips where she still felt the warmth of his. "Thanks for a wonderful evening. Hope to see you again soon." Tim said, put the car in gear, turned round and left.

"Good night." Kaja whispered and watched the car until its rear lights disappeared into the darkness.

'What a cheek.' Kaja thought as she walked with her dog towards the house. 'But somehow cute as well.' Obviously, it was not enough to see Tim as just an old childhood friend.

Outside her room, the dog suddenly started to growl again. "Shush, you're going to wake Mémé." But Zorro was still agitated and kept grumbling under his breath. Kaja shook her head disapprovingly and opened the door. What she saw in her room nearly made her faint. On top of the bed, there was a huge, shiny blue dragon. In panic, she slammed the door shut. 'Whatever Luc had in his whiskey...' she thought in exasperation. Somehow, today seemed to be going on forever. 'OK.' she told herself. 'I'm going to open this door again and everything will be alright.' She took a deep breath and pinched her arm, just to make sure she was awake. Then she swung the door open. But nothing had changed: The dragon was still sitting on top of her bed.

"Hello Kaja." the sound seemed to drone inside her head. 'I don't believe it.' she thought. 'This monster is talking to me. What am I going to do?' Her first instinct was to call Mémé. After all, this was her field of expertise. But then she straightened her chin belligerently. As if she couldn't deal with this beast herself! She plugged all her courage and said aloud: "Now look at that: You can talk and somehow you even know my name. Would you mind introducing yourself?"

"With pleasure: My name is Lance and I'm your personal dragon."

Again, the voice seemed to come from inside Kaja's head. This was weird. Quickly, she collected herself and said firmly: "Good for you Lance, but I'm quite certain I don't have a dragon and I can't remember inviting you into my room." She hoped the hint was clear enough. In the back of her mind, she remembered that creatures from the other world could only enter a room if they were asked in. Or did that only apply to vampires? Never mind, this was not the time to worry about such minor details.

The dragon was about to say something when she stopped him with a resolute gesture. She pointed to the door and repeated: "Lance, get out of my room. Now!" The dragon disappeared with a puff. Kaja was genuinely surprised that this had worked. Perplexed, she was still staring at the empty bed. Then she frowned. Somehow, it had been too easy. Should she speak to Mémé? No, it was too late, she decided. Mémé was most likely asleep and she was quite tired herself as well. She got out of her clothes, slipped into a comfortable night-time t-shirt and pyjama bottoms and crawled under the duvet, where her eyes fell shut immediately.

Mémé was still sitting at the kitchen table dealing with her business correspondence, when the dragon rumbled down the stairs and angrily slumped down on a chair. Mémé didn't even look up: "Well, did she give you your marching orders?"

"Marching orders? If only! She burnt them into my hide with a branding iron. - I'm gagging for an elderberry brandy." Lance complained.

Now Mémé did look up with a mischievous smile on her lips. 'Respect, Kaja.' she thought. 'I didn't think you had it in you.' "That's my girl." she said with pride in her voice. "I'm only surprised that you let this deter you. And she couldn't have branded you without a fire, could she." she joked.

"Haha, I knew you'd find this funny." he moaned. "I thought it'd be a good day's work to make her see me and recognise my name. That is the required ritual for her to accept my existence, as you know. It should make it easier to get in touch with her in the future."

Yes, Josephine knew this all too well. Many years ago, she had experienced it herself. She sighed, half with worry, half in anticipation of where this would lead her granddaughter.

"So you mean you behaved with polite restraint, do you?" she snorted in disbelief.

The huge blue mythical creature said with as much dignity as his kind could muster in such a small kitchen: "Of course I did. It was late anyway. I expected her to be back earlier. What's her business staying out so late? Honestly, Josephine, you should give the girl a serious ticking-off." the dragon blustered with a frown. In the meantime, Mémé poured the drink he had requested and put it in front of him.

"Here you go, enjoy. Firstly, the girl is a grown-up woman and she can make up her own mind when to come home and secondly I have no doubt you yourself are going to do your best to tell her what's right and what's wrong. Now be quiet, I still have some work to do." With that, she turned back to her papers.

8

When Kaja woke up the next morning, she only knew she urgently had to talk to Mémé. But for a moment, she could not remember why. The gap in her memory was filled rapidly when she saw the dragon sitting at the bottom of her bed, talking and fiercely gesticulating at a snarling Zorro. She buried her head in the pillow. There was a dragon in her room and she wasn't even surprised. 'Kaja, you need a shrink!' she told herself. Suddenly she realised that she could not hear the dragon's voice. This was strange because yesterday, she had heard him loud and clear. From under her duvet, she peeped out at the odd pair.

"... nothing bad. Please believe me."

Now, concentrating on him, she could suddenly hear his voice again. Unfortunately, both the dog and the dragon noticed that she had woken up and fell silent like two little boys caught being naughty.

"Oh, you're awake." the dragon commented lamely and hissed at Zorro: "It's all your fault. Why did you have to make so much noise?" The dog tried to snap at him.

"That's enough now. Stop it, you two. If you want to have a fight, you can go outside. Don't disturb me in my room before I've had my coffee."

55

She got up, opened the door and pushed them out. The dragon was taken by surprise, so much so that he followed Zorro meekly, who was halfway down the stairs already.

Kaja closed the door and leaned against it. 'Goodness, what was that? I need a shower to clear my head.' she decided.

After the shower, she put on her tracksuit and was looking forward to having a cup of tea with Mémé before being off on a run. She needed to tell her grandmother about the strange things that were going on in her house. With a spring in her step, she skipped down the stairs. 'Why am I in such a good mood?' she asked herself. But as she turned the corner to the kitchen, she stopped dead: 'Please tell me this is not happening!' Lance had made himself comfortable at the kitchen table and Mémé - yes, Mémé! - was just putting a bowl of milk in front of him, wishing him? bon appétit?

"No way!" Kaja erupted. "Is this a madhouse? Don't tell me you already know each other." Her good mood had evaporated in an instant. "I've had enough of this. Come on, Zorro, walkies!" And off she went. Zorro had to rush after her to avoid the closing door.

At first, Josephine and the dragon were speechless. Then she turned on him and said angrily: "Great, I couldn't have done it any better." Lance rolled up his eyes: "Women..."

For the next twenty minutes, Kaja ran uphill as if the devil was chasing her. From the top of the hill, she looked back into the valley. The fresh air and the sounds of the forest did wonders for her frayed nerves. She fell into a moderate jog and followed the ridge. She knew she had probably over-reacted and had to calm down. But seeing Mémé and this... this Lance on such good terms and Mémé not in the least upset about his presence, she felt betrayed. She felt excluded, as if everyone around her knew what was going on and only she was being kept in the dark. It was nonsense, of course. Mémé was her family and this was the only place on earth she felt secure, come what may. She also had no doubts that her grandmother was well aware of whatever was going on in her house. But still she was hurt. Perhaps because she felt the same way as she had in that disastrous meeting with her section leader. It was the sheer helplessness that had stunned her.

She never wanted to have that feeling again! In the meantime, she had left the forest and was enjoying the warm rays of the morning sun on her back as she jogged the last stretch of her route downhill. Back at the farmyard, she switched the music in her iPod from "The Strokes" to "Café del Mar" and went through her stretching routine while Zorro stretched out in the shade of a tree, still panting. When she had finished and was brushing some sweaty strands of hair out of her face, she suddenly remembered the night before and felt slightly hot when she thought back to Tim's unmistakeable glance. There were a few other moments that had surprised her. She hadn't expected him to make such a quick and almost daring move and was not sure what to make of the development. 'No need to rush it.' she told herself and went inside to take her second shower of the day. 'Let's hope we won't stumble across that dragon again!'

She was in luck: Without being bothered by any shiny blue monsters, she managed to freshen herself up and make her way to the workshop in search for Mémé.

"So, are you back to normal?" her grandmother asked kindly.

"Yes, I'm alright. Sorry I flipped earlier on. Too much stress recently, I guess. Seeing you serve breakfast to the subject of my hallucinations was just too much for me. I thought I was the victim of a global conspiracy." Kaja mocked herself.

Josephine gave her an understanding nod and said: "I'd get paranoid, too, if I was in your shoes. No wonder, after what happened to you over the past few days."

"Since you seem to know the monster, perhaps you could tell me a little bit more about him?" Kaja asked curiously.

"Hm, let me think. I cannot tell you much. You'll have to find out yourself. But to give you a rough idea, I can try to explain it like this: Do you remember the spirit animals I told you about as a child? When you were afraid or sick?"

"Yes, I know. My spirit animal was the wolf and he's still with me. They are... how shall I put it... animal helpers from an astral sphere?"

"Exactly. Dragons are similar, but consist of a different form of energy which manifests itself in the shape of a dragon."

"A rather pushy manifestation, I'd say. I've rarely met such an arrogant and self-righteous creature." Kaja grumbled.

Josephine had to smile. She understood her granddaughter only too well. She had felt the same when she met Lance for the first time.

"What else?"

"What do you mean: What else?"

"Can't you tell me anything else?"

"Unfortunately, I can't, apart from one piece of advice: It may be worth putting up with him for a moment or two seeing what you can get out of him."

"Great! And I thought you'd teach me a spell to make him disappear." Kaja sighed.

"And I thought you didn't care for my witchcraft?" Mémé said with a twinkle.

"I didn't, until I met Lance." Kaja snorted.

"Do you want to help me make those candles?" Mémé changed the subject.

"Oh yes, I'd like to. In fact, it would be brilliant. I haven't told you yet that Tim and I went to Luc's garage last night to ask about my car."

"No, you haven't. He must have been glad to see you. Did he manage to fix it? And did you have a good time with Tim?"

"Oh yes, he was happy. But the old codger came up with one of his eccentric ideas. To pay him, he asked me to make a candle for him. And what's even stranger: I'm supposed to make one for Tim as well. He insisted on me making the candles myself. He didn't want one of yours. I did try to explain that I'm not half as good as you are, but he wouldn't listen." Kaja finished her report, shrugging her shoulders.

Although Mémé had an idea what the business was with Tim's candle

- Luc, you old matchmaker! - she did not quite understand what the point of the task was in general. There was no doubt Kaja would be able to manage. Long enough she had watched and helped her. But it had been some time since she'd last done it herself. Mémé spread the selected and dried herbs on the table next to flasks with corresponding essential oils.

In the meantime, Kaja weighed the ingredients for the wax, hard paraffin and stearin flakes, in the correct proportions and put them in a large pot which then went onto the hob that Mémé had especially enlarged for her business. Kaja set it to the second lowest temperature in order to melt the ingredients very slowly. Then she went over to the old workbench where Mémé had already started to assemble the moulds. Kaja assisted her, cutting the wicks to correct lengths. The wicks had to be considerably longer than the finished candles because they were tied to a horizontal beam in the ceiling. By doing this, you could be sure that the wick ran straight through the middle of the candle and that the wax would later melt evenly around it when lit.

When all this was prepared, they both checked the temperature of the molten wax. It was important to wait for the right moment when the wax started to solidify but was just runny enough to be poured into the moulds. Now they had to work quickly and accurately, first adding the herbs and at the very last moment the essential oils. If you did this too early, the extremely volatile oils would evaporate and never give the candle its wonderful scent. If you waited too long, the herbs would clot and spoil the look of the candle.

They worked quietly together like a well-trained team. They fell into an easy rhythm. Without saying much, each of them knew exactly what to do. Kaja was surprised at how easily she managed and how much she enjoyed the work.

An hour later, they had finished. The candles now needed to cool down for 48 hours, before they could be taken out of the moulds, their wicks shortened and Mémé's signature applied.

Kaja was peeling a few spots of wax from her arm, when Mémé said from the storage room next door: "I have something here for you: Two of my old moulds, a reel of wick and some wax already mixed. Just choose your herbs and oils from the workshop. I'm happy for you to have all this."

"That's brilliant. I was desperately trying to work out where to get all the things from."

"Oh, and I forgot to tell you: Tim was here while you were out for your jog."

"Goodness, how many eggs does the man consume every day?" Kaja shook her head.

"He wasn't here for eggs. I think he came to see you. He was rather disappointed when I told him you weren't here."

"What did he want from me?"

"I think he's being called back to Switzerland at short notice. He left you a message, the note is on the kitchen table."

"A note? On paper?" Kaja laughed. "Did he also ask you for a pen?"

"Yes, he did, why?"

Kaja told her the amusing story of how they had tried to exchange telephone numbers the night before.

"OK, if you don't need me for now, I'll go and check the message."

"You do that. There's not much left to finish here. I'll be with you as soon as I can. By the way, I left some tea on the stove for you, since you ran off without having any earlier on."

"Thanks, you're a star." Kaja kissed her on the cheek and left the workshop.

Back in the kitchen, Kaja poured herself a cup of tea and took a large gulp. Then she went over to the table to read the note. 'Where is Zorro?' she thought but shrugged her shoulders assuming he might be outside dreaming of catching a rabbit.

"Dear Kaja. We had a wonderful evening and I enjoyed very much..."

Suddenly she felt as if someone was looking over her shoulder. She turned her head and "Waah!" she jumped sideways. The dragon was standing directly behind her, much too close for Kaja's comfort. For his part, Kaja's shriek had shocked Lance so much that he was now sitting on top of the stove at the other end of the room. 'At least we're keeping a good distance if we have to share the same room.' Kaja thought with satisfaction. "How dare you! Sneaking up on me like that. You scared me to death."

"Scared you to death? Don't make me laugh!" the dragon snorted, "It was me who almost fainted when I heard you scream. As if you were stabbed, murdered or some such." he ranted.

Kaja was surprised that she had almost got used to hearing his voice in her head. "And by squeezing into a tight corner between a hotplate and a chimney you tried to rescue me?" she enquired sarcastically. "I suppose dragons are not as brave as they used to be. Or the knights of old exaggerated their stories about your fearsomeness and strength. After all, they had to impress innocent damsels, didn't they?" she scoffed.

With as much dignity as he could muster in his uncomfortable position on top of the stove, the dragon climbed down to the floor and said with a peeved face: "I see. You're just as rude as your grandmother. Go on then, read the soppy letter from your fancy man. I'm dying to know what he's got to say." he teased her.

"Get off, you nosy parker. Do you know what the word 'privacy' means? Most likely not." she answered her own question. "Otherwise you wouldn't have turned up in my bedroom without an invitation."

"I think I should be honoured that you decided to speak to me." Lance wondered. He had made himself comfortable on a kitchen chair. Kaja was fascinated by the various shades of blue wafting around the kitchen. As soon as she concentrated, she could see clear contours and the shape of the dragon again. It looked as if the dragon was filling the whole room.

"Mémé said I'd have a hard time getting rid of you, so I might as well accept your presence. She says it'll be less stressful for me. But don't think you've won!"

"I see." he grumbled. "The old witch's been dishing the dirt again."

Although Kaja could sense the affection with which he called Mémé a witch, nevertheless she interrupted him in a sharp voice: "OK, here's my first rule for you, Lance: Never, ever speak ill of Mémé! Otherwise I'll have to stop speaking to you immediately. Is that clear?"

The dragon nodded in agreement. Although he had his own views with regards to any threatened consequences, he very much valued loyalty and respected the rule without objection.

"Good." Kaja was surprised. Well, that was easy. Perhaps she should take her chance and draw up a few more rules? But then she decided to do that later. She was sure an opportunity would present itself very soon. Distracted by their conversation and the amazing, constantly changing phenomenon of the dragon, she didn't notice that Lance had grabbed Tim's letter.

"... enjoyed very much being with you." the dragon recited. "I would like to do this again soon. -"

"Give it back to me." Kaja snapped and jumped at him. Unfortunately, the dragon was considerably taller than her and his arm seemed to extend to the ceiling. She tried to jump up and snatch the paper from his hand. Bang! She went straight through his body and ended up on the floor. Apparently, the dragon did not have any physical substance.

While she was struggling to get back to her feet, the dragon continued unfazed: "Unfortunately, I had an urgent phone call late last night. It was stupid of me to hand out my landline number to a colleague. I didn't expect having to deal with an emergency right now."

"Have you lost it completely?" Kaja hissed, fiercely staring at him. "That is my letter. Do you understand? Mine."

With a sigh, the dragon smoothly pulled his extended arm down from the ceiling and handed the letter back to her: "It's a whole lot of drivel anyway. Do you really need it?:"

"Whatever I need, want or desire is none of your business. Does that finally get through to you?" Kaja spat out.

Lance waited for her to finish reading the letter which also contained Tim's mobile number in case of any emergencies in Kaja's life. Then he said casually: "Is it also none of my business if I can help you achieve what you want?"

Kaja jumped. Her thoughts were still with Tim. "What was that? What do you mean?"

"How shall I explain it to you." he started but then looked at his wrist to check what Kaja assumed to be an imaginary watch. "Oh, is it that late already? Sorry, we'll have to continue our conversation another time. I have to leave for an urgent appointment..." he got up and disappeared through the closed door. "What the hell..." She jumped up and ran after him, but the dragon was nowhere to be seen.

Moments later, Lance was sitting on top of the roof enjoying the sun and grinning with glee to see Kaja upset. Hehe.

9

"I've had it with that dragon." Kaja fumed when Mémé opened the door to come in.

"Did he upset you again?"

"He's got nothing better to do all day. And as soon as I'm starting to get some sense out of him, he's in a rush to be off. Appointments..." she scoffed.

Josephine smiled: "Yes, Lance is a bit of a nutcase. But he's easily flattered, the old peacock. Just try it out on him, perhaps it'll make him more approachable. What are your plans for the day?" she wanted to know from Kaja.

"I think after lunch I'll walk down to the village and pick up my car from Luc. I'll need it to get back home tomorrow."

"So you've decided to leave me tomorrow?"

"I think I'll have to. I need to get my life back on track. At least I enjoyed an urgently needed break here with you. But you can't put problems off forever, can you."

"No, you're right. But you're always welcome here, you know that." Mémé replied and gave her granddaughter a big warm hug.

That afternoon, Kaja made her way into the village. Mémé had asked her to take the broken CD player along which she had forgotten the night before. Zorro came out of hiding and ran ahead of her. Suddenly he stopped and apparently barked at the thin air. Kaja peered to her right and saw the expected blue haze signalling Lance's arrival. "Calm down, Zorro, everything's OK. You'll have to put up with him for a while." Kaja said, gently tickling him behind his ear. Zorro whined and whimpered for a bit longer but then calmed down with surprising ease. He was happy and also a little bit proud, because thanks to his alertness, his mistress had finally noticed the dragon.

"How did you do that?" a bad tempered Lance demanded to know. "I've been trying to explain it to him for the past three days."

"What do you expect? Did you really think any ragtag monster can tell him whether to protect me or not? Of course he will only listen to me. He's my dog. Mine! Just as the letter was mine." Kaja retorted pointedly. "You don't seem to know the difference between mine and thine. I see potential for improvement here. Perhaps we should practise a little bit?"

The dragon poked his tongue out at her. 'Right.' Kaja thought. 'Now it's time for him to get upset after he's been doing the same to me every time we met.' Grumpily, she kept kicking a pine cone in front of her.

"Stop sulking, babe..."

"Don't call me babe." she flared up. "That's rule number two!"

The dragon sighed: "OK, Kaja, if you want to make it difficult for yourself, that's fine by me. What I wanted to say, Kaja,..." He tried to sound so posh pronouncing her name that he made her giggle. "I already like you much better like this. What I wanted to say is this: Let's think together what you should do next to get one up on that - what's his name? - Freddy."

"Oh, you know about him already?" Kaja asked with one raised eyebrow.

"SweeTheart." Lance started and earned himself another cross look from Kaja. "I've always been by your side for the past few days. It couldn't have escaped me."

"Ah." Kaja acknowledged. "Well, what can I say? I don't have a clue what to do. Any suggestions?"

"I'm not sure if it is relevant to your situation, but let me tell you a story."

"OK, go on then. I can do with a bit of entertainment on the way." she laughed.

"When I was a young dragon, many centuries ago, we had these trainee dragon contests."

"How old are you now?" Kaja asked in disbelief.

"I'm four hundred and thirty seven years old." Lance answered.

"437 years?" Kaja was sceptical.

"That's what I said. Do you want to hear my story or don't you?" When she nodded, he continued: "Then don't interrupt me with such unimportant questions. Where was I?"

"Trainee dragon contests." she helped him.

"Oh yes, right. Well, this is what happened: The competitions consisted of several tasks, such as scaring people, setting fields on fire, stealing a virgin - the prettier they were the more points we got, dragons do appreciate beauty - doing some mental arithmetic and reporting on a journey to a faraway land. - If the audience fell asleep, we didn't get any points for that, of course."

Kaja shook herself and tried to keep a clear head. Stealing virgins? Scaring people? Granted, this could have come from one of her childhood fairy tales. But mental arithmetic? Reading from a travel diary? She could not decide whether to dismiss the story as pure fantasy or to believe it. So she stayed quiet and kept listening. There was no doubt this was a fantasy story anyway, as it was obviously told by a born-and-bred dragon. "It could be a mental health issue." she murmured to herself. But since she was now ready to listen to him, not only with her ears but also with an open mind, his words turned into the most amazing pictures. She was so surprised at them that she a) missed the next part of the story and b) almost would have ended up in the roadside ditch had Lance not caught her at the very last moment. His arm felt cool and smooth but before she could establish what she found so irritating in that, he let go of her and she forgot the thought.

"Watch where you're going." he grumbled.

Kaja had to suppress a grin. The dragon obviously felt uneasy about being nice to her for a change.

But soon she heard his deep full voice in her head again and was immersed in a sea of light, of fabled shapes and smells, when he continued: "One of us, his name was Jerry, thought of himself as the greatest dragon of them all. He had dark blue scales and golden spikes on his back. And he was very successful with the girls. They obviously had a crush on him..."

"When you say girls, do you mean girls like me or dragon girls?" Kaja interrupted him.

"Both, it seems to be a universal appeal. You human ladies appear to be rather fond of this combination as well."

"Fond of blue scales and golden spikes?" Kaja said in disbelief. "Not to my knowledge..."

"No, you silly girl." he said and flinched from Kaja's look. "For you humans it would be blue eyes and blond hair. I think you call them 'Les Garcons de la Plage'?"

"'Beach Boys' is the name you're looking for." she giggled.

Lance sighed: "All these different languages, I'm getting confused. Here you talk French, over in Switzerland German and then you slip in some words in English. How is one supposed to know?"

"Do you speak every language?"

"Many, but I prefer our universal dragon language. Unfortunately, you wouldn't understand a word I'm saying. But that's another subject. We've gone completely off topic. Let me get back to my story: Jerry was indeed quite handsome, even for a dragon. We all have our beauty..." he took a narcissistic look at his reflection in a cattle trough. "He only had one problem. In order to be officially recognised and celebrated as the most successful of them all, he had to win all the annual contests that were held for dragons above a certain age."

"What was his problem?"

"Firstly, these were not 'Mister Dragon' contests where only appearance counts. Everyone of us had an equal chance to show different skills. Secondly, he had a more serious problem: He was afraid of flying, so trips to faraway countries were out. Finally: He was as thick as a brick. He could hardly count to three, never mind doing more complicated sums."

"Oh."

"Yes, oh. At least for him. The rest of us were not too unhappy. We thought now was our time to shut his big mouth up once and for all. But to our surprise, we watched him win the championship and take the most beautiful virgin back to his cave. I hope you understand that we were very angry and suspected foul play."

"So what did you do?"

"A few of us teamed up and tried to get to the bottom of it. It took us a while because we didn't know where to start. We came to the conclusion that he might have nicked the exam answer sheets which were stored in the castle. In order to prove our theory, my best friend Arturo and I sneaked into the castle. We had to do it in the dark and managed to get inside without being seen. Apparently, nobody was expecting us and security wasn't very tight. The old dragons didn't think anyone would be daring enough to risk being caught. This is similar to your situation. Your Freddy thinks he's safe because you're too embarrassed to talk about him and you're too distraught to stand up to him. Both the jury and Jerry fell for the same false sense of security, albeit for different reasons. We, on the other hand, were able to prove that it was possible to enter the castle, but it didn't get us any closer to an answer. We still couldn't prove that Jerry might have taken the same route before the contest. It was with a heavy heart that we decided to allow him the fame of being the best trainee dragon for yet another year but resolved to be better prepared for the next contest."

"Really? You managed to restrain yourselves for so long? I couldn't have. I must always have it out immediately. Or I'll give up."

The dragon was thinking. "That's not always a bad attitude. It will often give you a sense of purpose. But the best plan can fall apart when executed at the wrong time."

"I often find it difficult to wait for the right moment." Kaja sighed.

"'First do what you must, then do what you can and finally have a go at the impossible.' some wise man - or was it a wise dragon? - once said. And there is some truth in it. If you more or less follow that advice and keep your eyes and ears open, you'll find your opportunity."

"Hm." she replied, not completely convinced. In the meantime, they had reached Luc's garage and Kaja asked Lance: "Can you hold on to your story for a moment? You can tell me the rest on our way home. I'm really keen to know how you resolved the mystery."

"Hi Kaja."

"Oh, hello Luc, I didn't see you come." she stammered.

"No, I thought not. Were you talking to yourself just now? Or were you having an argument with your dog?" he wanted to know.

She looked at him surprised. Couldn't he see Lance? But she recovered quickly and joked: "I always talk to Zorro, didn't you know? Before I forget," she stopped for a moment and searched in her shoulder bag, "Mémé has sent you this CD player. Could you please have a look at it and mend it, if you can?

Luc took the appliance from her and inspected it from all sides: "What's wrong with it?"

"Hm, I think it was some kind of short circuit." she said slightly embarrassed. "But I'm sure your magic hands will get it going again."

"So, are you now..." he mumbled. "And you? Are you about to leave us, then? Knowing you, that's why you've come for your little car."

"Yes, I'm leaving tomorrow. But I'll be back." she tried to re-assure him.

"Only come back when you've found the right way, your own way. Promise me."

"Luc, what're you trying to say? I already noticed your cryptic hints yesterday." But he stopped her with a wave of his hand. "Not now. I'm rather busy. Be safe, sweeTheart."

At the back of her head, Kaja heard Lance grumble: "Why is he allowed to call you sweeTheart and I'm not? It's not fair." he complained.

"Shush." Kaja hissed at Lance, which made Luc startle. She quickly smiled at him and demanded: "At least you owe me a brief explanation. You can't leave me standing here without an answer."

Instead, Luc grabbed her with his huge hands and gave her a tight hug. "Goodbye, Kaja. See you soon. You'll know what I mean when the time has come."

With these words, he let go of her and returned to his garage. Somewhat dumbfounded by his sudden departure, Kaja watched him walk away without saying a word. She frowned. 'It'd be nice if someone didn't talk in riddles to me for once.' she thought.

Finally, Lance had had enough and whinged: "Can we make a move now or do you want to carry on staring into space?"

"Yes, I'm coming." Together they went over to the small grey Peugeot and Kaja opened the door for her two passengers to hop in. Zorro didn't seem happy having to share the back seat again. Scowling, he curled up in a corner. She found the key behind the sun visor where Luc usually put it and looked at the dragon in her rear view mirror.

"Why couldn't Luc see you? Or did I miss something here?"

"Only women can see me and only those women who are destined to meet a dragon. We don't deal with just anyone and definitely not with men. They're too thick to get the point and are not worth the effort."

he said with a dismissive gesture.

Kaja had to grin. She understood him all too well. What she didn't understand was the rest of his explanation. "So you seriously think I was destined to meet you? Goodness, I must have been quite a pain in someone's neck in my previous life." she moaned.

"On the contrary. Don't you know it is a special honour only very few find bestowed on them?" he protested.

"Yes, keep your wig on. I noticed that you are talking about dragons in the plural. Does this mean there are others as well?"

He turned up his eyes. "You weren't listening to me, were you? I'd have to have a whole army of multiple personalities if I wanted to represent all the different dragons in my story. I'd be just as bad as Jerry!" Horrified by the thought, he shook himself until sparks flew from his scales.

"OK, I believe you. But be careful not to set my car on fire." Kaja calmed him down, laughing. "It could've been a story you'd made up to teach me a lesson."

"This is indeed the case, only that my story is true."

"Well then, hurry up. I want to hear the end of it before we reach home." she demanded.

And again his voice was talking inside Kaja's head: "So we decided to wait for a whole year and get better prepared for the next contest. Finally, the time had come. Jerry was bold enough to claim his victory at every given opportunity even before the competition had started. All of us were furious, but we didn't show it and continued with our preparations. A week to the day before the start of the contest, we made our way into Dragon's Crag Castle again and exchanged to correct answer sheet with a faked one. We had to trust our instincts that the timing was right and that Jerry hadn't got hold of the original sheet before. On the day before the contest, we went back and repeated the swap, returning the correct sheet to its place."

"Of course, you didn't dare take a look at the answers yourself, did you?" Kaja said sarcastically.

"Of course not." Lance said with indignation. 'Kaja can be such a Miss Know-It-All.' he thought to himself. "Do you want me to continue or will you keep interrupting me?"

Kaja kept silent in anticipation.

"Again we were labouring through all those difficult tasks and struggling with the arithmetic riddles. Jerry finished first, which confirmed our suspicions that he had learned the results by heart."

In the meantime, they had reached the farmyard and Kaja switched off the engine. Curiously, she looked at the dragon: "And then? What happened next?"

"Well, the award ceremony was the moment of truth. Jerry came last, not first. He listened to the announcements in total disbelief. He even wanted to interrupt the judge but then thought better of it. As I said, he wasn't the brightest button in the box, but even he understood that he would have had a lot of explaining to do if he voiced his protest there and then." Lance finished.

"How did he do with his travel report?" Kaja wondered.

"We never found out, but it wasn't important any more."

"Thank you, that was an amazing story." Kaja praised him. After a short pause, she asked: "By the way: What did you do with the stolen virgins? Did you eat them?"

"Eat them? We're not cannibals!" Lance was outraged.

"So what did you do with them? Why all the fuss?" she seemed irritated.

"Have you ever tried to keep a dragon's den tidy?" Lance shook his head. "I can tell you, it's an enormous task. We needed the virgins to clean and wash and cook for us."

"That's slavery!"

"But in return they were safe with us." he justified the practice. "They didn't have to cope with all those bothersome princes pestering them."

"OK, that was then. How do you do it today?"

"Do what?"

"I mean your choice of virgins must be greatly reduced nowadays?"

"Well, the rules have been relaxed a bit..."

"Ah, as long as they can cook, you mean." Kaja jibed. "I should've known. We'd better leave it there. I'm going inside to have dinner with Mémé and then I want to have some quality time with Zorro."

"Was that a wide hint?"

"A broad one." Kaja automatically corrected him. "Exactly, I need a bit of space now. One last question: Who did win that second competition in the end?"

"Me, of course." the dragon answered.

"Of course. Fair and square, you did."

She left the dragon standing in the yard without waiting for an answer. He apparently was too busy inspecting his claws to hear that final remark.

10

On Sunday morning, Mémé went to the bakery at the crack of dawn to get some fresh pains au chocolat for her granddaughter's final breakfast with her. When Kaja was finished packing, they had a last cup of tea together in the kitchen.

"I'll give you a call as soon as I arrive in Zurich."

"You do that, I'll be waiting. And please let me know of any new developments at work next week." Mémé sounded concerned.

"I will, but I don't think my situation is about to change very much." Kaja said with a gloomy look.

"Oh, I'm sure you'll find a solution." Mémé tried to cheer her up.

"Yes, I know I shouldn't give up without a fight. That much has become clear to me over the past few days." Kaja said with determination. "So, we'll have to set off on our journey now."

She got up, put her cup in the sink and took in a deep breath of the familiar smells in Mémé's herb kitchen, as if she wanted to take them home with her. Mémé followed her to the car and watched her granddaughter load the luggage into the boot. She put her mobile on the passenger seat and a packed lunch within easy reach. Finally, she let Zorro jump onto the back seat and looked for Lance.

"Where is that creature?" she complained. "I thought he wanted to come with us."

"Don't worry about Lance." the grandmother calmed her down. "He'll turn up soon enough."

"But how can he?" Kaja was sceptical. "I have to set off now, I can't wait any longer." She gave Mémé a hug and said goodbye.

"Have a safe journey and look after yourself. If you happen to hear from your parents - as unlikely as it is - give them my regards."

"Yes, I will. At least it gives us something to talk about." Kaja said jokingly and pulled one of her faces. "Ciao, take care." She started the engine and drove off.

Deeply immersed in her thoughts, Kaja took the Route du Soleil north. Zorro was taking a nap on the back seat. A loud "Hello." startled her so much that she jerked the steering wheel and had trouble keeping the car in lane.

"Hey, have you lost it completely? I'm doing a hundred miles an hour here and you hop into my car without a warning?"

To make matters worse, Zorro started to bark in the back. He sensed very clearly how his mistress had received a shock and how this made her adrenaline levels leap. And all this because of that dragon! The dog barked as loud as he could, hoping to make the monster disappear.

"Zorro, please!" Kaja shouted, now completely unnerved. He stopped his barking madness. 'OK, your choice.' the dog thought and curled up in a sulk.

"Tss, tss." went the dragon in disapproval. "I tried to announce my arrival via telepathy but your intuitive system seems to be completely clogged up..."

Kaja sighed. He was starting to sound like Mémé. She couldn't bear it. "My thoughts were somewhere else, so what." she defended herself.

"Did my story help you?" he tried to start a more friendly conversation.

"Hm, at the moment I can't see its relevance yet."

Now it was the dragon's turn to sigh. Humans could be so slow-witted sometimes. He decided to let it rest there and help himself to a snack in the meantime. He was about to grab the food bag from the passenger seat when his protégée started to speak again.

"I think I'll just go back to work and try to find out what's behind this whole business." She looked at him. "As you said: first do what you must, then do what you can and so on and so forth. Even I thought it was a good piece of advice. Hey, what're you doing?"

The dragon had just started to eat an apple with obvious pleasure. "At least you could have asked." she told him off. "I would have given it to you if you'd asked me politely."

"I knew you would have. That's why I didn't want to interrupt your nice speech." he excused his behaviour.

"You don't say." she mocked him. "Anyway, how come you can hold and even eat an apple?"

"Huh, what kind of question is that?" Lance exclaimed and gave her a blank look.

"Well, when you took Tim's letter from me and I tried to grab your arm, I didn't feel anything. You were just like thin air. Yet barely three hours later, you stopped me from falling into a roadside ditch. I could clearly feel your arm then. I did think it was strange."

"Oh that." Lance said dismissively. "It can be easily explained. As an astral being, I am not bound by the laws of physics. - I just need to concentrate on focussing my energies. It's that simple."

"That simple?" Kaja was staring at him.

"Would you mind paying attention to the traffic, please?" the dragon reminded her with unusual politeness.

Kaja jumped and dutifully turned her eyes back to the road in front of them. "Sorry, I got distracted by your 'simple' explanation."

From then on, she kept concentrating on her driving. After the dragon had finished feasting on his pinched apple, he followed Zorro's example, curled up on the back seat and fell asleep. Fascinated, Kaja watched in her mirror as the huge monster shrank in size until it was hardly bigger than a cat, leaving plenty of room in the back of the car.

"Now you would almost fit into my handbag." she teased him. "I like monsters of a manageable size."

Lance only squinted at her with half-closed eyes but didn't reply. 'OK then.' Kaja thought shrugging her shoulders. 'So much for my in-car entertainment.' She turned up the volume of the stereo and made her way towards Switzerland to the rousing music of "Nightwish".

Just over seven hours later, she arrived in the street in front of her flat, totally exhausted. She had only stopped once for a comfort break and to give Zorro a chance to stretch his legs. Tired, she rubbed her strained eyes. Then she turned round, pulled the dragon's tail and tickled Zorro behind his ear. The dog was already awake and alert. As soon as they had turned into their street, he kept looking out of the window.

"You know we are home now, don't you, kid." she said affectionately.

The dragon stretched himself and started to expand to his normal size. Kaja got out of the car and opened a door to let them both out, leaving the holdall in the car for the moment. She wanted to take Zorro for a walk and allow him to do his business so she wouldn't have to go out again later. While she watched Zorro inspecting every tuft of grass and every shrub for new odour markers telling him who was new in his territory, she stretched her arms and legs to get rid of the stiffness from the long drive. She had only just got back to Zurich and was already missing Mémé. She was also a little surprised and annoyed that Tim was still in her thoughts. Although she was grateful that he had managed to take her mind off the disaster with Frédéric and - without knowing - had helped her re-build her confidence, she felt she had no further space for him in her life right now. Heaven knew she had enough on her plate. The last thing she needed was yet another man seeking her attention.

Back at the car, she heaved the heavy bag onto her shoulder and searched for the flat keys. She had moved here to Wollishofen on the outskirts of Zurich right after her graduation. After living in boarding schools for twelve years and in shared student accommodation for another five, she had been desperate to set up home in her own four walls. The flat was on the ground floor. Because of her dog, she was not afraid of burglars and even called a little patio her own. In the gaps between the concrete slabs, she had planted rosemary and thyme. When the sun heated up the area, the herbs enriched the atmosphere with a scent reminding her of southern France.

Finally, Kaja found her keys. She went into her flat, left the holdall by the door and casually dropped the keys on the dresser. After quickly flicking through the post, she kicked off her shoes and dropped onto the sofa. Her flat consisted of two bedrooms, a sitting room and an open-plan kitchen. This was unusual for such an old building. A wall had been removed so that the kitchen was now part of the living room. The furniture was mostly from Ikea, apart from a few antiques that Mémé had given her. She had restored the rustic kitchen cabinet herself. It had been hard work stripping away layer upon layer of old paint and sanding down the wood. She felt proud of her work that had completely transformed the unit after applying a thin coat of varnish. She tilted back her head and looked at the stucco ornaments on the ceiling. The house had been built in the Art Nouveau era with high ceilings and huge windows. They started at knee height and almost reached to the top of the rooms. From the kitchen, five steps led outside to the patio area. The pergola she had built last year was now finally fully covered in foliage and provided a good shelter from the rain. This was extremely important to Kaja. Having chosen a job that kept her inside for most of the day, she needed an opportunity to spend her limited spare time outside amongst plants. Lance finished his inspection tour of the flat and sat down next to her on the sofa.

As if he was able to read her thoughts, he asked her seriously: "Where do you like spending most of your time?"

"Outside." she said without hesitation.

"So why do you spend most of your time behind closed doors?" She turned her head to look at him.

"Sometimes, you don't have a choice. I have to earn my money somehow."

"Hm, the earning part seems to work rather well for you. But are you happy with your life?"

"Where's this conversation leading? Are you going to be my therapist now?" She asked slightly annoyed.

"No particular reason." he avoided the question. "I'll have a look outside." and off he went.

"Just for the record: I am happy with my life." she shouted after him.

"Obviously." the dragon mumbled to himself. "Which is why such a simple question can get you so upset. It seems like I touched a sore spot." he was satisfied with himself and slumped into the deck chair under the pergola.

Kaja dragged herself up from the sofa to make a cup of tea. The old kitchen furniture and gas cooker certainly added some character to the flat. It was a disadvantage of these old houses that they had outdated bathrooms and kitchens. But it was these features that Kaja was particularly fond of. While the tea was brewing, she looked around. There was a lot of chaos at the moment. She had been so busy over the past few weeks that she hadn't found the time to tidy up her place. The thought made her grin. The truth was, her work had been a welcome excuse not to do it. Procrastination at its best. She'd never been a stickler for tidiness. She only ever made sure the kitchen and bathroom were scrupulously clean. Her frantic search for the project documentation and her hasty departure had added to the chaos she was now returning to. She sighed and Lance put his head in through the kitchen door.

She registered with some amusement that after his brief, unauthorised inspection of her flat and his pushy questioning, the dragon had made himself comfortable outside.

Now he had a mischievous look on his face: "You do realise this is not Venice?"

"Why's that?"

"Because for the past fifteen minutes, you've been acting like you were standing on the Bridge of Sighs. It's rather disturbing for someone who's trying to take a nap."

"Well, look around you. Wouldn't you find this chaos distressing?"

The dragon gave her a blank look and shrugged his shoulders: "What's your problem? I find the place almost as homely as my own den."

She put on a grim face. "My home is not a den. And if I had any doubts whether to make an effort today, you just gave me the right incentive to make a start now. Thanks a bunch."

Pulling out the vacuum, a duster and a bin bag, she immediately set to work. The speakers of her stereo were blasting out "Mano Negra", her favourite cleaning tune. She was lucky not to have any direct neighbours. The flats above hers were used as studios by two architects and therefore nobody was in over the weekend. Dismayed by her enthusiasm, Lance escaped back to the garden while Zorro hid under the sofa. She was just clearing the mess of paper from her desk, when she suddenly had a hand-written note from Frédéric in her hand. She stopped. "SuperMan77!" This must be one of his unmistakable passwords, but she couldn't work out which program or gadget it belonged to. And why had he written it down? She frowned. For the moment, she could not make much sense of it. Turning the piece of paper over, she found a date on its back: 28th September 2012. 'That's three weeks from now.' she thought. Underneath, there was a name she'd never heard before and a telephone number. She played with the note in her hands trying to decide what to do with it. Finally, she thought it best to keep it safe in her trouser pocket, just in case she might need it again at some point.

Two hours later, Kaja was soothing her exhausted body in a hot bath while nibbling on the remains of the pizza bread Mémé had given her for the journey.

Pleased with her cleaning efforts, she leaned back and indulged in the aromatic scent of Mémé's bath oil. 'Actually, I'll have to thank Lance.' she decided. 'He made me turn this flat into a clean and homely place again.' She was just immersing deeper into the hot water and starting to relax, when the air took on a blue haze. No, not here! Not now! Lance was lolling against the washbasin and barely ducked in time to avoid the flannel she threw at him.

"Get out! I want my peace. You've got no business in my bathroom. Anyway, how do you always manage to enter locked rooms? Ah, it doesn't matter, get out of my sight."

She got out of the bathtub, loosely wrapped a bath towel around her and opened the door.

"Get out, before I really get angry."

Lance was grumbling but realised that he had chosen the wrong moment. He had almost forgotten how fussy the female kind could be about their bathroom time. Swearing, Kaja dried herself off, brushed her hair with rough strokes and hastily rubbed on some cream. 'Bang goes my relaxation.' she huffed. Then she put on fresh pyjamas and brushed her teeth. All she wanted now was to sleep. She was so tired that her whole body was aching. She stumbled barefoot into her bedroom and had to take a big step over Zorro who had curled up on the floor. Lying in bed, half asleep already, she felt something touch her shoulder.

"So? Have you got a plan?" Lance wanted to know.

Bewildered, Kaja watched him make himself comfortable in her bed. "What the hell are you doing?"

"I'm going to sleep. What do you think? Now you can tell me all about your plan." he repeated his question.

But Kaja was too tired to have a conversation. She was too tired even to throw him out of her bed, especially since he had shrunk himself into that neat little ball again. So she just murmured: "I've always wanted a little dragon cat. - Sleep well." And with that, she dropped off.

11

At 6.30 the next morning, the sound of the alarm tore Kaja from her deepest sleep. She was tempted to switch it off and stay in bed a little longer. But she knew she could easily carry on sleeping for another two hours. So it was better to get up now. Rolling over, she almost knocked the dragon off her pillow. What was that noise? Carefully, she moved her head closer to the sleeping miniature dragon and could hardly believe what she was hearing: That chap was snoring! Admittedly, he did so quite discreetly, but nevertheless he did. She poked him: "Come on, wake up, you snoring monster."

"Hey, are you mad? It's much too early to get up."

Lance tried to grab a corner of the duvet and hide under it. Finally, her words seemed to reach his sleepy brain and he emerged, looking at her with flashing eyes.

"I don't snore. Dragons never snore." he claimed majestically. Kaja didn't have time for an argument and left him in his belief.

"I'm going to have a shower and get dressed. If you want or need any breakfast, you're welcome to join me in the kitchen."

She still wasn't sure whether he ate because he was hungry, because he needed food or just for fun.

Lance was already waiting for her when she came into the kitchen. "Would you like anything in particular for breakfast or aren't you having anything at all?" she enquired as she opened the fridge.

"A bowl of milk with some elderberry brandy would be nice."

She raised her eyebrows at him. "Alcohol in the morning? If you were human, I'd register you with Alcoholics Anonymous."

"It is quite normal for us dragons. We have a completely different metabolism." he was quick to explain.

She poured some cornflakes into a bowl and added milk. Then she poured some milk into a second bowl for Lance. "I thought astral beings don't have a metabolism?"

"Exactly and that's is why a brandy doesn't do me any harm for breakfast." he agreed.

"Well, the only problem is that I don't have any elderberry brandy. What about a dram of whiskey?"

"If that's all you have. " the dragon answered, slightly disgusted.

Kaja was steaming. "I'm not wasting my good whiskey on someone who can hardly stand the thought of it."

"Have a look in your holdall. Perhaps Josephine put in a bottle for me." he sounded hopeful.

Lance had such an innocent look on his face that Kaja had to laugh and give in. She dug through the bag, not really expecting to find anything, but was all the more surprised when she pulled out a bottle.

"It seems she knows you very well." she murmured adding a tot of the strong brew to his bowl of milk.

With gusto, Lance took a large gulp and said "Thank you." with his mouth full.

"You're welcome. Enjoy." She joined him at the table and started to eat her cornflakes which had become a soggy mess in the meantime.

"When do we have to leave?" Lance asked.

"We? We're not going anywhere. You're staying here."

In order to give her words more weight, she poked her finger into his chest. "You stay here and look after my flat. You're the housekeeper now." With these words, she got up and cleared the table.

'Housekeeper?' Lance thought angrily. 'I'll give you the housekeeper, you'll see.'

Since the dragon did not answer back, Kaja stopped and looked at him suspiciously.

"You're not angry that you'll have to stay home?" she wanted to know.

"No, no I'm not." the dragon answered in his sweetest voice.

Not sure what to make of it, she was still looking at him. "I don't trust you as far as I can throw you, but I'm running out of time. Come on, Zorro, we're off." She grabbed her car keys and left the flat. Just before she closed the door, she blew Lance a kiss and said: "Thanks for your co-operation. At least I'll have no worries about this place." And off she went.

'Dammit.' the dragon thought. 'Why did she have to thank me? Now I'm obliged to behave.' he grumbled. 'It would've been much easier to be naughty.' he sighed. 'But I didn't promise not to visit her.' he realised and his mood suddenly improved considerably.

On her way to work, Kaja went through the plan in her head. First, she had the unpleasant task of talking to her boss. At least, she hoped to avoid meeting the section leader. She did not have an aversion to the new Qubus staff per se, but she could not stand this new superior with his cold eyes. The merger of the two companies made sense and seemed to benefit both. But despite those advantages, a lot of bad things had happened. For a moment she pondered: Could it be that she was the only one who felt so negative because she couldn't cope with the changes? She resolutely shook her head. No, that was definitely not the reason. She only encountered such problems in her private life. Otherwise, she would not have become such an outstanding computer scientist. It was a profession where things were constantly on the move. She was not emotionally attached to the work, apart from being rightfully proud of her achievements. She grimaced. This had already earned her a telling-off once: She wasn't identifying enough with the company, she was told. 'So what, I'm not married to you.' she thought. OK, the next action on her list was to get back to her work and discreetly find out where the bastard was hiding.

She also decided to tap into the rumour mill. She could start with asking her colleague Thea out to lunch. Thea worked in the mail room and had a reputation for knowing everyone and everything. Perhaps Kaja could even take her and the dog for a walk in return for a sandwich. Time might be of the essence and she could do with some help.

In front of the office block, she pulled into one of the visitor parking spaces and signed her name in the corresponding list at reception. These spaces were actually meant for employees visiting from other branches in order to join projects or attend meetings. But checks were not done very thoroughly. She had a strong aversion to public transport which was shared by Zorro and therefore she parked her car here regularly.

She was glad not to bump into anyone on her way to the office. Zorro made himself comfortable under the desk, as usual. She booted up the computer and had a look around her desk. Something felt strange. She squinted trying to work out what it was. Her papers. When she had rushed off last week, she had left a few papers lying around instead of locking them away in the cupboard as required by company policy. Now they were arranged in a neat pile on the right-hand side of her desk. She never made neat piles, perhaps she'd never succeed if she tried to. Her piles usually looked chaotic. She frowned and thought of possible answers: Either they were employing new cleaning staff or someone had gone through her things. She decided it must have been the cleaners, if only to dispel the uneasy feeling of being part of a B-movie industrial espionage. She banished such thoughts from her mind and opened the team agenda application on her computer to find out whether her boss was in. The sooner she was able to talk to him, the better. She signalled Zorro to wait and went over to her boss' office.

"Max, can you spare me a moment, please?"

Her boss looked up. For a moment, she could see the relief in his eyes, but then he asked indignantly: "Kaja, what's got into you, disappearing like that? Heaven knows how often I've tried to call your mobile."

She kept silent with embarrassment. She had found out last night when she finally checked her mailbox. Max had tried to call her twice on the day of her departure. Those were still rather friendly, slightly concerned messages. Normally, she got on well with him. He had not only been her boss since she started at PC Lux, but had also been her mentor. She had learned more tips and tricks from Max alone than throughout her whole university course. His later messages, however, had become increasingly impatient and he had been saying something about standby duty and availability. But it didn't make any sense to her. It wasn't as if a new release was imminent.

She turned her attention back to Max, who was talking himself into a rage: "At first I was relieved to see you managed to get the X3 program into production. I thought at least this important project won't get delayed by your absence."

It suddenly hit Kaja that the X3 project had been due last week. She had completely forgotten about it.

Max continued: "I assumed you'd taken it through the usual testing procedures, but I was wrong. The whole production line had to be halted and nobody knew where to find you."

As she was still completely confused, she confined herself to saying: "I'm really sorry, I just needed to get away from it all and realised too late that I'd forgotten my mobile."

This wasn't quite right, but there were a lot of things not right here and until she knew what the game was she tried to play along as best as she could.

"I'll do my best to find the error and correct it, right away."

She still couldn't understand how the program had gone into production without her approval, but she would have to find out later.

"That won't be necessary." Max boomed. "Luckily, we got hold of Frédéric Scherrer who used to be your team buddy until recently. He was very helpful."

"You asked Frédéric? Couldn't you find anyone else?" Stunned, Kaja stared at her line manager.

"Well, do you think it gave me any pleasure doing that? I tried to delay the decision as long as I could. But you were nowhere to be found. I didn't have a choice. Section leader Frentzen put me under pressure."

For the second time in a week, Kaja was sitting on a chair feeling totally numb. Feverishly, she tried to decide whether to confide in Max and tell him that it was not her who had sent the program into production. But then she concluded she needed to have a clearer picture herself first. She realised the situation wasn't improved if she tried to excuse one failure with another even if neither was her own fault. Without any proof, she would leave a bad impression whichever way she tried to explain it.

"Now go and do your work." Max ordered her harshly. She got up and said goodbye. When she had almost reached the door, he added: "And Kaja, pull yourself together, will you? I can't always fight your corner. Times are getting harder." She nodded without saying a word and left the room.

Kaja tried to contain her anger. The last thing she needed right now was a computer crash. When she came back to the office, Zorro just briefly raised his head and then fell asleep again in the comfortable knowledge that his mistress was back. 'Well then.' she thought. 'Let battle begin.' Obviously, someone had sent the program to production on her behalf and not without inserting a few errors. Of this second assumption she was quite certain. She had worked for hours on end, putting it through rigorous testing, both on the official testing servers as well as using her own debugger, an error-checking program. After a few teething problems, it had passed all processing stages without a hitch. All this she had achieved in record time hoping to earn herself a pay rise and a generous bonus.

What the hell had gone wrong then? One way or another, she would get to the bottom of this, she grimly promised herself. But now she had to deal with other matters.

She took a piece of paper and started to jot down a to-do list. Doing her normal work, she often made such lists, but usually mislaid them within the next ten minutes. 'I'd better get a post-it note and stick it to the monitor.' she decided. 'At least I'll always know where it is.' But then she stopped short: a post-it note with her password on was missing. They had been advised to choose a new password every four weeks. She found it impossible to memorise new passwords every month, so she had developed a habit of keeping the first four digits and only changing the remaining three. Anyone not familiar with the static part couldn't do anything with the remaining numbers noted down on a slip. She had not missed it when she first walked into her office, but now she realised the slip was gone. Her latest password was three weeks old already and by then she usually knew it by heart. She put this discovery on her to-do list as well. Kaja found herself using abbreviations when describing observations. She also added items relating to her official work and the meeting with Thea yet to be arranged. 'I hope I'm not getting paranoid.' she sighed. But then she resolutely dismissed all those gloomy thoughts in the face of the mountain of riddles to be solved.

Finally, she reached for the phone and dialled Thea's extension.

"Mail Room, Thea Marquardt speaking. How can I help you?" she could hear Thea's husky voice coming from the receiver.

"Hi Thea, it's me, Kaja."

"Hello Kaja, what a nice surprise. What have you been up to? I heard some unbelievable rumours about you."

"Not now, Thea, can we have a chat later?" Kaja answered hastily. "What about going for a walk over lunch? I have to take Zorro out and you can join me for a sandwich." she offered her colleague.

"Sounds terribly important if you have to resort to bribery." Thea giggled. "Let me see when I have my lunch break." she said, now sounding serious again. "I'm free from half past twelve, but not before."

"That's great. See you half past twelve by the fountain. What sandwich can I get you?"

"Cheese and onion." was her brief answer. Thea lived a vegetarian lifestyle with conviction. "See you then."

"Bye."

When she hung up, Kaja felt relieved. If anyone knew what was going on, it was Thea. You could trust her to have the news. Thea was almost sixty and responsible for all snail mail, as the traditional letter service was known, as well as electronic correspondence. She was both respected and feared by her colleagues. If you crossed her, it could well be that some information, usually of a rather private nature, suddenly became public knowledge. But she was always discreet and clever enough not to be officially identified as the source. On the other hand, if you were on good terms with her and tolerated her numerous quirks, she could be a loyal friend. Especially in her current situation, Kaja was glad to be counted among her friends.

Satisfied that she had managed to set up the meeting with Thea, Kaja spent the next two hours catching up with her work. She concentrated on two programs she had developed some time ago. This allowed her to make good progress. When she finished, a glance at her watch told her it was only eleven o'clock, which left her one and a half hours for some more investigations.

Luckily for her, it was almost impossible to operate a computer without leaving any traces. She typed in a few commands and tensely scrutinised the logbook entries of the server her machine was connected to. Where were the activity logs stored? Ah, there they were. She discovered the two expected entries bearing her ID number. Last Thursday, she had logged in at 7.30am and already logged out again at 10.42am, exactly ten minutes after her unsavoury conversation with the section leader.

She knew the next entry with her ID number should have been this morning. So she scanned all the entries since Thursday and soon found what she was looking for: Friday 9.20pm. 'Somebody was busy! Let's see what my doppelgänger was up to on my behalf.'

She followed the links to bring the relevant details up on her screen. According to the server, she had made a few final adjustments to the X3 program on Friday night, before sending it to production without any further tests. Afterwards, the mysterious stranger had logged off. For a moment, she wanted to make printouts of the entries but then changed her mind and only made electronic copies which she sent to her home e-mail address. As soon as the transmission finished, she completely deleted the e-mail from her machine.

Just in case... well, whatever. Better to be paranoid than sorry.

Next, she changed her password. This time, she renewed all the digits.

'So, my friend. Tough luck. That's the end of your secret visits.'

Thea was already waiting by the fountain. Kaja recognised her from afar. Her colleague liked to dress in bright colours and large patterns. Today was no exception as she wore a pink dress with bright yellow flowers. Her large plastic earrings matched the flowers and she had complemented her outfit with a necklace made of turquoise stones. Standing next to Thea, Kaja often felt her ordinary jeans and t-shirts made her almost invisible. Not that she wanted to dress like Thea, but this was the effect such a glamorous personality had on her. They greeted each other with three pecks and Kaja gave her the promised sandwich.

"Avocado with dried tomatoes and soft cheese - the ordinary cheese and onion sandwiches looked rather dry." Kaja explained.

"That's perfect, I like the filling." Thea answered and took a big bite. Kaja unwrapped her own lunch, a baguette with tuna, bean sprouts and red peppers, and started eating.

"Now go on, tell me, what's the latest news about me on the grapevine?" Kaja wanted to know while still munching her sandwich.

Thea swallowed and started to tell her: "They say you neglected your work, made a pass at your married team buddy, even harassed him at his home. After you were confronted with the facts, you suddenly disappeared -

which is true because I was trying to find you myself. Your disappearance, which became the office gossip very quickly - too quickly even for my liking - was generally interpreted as an admission of guilt. You should have known, Kaja. Where were your brains?" Thea criticised her with a worried look.

"I was definitely not in the mood to contemplate the consequences of my actions." Kaja replied in a sharper tone than intended.

"OK, calm down. That was only half the story."

"There's more to come? Give me strength." she groaned when her friend confirmed it with a sorry nod.

"Yes, there are more rumours, but they were harder to find, meaning not everyone was talking about them. They put the story in a different light but I doubt you'll enjoy hearing them." Thea warned her young colleague.

"Go on, it can't get much worse." Kaja remarked tensely.

"Let's put it this way: I know all your underwear - you really could be a bit more daring, darling - and they say you're quite a hottie in bed."

"But who would..."

"Well, have a guess. It looks like he wasn't as harassed as he makes out."

"I don't believe it. First he brings me into disrepute with the bosses and then he brags about having bedded me? What a cheek. I'll have to have a word with Max." She made to turn round and go back to Max's office to vent her anger.

"I wouldn't do that if I were you." Thea said, grabbing her arm.

"But why? You said yourself..."

"... that I only heard rumours." she gently completed the sentence.

"But I can't let him get away with it!"

"No." Thea said. "Of course not. But there may be subtler ways to deal with him. Perhaps you should first try to find out what the real issue is."

"You're right. I'm a little confused. Since last week, things have been happening at breakneck speed and obviously not in my favour. I want my old life back, like it was two weeks ago."

"Are you sure that's what you want?"

"Hm." Kaja grumbled. "At least most of it. Of course I can do without Frédéric."

They sat down on a bench by the pond and watched Zorro swim across trying to chase some ducks.

"Why don't you just tell me what really happened?" Thea asked.

So Kaja came to tell her story for a third time, but now adding the suspicion that her office had been searched and the fact that the X3 program had been altered and submitted to the production department without her authorisation.

"I'll have to look at it in more detail. Perhaps I can find out what exactly has been changed. And most of all, if Frédéric was involved. But he's the most likely candidate because of the required password. As we used to work together he probably saw me type it in. It wasn't top secret anyway. You know what it was like before the merger. Everyone knew the passwords of their closest colleagues and we only changed them every three months."

She frowned. "I don't understand what Frédéric has got to gain from it? OK, I can understand he was keen to win the competition. I can also understand that he thought the best way to get access to my stuff was to go to bed with me. But why all the rest...?"

"He had to discredit you in case you were trying to point the finger at him for having stolen your program. That way he could be sure you'd be too embarrassed to say anything. And if you did, nobody would believe you."

"That's what Lance said." Kaja mumbled to herself.

"Who is Lance?" Thea probed.

"Lance? Did I say Lance? That's... uhm... a friend of Grandma's." Kaja stammered.

Thea gave her an inquisitive look, but against her usual habit she decided not to ask any further questions in order not to confuse Kaja any more.

"I think he went through too much pain just for the sake of winning the competition." Kaja insisted.

"What was the prize?" Thea asked.

"Glory, honour and 10,000 Swiss francs."

"Those are pretty good motives."

"On the face of it, they are. But do you know how much he earns? Not to mention his bonuses?"

"Some people can't resist the magical attraction of money, no matter how much they've amassed already." Thea pointed out.

"Hm, it is possible, but to be honest, I'm not convinced. There's more to it, I can feel it."

"How come you suddenly listen to your feelings?" Her friend sounded surprised.

"I don't know." Kaja replied. "I just do. Listen, can you do me a favour and keep an ear out for me? If I come up with anything, I'll let you know as well. And please don't pass on my suspicions to anyone."

"I'll take them to my grave." Thea grinned, but she was dead serious.

"Good, let's go back to work. You don't want to be late."

She whistled for her dog who was lying in the grass enjoying the sunshine and the three of them walked back to the office block.

Back in her office, she wanted to eat an apple she had placed on the desk in the morning but her hand grabbed at nothing. She looked around and - to her horror - she discovered Lance sitting in the window sill with his clawed feet dangling. She quickly closed the door and drew herself up in front of him, hissing:

"What are you doing here? I clearly told you to wait for me. And I want my apple back."

She snatched the apple from him and was satisfied with the surprise in the dragon's face. "Ha, I'm quicker than you think."

Lance sighed: "Yes, I didn't think you were that quick. At least your reflexes are still working. To answer your question: I did wait for you. Here."

"Well, that's the problem. You were not supposed to wait here, but at home. What if somebody sees you?"

"Nobody can see me, apart from you and Josephine. She's your grandmother and therefore related to you, so that's quite natural. Do you have any other relatives working here? You don't?" When she shook her head, taken by surprise, he nodded with satisfaction and said: "So what's the problem?"

"What am I going to do with you?" Kaja found little comfort in his words and scanned the room trying to find a place to hide him.

Lance took a step forward and gently but firmly pushed her into the office chair. "You carry on with your work and I'll have a little look around the building."

"You can't just..." Kaja started.

"Yes, I can. And who knows? Perhaps I'll find something useful for you. Remember? I'm a master in sneaking around."

He winked at her and disappeared through a wall. 'I don't believe it.' Kaja thought shaking her head. As if she didn't have enough problems, she certainly did not need a dragon to keep under control.

Later back at home, she felt whacked out and went into the kitchen to make herself a cup of tea. While the water was boiling, she fed Zorro. But when she walked past the kitchen table, she only nodded at the dragon. She was not in the mood to have another argument with him.

"It's your emotions, you know."

"What was that?"

Kaja was woken from her thoughts and looked at him, forgetting that she had resolved to ignore him.

"You're so tired because of the intense emotions that got hold of you today and in the past few days. They are soaking up your energy."

"Can't you go and steal a virgin somewhere? I'm really not in the mood for pseudo-scientific discussions with a dragon right now."

Undisturbed, he continued: "You've built a lot of firewalls around you for the past few years, just to keep your feelings at bay. I presume you've learned to do that in your childhood and the long practice made you surprisingly perfect. These walls are also the reason why you don't receive the telepathic announcements of my arrival and why you insist on using an old-fashioned telephone to talk to Mémé. But deep inside, you are a very sensitive person, Kaja."

"I'm a toughie, that's what I am." Kaja murmured, clearly upset.

She quickly took a sip of her tea which had just finished brewing - and promptly scalded her mouth. "Ouch!" she said. "And why isn't the tactic working for me now?" she asked Lance in a stroppy tone.

"I presume it has something to do with the shock you had last week. Such a blatant abuse of your confidence is bound to throw you. Not forgetting that the whole story is a threat to your very existence. It must be gut-wrenching, your self-defence is in tatters."

"What're you trying to tell me? I was quite happy the way I was."

"See the positive side. You can't block the issue from your mind forever. You could've had an accident or got seriously ill."

Kaja looked at him for a moment without saying a word. Then she said: "I need to think." and disappeared into her room.

'That would explain why I've suddenly started to have premonitions again. They just strike me out of the blue.' she thought lying stretched out on top of her bed. She had tried to do some further investigations that afternoon, but hadn't made any real progress. She had found that it was indeed Frédéric who had used her password and sent the X3 to the production department. But he'd used an earlier test version instead of the final one. He was cleverer than she thought. Apparently, he had expected a call to resolve the problems. That way, he had been able to correct the errors in next to no time. He only had to replace the faulty version with the fully tested one and appear as the big saviour. This also explained the one call on her mobile that was recorded as "Unknown Caller". It was his new office number. Thanks to Thea, it had not been difficult to confirm. If only she could work out what his motives were. A personal vendetta was unlikely. They had not known each other long enough to justify all the effort he had put into his scheme. No, she decided, there must be something else.

12

Not much happened over the following few days. The dragon did not bother her too much and instead entertained her in the evenings with amusing stories over a glass of wine. Kaja was not sure how much to believe of his tales. But who cared if the story teller was a born-and-bred dragon. This alone was an absurdity in itself.

However, on Thursday afternoon she witnessed for the first time that occasionally even dragons can be thrown off track. Kaja could have had a good laugh about it, had she not been so surprised or even shocked.

That day, she left work early because she wanted to go to town to buy a book. She knew of a small second-hand book shop she had never visited before and where she hoped to find an odd, out-of-print publication she had wanted to buy for some time. Zorro lay curled up on the back seat and Lance had joined her in the front passenger seat for a change.

As almost to be expected, there were no free parking spaces near the bookshop. In search of one, she went round the block a few times but was unlucky. Disappointed, she was approaching a junction when she saw a blond woman on a rickety bicycle riding towards her. Kaja slowed down to give her more time to avoid a collision. But as she was just about to say something to Lance, she noticed that the cyclist made no attempt to change her direction. On the contrary. She was coming straight at her with her eyes wide open. Kaja tried to pull the car sideways, even scraped a parked vehicle by the roadside, but it was too late. The bicycle hit her front wing with a loud bang and the young woman dropped to the ground like a felled tree. Kaja was panicking with fear, jumped out of the car and knelt beside the stranger. A frightening amount of blood was coming from a large gash just below her hairline.

"Hello? Can you hear me?" Kaja shouted in desperation.

Why didn't anyone stop to help? She needed help quickly. The blond woman had her eyes closed and was not moving. With nervous hands, Kaja tried to feel for her pulse. It seemed unlikely she could expect any help from passers-by. She took a deep breath and collected her thoughts. She had attended a first aid course ages ago. So she suppressed her rising fear and concentrated on using a packet of tissues and her scarf to stop the bleeding. She was just putting the finishing touches to her makeshift pressure bandage, when the young woman suddenly opened her eyes. Her look was bleary and confused at first but then focussed quickly.

"Does it hurt anywhere?" Kaja tried to make her speak. The young woman must have been about the same age as herself, she registered. She slowly went up on one elbow and tried to move her limbs. Then she answered: "Only my head. Apart from that, it was only the shock. This graze here is not as bad as it looks."

Kaja felt a big wave of relief which soon gave way to anger.

"What were you doing? Are you on drugs or something? You went straight in front of my car. If you're trying to commit suicide, please don't involve me."

"Well, no. I didn't mean to. But do you realise you have a dragon in your car?"

"A what?" Kaja said sheepishly.

"Yes, there was a dragon. I couldn't take my eyes of the strange creature and forgot to pay attention to the road."

"Oh nonsense, that was all in your imagination." Kaja hastened to add while taking a quick look at the car to see whether Lance was still visible. He wasn't and she hoped he would keep out of sight. Then she turned to the woman on the ground again.

"Look, perhaps we should try and get off the road, if you are up to it. We're obstructing the traffic here. OK?"

Hours later she reached home, totally exhausted. She had taken Miri - this was the woman's name - to hospital, waited until her head wound got stitched and further tests carried out and had then taken her home. All this upheaval had taken a lot of strength and nerves, especially since Miri had been adamant she'd seen a dragon in Kaja's car. Kaja wouldn't have it and had blocked any attempt to discuss Miri's observation. This had been harder than expected as the little woman was quite temperamental. They had exchanged addresses and Kaja had promised to inform her insurance company to cover the bicycle which was beyond repair as well as possible after-effects of the injury. Miri had not wanted her to and claimed it was all her own fault. But Kaja had insisted. Now she was taking deep breaths and working her shoulders to get rid of the tension. At least the car was OK, apart from a small scratch on the front wing.

Lance had made himself scarce since the accident and that was just as well! Kaja was angry with him. Hadn't he promised that she was the only person who could see him? Apart from this afternoon's shock, she also felt a touch of jealousy: He was her personal dragon. There was no need for anyone else to see him!

Back at home, she could feel his presence. The air was full of blue energy. Where was he? Obviously not in the living room or the kitchen. As she walked towards the bedroom, she came past the office door which was slightly ajar. And there he was, sitting next to a pile of screwed-up sheets of paper and chewing on an old-fashioned fountain pen. Although he made a comical picture, she looked at him angrily when she demanded to know: "Do you have any explanation about what happened earlier on? I don't ever want to see this happen again."

Lance looked at her and tore at his non-existent hair: "Believe me, Kaja. I don't have a clue. That's never happened to me before. In fact, I didn't even know it was possible."

"Do you know what she said?"

"Yes, I was so shocked that I rushed straight here and started to do some calculations."

Without saying a word, Kaja picked up a sheet of paper from the floor and smoothed it out. It was covered in strange symbols that did not make any sense to her. "Calculations?"

"Yes, something like that. Probability estimates. But I haven't found the correct formula." He continued, adding some incomprehensible technical terms. "Listen, Kaja, I have to leave you for a while. I'll be back as soon as I know what's going on here."

Kaja simply nodded and left the room.

Soon after, Kaja was pacing restlessly around her flat. She did not know what to do with herself. She could clearly feel that Lance was gone. Apparently, she had got used to his presence more than she was ready to admit. She had not made much progress with her problems at work either and was pretty sure they were part of a bigger picture, but she could not see what it was. Even more frustrating was the fact that she was running out of avenues to investigate. Zorro watched her movements round the flat uneasily. In frustration, she dropped on the sofa. But with a sudden inspiration, she soon jumped up and grabbed her jacket which was hanging by the door. She searched its pockets trying to find the slip of paper Tim had left for her on his unexpected departure. Finally, she found what she was looking for and returned to the sofa. On the way, she picked up the cordless phone and, after a short hesitation, quickly dialled Tim's number. She knew she would go mental if she didn't have the chance to talk to someone. Too many things were going on in her head. She had expected to speak to an answer machine and was pleasantly surprised when he answered himself after the first ring.

"Hello?" his enquiring voice came through the receiver.

"Is your mobile always glued to your ear?"

"Kaja, it's you. You won't believe this, but I was just about to call you. This is why I had the mobile in my hand."

She blinked in surprise but then realised he could not see her. "Erm, yes that is a surprise."

"Maybe not, who knows?" he said in an insinuating tone.

"Oh, stop it." Kaja laughed. "You sound already like Mémé. Why did you want to call me?" she enquired curiously.

"Just to hear your beautiful voice." he teased her.

"Yes, I think I could make a living from telephone sex. What do you think?" she returned the banter. "But seriously. What's your reason for calling me?"

"I happen to be with my parents in Zurich tonight and thought you might want to go for a walk by the lake and have a beer with me?"

Going out? Tonight? Kaja briefly hesitated. She had already changed into her baggy home clothes. But - 'Hey, why not.' - she took a spontaneous decision. She needed somebody to talk to and might as well go for a walk while doing so.

"So, what do you say? Or am I calling at the wrong time?"

"No, not at all. I just had to push myself to get dressed up again. But Zorro will be eternally grateful." she added.

"I'll pick you up in fifteen minutes."

"Make it twenty, OK? That'll give me the slimmest of chances to make myself presentable."

She quickly washed her face and put on new make-up. 'What am I doing here, dolling myself up for Tim?' She grimaced, but couldn't help the urge to look her best. Maybe he'll see the grown-up woman in her for once and not the Ragamuffin of old. Suddenly she remembered that evening in France when he stole a kiss from her. The memory made her feel boiling hot. My god, she'd almost forgotten about it. Not that she hadn't enjoyed it, but at the moment she was lacking the energy for such games. What's more, she preferred to be in control of the how, when and where in her relationships. She had to laugh about herself. Most likely she was reading too much into the small incident which he might have totally forgotten by now.

Kaja couldn't have been more wrong. In fact, there wasn't a single day Tim did not have to think of her. Obviously he had fallen for the little... no, he corrected himself on the way to Kaja's flat... the big whirlwind. He had never fallen in love before. Granted, he'd had a few girlfriends in the past, but owing to his busy work schedule, they had not been more than fleeting affairs. He was not too unhappy with that, had never looked for a lasting relationship. And he thought it was entirely his choice, but maybe he simply had not met the right girl yet. He'd better try to make her see it the same way. He had to smile with a feeling she might be hard work. But then he pushed all these confusing thoughts aside, decided to simply enjoy her company and wait and see what the evening would bring.

When the door bell rang, Kaja took a last, nervous look in the mirror. Zorro noisily jumped at the closed door and Kaja hurried to open it for her visitor. Tim got almost bowled over by an enthusiastic bundle of fur flying at him.

"Uff." Tim gasped and tried to push the dog out of the way, but kept his hand on Zorro's head and tickled him behind his ears while greeting Kaja. She noticed with relief that he had no intention of continuing where he had left off on their previous date.

"Let's take a stroll to the lake, shall we?" she asked him. "It's not very far."

"Yes, I thought it might be a good idea."

He linked arms with her and they walked like friends towards the lake. Zorro was in front of them and his tail shone brightly in the darkness of the city which was only broken by the occasional street light. It was a mild September evening but nevertheless she was glad to have her jacket with her.

For a while, they walked next to each other without saying a word. They just enjoyed the walk until Kaja finally broke the silence and asked: "Why did you have to leave so suddenly?"

She noticed how he hesitated briefly before answering: "A friend of mine died."

Kaja was taken aback and kept silent. She did not know how to react to the news. Discreetly she asked: "Was it an accident?"

"No, he had cancer. So it didn't come out of the blue, but you always hope for a miracle." he said very quietly, more to himself than to Kaja. She took his hand and squeezed it gently.

"I'm sorry I reminded you. I didn't know..." She stopped and looked at him. He smiled at her and returned the squeeze of her hand.

"Don't worry. I'm glad I told you. But we mustn't let it spoil our nice evening. It wouldn't bring my friend back to life again. I'm sure Sandro, that was his name, is in a peaceful place now, a place without any pain."

His eyes glistened in the street light under her probing glance. You had to give it to him: there was more than she expected under his attractive appearance. Kaja suddenly realised that she hardly knew anything about the man she was walking with. She could sense an intimacy between them, but to a large extent it was down to the childhood they had spent together. She only knew the boy of her memories. They had taken their first steps into adulthood independently of each other. She suddenly felt curious and wanted to explore what kind of man had become of the boy from back then.

His voice woke her from her thoughts.

"Any news from your work?" he asked, honestly interested.

Kaja had anticipated the question. Calmly she told him what had happened in the meantime and what she had found out. Finally, she told him of her suspicions that something was wrong with the whole company, not only with herself.

"How come?" he wanted to know.

"Firstly, it does not make any sense to me. They could have fired me a long time ago, if they wanted to. I've given them plenty of reasons."

"Only because of the contest?" He frowned in disbelief.

Too late Kaja remembered why Frédéric denigrated her with her boss and that she had had an affair with that bastard. An affair that was in the past, she corrected her thoughts and blushed. She was glad it was so dark.

"Well, how shall I put it. There was... something else."

"What was it?" he encouraged her to tell him.

So she told him the rest of the story.

"I'm speechless at so much malice." Tim said stunned. "No wonder our species has got a bad reputation." he grumbled angrily.

"Your species?" Kaja looked at him not comprehending.

"Well, us men, I mean."

"Oh, those." Kaja giggled and felt her tension subside.

"That bastard." he raged.

"I know that now." Kaja replied grimly. "Luckily, it was only an affair." Now she had said it, she realised it was the truth.

It seemed she had not been in love with him at all. Otherwise it would have hurt much more. She simply felt humiliated and angry. Angry, because he had slandered her name with friends and colleagues for no apparent reason. She glanced at Tim trying to find out how he felt about her latest revelations.

"Are you shocked?" she said trying to sound cool. But she knew she would be disappointed if he was.

"Shocked? Why should I be shocked?" He sounded surprised. "No, I'm just angry that someone abused your trust in such an appalling way."

Kaja took a deep breath of relief. "Well," she continued, "if this was only about me, they'd have enough evidence to sack me. But they didn't, so it doesn't make any sense. Secondly, I have a funny feeling..."

She looked at him to see how he would react to this hint. But Tim had learned his lessons from Mémé and said without batting an eyelid: "So, what are you going to do next?"

In frustration, Kaja ran her fingers through her hair and kicked a stone into the water. Zorro jumped after it. "I wish somebody could tell me what to do next."

"Yes, that's exactly what you need." Tim teased her. "Because you're so good at taking advice on board."

"Hm, that's true, I normally find it hard." she admitted with a mischievous smile. "But at this very moment, I'm just lost."

He paused briefly and then suggested: "I have a friend. His name is Simon. Perhaps I should introduce you to him. He's a private investigator. Maybe he can help you."

"A detective?"

"Something like that. But I don't know if he's got any experience with bullying at work."

"I thought they rather like keeping unfaithful spouses under surveillance or something like that." Kaja was surprised.

"To be honest, I don't know what his field is. I haven't seen him for ages." He shrugged his shoulders with regret that he did not have any more information. "I do like my regular trips abroad, but they are counter-productive when it comes to keeping a social life in Switzerland. If you think he might be able to help you, I'll give him a call."

"Hm, it might be worth a try." Kaja agreed. "Yes, please give him a ring and give him a summary of my situation. If he thinks he can help us... help me," she quickly corrected herself, "I would like to have a word with him. But I'd prefer you to be there as well." She looked at him, unsure of his response.

"Yes, of course. He is my friend, after all." he reassured her. "I told you I'll be in Switzerland for the next two months and" he continued with a mock bow, "I'll be at your service, Madam."

"Oh, stop it." she gave him a little nudge to defuse the tension that had started to build again between them. 'Pull yourself together.' she warned herself. 'No time for games, least of all with one of the few best friends you've got left.'

Tim watched her expression become withdrawn and was disappointed. This did not seem the right time to give her another kiss. He remembered the previous occasion all too well. But something told him not to push his luck and rather to enjoy her company instead and be patient.

"Thirsty?" he teased her, when they reached one of the shore-side restaurants with panoramic views.

"Always." she said and linked arms with him.

13

The very next morning, Kaja received a phone call from Tim: "Good news, I managed to get hold of Simon and he thinks he might be able to help."

"Really? That would be fantastic." Kaja was excited. "What exactly does he do?"

"He'd better explain it to you himself. But he is living in Bern and I wanted to ask you if you would like to come over this weekend? That would also give us a chance to visit the exhibition, but only if you have nothing better planned, of course." he hastened to add.

"Yes, why not. It would be nice." she answered. Lance was still notably absent and she didn't expect to make much progress all by herself.

"OK, let's say 10 o'clock in Bern. I'll meet you at the railway station. You can pick me up in your car. I'll show you where the gallery is."

"Good idea. I was dreading driving through Bern on my own. I think the way to the station is about all I can manage." she mocked herself.

As soon as she had hung up, the phone rang again. The display told her that this time it was Thea's direct line. Kaja was surprised, and wondered if her friend already had some news for her. "Hi Thea, how are you?"

"Hello Kaja, I just wanted to tell you that the submissions for the programming competition have been uploaded to test server B."

"Yes, OK, but what's it got to do with me?" Kaja was not sure what to make of the information.

"I thought it might be useful for you to know, just in case you want to make some final adjustments to your entry." Thea answered. "Bye for now, got to go" Those were the last words Kaja heard from her friend before the phone went silent.

Thea had simply hung up. Kaja shook her head. What was that supposed to mean? She had never made an entry because Frédéric had stolen her program. But come to think of it: Indirectly, it was her entry. She should give him a taste of his own medicine and plant some bugs. But then she sighed. What was the use? Faults can be found and corrected. And she did not have access to his computer or his passwords. Unless... Excited, she jumped up and started to pace her office like a tiger in its cage. Unless he was so sure of his game that he hadn't changed his passwords yet! She looked at the clock. He must be at work right now. No use trying to gain access: The system would not allow a double log-on. But his lunch break would start in half an hour and Kaja knew he never missed it. She also knew he was meticulous in logging out of the system whenever he left his desk.

"Come on." she called Zorro who was asleep under her desk. "We'll take our walk early today."

As soon as they were back - Zorro had barely settled in his resting place - Kaja sat down in front of the computer, rubbing her hands in anticipation. Now she had to think carefully. His main password was MAC347, at least that's what he had used for the past three weeks. She typed it in - but nothing happened. Maybe he'd changed the last three digits. He had used her method occasionally himself after she'd explained it to him. The memory fuelled her anger and the computer started to play up. 'Take a deep breath.' she tried to calm herself. She could not afford to cause a system crash at this very moment. So she banished any emotions from her mind and tried to think rationally. His previous password had been MAC473, so why not try MAC734 instead? She quickly typed it in but again nothing happened. It was starting to drive her mad. This meant with some certainty that he had changed his password completely. It could have been made up of anything. She had exactly one attempt left, otherwise his account would be blocked and the security department would look into the cause for the three failed login attempts. They would find out very quickly that they came from her workstation. Dammit! Think, Kaja, think! Suddenly she had an inspiration. Where was that slip of paper she had found and kept while cleaning her flat? Frantically, she searched her handbag. She'd put it in there after it had almost ended up in the washing machine, together with her jeans. But it wasn't there, or was it? To save time, she quickly tipped the whole content of her handbag on the floor. Never mind all those pens, tampons, tissues and coins - there it was, half-hidden under her keys. The slip said "Superman77". Kaja typed it in and closed her eyes before hitting the Enter key. Please let it be the right one! When Kaja did not hear the usual Pling sound that came with an unsuccessful login attempt, she slowly opened her eyes and could hardly believe what she saw: It had worked. She got excited and started drumming her fingers on the desktop. So far so good, but what next? She glanced at the clock and realised that she had little time left. When Frédéric came back from his lunch break, she needed to have logged out. This left her about 10 minutes. She needed to establish whether he had changed his password for test server B. There was a good chance he hadn't as these passwords did not have to be changed as often. Yes, the test server responded. She logged out, both from the test server and the whole system, and then logged in again with her own ID.

Again, Kaja started pacing her office. This was all well and good, but what did she want to achieve? Inserting bugs into the program would not make any sense. They could easily be found and corrected. It was also against her work ethics to spoil her own work. She stopped in front of the window and stared outside. Suddenly she had an idea. What if, instead of sabotaging the program, she was to improve it somehow? It was, after all, an accounting program and dealt with money transfers. Feverishly, she went through the endless possibilities that computer technology presented. Yes, there was a way to do it, she decided. But first she had to find out where little Freddy had his new office. She didn't want these activities to be traced back to her own machine, even if she did not expect him to notice the minute detail she was going to insert, nor that he would even think of accusing her. He had too much to lose, but nevertheless she didn't want to run the risk of being found out. She searched the intranet and found his office was in the next building, on the third floor. Gaining access would not be a problem because both buildings had a common entrance. But she did not have a clue who else was working over there and at what time they usually left their offices. In frustration, she kicked a paper ball across the room. Zorro thought it was his playtime and tried to catch it, knocking over the waste bin as he jumped. Kaja's tension subsided and she had to laugh out loud at the chaos the dog had caused. When she calmed down, she pushed him back into his usual place, started to clear up the mess and put her things back into the handbag. Come to think of it, there was not much left to do here before the weekend. It was better to go home and carry on working there instead of going mad in this tiny office where she could barely sit still for a moment. On the spur of the moment, she went over to see Max.

"Can I help you?" he didn't even look up from his papers when she gently knocked and put her head round the door.

"It's only me. I just wanted to say: I have to be off early today, need to see the doctor."

He looked up in surprise: "Are you OK? Anything wrong?"

"Nothing's wrong." she calmed him down. "Only a routine check-up. Women's matters."

"Oh, yes, of course you can go." He sounded slightly embarrassed.

When Kaja left his office, she had to control herself not to start laughing. It was the only plausible reason she could think of and the only one she was sure he would not dare questioning. All men were the same in this respect, even if they claimed to be open-minded and well-educated. As

110

soon as you mentioned only the slightest detail of normal female bodily functions, they blushed and changed the subject. Max was no different as she could tell from his red ears. 'That's men for you.' she scoffed.

The first thing she did when she got home was to make herself a big jug of home-made lemonade and take a glass of it outside to the pergola. She shook the tension out of her shoulders and sat up straight to type her idea into the laptop which she had taken outside. For the next three hours, she concentrated fully on her task and only stopped occasionally to take a sip from her drink. Finally, she saved the work and stretched. A deckchair was certainly not the most suitable piece of furniture for work normally done in an office and she felt rather stiff from sitting in it for too long. Looking at her watch, she noticed it was 5 o'clock already. She often lost track of time while programming. "All I need now are little Freddy's login details." She murmured to herself. She knew she could get them from the Human Resources system tonight but realised she would have to wait for at least another fifteen minutes before it was safe to hack into it. She was not happy. There was no doubt she would get what she needed but she felt uneasy about staying too long in a place she was not supposed to be in. Suddenly she remembered something: A few weeks ago, she had transferred some money into his account. It had been stupid of her to think she owed him just because she felt he offered to pay their bills too often. What a silly cow she was! Women will go to any lengths to prove they are independent and in control. What a joke! At least it might help her now, she decided. She opened a browser window and connected to the Internet to log into her e-banking account. The heading "Past Transactions" contained numerous entries and it took her a little while to go through them as she could not remember the exact date. Stop. Now she had almost scrolled past it. She quickly copied his account details and sighed when she went through the correct log-off procedure. The events of the past few weeks had taught her a lesson. Before, she would have ignored the warning message and simply closed the browser window. Now she had become more cautious.

Next, Kaja went back to her programming editor window and inserted the account details into the code. A final test run showed her that everything seemed to work perfectly: "No errors found." It was a good sign, but not enough. She had to make absolutely sure and the only way to do this was to use the test server in the company, meaning that she had to go back there in the middle of the night. She saved her work on a USB stick and put it in the inside pocket of her jacket, just to make sure she would not forget it. All done. Now she had to hurry up if she wanted to use the last daylight for a jog.

She was almost out of the door with Zorro at her heels, when the telephone rang. 'Who's that?' Kaja thought. She did not recognise the number on the caller display. For a moment, she considered ignoring the call but then curiosity got the better of her and she answered the phone.

"Hello?"

"Hi, Kaja, is that you? It's me, Miri!"

It took Kaja by surprise. "Who? Oh, I'm sorry. I didn't recognise your name. Remembering them is not one of my strong points." she apologised. "How are you? I meant to ring you earlier and ask about your injuries, but I had a hectic day."

"Oh, don't worry." Miri reassured her. "I'm much better today. I was thinking: Shall we spend the evening together? I don't feel like going out yet, but you could come over for a chat." she bubbled away.

"Erm." It was too much for Kaja. Her head was spinning. She had other plans tonight and had to get on with them if her scheme was to succeed. Unless she was to take Miri along to... Well, what for? To ask her to keep watch? While she was doing some semi-legal or, let's face it, illegal manipulations? She could not do that. She hardly knew the woman. Why should she trust a complete stranger? But there was a voice in her head saying: "That's the whole point. She is not a stranger. In fact, she seems frighteningly familiar." Nonsense. She banished the silly voice from her head.

"Kaja, are you still there?" Miri's voice woke her from her thoughts. "It was just an idea I had. If you don't want to come, I'll understand." Her voice suddenly sounded insecure and less lively.

Kaja realised that it had taken her too long to come up with an answer, which was why she hastened to say: "No, it's a brilliant idea. It's only that I'm rather busy this weekend. Can we make it Monday night instead?"

"Great, Monday is fine with me. You have my address. Shall we say at seven?"

"Perfect. Can I bring my dog along?"

"If he isn't scared of cats, he's welcome." Miri joked.

By the time Kaja and her four-legged friend returned from their exercise, it was completely dark outside. She took a shower and changed her clothes. Then she sat down at the kitchen table and tried to calm her nerves. She had the USB stick with the code segment in her trouser pocket. All she needed now was to pluck up the courage and go through with her plan. But she still hesitated. It was unfortunate that little Freddy had moved to the other building. She had no idea who was working there and it would be hard to explain her presence even to people she knew. If only Lance was here to help. "For once he could make himself useful. Where is he when I need him?" she grumbled. He could have sneaked into the office building to find out if anyone was still at work. She sighed. At least it was Friday. Even the worst workaholics might tear themselves away from their desks to enjoy a few hours of the city's night life. What the heck... The kitchen ceiling light exploded with a bang and the air around her hummed and crackled with electric charge.

"Lance?" Kaja recognised his shape on the sofa, but not as sharply as usual.

"What are you doing here? I thought you had important things to do?"

Lance stared at her angrily. "I have indeed. And I had just reached the top of the queue for an audience with the head dragoness when you called me. Now I'll have to line up again at the back. Do you have any idea how long I had been queueing?"

"About 24 hours if I'm not mistaken." Kaja said slightly amused. "I didn't call you. But thanks for coming anyway." she winked at him.

"Of course you called me." he snapped at her. "Your words were 'If only Lance was here.' which means you need me."

Kaja stared at him in surprise. When she found her voice again, she tried to be friendly: "I'm really sorry. I didn't know I can call you like a genie from a bottle. It wouldn't have happened, if you had told me more about dragons in general and about yourself in particular." she could not refrain from adding.

Ignoring this last statement, he informed her stiffly: "It is my duty to come when you call me because you're my protégée."

"If that's the case and now you're here, let's get on with it and not waste any more time. Zorro, sorry my boy, you'll have to stay home today."

Zorro acknowledged the order with a desperate howl. When he realised Kaja had made up her mind, he retreated under the sofa with a grim face. Kaja looked at the dragon, grabbed her jacket from the chair and said: "Come on, time to go."

"Where are we going? Just wait a moment, what are you up to?"

"I'll tell you on the way. Come on, hurry up."

Kaja did not waste any time opening the car door for him and trusted he would use his usual dragon method to join her. By the time he realised, she had already started the engine, so he was quick to materialise next to her on the passenger seat.

"Are you going to explain to me what is so urgent that it required my immediate presence?" he asked crossly.

She briefly explained her plan and finished by saying: "It's your job to go inside and find out if and where people are still working. If at all possible, I want to avoid bumping into them. Please come back and tell me. Later, while I'm... finalising the program, you can keep watch outside the office and warn me of anyone coming." Pleased with her plan, she leaned back in the seat, relaxing for the first time this evening.

Lance stared at her in disbelief: "You just want me to keep watch? Is that all you called me back for?"

"Why are you so angry? I'm sure you can talk to that dragoness of yours another time. And as I said: I didn't call you deliberately. Come to think of it, I never invited you to interfere with my life in the first place." This last sentence sounded sharper than she had intended. So she added in a more conciliatory tone: "But now you're here, I don't see why you can't help me with my plan. And if you're honest, you find the whole thing just as exciting as I do. Or am I wrong?"

Lance broke into a laugh and raised his hands in surrender: "OK, I give up. I might as well help you. Although I still don't think this is right. I'm supposed to give you moral support, not to lead you onto the career path of a criminal."

"You're supposed to give me what?" Kaja was irritated. "I can't follow you." She flicked her hair back over her shoulder. "Anyway, we have more important things to do. And if you must know: It was you who gave me the idea with your story."

"Of course." he steamed. "Now it is my fault you that you're going down the slippery slope." Disgruntled, he looked out of the window.

"So what was it you wanted to discuss with this dragon lady?" Kaja enquired to distract him.

"She's not a dragon lady, she's a dragoness." Lance corrected her. "And she's not just any dragoness, but the oldest one, which is why she's considered our leader."

Kaja was impressed and tried to understand: "So does this mean she is something like your queen?"

"Yes, but she's not our ruler. Dragons don't like to be ruled. She is our advisor. I need her advice on the young woman that ran into your car yesterday and who claims she's seen me."

"Ah yes, Miri. I just had a phone call from her. We're meeting up Monday night."

"You're still in touch with her?" Lance sounded rather alarmed.

"Yes, of course. Why not?"

"I'd prefer you to keep this on hold until I know more."

"Oh, don't be silly. There's nothing wrong with me seeing her. In fact, I feel like I've known her for a long time. - But let's talk about that later. Here we are."

She got out of the car and took a deep breath of the cool night-time air. So this was it, time to put her plan into action. She straightened her shoulders with determination and went towards the building. Lance followed her closely behind. At the door, she was about to swipe her pass when she stopped. It did not seem a good idea to let the system register her card. "Lance, you can get in here without my help, can't you?"

"Of course I can." the dragon replied and was keen to give her a demonstration by disappearing and re-appearing through the concrete wall.

"That's a rather practical skill to have." she said with a touch of jealousy.

"Don't complain and be grateful. I wouldn't be here without it. But I take it you can't follow me? So how are you going to get inside?"

"That's a bit of a problem. Let me think... There's an emergency exit on the first floor. The door is not alarmed because it is used during the day by smokers to take their break. Can you try and open it from the inside?"

"Will do." Lance replied promptly and disappeared.

Kaja sneaked to the side of the building and climbed up the external fire escape ladder. The door on the first floor opened with a soft click. "Well done, partner." she praised him. "OK, listen, I'll turn left to go to my own office. You turn right, go three floors up and follow the corridor down to room 341. Once you have all the information we need, come back and report to me."

"Yes, Ma'am!" Lance replied with little enthusiasm and ambled off.

"And don't hurry. You might break into a sweat." Kaja added sarcastically as he left before she turned the other way to wait for his return in her office.

Lance had deliberately made it look as if he was having leisurely stroll in order to tease Kaja. His little hothead protégée needed to be taught a lesson. As soon as he was out of her sight, he rushed through the building like a flash and remembered exactly where he'd seen any lights on. He quickly inspected those rooms and registered who was there and what they were doing. Apparently, the cleaners had just finished this floor and were about to leave. Apart from that, he only noticed lights in two other offices. One of them was empty. Lance asked himself if the person had simply forgotten to switch off the lights but then realised the computer was still running as well. He frowned. This could be dangerous. If the employee returned while Kaja was in Freddy's office, they might bump into each other. She needed to take precautions. In the second office, he found a woman concentrating on her work. He left the floor as unnoticed as he'd entered it and returned to Kaja.

"What's the news? Did you see anyone?" she welcomed him impatiently.

Lance reported what he had seen and closed by saying: "Your only problem is the empty desk. What are you going to do if you bump into that person?"

Kaja dismissed his concerns with a shrug of her shoulders. "Maybe someone just forgot to switch off the computer and the lights. It does happen."

But Lance was not satisfied with her explanation. He stood in front of Kaja, blocking her way to the door.

"What are you doing? Let me finish my business. I thought you were on my side." she hissed at him impatiently.

"I'm here to help you. That is why I'd prefer you to explain what you are going to do, just in case somebody sees you."

"Listen, of course it wouldn't be ideal if someone saw me, but I'm authorised to be in this building. I'm an employee, just like everyone else."

"And you really intend to jeopardise your whole plan just because you can't find a better excuse for being here than your legal right?" he asked with unexpected gentleness.

Kaja stopped for a moment, surprised that he was suddenly so calm and friendly. Unfortunately, she had to admit reluctantly, he had a point. Her eyes caught a pile of paper and a project folder on her desk, which suggested a way to save the situation. She grabbed the documents and explained to Lance: "If I bump into someone, it will look as if I'm delivering something. Is that any better?"

"Hm, yes, it'll do. Let's go." - 'Pfft' Lance thought. 'Luckily the softly-softly approach did the trick.'

Kaja made sure one more time that the USB stick was safe in her trouser pocket and took a deep breath.

'Wish me luck, partner, I'm going to need it tonight.' she thought silently.

Lance gave her an encouraging nod. She straightened her shoulders and took the same route as Lance had earlier on, hoping not to run into any unexpected surprises. Without any hiccups, she reached Freddy's office.

"Please stay by the door and give me a warning if you see anyone coming." she whispered to her accomplice.

"I will. By the way: No need to whisper. Just think what you would normally say. I can hear your voice in my head just as well as you can hear mine."

She looked at him surprised. "Well, did you really think it was only a one way communication?" he asked impatiently. "Get your job over and done with. I want to go home and have an elderberry brandy."

'That's so typical of Lance.' Kaja was irritated. She turned away from him and towards her work, which was exactly what Lance had intended with his flippant remark.

She sat down at the desk and booted up the computer. It felt like an eternity until the machine asked her for Frédéric's staff ID and password. 'It's like watching paint dry.' Kaja remembered a popular saying. Spellbound, she watched the display until she registered with relief that her login attempt was successful, telling her that she had taken the first hurdle. She was tempted to snoop through his e-mail folders but then controlled herself. Just in time, it seemed. When she guiltily peered at Lance, she noticed from the look on his face that he knew exactly what she had almost wasted her precious time on. She realised it was not always an advantage to be hard-wired head-to-head with Lance. Time to get back to more important issues. She double-clicked the test server symbol on the desktop and was able to log in without a problem. Then she quickly scanned the programs stored there in order to find her own. It was easier than she anticipated because Frédéric hadn't even bothered to change the file name. After working on it for a whole afternoon, she did not have any trouble navigating through the code. When she found the correct spot, she plugged her USB stick into a port and inserted the new data as intended. Doing such familiar work calmed her nerves down and she was happy to start the usual preparations for a limited test run. It did not reveal any errors, but she did not dare starting a full test procedure as this usually triggered a number of log entries somebody might pick up on. So she manually checked the code again and scanned through it with her trained eyes. Something suddenly caught her attention and she stopped. This was unbelievable!

At this very moment, Lance interrupted her. "Quiet. I think I heard something."

For a few seconds, Kaja listened intently, but then she gave up. "I can't hear anything. Have to carry on now, come what may."

With these words, Kaja turned her attention back to the computer and only subconsciously registered that the dragon said he was going to have a look down the corridor. Kaja stared at the flickering screen. The idiot had not even changed the signature every programmer usually put at the end of each line so that it was possible to establish later who had done what. All through the program, the signature read "KJM" for Kaja Josephine Meyer. And nobody had even noticed! Disgusted by so much laziness and stupidity, she used the "Find and Replace" function to replace all instances of her signature with little Freddy's. Now her work was almost complete. All that was left was to replace the master source code. To do so, she borrowed the super user access ID from her friends in Support. She felt guilty for abusing their trust but had no choice. There was no other way to find out where the master source code was stored. As a super user, she had no problem finding and replacing the file. She had concentrated so much on her work that she was not aware her accomplice had not returned. Now she panicked when she suddenly heard his voice in her head.

"Kaja, be careful, two people approaching."

'Dammit' she thought. 'Not now, I'm almost done.' She bent down under the desk to remove the USB stick and promptly knocked her head with a dull bang. She had to control herself not to groan with pain. At the same time, she heard voices in the corridor.

"What was that?"

Kaja frowned. It was a female voice. And it sounded concerned that somebody might be in this office. Strange. She had to react quickly, pressed the key combination to shut down the computer, switched off the monitor and crouched under the desk. Not a second too early. This time, it was a male voice saying:

"I'm going to have a look."

"You're so brave." the female voice giggled.

'Popeye and his girlfriend Wilma? Give me a break!' Kaja rolled her eyes. The two strangers were so close now that Kaja could hear their footsteps on the carpet outside. She tensely tried to keep still in her hideout and barely dared to breathe. The door was opened a bit further and she felt someone enter the room.

"There's nobody here. They must have forgotten to switch off the lights."

'Just switch them off and go.' Kaja thought. 'It's rather uncomfortable down here.'

"I do like the darkness." the female voice said seductively.

Suddenly, the room went dark. This was to Kaja's advantage because it reduced her risk of being discovered. She would have preferred the couple to go somewhere else. But instead of the happy sound of disappearing footsteps, she heard a second person - obviously the woman - tiptoeing into the room.

"My hero, here I am. Did you miss me?"

What the devil were they doing? Now it sounded as if they were starting to kiss each other. The situation was so grotesque that Kaja had to pull herself together to avoid laughing hysterically. By the sound of it, they were in full swing on top of the desk... Hadn't Lance said she could have a two-way communication with him? Now was the time to put his claim to the test.

She concentrated all her thoughts on Lance, focusing all her panic-fuelled energies. "Lance, please help. I need you!"

"Ouch! No need to scream. I'm not deaf. What's happened? Did they find you?"

"Sorry." Kaja answered remorsefully and asked herself the amusing question what a remorseful thought might sound like in his mind. She shook her head to come back to reality. No time for philosophical questions. She had to get rid of these unwanted intruders.

"No, they didn't find me, but I'm having other problems." namely possibly being buried under a collapsing desk which was certainly not built for the sort of activity happening on top of it. "I'll explain to you when we get out of here. For now, I could just do with a distraction for our visitors."

"OK." Lance replied. "Coming up."

A few seconds later, loud rumbling and hissing noises came from the corridor.

"What was that???"

The strangers immediately stopped their canoodling and listened in horror.

"Let's get out of here. We don't want to be found out. I don't even know whose office this is." the male voice said.

In the meantime, Kaja's eyes had adjusted to the darkness. When the couple tiptoed out of the room, she risked a sneaky look. 'Fancy that! Isn't that Sabine, Max's PA? And Olli, the chief project manager at Qubus and right-hand man of the section leader? Even Thea will be in for a surprise when I'll tell her on Monday.'

"The coast is clear now." she heard Lance say a short while later.

Kaja came crawling from under the desk with some difficulty and tried to get the circulation going in her legs. She quickly checked that no clues were left in the room to betray their late-night visit. Satisfied with the result, she collected her alibi pile of paper, opened the door and checked the corridor. To her relief, nobody was in sight. She felt so tense that she would have run all the way but controlled herself until she had left the building. Lance was already waiting for her by the car. She rushed up to him, took his hands and danced around him.

"We did it. We did it." she exclaimed.

"Hm." he grumbled. "Imagine somebody seeing you in the middle of the night, dancing round your car like Rumpelstilzkin and talking to yourself. Do you really think this is a good career move?"

"You're a killjoy." she griped. But, once she'd calmed down, she got into the car and drove her shiny companion home.

Zorro gave Kaja an enthusiastic welcome while only having a sneer for the dragon.

"OK, big boy, OK. Sorry Mummy's left you here all by yourself. She's naughty, isn't she?"

She laid down on the floor next to the dog and tickled his belly. Zorro sprawled out enjoying the attention while Lance made faces at him behind Kaja's back.

"Stop that, you big monster." she scolded him.

Kaja could sense the surprise on his face without even looking at him just as she had felt his rolling eyes before. She let go of Zorro and gave the dragon a challenging look.

"Close your big mouth before I pull your teeth." she teased him. "It was you who told me to rely on my intuition. Now you'll have to bear the consequences."

But deep down even she was surprised it had worked so well on her first attempt. At least it had worked with Lance, she corrected herself.

She grabbed the bottle of elderberry brandy from the sideboard and poured them two generous drinks. "Here, Mr. Dragon, have a glass of your favourite tipple. Thank you very much for keeping watch for me. It looks like you can make yourself useful sometimes."

Lance took his glass and watched Kaja with raised eyebrows down her drink in one go. He looked at his own drink, frowning and asking himself how it was possible that he had ended up as the bodyguard of his protégée instead of guiding her in finding the right path in life. But he had to admit that he had always found this job description a bit of an exaggeration. Who believed in ideas like destiny nowadays? He shrugged his shoulders and knocked back his drink. Then he turned to Kaja to bid farewell: "So, time for me to go. - Hey, what're you doing?" Kaja had just finished her third glass and was about to pour herself a fourth one. "You're not binge-drinking, are you?"

She waved her hand laughing: "No no, but I am on such a high, I just need to celebrate a little bit."

"It looks like you're celebrating more than just a little bit." he grumbled. "I hope you have a dragon's constitution or you'll wake up with a massive headache tomorrow." he nodded at her.

"Oh, I almost forgot..."

Determinedly, she put her glass aside and started to prepare an Alka-Seltzer.

"Why, what's happening tomorrow? I thought according to your strange calendar, tomorrow is Saturday, a day when people usually stay in bed late."

"Yes, normally they do. But I have a date with Tim. To meet him I have to travel to Bern, which means I'll have to get up early."

Her thoughts were already on the meeting tomorrow and her eyes wandered absent-mindedly around the room. When Lance came into her sight, she paused.

"What's up with you, my big bad dragon? Why're you looking so grim?"

"Nothing's up." he scowled. "I'm just worried about you meeting him without me being there to protect you."

"What's your problem? I've known Tim for all my life. He won't do anything you need to protect me from. He's like the big brother I never had."

"Your big brother? You must be joking. That kiss told a different story."

Kaja was annoyed to feel her face blushing. And slowly she was getting angry. Really angry.

"I see. So you're spying on me. And I really thought you'd learned your lesson. You're lucky you can't come with me tomorrow. - I wouldn't have taken you anyway."

He snorted with contempt. "As if you could've stopped me."

Kaja was just about to reply with another snide remark, when she suddenly had a thought that stopped her. Could it be... and she decided to say it loud: "Could it be that Mr. Dragon is jealous?"

"Me? Jealous?" He was so shocked that his voice jumped a few octaves. "Bah. Do what you must. But don't come complaining afterwards that I didn't warn you!" With these words he turned like a prima donna and swept out of the room.

"A jealous dragon." Kaja pondered, feeling rather flattered.

The knowledge might come in handy later if ever he started getting big ideas again. She was grinning. Finally, she pulled herself to her feet, half-heartedly tidied up the kitchen and tottered off to bed, totally exhausted from the excitement of the day, but also very pleased with herself.

14

When Kaja woke up the next morning, she felt surprisingly fit. Her sleep had been deep and dreamless. For a moment, she stayed under the duvet and looked out of the open window. She always kept it open because she needed as much fresh air as possible and hated nothing more than closed windows. That was how she could now admire the clear blue sky without any visual obstruction. It was a wonderful morning and the weather promised her a pleasant trip to Bern. Kaja was looking forward to the day in front of her. Part of her was looking forward to meeting Tim's friend, although she didn't have high hopes he might be able to help. After all, she wasn't sure herself what she was looking for. And, being honest with herself, she was also looking forward to seeing Tim again. But she found the prospect a bit scary as well. Without doubt, there was a certain attraction between them that had not been there in the old days.

'That's stupid.' she cursed herself. Of course it had not been there ten years ago. Determinedly, she kicked off the duvet and stood up to face the cool autumn breeze. Luckily, it was only a few steps to the bathroom where she could switch on a small fan heater. Still shivering, she got under the shower and turned the water so hot that she could hardly bear it.

Ten minutes later, she'd had enough and wrapped herself in a bath towel she grabbed from the rail.

While Zorro was devouring his breakfast, she packed her bag. Her diary and mobile phone were already in there, she only had to add a few cereal bars from the kitchen cupboard. A full water bottle and Zorro's leash completed the set of necessities and she made her way to the door. Zorro jumped ahead of her with excitement. He knew Kaja had got up early enough to take him to the park before he had to endure a long trip in the car. She did not expect much traffic on a Saturday morning and enjoyed some playtime with her dog. While she watched him chasing his ball, she remembered how much fun he usually had on their visits to Mémé. She knew he was not a city dog and although she tried to give him as much exercise as possible, she felt sorry for him. She got the ball back from him and threw it again far out on the lawn. She would have preferred to live in the countryside herself, but could not imagine commuting to the city every day. 'I should be self-employed.' she sighed. But she wasn't. 'No use fretting over things you cannot change.' She threw the ball one last time before making her way back home.

Before they could finally be on their way to Bern, she had to go upstairs once more to fetch her car keys. Zorro promptly took the opportunity to chase a neighbour's cat round the block. The cat's owner was rather upset and Kaja had to spend another fifteen minutes calming him down. 'Lucky you that Zorro is not more of a husky.' she grumbled to herself as she put the car in first gear to pull out of the parking space. 'Otherwise your cat would be as dead as a mouse by now.' she giggled and Zorro pricked up his ears.

"You know what you've done, you little rascal. You deserve a severe punishment." she said sternly and tried to look serious.

His only reaction was to try and catch a fly that was trapped inside the car. When he realised it was too quick for him, he made himself comfortable on the back seat.

"I see. You could at least try and pretend to be scared of me."

She looked in the mirror and caught a glimpse of the dog raising his eyebrows, looking rather amused. She couldn't help but laugh.

One and a half hours later, Kaja was still happy. As expected, traffic wasn't too heavy and she made good progress. She had taken a short break at a service station to buy a takeaway coffee. A glance at her watch told her that she was well on schedule and might even be on time, against her usual habit. She pushed the watch away from her wrist as it restricted her movements. Kaja loved this old watch with its well-worn, soft leather strap more than anything. It had been a present from Mémé for her graduation. She had been so excited that she had made the mistake of telling her parents, on the phone of course. Her parents had always been much too busy to visit their only daughter, even for her university graduation. Most certainly, world peace would have been at risk if Mr. and Mrs. Diplomat had left their posts for a few days, Kaja thought cynically. But this did not prevent her parents, especially her mother, from interfering with her life.

"Kaja." she had said in her piercing voice - and it was an order rather than a piece of advice - "You cannot accept this present. You must give it straight back the next time you see her."

"But why?" Kaja had wanted to know.

"That watch is very valuable and part of our inheritance. When Josephine dies," she always called her mother by her proper first name, "It will come to me first and then it is up to me to decide whether it's right for you to have it."

"But Mémé is fit and well! How can you talk about your inheritance?" Kaja was rather disturbed.

"Don't be sentimental and do as I ask." was her mother's unfriendly advice.

Kaja remembered all too well what had followed next.

"No." she had said and hung up.

It had been one of the first instances when she rebelled against her mother. And she had no regrets. Seeing Mémé happy that she enjoyed her present so much was more than enough compensation for all the trouble. But following this incident, the relationship with her parents had cooled down by a further few degrees, if that were at all possible. Kaja sighed. Well, she didn't have perfect parents, but she had Mémé. Lost in her thoughts, she ran her index finger over the soft leather strap once more before fully concentrating on the traffic again.

One hour later, Kaja's mood had changed completely. Only six miles to Bern and the motorway was blocked solid with a traffic jam. This very minute she was supposed to meet Tim. Dammit! She bashed the steering wheel with the palm of her hand to vent her anger, which made the car stereo stop playing. Kaja was about to start swearing again but thought better of it and frantically searched her bag for the mobile phone instead. 'Let's hope this at least still works.' she was worried. But it looked like she was in luck. She dialled Tim's number and waited for him to answer.

"Hello Tim? Oh, am I glad to catch you."

"Why? What's up? Don't tell me you're calling to cancel? I would be seriously disappointed." he said with a dramatic tone in his voice.

"No, I'm on my way, but I'm late again. I am in the middle of a traffic jam and nothing's moving. I've already killed the car stereo and the way I'm feeling my mobile is going to pack up soon as well. Never mind, I'll be there as soon as I can. You'll hear from me when I arrive at the station. Bye for now."

Tim was a bit overwhelmed by this bubbly stream of information and barely managed to say: "No problem, I'll be here waiting for you." before she hung up.

Relieved, Kaja dropped her mobile on the passenger seat and tried to relax. She rummaged through the chaos in the glove compartment to find her "Nightwish" CD and put the disc into the player. In anticipation of the music, she drummed the rhythm of the first song on the steering wheel with her fingers and hummed the melody, but nothing happened. What was wrong now? 'Oh, I have a memory like a sieve.' she cursed herself. 'It's broken, isn't it?' Discontented, she wound down the car window to take in the fresh autumn air. On hearing the electric window, Zorro woke up and pushed his head past Kaja's headrest.

128

"You like that, don't you?" Kaja asked and massaged his neck.

Finally, the traffic started moving again. Perhaps she would make it to Bern, even before the end of the day by the looks of it.

A good forty-five minutes later she pulled up in front of the railway station. She'd finally made it, but was tired, exhausted and bad-tempered instead of beaming, fit and looking forward to the day, as she had been at the start of her journey. It couldn't be helped. She pulled her seat forward to release Zorro from his back seat, grabbed her bag and turned round without looking - only to stumble into a broad-chested man.

"What the hell..."

She tried to get away from the stranger but was trapped by the open car door. If only the sun wasn't shining straight into her eyes. She tilted her head back to get a better view but promptly lost her balance. In a reflex movement, she got hold of the man's jacket.

"If I'd known you fall into my arms the minute you see me, I'd have tried before to jam you between two cars." His voice sounded rather amused.

"Tim." she said with relief. "I hoped I'd meet you here."

When she realised she was still holding on to his collar, she abruptly let go.

"Though, I'm in a right fighting mood." she remarked and sniped at him: "Didn't I warn you before not to sneak up on me?"

When she pushed him out of her way and squeezed past, he raised his hands in surrender.

"I saw you coming and wanted to offer my help."

She looked at him suspiciously: "Your help? What for? With parking my car?"

"I know you girls always carry everything plus the kitchen sink with you. So I thought you might need a porter." He grinned at her disarmingly.

Kaja felt her heart pounding and hoped her cheeks didn't look as hot as they felt.

"I thought I was supposed to give you a lift? I only got out of the car to look for you."

"Simon is waiting for us in a café not far from here. I gave him a call when you told me you were late. It saves us time. We don't have to go to his flat."

"Oh. OK. Good idea."

She was a little surprised how well Tim had organised everything. Grudgingly she had to admit that he was making every effort to turn this day into a success. But to Tim she only said: "As I'm obviously a damsel in distress with too many odds and ends to carry, you're welcome to hold my bag."

Without batting an eyelid, he swung the bag over his shoulder, as if it was the most natural thing in the world to stroll through Bern with a lady's handbag on display. "Very well, madam." His eyes flashed with amusement.

"And don't call me madam. What's wrong with you men that you can't remember my name?"

"That's right." he mumbled. "I should have called you a witch instead." which earned him a dig in the ribs. At the risk of being hit again, he teased her, hoping to find out more about his competitors: "Who are the other men having problems with your name?"

"Lance..." she started to explain, but then added evasively: "Oh forget it. I was just talking to myself."

Tim didn't believe a word she was saying but decided not to question her any further. He knew from experience that Kaja's stubbornness was hard to break. He had known her long enough. "Let's go then. I'm sure Simon is already waiting."

He took her to a small café only a few minutes walk from the station. It was an old establishment with an informal atmosphere. On the left-hand side, there were two large wooden tables, apparently meant to provide plenty of space for dining and meeting people. Opposite the entrance there was a glass front offering views into a small, pretty courtyard which was obviously used as a beer garden in the summer. Inside the glass front, there were a couple of well-worn sofas providing a comfortable space to enjoy a cup of tea and some croissants while reading the Sunday newspapers. However, right now some guests had gathered there to use the chequered tops of the coffee tables to play chess. From the door leading to an anteroom, loud laughter could be heard above the unmistakable sound of a serious table football match in progress. On the right-hand side, there was a glass counter, framed with wooden planks. Large notice boards informed guests of the day's menu as well as the standard set of snacks and drinks on offer, followed by the sentence: "We are happy to serve you at your table." Kaja was overwhelmed and not sure whether she had entered a students' hangout or a philosophers' meeting club. The loudspeakers, positioned either side of the counter, were playing some pleasant background music by the Buena Vista Social Club. Kaja loved this kind of music which combined a zest for life with a melancholic mood. Automatically, she smiled and started to hum along to the melody. Tim caught her smile and returned it. It had turned out to be the right decision to show her this place, his favourite bar in Switzerland. He gently touched her arm and leaned forward to make sure she could hear him. Kaja was so busy taking in the atmosphere that she did not realise Tim was talking to her. Only when she felt his warm breath at her ear making her heart jump, she heard him say with amusement: "Are you listening to me?"

With a pang of guilt she turned round to apologise for her absent-mindedness. But before she could say anything, the thought evaporated. The abrupt movement had brought her so close to him that she could feel the warmth of his body. She slightly tilted back her head and stared at him, apparently unable to move or speak. Both of them stayed motionless for several seconds. Or was it for minutes? Kaja had lost all concept of time. His closeness confused her and woke a feeling in her she did not even know existed. 'I feel like a rabbit in front of a snake.' she thought with a touch of black humour. But he seemed to feel exactly the same. This observation relaxed her enough to put a smile on her face. She took a step backwards and at the same time poked her finger into his chest. She hoped this would disguise the fact that she was backing off from him.

On principle, Kaja never gave in and never ran away from anything. At least most of the time, she admitted to herself, remembering her escape to France.

"Didn't you want to introduce me to Simon? Is he here?"

"I was going to tell you before you decided to mesmerise me." he grumbled stroppily.

Kaja looked into his face trying to find out whether he was annoyed. The tone of his voice gave her reason to believe so. She decided to simply ignore his confusing remark just as much as his unfriendly tone and the wealth of feelings he had obviously caused in her. Instead, she insisted: "And? Where is he?"

"He's over there playing chess. Let's go and let him know we've arrived. Perhaps he'll speed up the cat-and-mouse game."

Kaja followed him through the crowd and asked with surprise: "How do you know he's going to win?"

"Because I haven't met anyone yet who could beat him. But wait, you'll see for yourself in a second."

She noticed with relief that his voice sounded less gruff. Whatever it was that had annoyed him, it seemed to have disappeared.

He said hello to a man with a dark military-style haircut and a distinctive face that made him look almost stern. She guessed he was in his mid-thirties.

"Hey Simon, how're you doing?"

"Hey Tim, let me quickly finish this game. Then I'll have time for you two."

"Oh please, take your time." Kaja tried to re-assure him but then she stopped as she was staring into the most piercing pair of blue eyes she had ever met. He briefly looked at her and was obviously satisfied with what he saw. He nodded in no particular direction and turned his attention back to the game.

"If you lend me your car keys, I'll take it to a different car park. At the moment, it's still in the drop-off zone. You'll have an expensive day trip if you leave it there." Tim abruptly broke in on her thoughts.

Gratefully, she handed over her car keys and watched him make his way to the door. What was wrong with Tim? She didn't know he could be so moody. That was usually her department. She shook off her thoughts and bent down to see if there was enough space under the table for Zorro. In theory there was, but in practice it was occupied by an exceptionally beautiful Malinois, a short-haired Belgian sheep dog. His yellow eyes looked at her, alert but friendly.

She put her head above the table: "Simon, is this your dog?"

"Yes." the absorbed player answered briefly.

Kaja's head disappeared under the table again and she respectfully approached the huge dog and offered her hand for him to sniff at. In the meantime, Zorro got curious and tried to squeeze under the table as well. Kaja managed to grab his collar and push him into a corner behind a chair.

"There's not enough space here for you to play. Be patient, please."

The other dog appeared to be completely good-mannered, but he was still a stranger. Zorro tended to be over-enthusiastic in his welcoming rituals, so she let one of her hands rest on her dog's neck while turning her attention back to Simon and his game.

"Checkmate." he just announced.

Kaja stared at the board in disbelief. Even she, having hardly any experience of the game, could tell that he was right.

She was genuinely impressed: "How did you manage to do that? You'd only just started."

"It's all tactics." he was laughing. While his face had showed pure concentration before, making him look stern, it now appeared soft and playful as he enjoyed his victory.

"Take a seat." he said pointing to a free place at the table.

She slowly sank into the chair and waited for him to say something.

"So you are Kaja." he asserted and gave her another inquisitive look. She was starting to get nervous under his scrutinizing gaze.

When she realised, she got annoyed, quibbing: "Have I grown a wart on my chin this morning or is there anything else you're trying to find in my face?"

Simon grinned: "I see your dog is not the only one willing to show his teeth. Tim's got his work cut out..."

Now completely confused, Kaja wanted to know: "What work? I was hoping you were going to do some work for me."

"Well, let's put it this way: Tim rarely asks me for favours, least of all to help a woman. The fact that he did this time made me curious to meet the girl that is apparently important to him. That's why I looked at you so closely. I'm sorry if it made you feel uneasy. It's part of my profession to assess people."

"Are you satisfied now?" she asked derisively. "And I'm sorry to disappoint you. Tim and I are only good friends. We've known each other for ages."

"We'll see about that." was Simon's cryptic answer. "Let's deal with your problem first. Perhaps you should tell me everything from the beginning. I need to get the full picture."

"Shouldn't we wait for Tim?"

"I'm sure he'll be back soon. And he already knows the beginning of your story, doesn't he?"

"Yes, he does."

But before she could start, a young waitress turned up at their table to take orders. Kaja chose a caffè latte for herself and one for Tim. As the waitress left, she whispered to Simon: "Now I know why they mention their service on the board. She's so slow, you might be tempted go to the counter yourself."

He smiled at her in agreement. She leaned forward and rested her arms on the table. Each time she had to repeat her story, it seemed more and more unreal to her. 'Next time, I'll start with Once upon a time and make it a proper fairy tale.' she thought and grimaced. "What's wrong?" Simon enquired. The searching gaze of his steely blue eyes did not let go of her. She told him her thought and they both had to laugh. Kaja relaxed and started to tell her story.

In the meantime, Tim took his time outside. After he had parked Kaja's car in a different location, he decided to go for a little walk. He needed the autumn breeze to cool him down and the distraction of the exercise to clear his head. He had intended to act like a good friend to Kaja because he sensed that this was all she wanted. But the bond between the two of them was becoming more and more important to him by the day. He could not remember anything ever being so important to him in his life. But he intended to take it slowly, to take every chance of getting closer to her. However, that accidental and surprising physical contact earlier on had confused him. Irritated, he ran his fingers through his thick, dark hair. It was impossible that the attraction he sensed each time he merely looked at her was only one-sided. Bad-tempered, he kicked a shard of glass out of his way. 'Or maybe it is.' he thought gloomily. He was swearing to himself in frustration. But then his face lit up. 'Nothing is stopping me from trying to change that.' Satisfied with this realisation, which had occurred to him before more than once, he straightened up and walked back to the café.

By the time Tim sat down at the table, Kaja had almost finished her story.

"Where have you been so long?" she enquired.

Tim mumbled something about having trouble finding a parking space in a big city.

"Just as bad as in Zurich." she replied absent-mindedly. Zorro had noticed that Tim was back and squeezed out from behind the chair to welcome him. He was so boisterous that he knocked the sugar bowl from the table. Kaja just managed to catch it before it hit the floor.

"Good reflexes." Simon seemed impressed.

Kaja was slightly embarrassed and played the incident down: "Just beginner's luck. But let me tell you the rest of the story. Tim hasn't heard this part yet either."

She leaned back and smiled at Tim, realising she was glad that he was back in their company. It just felt right. Slightly irritated, she glanced at him. Being confused was the last thing she needed right now. She pulled herself together and summarised last night's events for the two men. Of course she omitted Lance's part and made it sound less dramatic. But nevertheless, she made no secret of her pride at having pulled off the plan.

"But there's one thing I don't understand: What effect does your alteration have on the program?" Both of them looked at her expectantly.

"Oh, sorry, I forgot to explain." she laughed. "Of course you may ask yourselves: Why all the trouble? Here's the twist: I told you the program is to be used for accounting. At the moment, most payments are odd figures that need to be rounded up or down by five centimes."

She looked at each of them. "Are you with me?" When they nodded, she continued: "That's standard practice, but I modified the program in such a way that the figures are always rounded down and that the centimes taken off the payments are re-directed to little Freddy's private account. Am I a genius or what?" She looked at her audience expecting to be praised.

"I think I'm missing something here." Tim frowned. "All I understand is that you'll make that bastard even richer. Where's the justice in that? Where's your revenge?"

He first looked to Simon and then to Kaja.

"I think I've got it." Simon suddenly said. "I suppose you'll let the program do its work for a while and then play the whistle-blower?"

Surprised, Kaja confirmed his guess: "Good thinking. You have a quick mind, respect."

"Oh, stop it."

With a casual wave of his hand, he dismissed her compliment. "It was the only logical conclusion. But what am I supposed to do for you? It seems to me you have it all under control."

"Kaja suspects that all these events amount to more than just the ego trip of a single employee." Tim intervened.

"That's right." she agreed. "I'll tell you in a minute what aroused my suspicion. But first, perhaps you should tell me a little bit about yourself. I still have no idea what your profession is. Tim said you are a kind of private investigator? But I can't imagine what that involves."

"Shall we give her the short version or the long version?" Simon asked Tim in jest.

"I didn't know you could tell a long version." his friend joked. "You must know that Simon is not fond of long speeches. He likes to express himself in short and precise statements." he winked at Kaja.

"Oh, you poor thing. My long-winded story must have bored you to death." she apologised.

"And she hasn't even finished yet." Simon groaned in mock despair.

All three of them broke into laughter and only calmed down when Zorro jumped up at Kaja to join in and even Simon's well-trained dog did not want to stay still under the table.

"Tsar, enough of that. Lie down."

"You too, Zorro, sit."

They all calmed down and focussed on their business again. Simon summarised his work in a few short sentences.

"In essence, Tim was right. My partner and I are indeed private investigators, but we do very little traditional detective work. For instance, we don't keep unfaithful spouses under surveillance. But we have other services to offer. We can carry out covert investigations in business matters. And we can be booked for personal security."

"You are bodyguards?"

"Yes, that's part of what we do."

When he saw the awe in her face, he quickly added: "It's not as fascinating as it sounds. Switzerland is a very safe country. We are often employed just for show or to watch the spoilt kids of rich and important people. I don't suppose you came all the way to Bern to find a bodyguard?"

She laughed. "No, of course not. But your business investigations sound promising. Perhaps I should fill you in on the details and then I leave it to you to decide whether you can help me."

She went through all the events again and emphasised the inconsistencies.

"At first sight, it appears as if all this was directed at me, as if Freddy wanted to damage my reputation. But I don't think he's clever enough to have come up with it all by himself. On the other hand, if there is more at stake, I cannot see a motive. To be honest, I don't hold an important position within the company. Granted, I'm one of the best developers, but I'm certainly not worth all the effort. And, I have heard rumours about similar incidents in the company, always affecting former PC Lux employees. That made me suspicious. But I can't understand why the board hasn't just dismissed the involved staff members like me."

"If I understand you correctly, you want me to find out if something is afoot in your company?" Simon tried to ascertain.

"Well, to be honest, when I left Zurich this morning, I didn't have any idea how you might be able to help. But now I know what you do for a living, it would be great if you could."

Helplessly, she shrugged her shoulders and looked at Tim for support. "Or what do you think?"

He smiled at her: "Yes, that was my feeling, too."

To Simon, he said: "I knew I could rely on you, even if your remit is a bit vague at the moment."

"I'm used to that. It's quite normal in our business. It looks like we've covered everything. What shall we do next?" Simon sounded satisfied.

"I'll take Kaja to the exhibition and show her my pictures of Spirit Bear Island."

"Yes, I'm keen to see them. But Zorro would like to take a walk first. The poor thing is missing his exercise."

"Do you mind if I join you?" Simon asked the two of them but looked explicitly at Tim.

"No, not at all." he laughed. "As long as we go our separate ways afterwards."

Kaja frowned, her eyes wandering between the two men. Her intuition told her that there was a hidden conversation going on there. As she could not work out what it was about, she simply said: "Why not? Do come along. Your dog will enjoy it. What was his name? Tsar?"

"Yes, Tsar."

He proudly caressed the side of his dog which had come from under the table once he sensed it was time to go. Followed by their dogs, they left the bar. They had barely walked a hundred yards when Tim turned round and said: "You carry on, I'll be with you in a sec."

Simon and Kaja looked at each other with surprise: "Where is he going?"

"No idea, perhaps he's forgotten something."

"I'm sure he'll be back soon."

But then it took Tim a while to return, so they decided to sit down on a bench by the river Aare and wait for him. After another five minutes wait, he returned out of breath. "I thought" he said panting, "you might be hungry." and waved a brown paper bag in his hand.

"What a good idea. Well done." Kaja praised him, laughing. "But you're not fit enough to carry that." she teased him and tried to grab the bag.

"Hands off, I'm fitter than you think. I can take you for a jog tomorrow morning." he grinned.

He opened the paper bag and produced three sandwiches, one of which he threw to Simon.

"Egg and ham - that's for you."

With another look into the bag he announced: "That leaves one tuna and one cheese." he looked at Kaja waiting for her to make a choice.

"Tuna." she replied promptly.

He handed her the chosen pack and unwrapped his own. They sat together, quietly enjoying their snacks. Simon and Kaja sat on the bench while Tim rested on an old tree stump opposite. The two dogs had made friends and were chasing each other in the shallows.

"Mmh, how did you come to choose your profession?" Kaja wanted to know between two bites of her sandwich. "It's not a very common occupation."

"That's true." he laughed. "I told you it's a long story, but let me try to make it as short as possible."

"You see, he can condense even a whole life story into a few short sentences." Tim joked.

"Now we've got him talking, don't interrupt the flow of his speech." Kaja advised him mockingly.

"Be quiet and listen. Here's my story. Tim knows it already."

"Oh, I wouldn't miss the chance to hear it again for all the world." Tim was quick to re-assure him.

"After leaving school, I went to university in St.Gallen to study business informatics."

"Respect, I've heard that's a very challenging course." Kaja commented.

"Yes, but luckily I'm rather good at remembering things."

"Me too." Kaja grinned. "But carry on, I didn't mean to interrupt you."

"After my graduation, I was a bit at a loss what to do. The last thing I wanted was to waste away as a project manager in a bank. I had several work placements and knew from experience how uninspiring such jobs are. Senior management haven't got a clue what they are doing and constantly change direction, discarding decisions that are barely two days old. I couldn't work like that, not back then and not now."

"I know what you're saying." Kaja agreed. "We have the same problem in our company, especially since the merger. It used to be different." she added wistfully.

"So I decided to take a completely different direction and applied for a job with the police."

"The police?" Kaja was surprised. "Why did you do that?"

"Because deep down Simon is a thrill-seeker." Tim explained. He had been listening patiently and now winked at Kaja.

"There's some truth in that." Simon agreed. "I am always looking for adventure, only that police work isn't half as adventurous as you might think. Most of it is routine procedures requiring piles of paperwork and for the little time you've got left to work on the street, you have to deal with rather questionable elements of society. Granted, the situation here in Switzerland is harmless compared to other countries, but it's still no fun."

"What was your job with the police?"

"Well, it works like this: First you study at the police academy and then you have to go through the ranks. The whole system is strictly hierarchical. There's no fast track. For a few years, I was out on the beat and did other, similarly menial jobs until I finally received a recommendation for the dog squad."

"Ah, that's where you got your dog from." Kaja concluded immediately.

"Exactly. I owe my current career to Tsar and, strictly speaking, to the police. In that sense, the six years I spent there were not completely wasted. But I didn't fit into the rigid structures. More than once I got reprimanded for 'not being able to function in my subordinate role and questioning my superior's orders', as they put it. I thought I had fulfilled an ambition by becoming a dog handler but in reality I was rather frustrated with their training methods."

"I thought the police were exemplary in their dog training?" Kaja frowned.

"Well, that's what I thought as well. And part of it is true. I had an instructor called Josef who taught me a lot of extremely useful things. But on the other hand, there is immense pressure and rigid ideas on how long each training phase is supposed to take, without taking into account the individual strengths and weaknesses of the dogs. Don't get me wrong. I too have high expectations of my dog and I'm well aware that a police dog simply has to function when required. There's not much room for experiments. But on the other hand I think it would be easier for everyone involved if the basic training focussed on the strengths of the dog and so build up his confidence. Later, this makes it much easier to iron out his weaknesses. Josef tried to use this method and showed me in practice what I had vaguely guessed already. But many other handlers haven't managed to tune in to their dogs. They had no choice or they knew no better than to follow the rule book strictly. I think this was what annoyed me most, the obvious refusal to consider alternative ways to achieve the same goal."

"I can understand that." Tim agreed.

"It would mean questioning yourself and your methods, improving yourself. But most people have an aversion to change. It's always the same, isn't it? They can't think outside the box." Kaja was angry.

"Exactly. What I also found upsetting was that the dogs were kept in individual kennels until they were needed. This went against my feeling that I should be with him as much as possible, to keep Tsar under my desk." he grinned.

"I think Simon's idea of police dog handling was heavily influenced by Inspector Rex." Tim informed Kaja, referring to a popular TV series.

"It was no joking matter." Simon protested, but even he could not help a smile. "To cut a long story short, I stayed until Josef went into retirement and then quit the force. Tsar was used to me so I was able to take him with me."

"Very exciting, but it still doesn't explain how you came to start your business."

"Yes, first I took two months off to develop ideas about what I wanted to do with my life. Finally, I decided to combine the subjects of my training and education with my police experience. That's why we now specialise in business crime. As a sideline, we train dogs for our own use and for a few select partners. Unfortunately I don't have time to get involved with the dog training any more. I'm lucky if I find enough opportunities to train Tsar."

"But who is working with the dogs then? Don't you have the same situation as in the police? I mean, the problem seems to be individual people's attitudes, not the system as a whole."

"I'm in a position to pick and choose my dog handlers very carefully, based on their experience and abilities. And I was able to persuade Josef to become my partner in the company."

"Oh, now that explains a lot..." Kaja and Tim both laughed.

"It all sounds very exciting." Kaja commented.

"It is indeed. You're welcome to visit us once our investigations are under way. That'll give you the chance to see our work first-hand."

"Investigations - it sounds so serious." Kaja moaned. "I only hope my suspicions are true and I didn't cause all that trouble for nothing. But part of me also wishes it was all in my imagination and everything could stay as it was."

"I do think your suspicions are justified and nothing will stay as it was anyway. Too much has happened and changed." Tim reminded her gently.

For a while, Kaja kept silent and watched the river and the rambunctious dogs. 'Changes' she thought and suddenly saw Lance clearly in front of her.

"You're right." she said eventually. "I couldn't even tell what has changed more: me or the world around me."

"I believe everything and everyone is subject to constant change, but we often refuse to recognise it." Tim answered.

Kaja looked into his eyes and suddenly felt as if time was standing still. She could not believe that Tim understood her so well and was able to find words for what she had only felt very vaguely up to now.

Simon noticed that their mood had changed and cleared his throat to catch their attention. "Sorry to interrupt your philosophical debate, but I have to go. Kaja, I have your mobile number and you know how to get hold of me as well. I'll give you a call if I have any news or need more information."

"Yes, please do. And many thanks again for your help. I'm really grateful."

"You're welcome. As I said, Tim is a friend and I'm pleased to do him a favour." he said with an insinuating grin towards him. He called for Tsar, who came up to him promptly and they left. Kaja managed to grab Zorro by his collar before her dog could follow his new-found friend.

"Did you see how it is done, you little mongrel? Master whistles, dog comes. Nice and simple."

Zorro answered by violently shaking the water out of his coat. "Yuck! Zorro, did you have to do that? Now we are all wet." she angrily told him off.

"At least you're not the only Ragamuffin this time." Tim joked.

"What a cheek!" she shouted and threatened to push him into the water.

"Please have mercy." Tim begged. "Didn't you want me to take you to the exhibition?"

"OK, I'll let you off. But there's always another time." Reluctantly, Kaja backed off. Secretly, she was glad to find an excuse to let go of his arm. Direct physical contact with Tim currently had a very confusing impact on her feelings and reasoning.

On their way to the exhibition, they left Zorro locked in the car. He would have to wait there for them to return. He wasn't allowed into the exhibition and the autumn sun was not very strong so that he would be comfortable in the vehicle.

"Do you want to take the tram or shall we have a walk?"

"Ah, let's walk. I need the exercise to keep me warm."

In a spontaneous decision, she linked her arm with his. Five minutes later, she wished she hadn't done that. Not that she didn't enjoy it. Through the fabric of his jacket, she could feel his body warmth and she could smell the faint scent of his aftershave as well as something else. She wasn't sure what it was but it smelled so pleasant and familiar that she was tempted to bury her nose into his jacket. But it was this familiarity that completely confused Kaja. For the next few minutes, she walked silently next to her companion. Tim peered down at her dark hair and tried to work out what she was thinking. At first he had been pleasantly surprised when she had linked her arm with his, but now he felt that her emotions had gone cold and he didn't like it.

"Do you still have feelings for this... Freddy?" he suddenly blurted out. The question had been on his mind for a long time.

Kaja looked at him with surprise: "Freddy? What gave you that idea?"

"Well, you're so quiet all of a sudden. And I was wondering..." he tried to justify himself.

Kaja gave him a long look and then took a quick decision to be open with him. "I was never in love with Freddy. It was convenient to be with him for a while, that's all. But I don't like to be cheated on. No matter by whom. Even a casual relationship needs to be built on trust."

"Oh, I see." It was all Tim was able to reply. Now he had the answer he was looking for, he wasn't keen to hear any more details. Even the thought of this cheat having touched Kaja made him boil with anger. He was well aware that this was a rather old-fashioned attitude. He had never thought of himself as the jealous type, particularly with respect to past relationships. But it seemed the rule book had to be re-written when it came to Kaja. He sighed.

"Let's change the subject, shall we? I'm sorry I brought it up."

"Fine by me. I wanted to know more about your work anyway." she smiled.

A few strands of hair had come loose from her pony tail, which gave her a good excuse to retrieve her arm from his. Now she was definitely missing the feeling of closeness, but at least she was able to think clearly again... For the rest of their walk, Kaja bombarded him with questions about his work and the exhibition.

"You're wearing me out..." Tim begged her laughing after he had managed to answer almost all of her questions. "You'll see Spirit Bear Island and its inhabitants for yourself in a minute, because we're here."

They had arrived in front of a tall brick building.

"Is this a gallery?" she was surprised.

"Yes, in a sense. The building belongs to the Zoological and Botanical Institute of the University of Bern. One of my former lecturers is a specialist on the Great Bear Rain Forest, the Canadian nature reserve which includes Spirit Bear Island. I am still in touch with him occasionally and when I told him I was planning a research trip, he arranged the exhibition for me. Come on in, let's have a look."

He led her through a large entrance hall where people were queuing at a ticket counter.

"No need to waste our time with that." he said with a boyish grin and pulled her towards the staircase. Boisterously, he leaped up the wooden stairs, always taking two steps at a time. Kaja had trouble keeping up with him and quietly congratulated herself on her daily jogging routine. Otherwise she would have been out of puff very soon. When they reached the second floor, she panted: "This house must be jinxed. Isn't there any end to these stairs?"

Tim laughed and tried to cheer her up: "Only two more floors and we're there."

Resigning to her fate, Kaja carried on chasing Tim until they eventually reached the top floor under the roof.

"Hello Tim? The master in person, I'm honoured."

"Hello Frank." he greeted the doorman who had just finished checking the tickets of a group of noisy fourteen-year-olds. "I would like to introduce somebody to you."

He grabbed Kaja by her waist and pulled her close. "This is my very close friend Kaja. I would like to show her the exhibition. Can we go in?"

Kaja involuntarily stiffened when he described their relationship as "very close". But what else was he supposed to say? Any other explanation would have been too complicated. Or did he use this introduction for all the women he took here? She resolutely dismissed the thought and tried to relax. She gave the doorman a friendly smile while she examined him inconspicuously. Frank was a corpulent man with red, flabby cheeks and an unruly shock of grey hair. His golden-green eyes sparkled cheekily. "Ah, off you go then. And have fun, you two."

"Many thanks. Nice to meet you." Kaja replied politely and followed Tim through the door.

Deep down she thought Frank looked like an old lighthouse keeper. Still occupied with this amusing thought, she did not pay much attention to the room at first. Only when they reached the centre, did she look around her and stop with surprise. It was a huge exhibition hall. Massive wooden beams supporting angled walls were a stark reminder that it was located under a roof. There were large dormer windows in each direction, letting in the afternoon sun. Because wall space was limited, Tim's work had been mounted on free-standing display boards in order to create the best possible visual effect.

"Kaja? I'm over here."

She turned her attention back to her companion who had just noticed that she was not following him. She laughed and turned a full circle.

"This is such a wonderful room, just as if it had been purpose-built for your exhibition."

She pointed at some photographs close by. "The pictures form a harmonic ensemble in themselves and a nice contrast to the old architecture."

"Thank you. I'm rather pleased with the show myself." Amused, he watched her still bewildered looking face. "What did you expect? Would you rather have them put in a nondescript concrete bunker?" he teased her.

"Oh, I don't know." she looked away slightly embarrassed. "I didn't expect anything, but perhaps I was worried that might be the case." She grimaced. "I can't stand those cold, stylised art temples." she admitted.

Tim laughed and took her hand. "Neither can I. But now let me give you the private guided tour I promised you."

He guided her from picture to picture and left her enough time to look at the photos in peace before explaining how he had taken them and what they showed. Often he enriched his comments with amusing anecdotes about all sorts of mishaps he encountered during his work. He pointed to a series of photos showing a large white bear swimming to the shore and climbing out of the water. In the last picture, which happened to be slightly out of focus, the bear looked straight into the camera.

"I took these pictures from an inflatable boat close to the island. I couldn't believe my luck seeing this bear - I call him Papa Joe..."

"You gave him a name?" Kaja asked in disbelief and giggled.

"Of course, he was like a mate to me." he answered with mock innocence.

"How were you able to tell the animals apart?"

"Well, for one thing, the population is not very big and then each bear has very specific characteristics. Sometimes it is the way he or she moves or the shape of his mouth. Papa Joe, for instance, had a tear in his ear. Perhaps he got injured in a fight. But you need to take your time to familiarise yourself with the various animals in order to recognise the subtle differences between them."

"You must have the patience of a saint." Kaja was impressed. She leaned past Tim to get a closer look at the picture.

"That's what I thought I had." Tim murmured, desperately trying not to bury his face in Kaja's dark hair. A few unruly strands had escaped her attempt to tie them up with a rubber band. They tickled his nose and he could smell the flowery scent of the shampoo she used that morning. Abruptly she straightened up, oblivious to the turmoil she had caused in him.

"Now please, tell me why that last picture is so blurred." she asked, keen to hear his story.

Tim had to laugh at the eagerness in her voice. "I would love to if it wasn't for a little Ragamuffin constantly interrupting me."

"Don't blame me." she said impatiently. "I'm listening." She looked at him with anticipation.

"As I said, I was sitting in this inflatable and tried to get a good shot of the bear. I didn't want to use my paddles to get any nearer and possibly scare Papa Joe away. So I perched myself right at the front of the boat. I was so keen to get my shot that I didn't realise how far I had leaned out. The inevitable happened: The laws of physics made the back of the boat tip up and I tipped head-first into the water, apparently not without hitting the trigger of my camera. Papa Joe must have heard me and looked up that very moment."

"How did you manage to salvage the pictures? Didn't your camera get wet?"

"I must have managed to keep it out of the water. The first thing I did when I reached my boat, coughing and spluttering, was to dry it off and store it safely in its watertight carrier case to protect my precious pictures."

"Did you enjoy your dip in the water?" Kaja asked, hardly able to contain her laughter.

"Bah!" Tim poked his tongue out at her. "It was cold. You could hear my teeth chattering for miles."

Now Kaja could not contain herself and laughed out so loud that some of the other visitors looked at her disapprovingly. "I'm sorry, but I'm trying to imagine the picture of you falling into the water. It's just so funny."

Now Tim had to grin as well. "With hindsight, yes, it was. But just at that very moment, I cursed everything in the world: the bears, my work and even myself."

"What happened to Papa Joe? Did he run away?"

"No he didn't. It was really outrageous: he turned round, sat down and watched that poor little human trying to crawl back into his swimming vehicle." Tim was steaming, which caused Kaja to laugh even more. "Come on. Enough of that. There's more to see."

One hour later, Kaja was standing spellbound in front of the final picture. It showed an evening scene with a mother and her two cubs playing in the foreground.

"What's the matter?" Tim asked when he noticed Kaja looking at the picture in silence. Kaja shook off her reverie and turned round to him.

"I'm just impressed. I feel your pictures touch my heart..." she stopped trying to find the right words for her emotions. "You can see how much patience and hard work went into them in order to get the right shot. And yet they look so natural, they express your dedication and love of life." She went silent again.

Tim stared at her stunned. He had not expected this outburst. Of course he had hoped she would like his pictures. But he did not expect her to realise how important this work was to him and what drove him to do it. Such understanding took him by surprise. In fact, she had put it much better than he would have ever been able to express. While he was still pondering this thought, Kaja turned round and gave him a hug.

"I think I now understand what makes you shiver in the rain, jump into cold water, endure soaring heat, fight the mosquitoes, eat instant soup and canned food and travel to the most remote locations in the world." Her voice broke and only now did she realise what she was doing.

Tim immediately felt her stiffen and reluctantly let go of her. What was it that felt so good about this woman? He urgently needed some fresh air. Again. Today seemed to be his day for running away outdoors.

Kaja took a step backwards and pretended to study the picture again.

God, this man was dangerous! If she wasn't careful she could get used to lying in his arms. 'Hold your horses.' she told herself. 'I should get a grip on my life first before I can allow myself to think such things. And anyway, he's always on the go.' It was the last thing she wanted, she reminded herself and thought of her parents who, as long as she could think back, had always been away with more important things to do than watching their daughter grow up. The pain this caused her each time she thought of it was strong enough to kill any romantic inclinations.

"Shall we make a move?" she asked in a gruffer voice than intended. "I'm sure Zorro is waiting for me."

Tim noticed the change in her mood but decided to let it pass. She would eventually open up to him, in her own time. So he only replied: "Of course. Perhaps we can stop for something to eat on the way."

"Hungry again?" Kaja teased him and playfully pinched his side.

Together they left the university building and went back to Kaja's car. Tim noticed that the shadows had disappeared from Kaja's eyes and calmed down. But he couldn't help asking himself what the cause for her mood swings was. He watched her profile and caught himself wondering what it would feel like holding her in his arms. No, he corrected himself, he knew that already. After all, she had stumbled right into his arms this morning, outside the railway station. And the memory had been haunting him all day. All his thoughts focussed on how to get back to that situation. Permanently. He was not entirely innocent in what had happened. He had been so excited to see her again that he inadvertently tried to be as near her as possible.

The autumn breeze had picked up and ruffled Kaja's hair. A meddlesome strand kept flying into her eyes until Tim could not stop himself from brushing it away with two of his fingers. Kaja twitched away from him and stopped walking. Tim felt like a naughty boy and withdrew his hand.

"Sorry, I didn't mean to make you jump." he mumbled with embarrassment. God, he was behaving like a stammering sixteen-year-old. It wasn't like they were complete strangers. Kaja's face felt a burning sensation where he had touched it. Quickly, she turned away from Tim and said in a forced neutral tone: "No worries. We're almost there. Zorro's seen us already." Frustrated, he tried to catch up with Kaja. In the meantime, she had reached the car and released Zorro. The dog was so overjoyed that he jumped up at his mistress and knocked her over backwards, straight into Tim's arms again. He couldn't believe his luck.

He caringly closed his arms around her and whispered into her ear: "Are you running away from me, Kaja?"

"Of course not." she hissed at him and belatedly tried to escape from his unintended embrace. 'An unintended embrace that feels better than it should.' she realised with annoyance.

"Let go of me!" she demanded in a slight panic.

Immediately, he took a step away and asked: "So, what next? Hungry?"

"I, well..." Kaja's thoughts were all over the place. "I'm sorry. I have to be off. It's later than I thought." On impulse, she put her hand on his cheek. "Thank you for a wonderful day. I love your pictures." Hastily she withdrew her hand. "Time to go." She didn't trust herself enough to give him more than a quick glance before she turned round and pushed a completely confused Zorro back into the car before getting into the driver's seat herself. She had already started the engine when Tim knocked on the window. She wound it down and looked at him impatiently.

"And you are running away from me." he insisted.

She gave him an angry look, vigorously wound up the window and drove off.

15

On Sunday morning, Kaja woke up with a groan. She tried to open her eyes but immediately closed them again as she found the bright sunlight coming through the window too harsh. Her head was thumping. It took her some effort to try and remember why she was still lying in bed with a hangover at 10 o'clock in the morning. But she did not have the chance to sort her thoughts out. Zorro was already resting his paws on the side of her bed, pulling her duvet away with his teeth. 'Poor thing!' she thought. 'I'm sure you're desperate to get out.' She pulled herself together and vigorously sat up, only to sink back into the bed holding her head in pain. 'It looks like I'll have to take it easy today.' she thought grumpily. With Zorro following behind her, she opened the glass door leading out to the patio. She let the dog out so that he could do his business on a small patch of grass behind the pergola. Under normal circumstances, she didn't like that but today she didn't feel in a fit state to set foot outside her flat, never mind walk all the way to the park. In the meantime, she went straight to the kitchen to make herself a strong espresso and take an Alka-Seltzer. 'Better make it two.' she decided. While the coffee was brewing, she took a large glass of cool water from the tap and drank it in large gulps.

This helped her slowly wake up and suddenly she remembered the previous day. Pictures and emotions that she had seen and felt through her journey home came flooding back. She felt that she had descended into a maelstrom of events and was absolutely powerless to do anything about it. Kaja had not been able to stop the avalanche of thoughts rushing through her mind. Even taking a break from driving and going for a walk with Zorro had not helped. Normally, this was a reliable method for clearing her head and calming down. She frowned with depression. Yesterday had been such a successful and enjoyable day. But to her annoyance, she had to admit she was not at all immune to Tim's attraction. And this realisation caused her to panic, especially since she had found out he went abroad so often. Just like her parents...

She didn't dwell on the thought. Her mind went back to the rest of the evening. When she had finally arrived back home, she had made herself comfortable on the sofa with a family-sized packet of crisps and a bottle of Pinot Grigio while zapping through the TV channels, just to find some distraction. As Kaja looked round the kitchen, her eyes came to rest on the wine bottle next to the cooker in the kitchen. The tiny amount of liquid in it made her wonder: Had she really drank all that? No wonder her head felt like a herd of buffaloes was stampeding through it.

She was about to pour away the last of the wine - barely half a glass - when she heard a noise behind her. She put the bottle back down.

"Tut, tut." a disapproving sound could be heard.

Slowly, Kaja turned round, visibly annoyed. "You? What are you doing here? I thought you weren't back until tomorrow?"

Ostentatiously, she turned her back on him.

"Nice to see you, too." Lance replied in the same sarcastic tone. When Kaja refused to be drawn into a conversation, he sighed. "I was able to sort out the matter much quicker than expected."

"Good for you and now leave me in peace." Kaja was rather unimpressed.

"Hello? What's the matter with you? I'm doing this for you, you know." His voice had changed considerably.

She stopped inspecting the kitchen worktop and looked at him. The dragon looked chuffed to bits. He obviously had important news to tell but had caught her at the wrong time. It was too bad for him that she absolutely wasn't in the mood to talk to a dragon right now. She knew she had much more important things to do but momentarily struggled to remember what these were. So she just said said stroppily: "Welcome back. Sorry, I don't have time for you."

Lance, who had just decided to ingest the leftover wine, stopped dead, holding the bottle in mid-air. "What important things do you have to do? I thought Sunday was a day of rest or whatever you humans call it."

"Oh, this and that." she said evasively, hoping he would not keep questioning her. But there was little hope a pig-headed dragon could be fobbed off like that. "That doesn't sound very important to me." he promptly replied.

Now she completely lost her patience, which had been wearing thin all morning anyway. "What business is it of yours? When I say I don't have time for you, you'll just have to accept it as a fact." she hissed. Indignantly, she pushed herself away from the kitchen cabinet and accidentally banged her elbow in the process. "Ouch!"

Lance could hardly contain his glee. "This is what you get if you don't pay your dragon the respect he deserves." He commented as she whinged.

When she did not reply but marched off towards her room instead, he shouted after her: "Very well, if you want to spend your day drowning in self-pity, don't let me stop you. I don't want to run the risk of cheering you up."

Kaja did not deign to look at him and disappeared into her room.

Lance made himself comfortable at the kitchen table and put the bottle to his snout to gulp the last of the wine, smacking his lips with delight. How long would it take for her to see sense? Normally, he expected her to calm down very quickly, but his protégée could be surprisingly stubborn. 'No wonder.' he giggled to himself. 'After all, she is Josephine's granddaughter.'

While Lance was enjoying himself, Kaja hastily pulled some clothes from the wardrobe and put them on to go for a jog with Zorro. She had been so angry that she completely forgot about her sore head. But the exercise and the fresh air did her body good, although they did little to improve her mood. How dare that dragon pass judgement on her! She hadn't asked for his opinion. She had enough problems to deal with in her life without someone coming along and muscling in. And this wasn't just anyone. A dragon! That tells you something. 'At least it tells you something about my state of mind.' she thought ironically.

Engrossed in her monologues, she ran mile after mile. Zorro was elated how his morning had turned out after such an unpromising start, from a dog's point-of-view. In his excitement, he jumped up at Kaja and interrupted her dull thoughts.

She stopped and teased him: "Alright, at least somebody's happy. For once, you look like you agree with Lance."

The dog, rather offended, turned away and followed a mouse trail. Watching him, she shook her head. 'Sometimes, I could swear he understands every word I say.' she murmured. She closed her eyes and turned her face towards the sun, basking in its warm rays. Apparently, she had sweated out most of last night's alcohol. Her head was much clearer now. And she had to admit Lance's tactic had been clever. He had successfully distracted her from her worries, fanned her anger and spurred her to action. She sighed. He must be in cahoots with Josephine. She had no time for self-pity either. But what next? She might as well go home and face that impertinent dragon beast. She realised this might be exactly what Lance had intended. Uttering a few half-hearted curses, she started jogging again and made her way home.

An hour later, Kaja had finished her shower and came back to the kitchen in a much better mood to put the kettle on. Lance was still relaxing at the kitchen table, but he had replaced the empty wine bottle with a half-empty whiskey one.

"That doesn't happen to be my whiskey by any chance?" she asked him sternly.

"Well, I don't know. It doesn't have a name on it and looked rather lonely so I decided to keep it company." he grinned cheekily.

"You poor thing. Being in charge of the whiskey must be hard. But don't despair. I'm here to relieve you of your duty." she jibed and quickly locked the whiskey away in the kitchen cupboard.

"Hey, what're you doing?" he sounded annoyed.

Unfazed, she put a cup of tea in front of him. "If you're gobbling it like water, you might as well drink tea." And she poured another cup for herself.

Lance sniffed at his cup and grimaced. "Yuck! I believe dragons can get sick from what you call healthy stuff."

"I'll be your devoted nurse." she said in her sweetest voice and a beaming smile.

"You look like you're much better now." he grumbled.

"Well, that's partly thanks to you." she admitted reluctantly.

The dragon acknowledged the praise with unusual modesty. "Don't thank me, you did it all by yourself. I just forced you into action. Do you want to talk about it?"

"I have nothing to talk about. But what about your big news?" She looked at him expectantly.

"Don't think I don't notice when you change the subject. But very well, I'll let it pass as I have exciting news indeed."

"You can come off your high horse." Kaja laughed. "I'm all ears. I know you can't wait to tell me your story."

Lance grinned. "Well, you're right, I have lots to tell you. If you remember, I was going to enquire of the head dragoness why Miri was able to see me. When it was finally my turn to be called in for an audience, I was taken to a magnificent room. The walls were covered in mosaics shining in all colours..." The dragon was fully absorbed in the description of this obviously grand palace.

For a while, Kaja listened patiently to him until she begged, laughing: "Please get to the point. My eyes and ears are hurting from all that splendour. But I'm keen to know what the story is with Miri."

Lance pretended to be offended because she had interrupted his description, but then he was all too willing to answer her request: "Apparently, there are dragon sisters once every few centuries who are linked to each other through a common fate."

"Dragon sisters" Kaja tried to say the words a few times. They felt strangely familiar although her brain was unable to make any sense of them. She suddenly had a thought. "Does this mean you are her dragon as well?" she asked jealously. She had no intention of sharing Lance with anyone. If she had to deal with this annoying creature and his wisecracks, she wanted to do so on her own!

"No, I'm not." Lance re-assured her. "Thank heavens, I'm only responsible for you."

"What's that supposed to mean?" Kaja asked indignantly.

With unusual diplomacy, he replied: "I think we both have our work cut out with each other. I wouldn't be keen to look after somebody else on top of that."

"Yeah, right." She wasn't really listening as she tried to digest the news. "Dragon sisters. How many? Only Miri and me? Or is there another accident waiting to happen? I'm not keen to meet any others. Having said that, I'm getting on surprisingly well with Miri." she mused.

"There are always three sisters whose lives are inter-linked."

"So there does need to be another accident? But what if I don't want to meet the third sister?" Kaja asked rebelliously.

Lance smiled and explained: "It doesn't look like you have a choice. Certain things in life are beyond our control."

That was enough to shut Kaja up.

"Of course, it's up to you what you make of those encounters." the dragon tried to calm her down. "You're a free agent."

"Yes, I can see that. It was supposedly my free decision to call you." she steamed.

Lance frowned. He didn't understand why Kaja was so upset. She seemed to have returned to her gloomy mood of earlier that morning. "Hey, what's the matter with you? No need to start crying." He clumsily sat down on the sofa next to Kaja and gave her a hug.

"No." she sniffled. "I never cry." but immediately had to laugh, realising how silly her insistence was when in fact tears were running down her cheeks.

"That's a good girl." Lance replied, trying to preserve the little sign of cheerfulness. "Now come on, tell me what's really been upsetting you. I thought you'd be happy about my news. You seem to be fond of Miri although you hardly know her."

"You're right." Kaja blew her nose and took a deep breath. "Looking at this rationally, I find it exciting. I'm curious. But at the same time, I feel I'm totally losing control of my life and my feelings."

"And you like to be in control of your life, am I right?"

"Yes, even if it sounds stupid now you say it. I do like to be in control of my life and I have to be. It's the only way I can be sure everything is working as it should."

"And why is that so important to you?" Lance asked gently, although he knew the answer already. But it was important for her to see and understand her own motives. It was the only way to enable her to change the pattern.

"Because... I don't know why." She stopped, trying to collect her thoughts, something which wasn't easy in her current state of mind. "As a child, I always lived with Mémé. It was really wonderful. I wouldn't have wanted to be anywhere else. But I always wished my parents had been there for me and they never were. Most of the time, they were abroad, sometimes here, sometimes there. Whenever they turned up for one of their rare visits, I tried my best to please them. I thought if I was a good girl they would take me along." Her voice broke as she recalled the past.

"Not that I wanted to leave Mémé. I think I didn't even realise this would have been the consequence of me actually going with them. All I wanted was for my parents to love me enough to include me and to share their life with me. But I was never good enough. Quite the opposite, they always found fault with me or my life with Mémé. For many years, I felt helpless because I didn't have the chance to change anything. And then I decided to do whatever was necessary to avoid ever having that feeling again." All these recollections had exhausted Kaja.

"And now you think your whole life is in turmoil because you've met two new people?" Lance asked in a friendly but slightly puzzled tone.

Kaja looked depressed. "No, it's not that. They are just the straw that broke the camel's back."

"I didn't know you have a camel? And what's it got to do with Miri and me?" He sounded confused.

She smiled. "It's just a saying. Never mind. What I wanted to say was that my life has been turned upside down recently. First the trouble with Little Freddy and my employer. I almost handed in my notice but didn't know what to do with myself. Now the problem with Tim..."

"What problem with Tim?" Lance asked sharply. Now it was his turn to be jealous.

"I like him. I like him a lot, actually."

"And you have a problem with that? All the better for me, one less thing to worry about." Lance said smugly.

"It's no joking matter." she said bitterly. "He used to be my best friend."

"And now he isn't any more?"

"Well, yes, he still is, somehow. But there's more. More than there used to be."

"What more?" he enquired, although he was actually not too keen to know.

"More feelings... I can't explain it."

"So why all the headaches? I don't suppose the presence of my humble self is stopping you." he replied, hoping that this was exactly the case.

"No, not really. What's it got to do with you?" She didn't get his point. "Can't you see? Tim is a photographer and wildlife biologist."

He looked at her waiting for an explanation. "So? You say that as if he was a wanted criminal."

"He's constantly on the move." she said with a shaky voice. "Just like my parents. I couldn't bear him not being round for most of the time. Being away, far away without any common memories, being like strangers each time we meet again..."

"Hey, you sound like you were going to marry him?" Lance was shocked.

And so was Kaja: "Marry him? No way!"

The dragon was not really convinced and kept digging: "You could have fooled me. Why else would you be counting your chicken before they are born?"

"Before they are hatched..." she automatically corrected him.

"What?"

"It's hatched, not born. But never mind." she said with an enervated wave of her hand. "Anyway, I would appreciate it if you could stop making fun of me and take my concerns more seriously. I'm baring my soul to you." she was losing patience with her companion.

"Why don't you just forget about him, if he's that much trouble?" he was hoping to make sense.

"I've tried that already, but I can't. And he's not only trouble. He could actually be good for me, really good. Perhaps your comment about marrying him wasn't too far off the mark." she admitted. "I don't want to get married, not at all. But I feel a relationship with Tim could work very well." She stopped and thought back to how well Tim had understood her, how he had offered his help without being asked and immediately got into action. How he made her laugh, how nice his embrace had felt.

She tried to explain her feelings. "When he holds me in his arms, I feel safe. That's what scares me most."

Lance realised that he wasn't getting anywhere. In, fact, he was alarmed by what she had said. If his protégée felt safe being with this... What was his name?... Tim, it was obviously a rather serious affair. This meant he had to support her, even grudgingly, and put his own ambitions on hold. Being a dragon could be a lousy job sometimes.

He sighed. Kaja sighed. They looked at each other and broke into a liberating laughter.

After they had calmed down, Lance summarised: "First: If you have known Tim for such a long time, you should know whether you can trust him."

"I can, but not in this sense."

"Be quiet. Now I've decided to take you seriously, you mustn't interrupt me."

"Yes Sir." Kaja answered mockingly.

"Second: Why don't you give it a go and see how you feel about it?"

"But if it goes wrong, I'll lose his friendship too, most likely."

"Stop, I still haven't finished. Anyway, how did you survive the past few years without his valuable friendship?"

"But..." Kaja tried to protest.

"No buts. I'm right and you know it. And third: At this very moment, you're not in any danger of being seduced, getting married or whatever you're imagining in your pretty little head. Even supposing you were, you couldn't tell the outcome, could you?"

"No, of course not, but..."

"I don't want to hear any buts. All I want you to see is that you are getting worked up about a hypothetical situation which you may never encounter. And even if you wanted to, there is nothing you could do about it right now. So please tell me, what's the point of getting worried?"

"Hm, you're right, there is no point." Kaja was surprised and overwhelmed to admit. "The way you put it makes perfect sense. But my mind has gone haywire and isn't open to any sensible explanations at the moment." she concluded feebly. "We've digressed, haven't we? Our conversation started with my so-called sisters. What am I supposed to do with that information?"

Lance shrugged his shoulders. "I'm not very good at predictions about the future. I suppose you'll have to find out yourself."

"That's so typical of you." Kaja was furious and amused at the same time. "First you make a big deal about our shared fate and then you can't fill me in on the details. Well, never mind. I'm going to meet Miri tomorrow and then we'll see if you were right."

Lance was satisfied. He nodded and said: "That's right. Good girl."

"And how can I switch off those stupid thoughts rushing through my head?"

"Find some distraction, do something to occupy yourself. On the other hand, you could just sit here and meditate." he grinned.

"Meditate?" Kaja snorted with laughter. "Like 'Ommm!'" she tried and immediately fell into a giggle again. "Thanks, but no thanks. I'd rather try your occupational therapy." she decided and disappeared into the bedroom.

There, she dropped on her bed and stared at the ceiling. Her talk with Lance had gone surprisingly well although she still had no idea how to handle the situation. She sighed and remembered her promise to stop moping and find some distraction. But how? She frowned, realising that she could hardly remember the last time when she had been free of urgent projects that kept her busy after work. For the past few months, she had often been sitting in front of her home computer at night, developing software programs and trying to meet deadlines. Now she realised that she had not been given a new project yet. She jumped up but slumped back into her pillow immediately. Perhaps this was another issue not worth getting upset about. Today she was unlikely to get hold of a new project, but tomorrow, she would knock on Max's door and ask if he had anything lined up for her. However, this still didn't solve her current problem of trying to find a distraction.

"It looks like you need a hobby, Kaja." she scolded herself. Looking around her bedroom, she saw one of Mémé's candles. Perhaps this was the idea she was looking for. She still had to pay her debts to Luc and grimaced realising that those debts involved making a candle for Tim as well. So be it! Making candles was a good way of taking her mind off things. And Mémé had been wise enough to give her everything she needed. With renewed energy, she jumped from her bed and searched for the equipment and ingredients.

A few hours later, she was ranting and raving in despair. Full of enthusiasm, she had forgotten how well Mémé's workshop was equipped with tools and clever tricks and how inadequate her little kitchen was, intended for cooking the occasional meal but not for melting wax, mixing herbs and all the other steps required in the candle-making process. She had already ruined two of the few cooking pots she owned and was struggling to attach the wicks to the bottom of the moulds so that she could straighten them up by hand. When she finally succeeded, applying generous amounts of superglue, she realised she needed at least another pair of hands if she was to hold the mould, straighten the wick and pour the hot wax in.

"I wish I was an octopus." she grumbled.

But she wasn't. So all she could do was to hold the mould between her knees and the wick between her teeth. In this contorted posture, she shuffled her chair towards the cooker, hoping desperately that the wax was still liquid enough. To make matters worse, Lance had decided to give her practical advice.

"Don't you think that's a bit dangerous? What if you miss the mould with the hot wax?"

"Grmpf!" was the best swear word Kaja was able to throw at him with the wick between her teeth.

Carefully, she tried once more to pour the hot wax into the mould. At first, all seemed to go well until the superglue apparently gave way under the heat and the wick was released from the bottom of the mould. The hot liquid gushed all over Kaja's jeans and, together with her chair, she slowly dropped backwards to the floor as if she was re-enacting a scene from an early Hollywood slapstick movie.

"Wah, that's hot." she shrieked.

"Didn't I tell you." know-it-all Lance commented before breaking into loud laughter.

Kaja glowered at him while she struggled to her feet. "It's not funny." she hissed. "I'm trying to make something here."

"Oh come off it. The wax wasn't too hot I imagine and the look on your face was hilarious. And anyway: Your day's job is done, whether you managed to make the candles or not."

Kaja continued to try and look angry but finally gave up.

"You're right. A shame about the wax, though. Since I've already mixed in the herbs, I can't re-use the rest." she lamented.

"What rest?" the dragon giggled, earning himself another angry look from Kaja.

"Well, it can't be helped. I'd better clear up this mess and prepare my next attempt more carefully."

Exhausted, Kaja slumped on the sofa, switched on the TV and zapped through the channels. For the past two hours, she had been scraping wax from the parquet floor, ironing her jeans to remove the stains and cleaning the rest of the kitchen. Discontented, she looked at herself: Although she was wearing new trousers, her arms, and most likely her face as well, still bore the signs of the candle-making disaster. What the heck! Time to look forward to her pizza delivery (the kitchen now too clean to be cooked in) and leave it to the telly to distract her.

A few hours later, she sat up rubbing her eyes. The TV was still on and the clock in her ancient video recorder told her it was one o'clock in the morning already. All her worries about finding distraction had been unnecessary, she realised. Apparently, she had only made it halfway through the pizza before falling asleep over a boring TV programme. But wait, where was the rest of her dinner? The pizza carton was empty.

"Zorro and I shared it. You don't mind, do you? You didn't look like you wanted any more, the way you were snoring on the sofa."

"I don't snore." Kaja insisted indignantly. "And don't think I don't notice when you're trying to get into my dog's good books." she added ungraciously. "I'm going to bed now. And don't you dare touch that whiskey bottle."

The dragon rolled his eyes in mock despair and grimaced.

"And don't pull faces behind my back either." she added without looking at him.

16

The next morning, Kaja was in her office unusually early. Apparently, she had caught up on much needed sleep last night in front of the telly. So she had been wide awake by 6am and had thrown herself fully into this foggy and still rather dark day. Neither the dog's playfulness nor Kaja's exuberant mood had suffered from the dull weather. On the contrary, she was looking forward to her meeting with Miri tonight. She wasn't sure whether she should mention the dragon at all. Actually, she had no intention of giving the impression of a hallucinating maniac within the first five minutes of meeting her.

On the other hand, she mused, Miri had been able to see the dragon right from the start as well and had obviously accepted him as being real. Kaja sighed. Lance, that old rogue, would tell her yet again not to worry about things she could not change. And his advice was right. Annoying but right. Resolutely, she pushed any thoughts about the evening aside.

'I have other problems that need taking care of.' she reminded herself and decided to take the bull by the horns.

She jumped up from her chair and went over to Max's office. It was empty. Damn! Why couldn't anything go right for her just now?!

She opened the door next to it and spoke to Max's PA: "Anna?"

Guiltily, she jumped, but when she saw it was only Kaja, she immediately turned her attention back to the Sudoku on her desk and answered rudely: "Yes?"

"Erm, I just wanted find Max?"

"He's out." was the brief answer.

"Out where?" Kaja was irritated.

"I don't think that's any of your business, but I'll tell you anyway: He's on a training course for the next few days."

"And who will assign the next project to me?"

"How am I supposed to know?" Anna responded, obviously so bored that she had to pull a long, disgusting string of chewing gum from her mouth. Then she turned her back on Kaja and ostentatiously continued with her number puzzle.

Kaja left the office totally perplexed and none the wiser. Touchy bitch! She had only wanted to know her next project assignment. After tidying up various odds and ends last week, she had now run out of work to do. Out of work! Had she become paranoid or was she being kept away from large projects on purpose. Not only large ones, practically any, she steamed. In three weeks time, her staff review was due. Of course, it would create a great impression if she had nothing to show for the past three months.

"Has the penny finally dropped?" a disembodied voice suddenly said next to her.

"Lance?" She turned round and discovered the dragon sitting on a filing cabinet.

"Shhh!" he pressed one of his clawed fingers against his scaly mouth.

"What's up now?" Kaja was completely confused. After all, the day had started so promisingly.

"I thought nobody could see you apart from me?"

"Yes, but they can see you talking to a filing cabinet. I'm sure it would benefit your reputation of being a reliable, mentally healthy and resilient employee. Hehe."

Indeed somebody was giving her a worried look already.

"Hey you! Had a tough weekend?" Phew, luckily it was only Thea, today wearing a scarlet dress and yellow high heels.

"Wow, you're looking great today" Kaja tried to distract her. "What do you mean?"

"I thought I heard you talking to yourself."

"Oh that. I was just going through the to-do list in my head. Or perhaps not only in my head, as it seems." she grinned. "What are you doing here?"

"I'm looking for you." Thea promptly replied.

"What a coincidence. I was just going to call you as well. Lunch again?"

"OK, see you at twelve. I can't make it any earlier."

With that, she turned round and gave Kaja a quick wave before disappearing down the stairs. 'Rushing around like a scarlet whirlwind.' Kaja smiled to herself.

"Uh, that was a close shave." she said to Lance.

"You're doing it again." Lance reminded her in a slightly enervated tone.

"Doing what?" she asked absent-mindedly as her thoughts had wandered off elsewhere.

"Talking to me with your voice. How often have I told you that you can use your thoughts to communicate with me?"

"Oh yes, you're right. Still haven't got used to it."

"You'd better pull yourself together if you want to keep working in this place."

Kaja gave Lance a questioning look but decided it was better to continue this conversation in her own office rather than hanging around in the hallway. It took her only a few steps to reach her office and, glancing at the clock, she was about to start talking to Lance again.

'That girl can be so stubborn sometimes.' Lance thought shaking his head and quickly put his hand over her mouth before she could say a word.

'What the...' she didn't have time to finish thinking the curse and only stared in surprise at the person sitting at Frédéric's old desk. The man was wearing an expensive suit and white trainers. He had styled his medium-length hair in current fashion using at least one whole tube of gel, combing it forward onto his forehead - a look that was absolutely not to Kaja's taste. He had taken off his tie and thrown it carelessly over the back of his chair. The top button on his pink shirt was open. A pink shirt. Whatever next. Never mind fashion trends, not many men can really wear that colour. Most should definitely stay off it. But this one seemed quite comfortable and had made himself at home already.

"Hello, I'm Michael." He came towards her offering his hand and displaying a set of gleaming white teeth. Kaja returned the handshake and was going to ask what he was doing here when he continued: "I'm sure we'll get on well with each other. I've heard a lot about you and your talents." he smirked.

Kaja froze. "I'm sorry?" she said in the coldest tone she could muster although she was fuming inside. It took all her willpower not to let her anger get the better of her. The last thing she needed right now was a computer crash.

"Channel your thoughts." she heard Lance's distant voice in her head.

"You know what I mean." Michael replied boldly and had the audacity to give her an insinuating wink.

Kaja was about to explode when she realised what her sometimes useful dragon had been trying to tell her. She forced herself to appear calm and took a step towards this obnoxious Michael.

"You don't happen to be my new partner, do you?" she said seductively while straightening the collar on his shirt with two of her fingers and slowly pushing him towards his own desk, away from hers.

"Erm, yes, I am." he stammered, pleasantly surprised that all those fantastic rumours about Kaja appeared to be true. Boy oh boy, this girl was hot!

"And you think we'll work well together? In all respects?"

Michael, who obviously had a healthy ego, missed the barely disguised sarcasm in Kaja's voice.

"Oh, I'm sure we will." It had also escaped his attention that he was now backed up against his desk, trapped between the worktop and Kaja. In the meantime, she concentrated on building a mental barrier between the two workstations facing each other in the room. In her sweetest voice, she asked him: "Please tell me all the things you've heard about me. I can't get enough of them."

"Oh, you're into dirty talk? All the better..."

At this point, he was suddenly interrupted by Kaja. Earlier in their conversation, she had playfully tickled his arm but now she grabbed it hard and twisted it round his back. "Listen carefully, my friend. You will take your things now and leave my office at once. Is that understood?"

Zorro, who had followed the exchange with interest, commented on the latest development with a deep growl.

"But it was Frentzen who put me here." Michael, who had lost much of his cheerful mood, winced. "And please, call your beast off." Now the panic was clearly noticeable in his voice.

"I don't care who put whom where." she hissed. "But one thing I know for certain: I'm not going to share my office with a chauvinistic piece of shit. Now piss off."

With these words, she pushed him across the office and let her anger loose. With a loud puff, his screen exploded, presumably killing the whole computer with it.

"What..." Michael stared at the machine in disbelief.

"Oops." Kaja said, back to using her sugar sweet voice. "The problem seems to have solved itself. You can't get any work done without a working computer. And we wouldn't want that to happen, would we?"

Michael's eyes wandered in terror between her and the computer. If he weren't sure both her hands had been busy holding him, he could have sworn the damage was her work. In panic, he snatched up his belongings and fled the room. Just outside the door, now feeling safe from Zorro, he turned and barked: "You will regret this, you frigid cow."

Kaja's anger immediately flared up. "I'm shivering with fear." She registered with satisfaction that the mobile in his jacket started to make funny noises and was obviously on the blink.

"Perhaps you should be afraid." Michael ranted, his face turning red. "If I were you, I wouldn't be so sure my job was safe."

Alarmed, she looked up at him.

"Well, you didn't think I was that well-informed, did you." he gloated. "Tough luck. You lost your chance to know what I know."

Kaja got up, closely followed by her canine protector and demonstratively slammed the door in his face. Then she slumped into her chair and sighed: "What has happened to my life?" The dog poked his nose towards Kaja and then turned round to fetch his ball from under the table. Unexpectedly, this made her laugh.

"That's your logic, isn't it? If the ball can cheer you up, surely it will work on your mistress as well?" Affectionately, she massaged him behind his ears and he wagged his tail with delight.

'See? I knew it. It does work.' he thought.

"Obviously, it does work." Kaja immediately confirmed. Triumphantly, the dog looked at Lance and said: "You see? I can talk to her as well."

"OK, so you can. What do I care? Now be a good pet and leave us in peace. We have more important things to discuss." Offended, Zorro retreated under the table. Kaja frowned and looked at the dragon.

"Is it your turn to talk to yourself now?"

"Me?" Now it was Lance who looked confused. "No, why? I was talking to Zorro."

172

"You don't say, tell me another one. Can we deal with the more important issues now?" she asked brusquely, assuming Lance was mocking her.

"That's exactly what I was saying." Lance answered piqued, shaking his head at his protégée's limited imagination.

Kaja had just decided to ignore Lance and his drivel when her mobile phone rang. Simon. What did he want? Did he have any news for her? Unlikely, he'd hardly had enough time to start his work.

"Why don't you answer the phone and ask what he wants instead of guessing?" Lance asked amused. Kaja quickly answered the call.

"Hello?"

"Hi, it's Simon here. Are you OK?"

"Hm." Kaja answered vaguely. "Is there anything you need?"

"I just wanted to ask if you could lend me your badge tomorrow."

"My badge? You mean my work ID?"

"Yes, exactly. I may have to come over to have a look around your workplace and it would be useful."

"Erm, yes, of course. Have you found anything out yet?"

"Nothing solid. I'm following a few leads and tying up some loose ends." he answered evasively. "I'll pop round to your flat tonight and collect the badge. Is that alright with you?"

"Yes, of course. Actually, no, it's not. I'm not at home tonight. Damn!"

"Just put it on the kitchen table. I'll collect it from there."

"OK, good idea." Kaja said without thinking. "See you later."

"Bye then."

"This Simon character is getting rather interesting." Lance observed.

"Why? What do you mean?" Kaja was irritated.

"As you know, we dragons can easily pass through closed doors but I'm quite sure you humans have a problem with it." he briefly paused to maximise the effect. "Or are you the last of them to miss the trick?" he teased Kaja who threw a screwed-up paper ball at him, which he managed to avoid with a laugh.

"I'll have to leave the door unlocked for him. I'm sure that is what he meant."

"I don't think so. Otherwise, he would have specifically asked you to leave it open, in order to make sure he doesn't come all the way in vain. I suggest you lock your door and watch what happens."

"Hey, Simon is on my side. I don't want to make it difficult for him."

"Yes, I do know that. Keep your wig on. I only thought it might be interesting to see how he manages to get to the badge." the dragon defended himself.

"Let's see." was Kaja's only answer.

"And? What's next?" he enquired curiously.

"To be honest: I don't have a clue. But I don't have time to rack my brains. Got more important things to do." She got up, took Michael's pink and purple tie and marched out of the office. Lance scurried after her, curious what she was going to do.

"I'm surprised this thing doesn't have Mickey Mouse patterns." she murmured disgustedly.

"Are you heading for any particular place?" her companion wanted to know.

"You'll see in a second." she fobbed him off. When she reached the end of the corridor, she turned right into an open space that served both as a staff room as well as the location of commonly used office machines such as a colour laser printer, a fax machine and a shredder. It was this last device she was aiming at, smoothly feeding Michael's tie into it.

"Right." she stated with satisfaction. "That's done. What next?"

"Don't ask me, you're the boss." Lance said with unusual restraint.

She had impressed him considerably. He didn't know his protégée could be so determined and decisive. Kaja acknowledged his unusual comment with a suspicious look as if she wanted to say: That'll be the day! But she didn't condescend to give him an answer. On their way back to the office, Lance teased her: "Perhaps you should have kept that Michael near you? Apparently, he manages to bring out the best in you." Instead of an answer, a strip light exploded above their heads.

"Only the best in me, is it?" Kaja replied. The corners of her mouth twitched while she was trying to keep a straight face.

"Ah, I see." Lance noted. "Now you've got the hang of how to limit the damage, you seem to enjoy destroying things."

Kaja poked her tongue out at him but could not help a satisfied smile sneaking onto her face.

"You look like the cat that got the keys to the milk float."

Kaja giggled and corrected him: "Like the cat that got the cream. I should start collecting your mangled proverbs and publishing them. They would sell like hot cakes."

"At a bakery?" Lance appeared quite irritated. He had never been good at taking criticism.

Kaja, well aware of that by now, just waved her hand and laughed: "Don't get into a strop, we have more important things to do. At least I have. I need to find out where Max is, what my job prospects are and later on, I have a meeting with Thea."

Kaja hung up the phone in frustration. She had tried to call Max, but apparently it was impossible to locate him. It was as if he had disappeared from the face of the earth. A training course might be a good excuse for not being at his desk. But what kind of training was he on? Where was it supposed to be taking place? And when was he expected back? Nobody could, or rather would, give her an answer to all these questions. She had a feeling of being strung along. She had even brought herself to call Frentzen, but his cow of a secretary had fobbed her off claiming he was busy with meetings all day. And currently, she did not have the courage to storm into his office and check if it was true. She sighed. As if all this wasn't enough, Tim and the kiss kept occupying her mind. The kiss?!? They hadn't shared a proper kiss yet. Well, apart from that tiny one he stole on their first night in France. And this tongue-in-cheek, almost innocent attempt had nothing to do with the pictures in her head and the feelings in her stomach and other parts of her body. She sighed. Now she was already having slightly erotic day dreams in which Tim played a part. Whatever next? 'Have I involuntarily mutated to a gushing teenager and totally lost control?' she asked herself, feeling disgusted.

"That film in your head should be adult-rated..." Lance promptly mocked her.

"Shut up and get out of my head."

She felt her ears turning hot. Great. Now she was blushing and all this because a mythical creature, which was not supposed to exist anyway, was pulling her leg. Bang! The next moment she landed on the floor.

"Hey, what did you do that for? I didn't ask for a wrestling match."

"You told me to pull your leg. What do I know what you needed that for?" Lance defended himself.

Zorro interpreted the situation as an invitation to play. He jumped on Kaja's belly and started licking her face. "Eh, get off me!"

"What are you two up to?" an amused voice came from the door.

"Uh, oh, Thea. do come in." Kaja's cheeks were burning. "Zorro and I only had our mad five minutes just now."

"That's not fair." Zorro grumbled next to her. "I was only joining in the fun."

"That's humans for you." Lance replied to him, nodding sympathetically. "They can never make up their minds."

"Zorro, be quiet. Stop that squeaking. We're going out in a minute."

She shut down her computer, took her badge and the leash and followed Thea outside, accompanied by a fully wound-up Zorro.

This time, Thea had organised the food and they let Zorro roam free on the bank of the river Limmat as they tried to have a reasonably coherent conversation between bites from their baguettes.

"Hm." Kaja grinned with her mouth full. "Meetings over lunch have their pitfalls." she mumbled.

Thea was busy chewing as well and took a moment to reply: "Mmh, that's true." and, after swallowing hard: "Perhaps we should first enjoy our great organic bread rolls, guaranteed free from GM technology, made from naturally grown wheat, without any antibiotics or pesticides, but with lots of yoghurt sauce or coarse mustard and a number of other secret ingredients." she added acting like a market trader. "Why don't we have our chat on the way home?"

"OK, it may be more practical." Kaja laughed before she tackled the next big bite from her turkey baguette with mustard, gherkins and black olives.

They sat down on a bench, happy and satisfied. The weather had turned colder lately. Although the sun was shining, a cool breeze stopped many people from taking a break outside. During the summer, this area would be packed with people having their lunch breaks. Now there were only a few businessmen trying to catch a little bit of sunshine before they plunged into their November depression. There were also a few other dog owners - to Zorro's delight -, plus a mother and her toddler feeding the ducks, and of course the two of them.

"So, now tell me: Why did you want to see me?" Thea wanted to know from Kaja.

"No, you go first. After all, it was you who came looking for me."

"Whatever. OK, I'll make a start."

"That sounds rather serious." Kaja commented, who slowly but surely felt the butterflies in her stomach waking up. "I feel like a schoolgirl being called to the headmaster's office without knowing why. My guilty conscience used to work overtime when that used to happen back then." Kaja sighed. "Go on then, give me the bad news."

"I would love to" Thea answered amused. "If only you could let go of your childhood memories for a moment, I will tell you my story. And it's not as dramatic as you might expect."

"I'm not so sure about that." Kaja said with a half-hearted smile. "My day already had a dramatic start, but I'll tell you later. I'd better shut up now and let you get on with it."

"You shutting up? That'll be the day..." Thea snorted with a smile. "OK, first of all, there is a rumour out there that some of the most senior employees are to be sacked. Or perhaps that's not the right word. They want to get rid of them, but not through official dismissals as that would entitle them to months of redundancy pay and even the odd extensive compensation."

"Get rid of them?" Kaja asked incredulously. "How is that going to work?" In her mind, she already saw IT specialists going missing in large numbers.

"No no." Thea was quick to calm her down, when she saw the terror in Kaja's face. "It's not what you think. You shouldn't watch so many B-movie thrillers on the telly or go to bed earlier, if you're becoming paranoid."

"With everything that's happened to me lately, is it any wonder if I'm becoming a little paranoid?" Kaja defended herself.

"That's another story. But I did tell you it is not quite as dramatic as it seems, didn't I?"

"Yes, you're right, but even so: It is dramatic and fits in with what I have been through this morning. But please finish your story first."

"The intention seems to be to provoke these people into handing in their notice. That way, the company would be off the hook."

"They would like that, surely." Kaja was enraged. "But what is someone like Edi supposed to do?"

Edi was a veteran of PC Lux Solutions, he had been there when the company was founded and was irreplaceable due to his wealth of knowledge about relational databases. Although he had attended various training courses over the years, Kaja did not believe it would be easy for him to find another job. He was almost 60. Even if he did find a new employer, the question remained if he would be able to cope with the change. He wasn't an easy person to get on with anyway. You had to be persistent if you wanted to get to know him. He usually fended off any such attempts with his acid style of cynicism. That way he could be sure to be left alone to do his work. In her first year, Kaja had found it hard to get on with him and decided to avoid him as much as possible. But later on, she had to rely on his help with one of her projects. There had been absolutely no-one else she could have turned to. She had tried all avenues, questioned other employees, even tracked down her old university lecturer, searched the net for solutions - but to no avail. So she finally plucked up the courage and entered the lion's den, which in itself had been a major challenge. His office looked much like a hazardous rubbish tip, a concoction of old pizza boxes, empty cola cans and huge piles of paper covering the whole room. Or you could see it as a unique piece of art, depending on your mood and inclination. She had told him that when he had tried to send her away with an unfriendly grumble, Kaja remembered with amusement. She had called him a biological hazard and threatened to report him to the local health authority if he wasn't prepared to help her. Of course, she had only been bluffing and they had both known it, but her resourcefulness had apparently impressed him. He had agreed to help her. From that point onwards they had regularly worked together, not only when she needed help with her own projects, but also on several occasions in a team. She thought of the old codger with a melancholic smile and resolved to visit him again soon in his "den" as he occasionally called his office in jest. She felt bad for not having been in touch for so long.

"Are you still listening to me?" Thea interrupted her musings.

"Yes, sorry, my mind got distracted."

"Quite obviously." her friend grinned. "That's nothing new with you. But let's move on with my story. One aspect is most fascinating, if not to say suspicious - I'm slowly getting paranoid as well, you see." she added frowning. "All the colleagues currently in trouble or rumoured to be in trouble soon are former employees of PC Lux Solutions."

"Hang on. You mean not a single Qubus employee is affected?" Kaja interrupted her incredulously.

"Exactly and..." Thea hesitated and looked at Kaja, not sure whether it was a good idea to continue or not.

Kaja caught her glance and commented dryly: "Go on, give it to me. I can cope." While Thea was still humming and hawing, she spelled it out: "Let me guess: My name appears on this unofficial sacking or non-sacking list as well. And probably quite close to the top."

"Yes, it does." Now that the awkward truth was finally out in the open, Thea started to relax. "How did you know?"

"Well, it wasn't difficult to work out. That faked story about my X3 program, the way I have been treated by Little Freddy... And this morning, another creep had the audacity to tell me straight to my face that I didn't have a future in this company."

"What? Who did that? And when? Haven't we just met this morning?"

"I hadn't been to my office when we did. There, I found a rather charming fellow named Michael." Kaja told her sarcastically. "Apparently, he had heard a lot about me and was convinced we had known each other for ages and were ready for some special, intimate co-operation."

Thea was shocked. "Intimate co-operation? What an odd choice of words. What are you trying to imply?"

"Do you remember what you told me when we last had lunch together? That the in-house rumour mill had me down as a hot number of loose morals?"

"Now that was a rather good choice of words." Thea smiled. "Yes, of course I remember."

"Well, obviously, this Michael was told by Frentzen to be my new work buddy, as a replacement for Frédéric. I presume at least that part of the story is true."

"Little Freddy." Thea promptly corrected her.

"Little Freddy. Michael must have heard those rumours and must have believed them to be true."

"Pfffh." Thea snorted. "What did he expect? That his teenage dreams might come true?"

"I don't know." Kaja sighed.

"And?"

"What do you mean: And?"

"Well, what did you say to him? I don't suppose you started unbuttoning your blouse?"

Kaja had to laugh. "I almost did."

"You did what?" Thea sounded genuinely shocked.

"Calm down. Only to get close enough to him to twist his arm round his back and give him a rather unfriendly push out of the door. Zorro was a great help."

Zorro, exhausted from unsuccessfully chasing the ducks, had lain down in front of the two women. Now he wagged his tail on hearing his name.

"Yes, big boy, I'm talking about you. That was very brave of you." Kaja confirmed again and rubbed his head. Then she turned back to Thea. "As you can imagine, he wasn't best pleased with the development and shouted a few rather unfriendly things at me. Among them was the information that I was not likely to work in the company for much longer. I'm quite sure I wasn't supposed to hear that, but he must have been so frustrated that he couldn't keep his mouth zipped."

"First, it must have knocked you for six to hear it from him and now I'm giving you the same information? My God, how can you keep so calm?"

"I don't know. It didn't come as a complete surprise after all the events of the past few weeks. And there's not much I can do about it apart from sitting it out. There's no point getting stressed." - 'That's a bit rich.' Kaja thought. 'Yesterday, I was a nervous wreck from worrying.' But when she examined her emotions now, she realised that this was no longer the case and she felt pretty relaxed.

Thea stared at her in disbelief: "Tell me: Did you use your absence from work for a course in meditation or something?"

"No, I stayed with my grandmother. Sometimes, she has the same effect on people. But let's not dwell on my emotions. The most important question is: Why is all this happening?"

"What do you mean?" Still stunned by Kaja's relaxed attitude, Thea, who was normally quick to respond, was a bit slow on the uptake.

"Well, think. At first I thought it was a personal vendetta against me. But it looks like I'm not the only one affected."

"No, that's true." Thea agreed. "And it looks like it is aimed at us former PC Lux employees."

"Exactly. Don't you smell a rat? Especially so soon after the merger?"

"That was at least half a year ago."

"Which is not much in terms of company history, come to think of it." Kaja insisted.

"OK, let's assume you're right and the Qubus people are behind it. It doesn't make sense. What do they stand to gain from driving away some of the best staff?"

"That's what I mean. 'There must be more to it.' That sentence has always been on my mind since my affair with Little Freddy. But I can't work out what this 'more' refers to."

The two friends kept on discussing for a little bit longer, imagining various scenarios only to dismiss them soon after as being unlikely. Finally, Thea said regretfully: "I have to go back now. As far as I'm aware, they haven't put me on the list yet. To be honest, I'm not keen to be included which means I need to keep my head down, stick to working hours etc."

"Of course you do." Kaja answered and linked her arm with Thea's on their way back.

Just before they reached the imposing concrete building, Thea stopped and asked: "By the way: Why did you want to see me?"

"Oh, I almost forgot. Do you know where Max is? I was told he is on a training course and made several enquiries to find out the location and subject but I didn't get any information." She looked at Thea hoping for an answer.

But she only shrugged her shoulders. "I don't know. I can try and find out. Will let you know as soon as I have something for you."

"OK, thanks. We'll have to meet up again soon."

"Yes, of course. By the way: Are you coming to the company ball on Wednesday?"

"Is it this Wednesday already?" Kaja thought for a moment, frowning. "It looks like I'll have to show my face."

"Why? Do you expect anything special to happen?"

"I'm short-listed for the Super Brain Prize that is awarded every year."

"Wow. So we'll meet there?"

Kaja nodded without much enthusiasm.

17

For the rest of the afternoon, Kaja sat in her office with little inclination to do anything. It was something she had never been able to cope with - having to be present without anything to do. It was a horrible feeling. She tried to contact a few other colleagues in order to find out which training course Max was attending. But as expected, her efforts proved to be fruitless so she eventually gave up. Then she aimlessly surfed the Web. But by four o'clock she had finally had enough.

"This is no good, Zorro. Come on, let's go for a jog in the forest. Tonight, we're invited to Miri's. At least we'll be done with our keep fit programme."

"I was wondering how long you were planning on hanging around here." Lance's voice came out of nowhere.

"Aren't you lucky that I have such steady nerves." Kaja sighed as he slowly materialised next to her. "Otherwise you'd have to resuscitate me every so often."

"No sweat. We dragons are used to dealing with delicate virgins. And you - come on, admit it - you've got so used to it, you'd miss me if I didn't turn up now and then." He fluttered his long eyelashes in exaggeration.

Kaja pretended to be annoyed, rolling her eyes as she packed her clothes. "Dream on, darling. Although, come to think of it, you're normally so meddlesome and such a chatterbox that I wonder what kept you from lightening up my otherwise boring afternoon?"

"Oh, I had a few things to do." the dragon replied evasively.

Kaja shrugged her shoulders. "You don't have to tell me, if you don't want to. Zorro and I are on our way home and we're going for a jog later on. Would you like to join us?"

"Me? You want me to come jogging?" Lance asked flabbergasted.

Kaja grinned. "That's a trick to remember: Ask a big, bad dragon if he wants to do some exercise and he'll break into a cold sweat. Your face was hilarious just now. But why not? You could fly next to us. Is it hard work?" she asked curiously, letting Zorro jump into the car.

Lance pulled a disgusted face. "It's simply not worthy of a dragon."

"Ah, I see." Kaja could not stop grinning. In the meantime, Lance sat down in the passenger seat and stared majestically out of the window.

"You're a wimp." Zorro barked from his back seat.

The dragon decided to ignore this comment and Kaja, who again misunderstood the situation, said: "No worries, big boy. We won't let a lazy dragon spoil our fun."

Two hours later, Kaja and Zorro returned from their exercise. While Kaja had a quick shower, Zorro, happy and exhausted, retreated to his resting place in the front room. Lance was apparently still sulking. At any rate, he was nowhere to be seen. But perhaps this didn't mean much for a creature who was not supposed to exist and was invisible most of the time anyway. And even this was putting it mildly because most people could not see him at all. For them, he simply didn't exist. But now she was going to meet a woman who was able to see the dragon. She still could not believe it and shook her head as she pulled a random pair of well-worn jeans from her wardrobe. After getting dressed, she sparingly applied some make-up in front of the mirror, a bit of eye shadow, some mascara, that was more than enough.

185

Without giving her image in the mirror a second look, she rushed to her desk, trying to find Miri's address in the chaos. She had already started to panic when she finally found it underneath today's newspaper. Schmiede Weidikon was not exactly an area she would have chosen to live in herself. She shrugged her shoulders. Perhaps she had been extremely lucky with her flat. And anyway, what gave her the right to judge Miri by her choice of neighbourhood? Maybe she was doing it because she was nervous. After all, she hardly knew the woman.

'No, you do know her - perhaps you've always known her. ' There it was again, that nagging voice in her mind.

"What a mess." Kaja said to herself. "First I see fabled creatures in broad daylight and then I hear voices. I'm definitely cracking up."

"Are you talking to yourself again?" Lance commented, now clearly visible on the sofa, making himself comfortable with a drink in his shiny blue claws.

Kaja raised her eyebrows at him: "I don't suppose you're just having a glass of water there?"

Imitating her expression, the dragon also raised an eyebrow and replied: "You're quite right. I've treated myself to a shot of elderberry brandy from my friend Josephine. At least she knows how to treat a dragon with the respect he deserves."

"Oh, get off your high horse. I won't deny you an elderberry brandy..." she said in an attempt to placate him, but could not refrain from adding "... most of the time. And don't scare Simon when he comes in, OK?"

"Just a moment. What do you mean? I thought I was going to Miri's with you?"

"No, Lance, this is something I'll have to do on my own. You are my dragon and I don't intend to share you. Not with all your antics I have to put up with." She jokingly explained. "If Miri and I really do have a deeper and continuing relationship - or whatever the right word is for it - I want to find out the details on my own."

"Hm, granted. I can see where you're coming from. In that case,

I'd better have a friend to keep me company." he said raising his glass.

"What's up with you?" Kaja turned to Zorro who had sneaked up on her from behind and was now gently dragging her to his food bowl by the hem of her pullover. "OK, I'm coming. How could I forget to feed my other monster?" she laughed.

When Zorro had finished his meal, she took the leash and put on her jacket.

"Look, Zorro, how lucky we were. It's started to rain and we would be rather wet by now if we were out jogging."

The two of them took a short sprint to the car. Ten minutes later, they were close to Miri's flat. Kaja was glad to find a parking space. Although it was some distance away from Miri's door, she decided to take it and park there.

"Looks like we'll be getting wet after all, Zorro."

She did not know the area very well and did not want to risk getting lost searching for another space, which could easily happen with all the one-way systems in this neighbourhood. Two streets further and well soaked, Kaja was finally standing in front of a dirty, grey block of flats. Zorro squeezed himself into the doorway to escape the downpour as best he could.

"Don't be such a fair weather dog." Kaja scoffed and bent forward to find Miri's name on the bell panel. She pressed the button and waited nervously. At first, nothing happened but then she heard someone running down the stairs taking several at a time. A key turned in the lock and Miri opened the door, still panting.

"Hi, I'm sorry. It takes me a while to come down from the fourth floor. We don't have an intercom, but the rent is cheap. - Oh, I'm rattling on, keeping you out in the rain. Do come in."

"I'm sorry as well. Zorro and I are soaked. Hope you don't mind?" Kaja asked hastily.

"No, no." Miri was quick to reassure her, as they both made their way up the old wooden staircase. Zorro rushed ahead, excited at having a new place to explore.

"You have it easy on your four legs." Miri laughed, seeing him disappear round a bend. When they reached the top, they were greeted by a picture to behold: Zorro had stopped mid-move and was facing a huge cat with a red-striped coat. It was about half the size of Zorro, who was not a small animal himself, and hissed at him angrily.

"Ah, and you were worried about your cat?" Kaja commented with an insecure smile. "That's a huge b..." she just managed to swallow the word "beast".

"Don't worry. You can call him a huge beast." Miri confirmed, grinning. "This is Chili, my Maine Coon tom."

"Wow, I'm impressed."

"And so is Zorro." she added laughing.

Miri bent down and picked Chili up with a sweep of her arm. "Come on, let's go in."

Kaja followed her into the flat with Zorro, still perturbed, at her heels.

"You can hang up your jacket on one of the hooks by the door." Miri's voice came from another room.

Kaja looked around and discovered several colourful coat hooks on the wall. They were designed in the shape of animal heads. Fabled animals, as Kaja realised when she took a closer look. There was a troll, several elves, a unicorn... And of course, as she almost expected, a fire-breathing dragon. She followed the hallway until she reached a small room that apparently served both as a bedroom and sitting room. The bed had been casually covered with a bedspread, embroidered with numerous small flowers. Every possible space in the room was covered with small pots, growing flowers, ferns and other plants. In one corner, there was a tree in full bloom. The cheap lino flooring had been cleverly covered with various patchwork rugs. Diagonally opposite the bed, next to the window, there was a worn-out sofa and in front of it an old wooden box, turned upside down and obviously used as a coffee table. Right now, it looked to Kaja as if it was completely covered in craft tools.

"I was wondering: Did you make those coat hooks yourself?" she shouted into the adjoining room. Miri came whirling through the door.

"I, well..." she pulled sheepishly at her huge pink sweatshirt. In combination with her black leggings and the short ash-blonde curls framing her face, she looked like an elf herself, Kaja thought. A rather curvy elf, she found, torn between jealousy and admiration.

"You did? They're all your own creations? And what about that one over there?" Kaja pointed to the wall behind an old TV set. A picture of a forest clearing created an impression as if the viewer was entering a fantasy land.

"Yes, I make them in my spare time."

"Do you sell them as well?" Kaja hesitated, not sure if Miri appreciated her asking so many personal questions. "Sorry, none of my business." she added quickly. "It's just that I like all these things here, your whole style."

"No worries. I'm glad you like them. But do you really think somebody might want to buy

them?"

"I don't know. Personally, I would buy them. It might be worth a try."

"Hm. Let me clear this away for you. We need some space for our tea cups."

"Can I help you? Perhaps we can have our tea in the kitchen and have a chat there. You don't need to tidy up especially for me."

Miri laughed out loud: "Only someone who's never seen my kitchen can make such a suggestion. Come on, follow me."

She led the way and Kaja followed her, curious - but only made it to the door. The kitchen already seemed over-crowded with Miri in it. The small room was furnished with a huge American fridge and a small, old-fashioned kitchen unit with two hobs. Above the sink, there was a tiny window and on the window sill stood several pots of fresh herbs.

Miri turned round bearing a tray with a steaming teapot and two slightly chipped cups in her hands. They almost bumped into each other..

"Oops. Be careful. We don't want to have another accident." Miri said.

"Oh, by the way: How are your injuries? Sorry, I should've asked earlier. I was too busy admiring your flat."

"That's OK. I'm not used to visitors admiring my flat. But it's much nicer than any formal pleasantries. And anyway, they're almost healed." She turned her head to show Kaja the scar which indeed looked quite promising, apart from a big yellow bruise that was still visible around it.

"Anyway: How's your dragon? I'm surprised you didn't bring him along."

Kaja raised an eyebrow: "I thought we'd agreed there never was a dragon?"

Miri grinned: "As far as I can remember, it was you who insisted there never was a dragon. And I simply stopped pestering you. But it doesn't mean I've changed my mind. I remember very clearly what I saw that day."

"On that day, you received a serious blow to the head." Kaja groaned in mock despair. "But OK, if you insist, let's talk about imaginary dragons."

Miri threw a cushion at her which she avoided with a laugh. After that moment of playful fun, they sipped their tea, slightly embarrassed. "I'm so glad you came. I feel as if we've known each other for ages."

"I feel the same." Kaja replied spontaneously and was surprised. "Isn't that strange?"

"Not any stranger than being acquainted with a dragon, I suppose." Miri gave her a meaningful look. "Don't get me wrong. But isn't it time we stopped this charade? I don't have any patience for this." she bubbled on. "And to be absolutely clear: I don't want anything from your dragon."

Kaja blushed. "Yes I know. It's only that the dragon subject is extremely personal to me. I'm not used to talking about it to anyone. I can't even mention him to Mémé without being flippant. To a certain extent, I accept that he belongs to me. But if any other people start seeing Lance - that's his name. - it all becomes a little bit too real."

"Who is Mémé?" Miri wanted to know.

"Mémé is my grandmother."

"And she can see your dragon, too?"

"It even looks like I've inherited him from her." Kaja explained grumpily. "You see, as soon as I start talking about Lance, I forget my good manners and turn moody. I hardly understand how you can keep so calm while I'm telling you all this."

"Well, I wouldn't be as cool if I wasn't pre-disposed that way. Having seen a real dragon last week is only part of my dragon experience."

"You sound as if you were talking about an exotic pet." Kaja was amused to observe.

"Not at all." Miri defended herself indignantly. "I'm sure you've experienced for yourself that dragons can be rather pig-headed."

"Yes, you might say that." Kaja gave an exaggerated sigh.

"You see? And that's why I was surprised that he - what did you call him? Lance?..."

"Yes, that's his name."

"That Lance didn't come with you."

"I've learned a few useful tricks from Mémé on how to handle him. But tonight, I simply asked him to stay behind and so he did."

"Oh, I'm impressed."

"But what about your dragon experience? Do you have one of your own? Or did you attend an introductory weekend course 'How to find a dragon'?" Kaja joked.

Miri suppressed a giggle: "I used to have one when I was a child."

Miri looked absent-minded as she remembered her childhood. Kaja brought her back to reality, asking: "And where's he now?"

"Oh, I don't know. At some point she - it was a female dragon, actually a dragon girl - just disappeared. I can't even tell you exactly when that happened. She used to be my best friend." She shrugged her shoulders. "It must have happened when I was between four and ten years old." She jumped up. Being a bundle of energy, she wasn't able to sit still for very long. Pacing up and down the little room, she recalled a few amusing stories from her childhood. "On the one hand, this dragon girl was terribly opinionated and appallingly wise, which I often despised."

"Why was that?"

"She used to convince me that my Mum was right telling me off when I had been naughty. And most of the time, she even tricked me into coming to the same conclusion all by myself."

"That sounds familiar. If you found it annoying as a child, can you imagine how hard I'm finding it now to cope with Lance?" Kaja grumbled.

Miri briefly sat down on the sofa next to Kaja and patted her arm in sympathy.

"Poor thing. But if the relationship between you and your dragon is similar to mine, I'm sure you're having lots of fun as well. Maxi often used to help me come up with perfect practical jokes."

"That's true." Kaja admitted, laughing as she thought of the night when she and Lance had broken into the company offices together.

Her thoughts were interrupted by Miri who had jumped up again and flicked a pack of cards through her fingers. "What I still cannot understand is: Why can I see Lance? He's your dragon, isn't he? Or can dragons be shared?"

"Not likely. Well, I don't know, but Lance is definitely my dragon!" Kaja blushed slightly as she realised how sternly she had said this. "I'm sorry. I know you have no intention of taking him away from me. But despite having conflicting feelings about Lance, I've become a little bit possessive of him." she concluded lamely.

Miri gave her an understanding smile, put the large cards back on the window sill and poured some more tea. "I would have been mad as hell at any suggestion that somebody else might be able to see my dragon. Now that's been cleared up, can we work on the question together? Where shall we start?"

"Isn't there a weekend course '1001 questions and answers about your dragon'?" They both snorted again with laughter.

After they had calmed down, Miri asked: "Do I detect a slight aversion to weekend courses?"

"No, not normally. But if you read some of the ads in the local newspaper, such as 'Become a shaman overnight' or 'Learn white witchcraft in a day' you know they cannot be taken seriously."

"You don't believe in such things?" Miri was interested to know.

"No... Yes... Oh, it's difficult to explain."

Miri dropped into the armchair opposite Kaja.

"Go on, tell me. I have lots of time - and you?"

"OK then, I will. It's all rather weird. But since we're talking about dragons as if they were the most natural thing in the world, it may not be too far off-topic."

"I think you're right there." Miri agreed impatiently.

"Mémé, the grandmother I mentioned before, is what people often call a witch."

"Hey, that's cool."

"Yes, quite cool if you're called a witch's daughter when you're just twelve years old." Kaja replied sarcastically.

"Oh." Miri said sheepishly.

"It's OK. Today I'd be the talk of the cocktail party as everyone is into esoterics. They all have Amerindian dream catchers at home or, if they are rich enough, they've been on self-discovery trips or experienced swimming with supposedly spiritual dolphins."

From the corner of her eye, Miri glanced at her own dream catcher, quite visible on the wall above her bed. Kaja followed her eyes and now it was her turn to utter an embarrassed "Oh!"

"Listen, I'm sorry. Sometimes I can be such a clumsy idiot. Diplomacy is not one of my strong points, even though both of my parents are in the diplomatic service."

Miri had to laugh. "To be honest, I just had to look at it, but I'm not personally offended by your description. I know the kind of people you mean: those Sunday afternoon gurus."

"Exactly. I'm not an expert, but I suppose the fact that you used to have your own dragon and that you can see Lance does qualify you to have a dream catcher." Kaja quipped and Miri poked her tongue out at her.

"Now please carry on with your story."

"Well, Mémé is into the old-time beliefs, knows all sorts of herbal remedies, talks to plant spirits and anyone in the village with a problem will sooner or later end up on her doorstep asking for advice. She has the ability to make them feel better or even point them in the right direction to solve their problems. I watched and learned from her throughout my childhood and realised that there can be no such thing as a part-time witch. It's an attitude to life that you cannot switch on or off as you please."

"And you? Do you also have a close relationship with nature and the Goddess?" Miri wanted to know.

"Actually, no, I don't. I am kind of Mémé's life-long project. She doesn't try to convert me or anything like that." she hastened to add. "She rather tries to introduce me to her world, give me access to her secrets. And of course, I'm always confronted with them when I visit her. But I'm rather reluctant to get involved. Perhaps those schoolyard taunts taught me to keep away from any intuitive stuff."

"I see."

"What do you see?"

"I suppose you're quite in turmoil since you've found out you have to cope with a dragon. Isn't that the case?"

"Well, you may be right." Kaja was reluctant to admit.

"It sounds exciting. But we got distracted from our more pressing question: Why can I see your dragon?"

"I do have some idea. In fact, I asked Lance. I cornered him about it." she grinned. "Of course I wanted to know immediately why a complete stranger can suddenly see my private monster."

"And? What did he say?"

Miri sat up in her chair expectantly and crossed her legs tailor-fashion.

"He didn't know the answer himself at first. So he went to consult the dragon council."

"The dragon council?" Miri looked a bit puzzled.

"Never mind." Kaja laughed. "It's another long story and we want to get to the point."

"That's right."

Kaja gave Miri a summary of what Lance had found out. When she finished, Miri asked in disbelief: "Dragon sisters?"

"Yes, I know it sounds out of this world. But on the other hand," she paused briefly, "dragons are no common pets either."

Miri grinned. "Yes, that's true. You're lucky Lance is not here. I'm sure he wouldn't be pleased to hear what you've just said."

"Hear what?"

"Well, your comment about pets."

"Oh, I'm not afraid to tell him." Kaja giggled. "His huge ego needs a bit of cutting down to size now and then."

"And how are we supposed to find our third sister?"

"Hm, Lance couldn't tell me that either. I only hope I won't have to knock her over like I did with you."

"Such situations can drive me up the wall." Miri, who had started pacing the small room again, exclaimed. "I hate it when all you can do is sit and wait for something to happen, not knowing what, how, where and when it's going to hit you."

"Tell me about it." Kaja agreed. "The mad thing is that this applies to all aspects of my life at the moment."

"How come?"

"Right now, I have a rather strange situation at work."

"What's your job anyway?"

"I'll tell you in a minute. Let me first ask you a cheeky question."

"OK, I love cheeky questions. Go ahead." Miri encouraged her.

"Have you had anything to eat yet?"

"No, I wasn't sure how long our meeting would go on. So I didn't prepare anything." she apologised. "It was rather stupid of me since I had a strong feeling my oldest and best friend was coming to visit."

"You felt that, too?" Kaja looked at her in surprise.

"Yes, although I don't even know what that should feel like. I don't have a best friend, never had one."

"Yes, same here, never had one either."

"Well, now we know we're supposed to be dragon sisters, it makes sense. I'm curious to meet sister number three. Do you think we'll get on with her just as well as we do?" Miri pondered. "Let's deal with our real-life issues first. Pizza delivery?"

"Good idea. One pizza Hawaii for me, please."

"Yuck!" Miri shivered with disgust. "Fruit on a pizza, that's vile."

"No it's not. And I won't share it with you anyway." Kaja warned her.

Zorro, whose ears had pricked up at the word pizza, worried that the threat was aimed at him. Whimpering, he turned to Kaja and put his paw in her lap. "I didn't mean you. Of course you'll get your share."

Miri watched them and couldn't help laughing.

"Yes, I know, he shouldn't have pizza, but I can never turn him down and he's already much too spoilt." Kaja grimaced.

"I didn't say anything."

"No, but you grinned."

"I did, but for a different reason."

"Why?" Kaja wanted to know.

"Well, the reason I always order a tuna pizza has a name: Chili." Miri admitted, pointing to the huge tomcat who, despite his size, had managed to sneak up on them and was now sitting enthroned on the window sill. From time to time, he hissed at Zorro when he felt one of the dog's ears was pointing in the wrong direction.

Miri ordered the pizzas over the phone and brought a bottle of red wine from her tiny kitchen. Kaja made herself comfortable and they raised their glasses.

"Here's to us, our new family."

"To our new family."

They both sipped from their glasses at the same time and beamed at each other. "I've always wanted to have some sisters." Miri admitted.

"I've always envied my neighbours for being a big family." Kaja responded.

"I wonder what kind of person she might be."

"Who?"

"Our third sister."

"I think we'll find out in due course. There's no point racking our brains right now."

"Hear, hear. Some sound dragon advice." Miri jibed in good humour.

"OK, I admit it." Kaja laughed. "That was one of Lance's gems. But I recently learnt that some dragon advice can be indeed useful."

"That's the annoying thing." Miri commented with a smile. "Of course he's right. But I'm extremely impatient. It's part of my personality.

And I can get totally excited making guesses."

"I'm basically the same. But once I get started, I can't stop and I'll soon have my head full of all sorts of scenarios."

"It can be rather stressful."

"Exactly."

Twenty minutes later, the door bell rang. Miri jumped up, closely followed by her cat and Zorro, who kept a five foot distance to be safe. "Can I help?" Kaja called after Miri.

"No, stay there. We'll be back soon."

"Be careful that our vultures don't snatch the food from you on your way back."

The door opened again and an appetizing smell of pizza wafted into the small sitting room.

"Somehow your procession reminds me of the story of the The Musicians of Bremen: the donkey, the dog, the cat...: Kaja joked. "Only the cockerel is missing."

"Thanks very much for making me the donkey." Miri scoffed playfully. Kaja quickly took her pizza carton before Miri had any silly ideas.

For the next few minutes, they quietly enjoyed their meal together. When they had almost finished, Miri picked up the conversation again. Still chewing on a piece of pizza, she asked: "So, what's going on at your work?"

Kaja swallowed hard and licked her greasy fingers. "Can I have a glass of water, please? Your wine is delicious, but unfortunately I'll have to drive."

"Of course you can. I also have Appletizer, tea, coffee and of course water, although only from the tap. What would you like?"

"Water will be fine, thanks."

Miri went to the kitchen to get a glass of water while Kaja filled her in on the events of the past few weeks.

"I've been telling my story so often, I could write a book about it."

"Why not? Sex it up and sell it as a thriller."

"You think so? What do you know about it?"

"I read a lot and I work in a bookshop."

"Don't tell me you work in that little corner shop where we had our accident?"

"Yes, that's the one."

"What a coincidence. On that very day I wanted to visit your shop. Our paths would have crossed anyway."

"Not necessarily." Miri said reluctantly. "I'm usually in the back office, placing orders, doing accounts and all the other admin chores. The shop is owned by my uncle."

"It must be great to have free access to all those books." Kaja was excited.

"Actually, it's not as rosy as you think. My uncle and I are not exactly a 'dream team'. He's the most tight-fisted person in the world and doesn't particularly like me. And to be honest, the feeling is mutual."

"Then why are you working for him?"

"At the time, I was broke, had quite a few debts and was desperately looking for a job. I guess I should be grateful." Miri grumbled. "And for the first few weeks I was. Until I realised he only offered me the job in order to have me under his control and to wear me down."

"Is it that bad?" Kaja was shocked.

"Yes, quite that bad. I'm not supposed to talk to customers because he thinks I'm a disgrace, the way I dress, the way I speak... He thinks I'll scare them off. And if I happen to make a mistake..." Miri swallowed and looked away.

"What happens then?"

Miri pulled herself together and straightened her shoulders. "Then I have to listen to never-ending monologues on how stupid I am and that it must be the punishment for my mother committing the sin of sleeping with my father and getting pregnant out of wedlock."

"But..." Kaja was struggling to find the right words. "He does know we're living in the 21st century, which followed the 20th and is a long way from the dark ages?" She asked in disbelief.

"Phew." Miri exhaled audibly. "I'm sorry. I always get very upset. I know I should rise above it, but I can't. I'm taking it too personally." She blew her nose noisily.

"I can understand how you're feeling. It must be hard to listen to this now and then, but having it rubbed in every day is just too much."

"Perhaps I'm particularly sensitive." Miri added. "I haven't told you yet that I have some learning difficulties. Going to school used to be torture for me."

"Learning difficulties? What kind?"

"I used to be dyslexic. I couldn't form letters into words and wasn't very good with figures either."

"How did you deal with it?"

"For the first few years, I made good progress. My mother had read somewhere that yoga might help. Apparently, among the possible causes for the deficiency are some missing links between the hemispheres of the brain. And yoga can improve that."

"And? Did it help?"

"Yes, surprisingly it did. I had lots of fun and remember doing the exercises together with Maxi. Can you imagine how funny a dragon looks when tied into a knot?" Miri grinned.

Trying to imagine the picture, Kaja had to laugh.

"Unfortunately, my parents both died in a car crash and I had to move in with my aunt and uncle. That was the end of my yoga and painting therapy. In fact, it was the end of my childhood. - But let's change the subject. I'd rather like to enjoy the evening."

They spent another hour talking, but then Kaja reluctantly pulled herself up. "I'd better be going now. Otherwise I'll never get out of bed in the morning. Come to think of it, perhaps it doesn't matter anyway." She concluded their conversation with a little sadness in her voice.

"That's what I think every evening. Perhaps that's why I'm such a night owl. A typical attitude of denial. If I don't go to bed tonight, morning will never come." Miri grimaced. "Why don't we set up another meeting. It'll give us something to look forward to."

"Good idea. What about Thursday night? You can come to my place for a change." Kaja suggested.

"Thursday... I need to be home by eleven, but I could come over before. Is that OK with you?"

"Yes, great. Perhaps we'll know by then who our third sister is?" Kaja said cheekily.

"That would be amazing. Thanks for a nice evening. Drive carefully."

"I will. Bye for now."

From her open window, Miri watched Kaja walk to her car, with Zorro jumping up at her in excitement. She saw Zorro take his place on the back seat, Kaja get in the driver's seat and finally drive off. Then she thought about the evening they had spent together. She had thoroughly enjoyed herself and didn't even feel her usual restlessness. On the other hand, it had been slightly irritating to talk to someone about dragons. It was certainly a first. Not even her mother had understood that Maxi had been more than a child's fantasy. She used to be very understanding, but that was one point she never got. Miri sighed. The evening had been both painful and consoling. Painful, because the dragon was Kaja's and not hers. She quickly banished any thoughts of feeling abandoned and concentrated on the consoling aspect, namely not being the only person who appeared to be slightly off her rocker. A cold gust of wind woke her from her thoughts and reminded her that she was still standing by the open window. She rubbed her shivering arms and closed it resolutely.

When Kaja reached home, she quickly took Zorro to the park and waited for him to do his business. In the meantime, she reflected on the evening. Miri was one of the nicest people she had ever met. Everything had seemed so easy.

Deeply immersed in her thoughts, she opened the door, entered the flat and found Lance sitting on the sofa with a disapproving look on his face. "So you made it home, then." he drawled.

"Erm yes, I did. I don't know what business of yours it is when I come home, but yes, here I am." Kaja answered slightly irritated.

"I'm just worried about you. I almost put out a dragon emergency call."

Kaja rolled her eyes. "Why didn't you come over? You would have seen me having a wonderful time."

"You told me to stay away." Lance commented indignantly.

"As if that would stop you from doing whatever you want." Kaja steamed.

"And? How was it?"

"Good, really good." Exhausted, Kaja dropped next to him on the sofa. She started to feel the effect of the bottle of red wine she had shared with Miri. "We talked and talked, had a pizza and then talked some more."

Now it was Lance's turn to steam: "Women... no matter if they are human or dragon women. They're all the same."

Kaja giggled: "Yes, that's us."

"And, did you come to any conclusion?"

"Why did we have to come to any conclusion? We just wanted to get to know each other. It's not as if the three of us are destined to save the world, or is it?"

"Hm, I don't know. At least you talk about the three of you quite naturally. Did you have any inspired ideas who your third sister might be?"

"No, not at all. Neither of us knows anyone who fits the description." Kaja joked.

"What description?" Lance was interested to know.

"You know: chaotic lifestyle, slightly deranged, obsessed with dragons." she answered casually, which earned her a poke in the ribs from Lance. "So, time to go to bed." she said getting up from the sofa, yawning.

"Not yet, stay here for a minute. Haven't you noticed anything?"

"What should I have noticed?"

Kaja rubbed her eyes and looked around the sitting room.

"Your badge is gone."

"Of course it's gone. Simon said he'd pick it up." she replied impatiently.

"Yes, but the question is: How did he do it? You locked the door when you went out and unlocked it when you came back in..." Lance waited for the message to reach Kaja's drowsy brain.

"Oh... How did he do it, then?"

Lance replied with a counter question: "What do you think his profession is? A career burglar?"

"Erm, no, I don't think so."

"Anyway, he got in here in less then three minutes and left just as quickly."

"Amazing." Kaja mused. "But I still need to go to bed now."

Lance looked disappointed that his news did not draw any more excitement, but then resigned himself to the fact and disappeared into Kaja's room to wait for his protégée. On her pillow, of course.

18

"Hey, what's the matter?"

Lance looked rather confused as he watched Kaja rush from the bathroom into her bedroom and back while clumsily trying to attach an earring to her earlobe with one hand and using the other to pull impatiently at the zip of her knee-length, greenish-blue, low-cut pinafore dress.

"Mgunnubeleyt!" she mumbled holding a hair clip between her lips.

"Relax, stay still and take a deep breath." Lance told her.

While pulling up the zip like a gentleman, he tried to calm her down: "You have another half hour until the ceremony. I'll take care of the traffic and when they see you in this..." he searched for a word to express both his disapproval and admiration. "...slinky rag, they'll forget to look at their watches anyway."

Despite feeling tense, Kaja had to laugh and roll her eyes.

"Thanks." she said. "If you ever become unemployed, you'd make a good valet." she added with a mischievous grin.

"As I prefer you relaxed and cheeky, I'll pretend I didn't hear that comment." he shouted after Kaja who had already put on her coat and was trying to squeeze her feet into a pair of high heels.

When she straightened up with her face already showing signs of pain, he smiled with satisfaction.

"I knew you'd find this funny." she scoffed at him half-heartedly.

She threw Zorro a dog biscuit to compensate him for staying home tonight, grabbed her girlie handbag and tried to run to the car as elegantly as possible. For someone who had hardly had any practice wearing four-inch heels for the past year, it turned out to be quite a challenge. Once they were sitting in the car, she kicked off her shoes again and answered Lance's questioning look by saying: "I can't drive in these!"

Lance just whistled.

"Yes, I know, it's my own fault etcetera etcetera. But the effect more than makes up for it, doesn't it?"

Satisfied, she registered that it was now Lance's turn to roll his eyes.

It was hard to believe, but apparently Lance had managed to tweak the city traffic in their favour. It barely took them fifteen minutes to reach the congress hall which the company had hired especially for the ball. They even found a parking space right by the entrance.

She got out of the car and blew Lance a kiss: "Sometimes, you're indispensable."

"I know." the dragon replied self-importantly. Kaja had already been spotted by some people she knew and had to engage in conversation.

"Hey Kaja, nice to see you."

"Hello Sonja, likewise." she replied with strained cheerfulness. She couldn't stand Sonja. The feeling was mutual, but didn't stop them from conducting meaningless small talk. Once the obligatory pecks on the cheek were exchanged, Sonja asked: "Did you bring a partner?"

She craned her neck to see who might be behind Kaja.

"Why? What're you talking about?"

"Well, I thought I saw you blow a kiss to someone just now."

"Blow a kiss?" Kaja looked back at her car in irritation, until she remembered the brief conversation she had had with Lance. "Erm, I always say goodbye to my car like that. It stops it from being nicked." she explained lamely for want of a better excuse for her behaviour.

"Oh, I see... For a moment, I thought you were introducing us to your latest conquest. We've heard some amazing stories about you." Sonja smiled cynically.

Kaja's initial irritation turned into cold hatred. Only Lance's calming presence behind her back stopped her from starting a cat fight. "So, have you really?" she finally managed to say with a sweet smile on her lips. "Jealous?"

With that, she left Sonja, who stared after her with her jaw dropped.

"That expression on her face was certainly worth more than the broken finger nail you might have sustained in a fight with that bitch." the dragon whispered in her head. Kaja had to giggle which earned her surprised looks from some of the other people close by.

"I thought you didn't want to attract any attention." the dragon teased her and received a dig in his ribs as a reply. At least the dig was meant for him, but instead Kaja's elbow ended up hitting another bystander in his stomach.

"Wow, hello."

Kaja blushed. "Oh, I'm sorry. I can be so clumsy sometimes."

"Tut, tut." she heard the dragon in her head.

"And you be quiet." she hissed at him, unfortunately using her voice again instead of her thoughts.

"What was that?"

Kaja closed her eyes and prayed the situation would not get any worse.

"Oh nothing, I was talking to myself. Are you OK?"

The man looked at her as if she had grown a second head and hastily retreated from her immediate vicinity.

"Great move." she grumbled "From office tart to mad woman."

Lance was in stitches and gasped for breath. Kaja tried to concentrate and ignore the dragon, which wasn't easy to do with a creature that was constantly by her side, six feet tall and shiny blue. At least to her eyes he was, she grimaced.

"Hey, what's wrong with you today? That sour face doesn't go with your stunning dress."

"Thea!" she shouted with relief. "I never thought I'd find you in this crowd."

"How can you miss me?" her friend laughed. "After all, I've made absolutely sure I'll stand out tonight."

She turned a full circle to let Kaja admire her fiery orange dress. She had dyed her hair a dramatic red and used some golden clips to hold it up.

"Wow, you've excelled yourself!" Kaja praised her dutifully.

"Thanks, but today I can return the compliment."

"Only today?" Kaja asked in mock offence.

"Well, I don't consider your usual outfit of jeans, trainers and a t-shirt competition for myself." Thea admitted openly.

"I know, I'm only pulling your leg." Kaja replied and linked arms with her.

"Hang on, you don't have a drink yet?" Thea observed. "We certainly can't have that!" with a swift move of her hand, she took a glass of champagne from a passing waiter and put it into Kaja's hand. "You need to be drunk to survive this occasion." she advised her.

"I'm afraid you may be right." Kaja agreed.

"Of course I'm right. I'm always right." Thea grinned. She proposed a toast. "To an unforgettable evening."

Kaja raised her glass as well and murmured: "I'd rather make it an unremarkable evening."

"Come on, let your hair down." Thea protested. "Let's find some good seats. You'll have a prize to collect later on."

With little motivation, Kaja followed her into the conference hall where the prizes would be awarded before the ball started. Ball was much too grand a word for the bopping around that was likely to take place here later on. Although she had grown up with Mémé, she was too much the daughter of diplomat parents to confuse a ball with a simple party. This was so typical for the development that had taken place in the company she used to feel so much attached to. Don't do things by halves - or at least appear not to.

"You don't drink fast enough. Stop brooding and try at least to look as if you're having fun." Thea lectured her and pointed disapprovingly to Kaja's glass which was still almost full.

"You're right."

"We've been through that already." Thea said ironically. "Now can you just pretend you actually believe me?"

"OK, OK, I give up." Kaja bravely knocked back her drink before quickly replacing her empty glass with a full one.

"Can I have some as well?" Lance's voice sounded in her head. Kaja was distracted with all the people around her and the champagne was starting to take its toll. This was why she quietly, but quite audibly hissed: "Why can't you take care of your own drinks?"

"Kaja, I'm getting worried. What's wrong with you?"

Perplexed, Kaja turned to Thea, who looked at her rather concerned.

"What was that?"

"Well, I noticed you keep talking to yourself. Are you stressed out?"

"Talking to myself? Stressed out?"

Kaja was a bit lost until she realised she must have talked to Lance aloud again. A quick look at the dragon confirmed her fears. She pulled herself together and hissed at him thinking: "Why do you constantly have to interfere?"

"Me? It's you who's shouting for the whole world to know." she heard him grumbling.

"Perhaps I'm a bit nervous about the prize award. Can I have some water, please?"

Thea, still looking sceptical, decided to drop the subject for the moment and went to get a glass of water. "Look, I think they're about to start." Kaja said when she returned.

However, it took another ten minutes for everyone to quieten down. Kaja and Thea were leaning against a wall to the side of the hall. Knowing what was going on in the company, the prize had lost its glamour for Kaja, although she was still proud of the work for which she would receive it. Fortunately, Lance had made it his mission to cheer her up. That way, she hardly noticed people's names being called out and how they made their way to the stage, looking either embarrassed or confident, depending on their personality. She was grateful for the distraction although she would never have admitted it to the dragon.

Otherwise he would become totally deluded, she thought to herself and had to smile.

The expression hadn't escaped Lance and he became suspicious: "What's there to grin about?"

She was still thinking of a glib reply when her name was called up.

"You had a narrow escape there." the dragon grumbled in her head while she made her way to the front, confidently ignoring everyone except for the Qubus boss who handed her the prize and pressed three unwelcome pecks on her cheeks.

The award ceremony went on for another ninety minutes before the pleasurable part of the evening began. However, it took just two dances to turn Kaja off the entertainment completely. Those two dancing partners had been bold enough to think she would fall for suggestive compliments and enjoy being touched up by strangers. Luckily, Lance had come to the rescue and made them trip over his feet so that Kaja didn't have to think of an excuse to get rid of them. She went to the cloakroom and collected her prize - a CD with her own program, mounted on a large piece of rock - and went to look for Thea. As Thea had remarked earlier on, she was not difficult to find in the crowd, thanks to her bright dress. Just before she reached her, she could hear Lance ask her telepathically: "Are you sure she's not a virgin any more? I could do with one... especially such a flamboyant one."

Kaja giggled.

"Would you like to share your joke with me?" Thea was interested to know.

"Erm, let's just say I've just heard someone say something very flattering about you."

"Oh." was all Thea could answer, blushing slightly.

"Listen." Kaja interrupted her thoughts quickly, before Thea could ask any further questions. "I'll call myself a taxi and go home now. I'll pick up my car tomorrow. Can't stand any more suggestive invitations."

"Is it that bad?" Thea wanted to know sympathetically.

"Even worse. See you in the office tomorrow. Alright?"

"Yes, of course. Have a safe journey home."

"I will. And you have fun."

In the lobby, a group of young men was standing by a champagne fountain, passing their time drinking and smoking cigarettes. Accordingly, they were in a boisterous mood. Kaja didn't pay any notice and was about to walk past them, when one of the men blocked her path.

"Now look at that. Who do we have here?"

'Oh no, not him.' Kaja sighed silently. It was one of the two men she had danced with. What was his name? She was desperately trying to remember. Peter or Paul? It didn't matter. All she wanted was to get home. But it seemed fate didn't want to spare her anything that night.

"It's our ice princess, isn't?" a second voice could be heard.

Irritated, Kaja turned round to identify the speaker. Oh no, it was Michael! Not him again! From the corner of her eye, she noticed that Lance had positioned himself sideways behind her using his energy-laden presence to boost her confidence. Although she felt the tension rising, she said in as cool a voice as she could muster: "Did I forget to tell you something when we last met?" She frowned as if she was trying to think hard.

"No, I don't think so. So have a good night and goodbye."

She turned round to leave, but Michael stepped in front of her and grabbed her arm. The alcohol must have clouded his memory, Kaja was surprised to observe. She couldn't believe he had the audacity to tangle with her yet again. Apparently, she had hurt his delicate male pride enough to make him careless.

"Be on your guard, he's not on his own this time." Lance warned her telepathically.

There was some truth in it. Kaja had failed to notice that the other lads had formed a tight circle around her. She couldn't quite work out whether they wanted to join in whatever Michael intended to do to her or if they were just keen not to miss anything. She decided it didn't matter. The truth was, she had definitely had enough of this bullshit.

"You'd better let go of my arm. Now!" she hissed at Michael.

"You'd like that, wouldn't you?" he leered at her.

She felt Lance trying to give her even more energy to support her.

"Don't worry." she signalled him, for once inaudible to the others. "I can manage. You taught me how, remember?"

She winked at him before turning back to Michael. Then she hesitated for a moment, taking a long look at his hand which was still holding her arm, just long enough to give him a chance to change his mind. When he didn't make any effort to obey her order, she focussed all her anger into pushing him into the nearest champagne fountain. The glasses tumbled down with a loud jangle and clatter and the other men jumped sideways to avoid a spray of champagne.

Kaja looked at Lance with a mischievous grin on her face: "It looks like we can finally go home now."

The dragon could not make up his mind whether to laugh out loud or to stare at his protégée in admiration. The altercation, followed by the noise of the collapsing fountain had attracted some onlookers.

"Move." Kaja said with an impatient nod of her head. "Let's not hang around here any longer. Or we'll end up in another traffic jam."

Behind her, the first people were starting to applaud. But she did not look at them and left the congress hall with her head held up high and her hips swinging, the invisible, laughing dragon by her side.

19

The next morning, Kaja woke up surprisingly refreshed. Perhaps it had been a good idea to take an Alka-Seltzer and drink a bottle of water before going to bed, she thought. She looked at the clock: Only half past five. No wonder it was still pitch-black outside. Why had she woken up so early? She noticed that her mobile phone on the bedside table was flashing frantically, obviously trying to tell her that she had received a text or missed a call. Who was trying to contact her at this time in the morning? She reached over to get to the device without disturbing Lance, who had made himself comfortable on her pillow as usual. But the phone was too far away, so she lost her balance and dropped on top of the dragon. Shocked to be woken up so abruptly, he started to spit blue flames and wave his arms wildly. They ended up having a wrestling match as they both got entangled in the duvet. By the time Kaja finally broke free, Lance had managed to get himself under control and was now merely spouting black smoke from his ears instead of fiery flames. But now his mouth was in full swing and he gave his protégée an ear-bashing.

"... walking disaster... deserve danger money... women..." As Kaja did not know how to stop him, she just took the glass of water still standing by her bedside and poured it over his head.

"Huh...?"

"Shut up! I'm sorry I've woken you up so unexpectedly. But that's no reason to make such a fuss."

"And what did you do that for?" Lance steamed, pointing at the wet top of his head.

"Oh, I've recently learned that agitated or annoying male creatures can do with a bit of cooling down now and then." She said with a cheeky glint in her eye.

"Ah. And why are you awake anyway? You're not exactly an early worm from what I've noticed over the past two weeks."

"You mean I'm not an early bird." Kaja corrected him automatically. Then she sat up and said: "That's what I was trying to find out..." and, pointing at the mangled duvet on the floor, she added "...before we had our pillow fight."

"You wanted to get your mobile? Why didn't you say so? I'm always at your service, you know. No need to pin me down." he grinned salaciously and threw her the phone.

"You're obnoxious. You really are." she said shaking her head but couldn't help a smile. The phone displayed one missed call. Who in the world was trying to get hold of her at such an unearthly hour? She pressed a button to bring up the list of missed calls. Simon! It must have been pretty important. With another press of a button, she called her voicemail.

"Hey Kaja. I hope I didn't wake you up? Listen, I think I'm on to something and will be out and about quite a lot. If you want to talk to me, please call me on this number." Then he quickly quoted a number and Kaja kept gesticulating at Lance, hoping he would fetch her a pen and a piece of paper. But it was already too late. Simon's message went on: "... if you know a senior manager you can trust, I would like to ask him a few questions. So now you know how to get hold of me. Talk to you soon."

That was the end of the message and Kaja hung up. She sighed and stretched. Last night's champagne had left her with a slight hangover. But at least she was awake now. Before listening to the recording again and noting down Simon's new number, she decided to get up and make herself a cup of coffee. Perhaps Simon's cryptic message would make more sense afterwards.

Half an hour later, she was dressed for work, sitting at the kitchen table with a steaming cup of coffee in front of her. She had written the phone number neatly on a notepad and listed her most pressing questions underneath:

1. Who had initiated the merger between the two companies?

2. Who was likely to know the corresponding agreement in detail?

3. Are there any other employees who had experienced similar difficulties recently?

4. Which company did they belong to originally?

5. Where is Max???

Max was the only superior that Kaja could think of as trustworthy. But this realisation was of little use if she didn't know how to get hold of him. She got up and poured herself another cup of coffee. With the steaming pot in her hand, she glanced over at Lance who seemed to be having fun with his elderberry brandy and a pack of playing cards.

"Oh, my wise and mighty dragon. Do you have any idea where I can find Max?"

"Uh." Lance looked at her absent-mindedly. "Are you talking to me?"

"Not particularly, but I'd be grateful if any one of you could give me some attention." she answered sarcastically. "Of course, I'm talking to you. Or at least I would be if your highness were not too occupied to listen to my trivial problems."

"Eh? It was me who got doused in cold water this morning. How come it's you who's so bad-tempered?" Lance complained.

"I'm concerned for Max! And I have a slight hangover, not a massive one, but bad enough to make me bad-tempered, as you put it. And on principle, I don't need to justify myself to you. It was your decision to become my companion. As they say: In for a penny, in for a pound.

I'm sorry!" Now she did have to grin.

"I see. You know very little about destiny, don't you?" the dragon grumbled.

"I may get a better picture soon, if your information about me and my sisters is right." she grimaced. "I'm already making progress. Miri is coming over tonight."

"She's what? You didn't tell me!"

"I'm telling you now." Kaja briefly informed him.

"Does this mean I'll have to make myself scarce again?"

"You can sleep in a doorway or under a bridge for all I care." she pulled his leg. But when she saw how offended he was by this remark, she was quick to add. "No, actually, you can stay here, if you want to. I'm sure Miri will be curious to meet you."

"Really?" The dragon honestly seemed to be looking forward to the meeting. He started strutting up and down excitedly between the sitting room and the kitchen, mumbling unintelligibly.

"Don't get me wrong. This is my appointment with Miri and we don't intend to spend our time adoring you."

Not even this comment could spoil his happiness. Kaja wasn't even sure he was listening to her. She sighed. It looked like she had to solve the mystery around Max on her own. She gathered her things, slipped the notes into her handbag where she had already stowed some other documents to take with her to work and put her jacket on. "Zorro, hurry up." she shouted and jingled her key ring. The dog was checking for the umpteenth time since breakfast whether he had missed the odd crumb of dry food in his bowl. But at her call and the familiar sound of the keys, he jumped up and leaped out of the door. The two of them first went to Zorro's park and then to the congress hall where Kaja's car was still parked from last night.

At the office, Kaja got herself a visitor's badge, but realised she had to get hold of Simon as soon as possible because her excuse that she had forgotten her own was starting to wear thin. Then she went straight to Thea.

"Hi, heroine." was the welcome she received.

Confused, Kaja looked at her friend: "Heroine?"

"That's what you are. If you thought your heroic exit yesterday had gone unnoticed, you're wrong. So much for the unremarkable evening you wanted to have."

"Oh that." she replied embarrassed. "It was nothing."

"No, nothing at all." Thea said with a twinkle in her eye. "Only that they'd already started to place bets."

"Bets?" Kaja looked blank, until she understood what Thea wanted to say. Now she grinned as well, asking: "And, did you win?"

"Of course I did, I cleaned up."

Kaja grimaced. "That's so typical. I'm sure the majority of the punters were men who, if not convinced that a girl like me was able to take on a real man, were at least supporting my opponent out of gender solidarity."

"That's exactly what happened." Thea confirmed. "And it wasn't my place to educate them as I had to protect my odds." Thea looked very satisfied with herself.

"By the way: Who managed to get the betting going so quickly?"

"Oh, I don't know. Must have been someone..." Thea replied and and smiled as innocently as the Mona Lisa.

"Sure. Can I have a share of your winnings?" Kaja grinned.

"No way! - But I can ask you out to lunch instead. Are you free?" Thea suggested.

"Great, I was about to suggest the same. In fact, I need you and your treasure trove of knowledge to clarify a few things that I find strange."

"Can you be a bit more specific?" Thea asked curiously.

"For instance..." Kaja stopped and looked round the mail room. "Let's talk about it later, shall we? I've got some work to do." Kaja demonstratively checked her watch and said: "OK, half past one, same place as usual? See you then." And off she went without waiting for an answer.

Thea was dumbfounded. Kaja was behaving ever more strangely recently. She shook her head. 'Well, I'm sure she's got her reasons.' she thought.

Back in the office, Kaja sat down at her desk and threw a dog biscuit to Zorro who had settled down in his usual place, while waiting for her computer to boot up. Without looking, she reached for a pack of Post-It notes that she always kept handy on the right-hand side of her desk. When her hand could not find it, she stared at the empty space, irritated. What was wrong now? Looking around the desk, she found what she was looking for on the left-hand side, on top of the in-tray. How had the notes got there? Perhaps it was the cleaning lady, she tried to re-assure herself but wasn't entirely convinced. Exhausted, she rubbed her face and took a deep breath.

"I can't go on like this for much longer." she said to herself. "No wonder I'm getting paranoid." A few minutes later, she mumbled again. "Perhaps I won't have to go on for much longer." In the meantime, she had opened her electronic project folder, fully expecting to find the next major assignment there. But the folder was as empty as it had been yesterday and the days before. Her e-mail inbox was the same. No e-mails about a new project. And no e-mail from Max either. Great! A few hours of spare time wouldn't go amiss if only she didn't have to spend them in the office. She tried again to reach Max while nervously pacing up and down the tiny room but couldn't even get through to his answer machine. She had two more product descriptions to finalise but those were all the tasks on her agenda. Something was definitely wrong if she had nothing else to do than dealing with tedious paperwork. In the fast-paced world of IT, you normally don't have time to produce proper documentation as you're immediately catapulted into the next project.

She sighed, stopped walking around and sat down in front of the computer again. As she was unable to get hold of Max, she had to get in touch with that unpleasant section leader to ask for a new project, whether she liked it or not. But she couldn't even get through to the direct line of her "boss' boss" and only reached his secretary instead. Irritated, she put down the receiver when she was told to apply for a new project by e-mail and wait for it to be delivered to her personal folder on the server.

Thank you very much, I might as well invent one myself. Restlessly, she jumped up to start her pacing again, when Lance suddenly appeared in front of her. As she had got used to him turning up at any time, whether convenient or not, she didn't even waste a moment trying to appear surprised but immediately made him the target of her frustration.

"You're leading a good life, aren't you? Coming and going as you please, no obligations, free access to spirits..."

Lance stopped her outburst by holding a pack of playing cards in front of her. "Care for a game of Crazy Eights?" he asked without even responding to her rants.

The disarming offer made Kaja laugh and her tension subsided. "Crazy Eights? I haven't played that for ages."

"All the better for me. So you won't notice me cheating."

"You cheat?"

"All dragons cheat. It's part of our make-up as much as breathing is part of yours."

"Oh, is it that bad?"

"Let's play." the dragon demanded. He obviously wasn't keen to explain.

Just after half past one, Kaja reached the agreed meeting point, slightly out-of-breath but in a much better mood than two hours earlier. Thea was already waiting with a kebab and a falafel in her hands. "Here is something nice for you two vultures." Thea commented and handed Kaja the kebab.

"Thank you, it smells delicious."

"You're late. Did you get much work done?"

"Work? Not at all, I was just killing some time playing..." she feverishly thought of a game she might have played on her own. "...solitaire." Phew, you had to keep your wits about you if you wanted to explain away time spent with a dragon.

Today, they chose a bench in a small park close to the office block for their lunch break. Thea, curious by nature, asked Kaja between two bites of her falafel what the latest news was.

"Um, do you remember our last conversation?" Kaja managed to say with her mouth full.

"Yes, what about it?"

"You were saying that I was not the only one with such problems. Have you managed to find out any more details?"

This time, Thea took her time to wash down the food with a sip of water. "Yes, I have and it took me by surprise to see how many people were affected when I compiled my list. If you get the information in dribs and drabs, you may be forgiven for thinking they are all isolated cases."

"How many did you finally pick up on?" Kaja was keen to know.

"I know of twelve cases."

"Twelve? But that's..."

"... more than a third of the old PC Lux staff."

"That would have been my next question: Where were the victims, if we can call them that, originally employed?"

"Yes, we can call them victims." Thea confirmed. "Although I do understand why you don't like the term. Nobody wants to see themselves as a victim."

"It doesn't matter." Kaja interrupted her impatiently. "We can do the psychoanalysis later, for instance when I've been made redundant." she added with a sarcastic tone in her voice. "Well?" she looked at Thea expectantly.

"Apart from two, they're all former colleagues of ours. What also struck me is that all the female programmers are among them."

"Even Jasmine? And Natasha?"

"All of them. It looks as if you were intentionally snowed under with work, on top of being paired up with a team buddy from Qubus."

"With hindsight, they wanted us to lose contact with each other?" Kaja got worked up. "And I thought it could never happen to me."

"Never say never..." a voice said in her head. Kaja rolled her eyes. It was so typical of him that he managed to get a saying right when he put his mind to it. She glanced discreetly around to see if Lance was physically present or if he was only hiding in her head. No, he was nowhere to be seen. So she turned her attention back to Thea.

"Don't be too hard on yourself." she was showing concern because she naturally interpreted Kaja's rolling eyes as being directed at herself. "We're all powerless against that kind of conspiracy." She thought for a moment and then had to grin. "I guess the boys were even easier to rope in than the girls. If I got it right, they were all presented with attractive female colleagues: young, long hair, long legs... You get the picture?"

Now Kaja cheered up as well. "OK, looking at it from this angle - which is not easy for me as I'm affected myself - the whole setup has a funny side to it."

"Exactly. Now you can stop feeling sorry for yourself." Thea quickly retreated to the other end of the bench to avoid Kaja's playful punch. "Hey, you really should! - Now let's think what we can do about the situation."

"I've already done something about it." Kaja replied.

"Oh? Have you? What did you do?"

Kaja briefly told her about Simon, but omitted Tim from her report as much as possible. She had successfully managed to banish him from her thoughts for the past few days and wanted to keep it that way. When she finished, Thea wanted to know if Simon had come up with any useful information yet.

"Not much, as far as I know. I only met him a few days ago. But I received a phone call from him this morning. He seemed in a hurry." she added and continued: "He wanted to know if I had a line manager I could trust in order to discuss some pressing questions with him. That brings me back to Max. Obviously, he is the only one that came to mind. But it looks as if he's disappeared from the face of the earth."

"You're right." Thea interrupted her. "Despite my links to the clandestine cyberworld of PC Lux Solutions," she had to grin saying that, "I haven't managed to find out where his training is supposed to take place." she concluded in an apologetic tone.

"Don't you find that strange? Normally, training courses and contact numbers are available on the intranet, at least the ones for senior management."

"Of course they are. If you ask me: He isn't on a training course at all."

"But..." Kaja hesitated. "Do you think he might be suspended?"

"He could be." Thea said, but didn't sound convinced. "But he's not on the sacking list I mentioned to you the other day."

"Hm." Kaja was thinking hard. "If only I had his mobile number or home address." It seemed rather strange: She had been working with Max for several years now but knew so little about him.

"Oh, I can help you there." her friend interrupted her thoughts. Kaja whipped round and looked at her wide-eyed. With a proud face, Thea produced a piece of paper."I rather wanted to give it to you on paper instead of sending it through the network. Who knows where it might end up otherwise."

"But how..."

"Don't look so surprised. I have my sources, including a reliable contact in Human Resources." she explained.

Kaja cocked her head and gave Thea a scrutinising look while tickling Zorro behind his ears. There had been something strange in her friend's voice when she had said that last sentence.

"Who's your contact?" she was curious to know.

"You know him... It's Thomas." She replied reluctantly with a dismissive wave of her hand. Obviously, she wanted to play the information down, but the colour of her neck told a different story.

"And? What's going on between the two of you?" Kaja tried to dig deeper.

"Nothing, really. - OK, we went out a few times, but that's all."

"Well, I'm glad for you." Kaja was genuinely happy for her. "Am I invited to the wedding?" Ever since she had met Thea, she knew she dreamt of a big wedding, which had to happen soon and had to be all in white. Kaja could not imagine that part, but she could see Thea having her own family and wished she would find the man of her dreams soon.

"Now hold your horses." Thea laughed. "We're not there yet." She restlessly glanced at her watch and said: "Oh, is it that late already? I'll have to go."

Kaja had to laugh at this scarcely disguised attempt to change the subject. "Alright, I'll leave you in peace. But next time I won't let you off so easily." Zorro felt that the two women wanted to go. So he jumped up and circled them in excitement. "Stop it, you rascal." Kaja told him off half-heartedly.

"Let me know when you get hold of Max, OK?"

"Of course I will." Kaja promised.

On her way back to the office, Kaja recollected all the information she had gathered so far. She was just watching Zorro scavenging for food in the little park when, out of the blue, she felt a huge paw resting on her shoulder. It was Lance.

"Hey, you." Kaja smiled at him. "It looks like I've got so used to you that you can't shock me any more."

Lance was offended. "Do you really want to hurt my dragon pride?"

"Far from it." she was quick to re-assure him, although she had to grin. "No, honestly, for once I didn't intend to hurt you." She was briefly distracted by her dog who had stuck his whole head into a litter bin. "Hey, leave that alone." she ordered Zorro, but got no reaction. It was so typical. She ran over to pull him away from the bin. "Will you stop it? I give you enough food at home." Zorro looked wistfully back at the treasures he'd found and was not convinced his dinner would be any better, but then he decided to follow his mistress.

"Can you help me sort out the chaos in my head?" she asked Lance.

"I think I need to mark this day in my diary: My protégée's asked me for help!" Lance commented.

"Don't let it go to your head." Kaja grumbled. "Or I'll withdraw the question." But this didn't stop the dragon from skipping about with joy until Kaja had to laugh.

20

Holding the keys between her teeth, a large shopping bag in one hand and the laptop in the other, Kaja was desperately trying to push the flat door open, when Zorro stormed past her through the narrow gap and into the hallway, almost knocking the shopping out of her hand.

"Hey, are you nuts?" she shouted angrily after him, only to be pushed aside again by her shiny blue dragon friend. She shook her head and re-adjusted the load in her hands. She had been waiting in her office for any electronic instructions to arrive regarding a new project. But soon she had had enough, gathered her things and went to the nearest supermarket. Today was the day of Miri's visit and she wanted to cook something nice instead of relying on yet another pizza delivery. Since her fridge was completely empty, she had filled the shopping bag with lots of ingredients for a delicious meal and small sticky tartlets for pudding. When she finally made it into the flat, she put the shopping on the kitchen worktop and looked through her post. Only newspapers and junk mail. Straight in the bin, she decided. Next, something on the sitting room table caught her attention. She went closer to find out what it was: Her ID badge! How did it get here? Irritated, she inspected the room.

"It must have entered the same way it left." Lance commented laconically in between fighting with Zorro over a large bag of crisps. Hadn't she just bought that? Before the observation could fully sink in, she noticed a piece of paper under the badge: "Everything went well. Please keep tomorrow night free, we'll pick you up at eight for de-briefing." it said in military style.

'We?' she asked herself but then shrugged her shoulders presuming he would bring a colleague. She was free tomorrow night anyway and it was high time they made a start on solving the mystery. Then her attention turned back to her two flat mates.

"Hello? Do you mind?" No reaction. The two of them were fully occupied stuffing themselves with the contents of the bag (it was indeed the one she had bought just an hour earlier). Resolutely, she stepped in to break up the quarrel and tried to grab them by the scruff of their necks. With Zorro, it worked and he howled in pain. (Not that she had actually hurt him. But she still might. he thought.) Lance, of course, de-materialised in her hand and re-appeared in the opposite corner of the room.

"So, gentlemen, I think I need to have a serious word with you." she was not sure whether to laugh or to cry. The whole room was littered with the remains of the crisp bag and its contents. Zorro kept a low profile, well aware of what he had done, and guiltily retreated to his basket while the dragon appeared occupied looking intensely out of the window, as if the whole rigmarole had nothing to do with him.

"Lance, what have you got to say for yourself?" She demanded to know, looking sternly at him.

"Me? It's got nothing to do with me."

"Spare me the innocence. I saw you stick your whole head in the bag."

"Why don't you ask Zorro?" he complained.

"It's easier to talk to you. And besides, I know he is rather partial to crisps but he'd be too clumsy to snatch the packet from the shopping bag without pulling the whole thing off the shelf." In order to give her argument more weight, she gave the shopping bag a meaningful look, pointing out that it was still sitting on the kitchen worktop next to the sink, apparently untouched.

"OK, OK, if you must look for a villain, I surrender." Apparently deeply offended, he looked out of the window again.

"No no, I'm not letting you off so easily." she was laying into him but stopped when she saw a big tear running down his scaly face. "Lance?" she asked and took a step closer, only to notice a revealing cheeky twinkle in his eyes. She couldn't help but grin. "I should register you as an actor. You might win an Oscar."

"You see? It worked. I just wanted to make you laugh."

"And you thought the best way to achieve that was to have a feasting orgy with Zorro!"

"Exactly! Just imagine the sacrifice I had to make. I usually detest crisps." He said in all seriousness.

Kaja shook her head in disbelief. "You know what?"

"No, what?"

"The next time you want to cheer me up, just tell me an old-fashioned joke." she advised him angrily before starting to tackle the chaos in her home.

She had just managed to finish blitzing the sitting room - to which Lance had greatly contributed by not being in the way - chop some vegetables and prepare a dip of sour cream with herbs from her garden, when the door bell rang. She quickly dried her hands on a tea towel and gave the two troublemakers a warning look not to touch the dip with their paws or claws. Then she hurried to open the door for Miri.

"Hi sister." Miri greeted her with a cheeky smile on her face. Relieved that the chemistry between them still worked, Kaja asked her in. Zorro, who obviously felt that he must have done enough repentance for his behaviour earlier on, jumped up from his basket and rushed up to Miri to welcome her. Once he'd had enough of the tickling and patting, he went to the open door and looked outside in anticipation. He was apparently missing something or someone and looked at the two women for an answer. "No, Chili is not coming today..." "Chili is not coming today..." they both started simultaneously, stopped, looked at each other and snorted with laughter.

"What a promising start." Lance interfered without being asked.

"So, you can talk to animals?"

"Of course." Miri answered. "But you know that already and Kaja does the same."

"Well, yes, she does but denies it." he answered.

"I don't deny anything. It's a fact that I don't."

"And what about earlier on? What happened then?"

"Oh, it was nothing. I just knew what he was thinking."

"I see." Miri opened her mouth to say something but then thought better of it. After all, she had not come here to argue with her new-found sister. Although, she suddenly thought, wasn't that what sisters were supposed to do? She decided to put this realisation to the test at a later point. "I brought you some freshly pressed apple juice. Hope you'll like it."

Kaja was about to give her the usual "Oh, thanks, but you shouldn't have." but then changed her mind and said: "Great, we can have it tonight." And Miri was pleased to have made the right choice.

Kaja put the bowl with the dip, a plate with cucumber and carrot sticks and two glasses for the apple juice on a tray and said: "Come on, let's sit outside."

"You have a garden?" Miri was excited.

Kaja grimaced. "Well, the word garden is a slight exaggeration. It's more like a large balcony with a few patches of grass." she said and winked at Miri.

"Better than no balcony and no plants at all." the girl sighed as she stretched out on one of the sun loungers. Without being asked, Lance turned up, holding another glass in his hand and Zorro kept close behind him. "May I join you?" he asked, expectantly looking at Miri as she poured the drinks.

"'course you can" Miri was quick to respond. "After all, it's thanks to you that we met."

Visibly pleased at the compliment, he made himself comfortable on the lawn opposite the two women. They both looked at him in anticipation and waited until Lance asked irritated: "Are you waiting for something?"

"Don't you want to say something to us?"

"Me? No, I'd never interfere with your conversation. Just pretend I'm not here."

Kaja gave his shiny body, which was currently expanded to its full size, a meaningful look. "Of course, we can hardly see you. It's as if you were invisible." she joked. She turned to Miri to ask how she had spent the last few days, but Lance interrupted her yet again.

"What I wanted to ask you: Who is your dragon?"

"I knew it." Kaja rolled her eyes.

"You should ask: Who was my dragon?" Miri corrected him with a little sadness in her voice.

Lance didn't know what to make of it: "Was?" which earned him an angry look from Kaja.

"Don't you realise it's a sore subject? Why do you have to give her a hard time?"

The dragon wanted to reply and explain his reasons, but then decided otherwise and waited for Miri to continue.

"Her name was Maxi and I grew up with her." Miri stared into space, obviously lost in pleasant memories.

"Maxi?" Lance asked excitedly. "I know of an elegant dragon lady of the same name with shiny purple scales."

"Yes, it sounds like her. Do you know her? How is she? What is she doing these days?"

"Of course I know her... I knew her." he quickly corrected himself.

"When did you last see her?" Miri was beside herself with excitement.

"Let me see..." he said with a vague wave of his hand. "It must have been some fifty years ago. You know what it's like with us dragons."

"Oh." was Miri's only answer. Kaja, who sensed her disappointment, was quick to change the subject.

"Have I told you about the company ball?"

"No, how was it?" Miri was grateful for the distraction.

For the next hour, Kaja gave her a colourful account of every embarrassing detail of the previous night and the two giggled away.

Suddenly, Kaja asked: "Are you hungry? Shall I start cooking the meal or...?"

"Or what? I don't really need any food right now. Your veggie nibbles were quite filling."

"I told you about Mémé, didn't I?"

"Your grandmother?"

"Yes, her. I'm not sure I mentioned that she hand-makes scented candles with herbs from her own garden. When I'm there visiting, I usually help her. I love the smell of the hot wax mixing with the aroma of the dried herbs. The work calms me down and reminds me of bygone winter evenings with Mémé."

"Does she only make candles in the winter?"

"She used to, but now she makes them all year round as the business is doing very well. Of course, the winter is preferable. Melting the wax heats up the house nicely and because the days are so short, you're stuck inside anyway."

"It sounds very interesting. Can you show me how to do it?"

Kaja had to laugh. "I was hoping you'd ask. I promised to make a candle for a friend. My first attempt was quite a disaster and I was wondering if you wanted to help me?" She looked at her friend, waiting for a positive answer.

"Of course, I'd love to."

"What are we waiting for? Let's go inside. I'll get all the things we need."

As Miri helped her take the leftovers from their snack inside, she asked: "Why was your last attempt a disaster? Are you out of practice?"

"Hm, that as well." Kaja mumbled with her head in the fridge looking for something. "But most of all, I didn't realise how well Mémé's place is equipped. The work almost does itself. In comparison, this" she made a gesture round her open-plan kitchen, "is not exactly what I would call an ideal workshop."

"OK, I can see your point." Miri agreed while casting a curious look round the flat.

Kaja had noticed the glance and encouraged her: "Feel free to snoop around, but if you want a guided tour, it'll have to wait until later."

"I see, you're keen to make a start. Is that because you enjoy it so much or because you want to get it over and done with?"

"To be honest, a little bit of both. It's part of Mémé's home and lifestyle, but here, where it gets so complicated, I found it hard to bring myself to do it. I've been putting it off for a while now."

"But now you have me for moral support."

"Not only for moral support, I'll need some hands-on help, too." Kaja quipped.

"Just tell me what to do."

"Here, smell this." Kaja handed her a few small, brown paper bags. "This is lavender. Here is some orange blossom and that..." she paused to stick her nose in the bag. "Oh yes, that's rosemary."

"Amazing." was Miri's only comment. As Kaja weighed the various ingredients for the wax, mixed them in a large old pot and explained the production process to Miri, she could hear Mémé's voice doing the same with her when she was a child. Miri listened to her intently and didn't interrupt. When the wax started to melt, Kaja put several flasks with essential oils in front of her.

"Now we're coming to the creative part. What kind of scent do we want to give our candles?" It was a lucky co-incidence that Mémé had given her three moulds. This way, she could make a candle for Miri as well, as a reward for her help.

"Do you have any special criteria?"

"Hm, it depends." Kaja replied, concentrating on the melting wax in the pot. "If you want to sell the candles, you'll have to think which emotions buyers might want to evoke, such as Christmas, relaxation, rejuvenation, love... You know what I mean?"

"Yes, you need to take very down-to-earth and business-like decisions."

"Exactly, if the candles are supposed to sell, you have to think along those lines. People find it easier to read a name first, smell the candle and then decide whether they like it or not. Many buy one candle off the shelf, but then come back to talk to Mémé and have their very own scent created." Kaja was genuinely proud of her grandmother. "Mémé is an old fox when it comes to selling. But I think the secret to her success is actually the effort she puts into getting the scent right. Her comprehensive knowledge of herbs and her intuitive ability to assess various moods are a great help as well."

"I'm sure that's all the more important when making personalised candles."

"Yes, it is, but then she can rely on specific information on what the person is looking for. I personally find it easier than creating a theme that needs to appeal to many people."

"It makes sense. Everyone seems to associate different things with different smells."

"Christmas is a relatively easy one, because of the local baking ingredients often used. But anything else can be tricky."

"Well then, let's make a start." Miri simply said.

Kaja put a small bowl for the first herb mixture on the kitchen worktop and briefly introduced Miri to Luc's life. She finished by asking: "So, now you have a good picture of him. Think about it. What comes to mind?"

"Me? I have absolutely no experience in such things." Miri fended her off.

"You don't have to. Just think what your first impression was. What is it that Luc might enjoy in his life? I'll show you some herbs and you tell me if they match your ideas."

"For someone claiming to have no intuitive side, you're quite committed."

"Ah, at last someone else is telling her, apart from me." Lance could be heard from the background.

"Quiet there in the cheap seats." Kaja shouted cheerfully. "This is completely different."

"Sure it is." the dragon and Miri said simultaneously and both rolled their eyes.

"Stop it now, Miri has to concentrate." Kaja told them off but could not help a grin. She was surprised how much fun this was. It was the best evening she'd had for a long time. Well, perhaps apart from her last meeting with Tim. Tim! His candle had to be made as well. She quickly dismissed the thought. It'll have to wait for another five minutes, at least. She turned back to Miri who was deeply immersed in her thoughts. "So, what do you think?"

"At first I thought of something bright and cheery. You said he can be quite grumpy at times?" She looked at Kaja with a questioning, insecure smile, anticipating feedback.

"Good idea, you're right." Kaja shook her head. Amazing how easy it was to miss the obvious if you knew someone too well. Kaja frowned, inspecting her bags of herbs. Apparently, she could not find what she was looking for and disappeared into the bedroom without saying another word. When she came back, she had a satisfied smile on her face and in her hands, she was holding a few dried twigs and leaves. "Please smell this and tell me what you think."

Miri carefully took the dried herbs from her and smelled them. "Hm, perfect. What is it? I don't really have green fingers and cannot tell."

"Last summer's lemon balm."

"Did you grow it on your patio?"

"No, I brought it from France last year, when I visited Mémé."

"From what you've told me about her, I feel like Mémé is someone I'd like to meet."

"Sorry, don't get me wrong." she added after a moment, when she realised Kaja wasn't going to reply. "I wasn't trying to invite myself."

"No no, I didn't think you were." Kaja was quick to re-assure her as she stirred the hot wax. "It's actually a good idea. We could go there together. But let's concentrate on the oils and herbs for the three candles now. Any more ideas about Luc?"

"Something to give him clarity."

"What do you mean by 'clarity'" Kaja frowned.

Miri was searching for words. "Clarity in the sense of being less absent-minded. I understand that he's quite clever, but also a bit of a scatterbrain. Is that right?"

"Perfect." Kaja chose one of the flasks and held it under Miri's nose.

"Exactly. Even I know this one: it's peppermint."

"Good. That's candle number one done. Now to candle number two..."

"Who's this one for?"

"This one, uhm, is also for a... sort of... friend." Kaja replied rather unconvincingly. It didn't help that Lance wolf-whistled in the background.

"Oh, I see. That sort of friend." Miri taunted her and winked at Lance in secret understanding. Kaja kept silent and appeared to be concentrating on stirring her wax. "Well, if you don't want to talk about this friend, I can't help you with selecting the right herbs for him." As Kaja was still not saying a word, she kept on digging: "So how come this unimportant friend deserves one of your candles?"

"It was Luc's idea." Kaja grumbled as a reply.

"I see."

"What do you see?"

"Nothing. If that's all you can tell us - no problem."

"Alright then. His name is Tim. When we were children, we used to be best friends. I hadn't seen him for a while but bumped into him on my last visit to Mémé."

"And?"

"What else do you want me to say?"

"You haven't even told us half the story. The better half is still missing." Lance butted in.

"Be quiet back there." In mock desperation, she turned to Miri: "Why can't dragons allow for a little privacy now and then?"

"Because not even best friends do." Miri joked. "Come on, spill."

Kaja selected one of the essential oils and smelled it herself before handing it to Miri: "This is the feeling he gives me right now."

"Warmth, security, reliability." Miri stated. "All perfect for a best friend." She looked over to Lance who gave her a knowing smile and an almost imperceptible shake of his head.

"The first two descriptions are spot on, but I'm not so sure about the third one - reliability. By the way, it's sandalwood that's commonly associated with these emotions." Kaja sighed.

"Hm, sandalwood has a very sensual smell. Why aren't you sure about his reliability? Has he given you any reason to think he might be unreliable?"

"No, I didn't mean it like that. What I feel being close to him is not so much down to reliability, it causes a complete emotional turmoil in me."

After this revelation, Miri decided not to tease her any further and asked: "Have you seen him again since you came back from France?"

"Yes I have, twice already."

"That's great news. Or isn't it?"

"Yes, I enjoyed each of our dates. And this is what scares the hell out of me." Kaja decided she had talked enough about Tim for the day and distracted herself selecting more herbs for the candle. "I'm going to add this one as well. Do you recognise it?"

"It smells like pizza to me. Is that the idea?" Miri asked back cheekily as she realised Kaja wanted to change the subject.

"I'm not surprised you made that association. It's rosemary, a staple ingredient in any pizza recipe."

"And why do you want to give the man a pizza candle? Do you want him to take you to dinner?"

"If he takes it as a hidden hint, why not?" Kaja giggled. "But it's something I learned from Mémé: Rosemary is a strong protective plant."

"Hm, from what you've told me, the man doesn't seem to need much protection, although you've kept suspiciously quiet about his appearance." Miri could not refrain from adding.

"Tall, broad shoulders, beaming blue eyes, dark hair. - You get the picture or do I need to say any more?" Kaja retorted cleverly.

"Oh." was all Miri was able to say. 'What in the world is stopping Kaja from falling head-over-heels in love with this Mr. Perfect?' She asked herself with a touch of jealousy. She quickly shook off such dark thoughts and reminded herself that she would be out on a date in an hour's time and might finally meet the man of her dreams herself.

Her thoughts were interrupted by Kaja saying: "Yes, he needs protection because he travels a lot, visiting wild bears."

Miri sensed the underlying tension in this casual remark. So that was the real problem! Miri realised that, although it felt as if they had known each other for ages, there were many areas in Kaja's life that she had yet to understand. But with time, she certainly would. She noticed that Kaja had started to assemble a third mixture. "And who's the third candle for?"

"This one's for you."

"For me? Let me try." Miri demanded excitedly.

"Go away. You can smell it when it's finished and decide whether you like the scent. And if you don't, I'm happy to make another one for you."

"Wow, I didn't expect that."

"That's the whole point of making presents." Kaja informed her. "But first I need your help. Look, at the bottom of the moulds, just here, I've attached one end of the wicks. And I fixed the other ends to this bamboo stick. I'd be grateful if you could hold the bamboo stick so that all three wicks point straight up to the ceiling. That's where it went wrong when I tried to do it on my own the last time."

"No problem. Give it to me." While Miri kept the wicks straight, Kaja poured the molten wax into the moulds.

"And now you're going to add the herbs?"

"No, we'll have to wait until the wax is almost solid. It must be as cool as possible and as liquid as necessary. It needs to be rather gooey, before the herbs and oils can be added. If we did it now, the essential oils would evaporate and the scent of the candle turn out much weaker."

Miri was impressed with this expert explanation and tried to remember as much as possible. "Do you want me to take over?" Kaja asked.

"Yes, that would be nice. It's quite strenuous having to hold my arm up for so long."

As they were waiting, Kaja suggested: "Would you like to come on a long walk with me and Zorro on Saturday morning? I can pick you up. I just need to get out and clear my head."

Miri cautiously asked: "What time did you have in mind?"

"I'm usually up quite early, but I can work around you. When is convenient?"

"I'm going out tomorrow night and might come home late..."

Kaja remembered that she was supposed to meet Simon on Friday. "I'm meeting someone as well. Why don't we give ourselves enough time to get up? What about ten?"

Miri swallowed hard. Normally, she wouldn't be seen out of bed before ten thirty on a Saturday morning. But she put on a brave face: "Yes, great. Keep ringing the door bell, in case I'm still in the shower and can't hear you." - 'Or in case I'm still in bed.' she thought.

"That's booked, then." Kaja carefully touched the wax with her index finger. "Now we have to work quickly. Can you take the stick again, please?" She handed the bamboo stick back to Miri and started to scatter the herbs on the wax stirring them in with skilful movements of her hand, using a wooden stick. Finally, she added a few drops of the essential oils. "So, that's it. Another five minutes cooling down and we can cut the wicks to size."

Miri looked at her watch. "Oh, is it that late already? I'll have to be off soon. I'm meeting some colleagues for a few drinks."

"Nice people?"

Instead of an answer, Miri leaned forward to smell her candle. "That's absolutely wonderful. May I ask what you've put in?"

"Rose petals and orange blossom oil."

"Ah, that's strange. I don't see myself as a flowery girl." You could see in Miri's face that she found the scent very appealing, but now she knew how it had been created, she wasn't sure whether it was appropriate for her to like it.

"Come on, don't look so disappointed." Kaja pulled her leg. "It's only a candle, not a full psychoanalysis."

"That's not what you sounded like when making the other two." Miri complained. "I do admit I find the smell sensational. Only I'm not sure what it says about me."

"Don't dwell on it too much. It was just an inspiration I had. And as I said: I'm not as intuitive as you are."

Miri glanced over to Lance in disbelief, as she tried to take in Kaja's explanation. But he pretended not to listen and intensely inspected his claws instead. 'OK, have it your way. I can be ignorant, too, especially when it comes to obviously absent dragons.' she thought and said aloud: "Anyway. I'm sorry I have to leave you now. But my mates are waiting."

Kaja was slightly taken by surprise by this hasty departure, so she just confirmed: "Are we still on for Saturday morning ten o'clock?"

"Yes, I'm looking forward to it. See you then." Miri picked up her handbag, slipped on her jacket, briefly tickled a sleepy Zorro on his belly, gave Kaja a quick hug and rushed off.

"I don't think her dragon taught her any manners." Lance said as soon as she was out of the door.

"What?" Kaja looked at him, irritated.

"That's so typical of you. You didn't even notice, did you?"

"What didn't I notice?"

"Well, she left without saying goodbye to me. That's what!"

"Now keep your wig on. You behaved so inconspicuously that even I almost forgot you were here. You were so busy grooming your fur. And besides, it's not as if I'd received a formal leaving ceremony myself."

"Excuse me? We dragons have scales to look after, not fur. And anyway, dragons can multi-task."

Kaja snorted with laughter. "Yes, of course, lots of men claim they can. But you didn't look too clever when she was turning to you for support."

When she saw the surprise on Lance's face, she smiled. "You didn't think I'd notice, did you? Now that's the fine art of multi-tasking. But as much as I enjoy our little banter, would you mind helping me clear up, please?"

"Oh, I just realised, I have an urgent appointment..."

"Nonsense! I need you here." But it was too late, Kaja was already alone in the room talking to herself. "An appointment, don't make me laugh. He's probably meeting my pillow right now." she steamed and started tidying up.

"You can come out from under your rock." Kaja shouted into the empty living room where she had settled down on the sofa, nibbling on the sweet sticky tartlets that had been sitting on the kitchen top untouched all evening. She realised that she hadn't felt this relaxed and satisfied for a long time. She decided it was Miri's visit that had caused this positive effect.

"Dragons live in caves and sometimes in castles, but never under rocks." Lance lectured her indignantly, as he materialised next to her on the sofa.

"Of course, whatever you say." she replied peaceably. Tonight, she did not intend to let her dragon spoil the buoyant mood she was in, even though she usually enjoyed their banter. She playfully swirled the last of the wine in her glass. "I was wondering: Was it really fifty years ago that you last saw Miri's dragon?"

"Why do you want to know?" Lance asked cautiously.

"Because Miri told me she grew up with Maxi. They must have been about the same age, which is to say Maxi must have been a dragon child back then. In that case, it would be impossible for you to have met her fifty years ago, because Miri isn't that old." she explained, obviously proud of her powers of deduction.

"Oh, that. Even though Miri was under the impression Maxi was the same age as her, Maxi must have been at least 132 years old. That's our minimum age before we can be assigned a protégée. It's still a very young age for a dragon, no wonder she must have had a child-like appearance."

"I see." It seemed rather surreal for Kaja to sit there talking to a dragon and to accept his explanations without questioning them. But it didn't matter any more. There was no point doubting him. After all, waking up in the morning, she had stopped asking herself whether the cute little creature next to her was a fluffy toy or not. Kaja yawned and the dragon did the same. "Let's go to bed. Tomorrow is another day." he suggested.

"Good idea. And please try to remind me to call Max on his mobile. Perhaps I'll be able to tell Simon tomorrow night how to get hold of him."

"OK, I will." Lance acknowledged, although he had serious doubts if it would be that easy.

In the meantime, Miri was sitting in a smoky bar, had just ordered her fourth tequila and was seriously wondering what in the world had driven her to abandon a relaxed evening with Kaja for this let-down experience. The music was as bad as it was loud and it was so dark that you could hardly see your own hand in front of your eyes. She quickly licked the salt from the back of her hand, downed the tequila and sucked the piece of lemon. On the positive side, the drink didn't burn her tongue any more as it got completely numb after the second shot anyway. Bored, she watched some of the party-goers dance with varying degrees of enthusiasm, if you could call their bouncing movements dancing at all. It had been a complete waste of time coming here tonight. Suddenly she felt a hand on her hips.

"And? Have you missed me today?" a voice whispered in her ear.

'Today?' she thought enervated. 'More like for the past two weeks.' Demonstratively, she turned away from the person although she could feel his hot hand turning the butterflies in her stomach into a burning fire.

"Don't play hard to get. Admit it, you're glad to see me, too." he muttered and pulled her closer. "Let's get out of here." Miri silently sighed. Maybe it had been worth coming here after all, she thought, but was surprised to find that her initial excitement had worn off. She turned towards the man, linked her arm with his and let him guide her outside, into the dark night.

21

It was Friday morning and Kaja tried to reach Max on his mobile, but all she got was a soft female voice saying: "The person you are calling is currently unavailable. Please try again later."

Kaja started to get seriously worried for her boss as she couldn't find out where he was. What if something had happened to him? With little enthusiasm, she finished her morning coffee and prepared for another dull day at work. Her next project still hadn't arrived. She sighed. Sitting in an office with nothing to do, just for the purpose of being present, was something she seriously resented. Luckily, she had not been in this position for the past two years as she had always been busy with one project or another. Absent-mindedly, she played with the keys in her hand. Zorro was already waiting for her by the door, wagging his tail.

"You don't have a worry in the world." she snapped at him grumpily, but had to smile when she saw the innocent expectation in his eyes. "You're right. It doesn't make a difference to you whether I'm working hard or just solving sudokus on my screen. In either case, you just make yourself comfortable on the office floor. Come on, let's go."

After having spent two hours doing nothing, she pushed herself away from the desk. "Argh! I can't stand it any longer."

"What can't you stand any longer?" Lance asked innocently. He was sitting on the window sill, relaxed as if he had been there for ages.

"You're just like a cat." Kaja said to him instead of an answer.

"A cat?" the dragon was genuinely surprised by this turn in their conversation.

"Yes, cats also create the impression that they have been sitting or lying in the same spot for hours, if not days." She waved at him. "So, time for me to see the section leader." But she hesitated to pluck up the courage. "I'm really not keen to talk to him, but this here is no good either."

"What is?" Lance had not been listening and was rather busy nibbling at her sandwich instead. Angrily, she took it from him, but after a brief look at it, she handed it back. She was certainly not squeamish, but a sandwich chewed up by a dragon didn't look very appealing.

"Why do you need to have a go at my lunch if you only live on dragon energy anyway?" she wanted to know.

Lance shrugged his shoulders. "I don't know. It was there looking at me."

"Oh, never mind. I'll go and see the section leader now."

"Hey, wait, stop! You're not normally so quick off the mark. Don't you want to tell me what this is all about?"

"Sorry, I don't have time for you right now or I'll be stuck on that mark forever. - to use your own expression."

Stunned, Lance watched Kaja leave the room. "My furry friend, can you tell me what's the matter with her?" Zorro raised his eyebrows at him. "OK, I get it. I should have listened to what she was saying." the dragon admitted.

"I thought you knew everything? So figure it out yourself." Zorro mumbled casually and turned to the other side to continue his office nap.

In the meantime, Kaja had made it as far as the section leader's secretary, who looked almost exactly the same as the secretary working for Max. Although she felt very tense about the impending conversation, an absurd thought crossed her mind that all these secretaries might have gone through the same training academy. She almost laughed out loud but then controlled herself. If she wanted to get past this one, she had better make a good impression.

"Can I help you?" the assistant asked in a bored tone.

'She sounds just like the other clones.' Kaja thought and had to bite her lip to stop a mischievous grin from creeping across her face. "I have an urgent problem to discuss with the section leader."

"Oh, do you? Have you got an appointment?"

"No, I don't. But as I said: it's urgent."

"That's what they all say." the secretary commented, unimpressed. "But we have a rule here: no appointment, no meeting."

"OK then, when can you schedule a meeting with him, please?" Kaja asked, hardly able to contain her anger.

"Just send me an e-mail requesting an appointment. We'll look at it early next week and you should be able to see him towards the end of the week."

"But now that I'm here, why don't you just look in your diary and tell me when the next appointment is available?" Kaja insisted.

"It's against the procedure."

Kaja stared at the assistant in disbelief. "You don't honestly mean that, do you?"

"Of course I do." came the cold answer.

Kaja felt she had reached the end of her tether. After having built up all that anticipation, she couldn't let such a self-important bitch stop her from seeing it through. She quickly turned on her heels and marched towards the section leader's door.

"But you can't..." were the last words Kaja heard from her.

She carefully closed the door behind her. Now that she had crossed the threshold, she did not feel as confident as she had been just a few minutes ago. 'It's too late anyway.' she told herself. Just show some bravado, Lance had advised her. Automatically, she straightened her shoulders and turned round.

"Oh, hello, my dear. What a coincidence. I urgently wanted to see you, and here you are." the section leader welcomed her with a slimy smile. He had been sitting at his desk, but now he got up and came towards her in large strides, offering his hand.

My dear? Urgently wanted to see me? Kaja deliberately ignored his stretched-out hand and tried hard not to show her irritation. What in the world was going on here?

"Keep calm and carry yourself." Lance whispered in her head.

"Carry on." Kaja corrected him automatically. "What are you doing here?"

"Oh, I won't keep carrying on, but I thought you could do with a little bit of support. Something's wrong here, very wrong."

Kaja was relieved. "So it was not just my imagination." she replied telepathically. "I feel like I'm being taken for a ride and I don't know what to make of it."

"Kaja, Kaja, I have to admit your actions took me by surprise, especially since your line manager had vouched for your excellent qualifications. But it seems you've found some more exciting ways to occupy yourself." he said in an ambiguous tone, giving her a conspiratorial wink.

For a moment, Kaja was so stunned that she was unable to react to his unsavoury insinuations. Suddenly, his mood changed completely and he angrily shouted at her: "At least that would explain why you're stalking

Max with phone calls."

"Is it against the rules now to call my line manager?" she asked, visibly irritated, while secretly wondering how he could have found out.

Had Max complained about her? She could not imagine he had. 'That would indeed be interesting to know." Lance silently confirmed. Obviously, he did not believe either that Max was the source of such accusations.

"Of course it's not against the rules, but it is rather unusual to call a private mobile number while the person is on a training course. I don't think his wife would be amused." Wouldn't she now? This was getting rather interesting as Kaja knew for a fact that Max was not married. She was about to say something to this effect when Lance warned her, gently squeezing her arm.

"Wait and see where this is going. You don't need to put all your cards on the desk at once."

"...on the table. But yes, you're right." she agreed and tried not to show any emotion. Apparently, the section leader had not noticed her silent conversation and continued unfazed with his monologue. "Your behaviour is even less excusable considering that you've just received an official warning for sexual harassment."

Kaja could feel the pulse throbbing in her neck and the blood singing in her ears.

"Take a deep breath." the dragon implored her. Kaja exhaled and tried to distance herself from this surreal situation. She let her thoughts wander and just caught the end of the man's lecture.

"Therefore, we have no other choice than to dismiss you with immediate effect. Of course, we regret losing someone with your credentials, but your behaviour cannot be tolerated any more. In fact, the quality of your work has also suffered recently." he finished with a malicious grin.

It took Kaja all her strength to control her anger, but the fact that she still showed no visible reaction was enough to irritate the section leader.

"Don't you have anything to say?"

"Where is Max?" she hissed between clenched teeth, which was the only articulate question her brain was able to produce at this very moment.

The unpleasant man looked at her shaking his head. "I see we don't seem to be getting anywhere. OK, two of our security guards will take you to your office now where you can pack your personal things."

Dumbfounded, Kaja looked at him: "You're serious, aren't you?"

"Of course I'm serious. What do you think? - Ah here they are. Please excuse me now. I'm busy."

In disbelief, Kaja watched the two security guards approach her.

"If you would like to follow us?" one of them said in a authoritative tone, not unfriendly, but sternly enough to make it sound like an order, not a question.

"What am I going to do?" she whispered to the dragon.

"Just go along with it, at least for now." he advised her and compassionately patted her shoulder before disappearing discreetly.

Back in her office, some IT technicians were already busy re-programming the computer while Zorro sat on his blanket, looking disturbed and unsure what was expected of him. Kaja calmed him down and tickled him behind his ear. "Good boy. Nothing to worry about." She put her belongings in one of the cardboard boxes that someone had conveniently placed on the desk. 'How considerate.' she thought sarcastically. Luckily, she had left her laptop at home today, otherwise they might have erased its hard disk as well. She pushed Zorro off his rolled-up faux fur blanket to put it on top of the pile of things. After a brief argument with one of her minders, she was allowed to go to the staff room to get her coffee mug and put it in the box as well. Finally, she took the blanket under her left arm, the cardboard box under her right and nodded to the security guards signalling she was ready to leave. All three of them made their way downstairs, followed by Zorro.

She was just about to squeeze through the exit turnstile when one of the guards held her back: "Ms. Meyer, I think you forgot something."

"What do you want?" she replied nervously.

"Your badge, please."

Ah, of course. Luckily, Simon had returned it yesterday. He would be in for a surprise tonight! For a moment, she struggled with her load in order to reach the badge until finally one of the security guards was kind enough to hold the box for her.

"Thanks." she mumbled and gave him the badge in return for the box.

Kaja carried her belongings to the car (luckily, she had come by car today) and put everything in the boot. Zorro took his usual place on the back seat and looked at her expectantly. Despite her foul mood, Kaja had to laugh.

"From your point of view, it must be the perfect day: Three hours in the office and we're on our way home again. That's what you like, don't you? I'm sure you're already asking yourself what other exciting things we're going to do for the rest of the day." She got into the driver's seat, but didn't start the engine yet. Yes, it was a good question. What was she going to do now? It was not every day that she got unexpected free time. She tried to grasp the feeling: Free! Her brains and stomach were filled with a wealth of emotions. Anger, yes. Insecurity, most definitely. - But to her surprise, she also felt a good measure of freedom. It shouldn't have come as a surprise. Working here hadn't been much fun recently. The only aspect that made her sad was the fact that she wouldn't see Thea as often as she used to. But they could always arrange to meet outside working hours. Nobody could stop them from doing that. Satisfied with this solution, she turned round to look at Zorro, who was bravely trying to ignore Lance sitting next to him.

"You're back?" she asked cheerfully.

"Yes, I am. And I notice you've used my absence to ponder the positive aspects of this latest development." the dragon said with satisfaction.

"Exactly. And that's why we're stopping at home just briefly to change clothes and then go on a little trip." Zorro, who recognised the word trip and sensed Kaja's adventurous mood, started to bark excitedly.

248

"Be quiet now." Kaja shouted with a restrained giggle in her voice and drove off.

22

At home, Kaja put the cardboard box on the kitchen worktop. Then she went over to the sitting room table where she had left her laptop and switched it on. She quickly wanted to send Thea an e-mail to explain what had happened. While the computer was booting up, she changed from her usual office jeans into a more comfortable pair of khaki cargo pants and complemented them with a fleece-lined cardigan to keep off the autumn breeze. She started the mail application and had to grin seeing a message from Thea already waiting in her inbox.

"So it was your turn now? Waiting for details. Any luck with M.?" she had written in telegraphic style.

'Why am I not surprised? Thea is always well-informed.' without even sitting down, she wrote a brief reply, suggesting a meeting over lunch next Monday. Then she made herself a sandwich, using peanut butter, mustard, cucumber, soft cheese and ham.

"That's mine!" she said sharply when she saw, from the corner of her eye, Lance sneaking up behind her.

"Spoilsport." he complained.

"I don't think it's part of your job description to keep nicking my sandwiches."

She was just filling an empty plastic bottle with tap water when the phone rang. She looked at the caller display: 0033 - France... Who could that be? It wasn't Mémé's number, not even her area code. So, to her relief, it was unlikely that something had happened and someone was trying to get hold of her. She was in two minds whether to answer the call but then curiosity got the better of her. "Meyer?"

"Kaja, it's your mother."

"Oh, hello Maman." Kaja replied in a flat voice. "Where're you calling from? I thought you were somewhere in the Indian Ocean?" and added in her thoughts: '...or somewhere else far away, as far away as possible."

"We've been invited to a reception in Paris by..." And then her mother ran through a list of names that Kaja had never heard of before.

When she detected a slight pause in that avalanche of words, she quickly interrupted her mother and said abruptly: "And why are you calling me?"

"Why? Can't a mother ask her only daughter how she is? Since you're not calling us any more, I decided to call you myself."

That was Maman in all her glory. She always distorted the facts and tried to make you feel guilty. Kaja was so fed up with it. She used to call her parents regularly only to be told more than once that they didn't have the time or the nerves to spend hours on the phone speaking to their daughter.

That was why she wanted to keep the conversation as brief as possible, but she could not refrain from saying with a hint of satisfaction in her voice: "I'm OK. Just got sacked and not sure what I'm going to do. But otherwise I'm fine."

This triggered a renewed monologue from her mother, surmising what Kaja must have done wrong to get into this predicament. Kaja held the phone receiver three feet away from her ear. She knew exactly where this was going and she didn't intend to listen to the whole lecture again. Lance gave her a sympathetic look and she pulled a face at him.

When there was another brief break in her mother's speech, she interrupted her again and said: "By the way: Mémé sends her regards. Thanks for calling but I'm a bit in a rush." Without waiting for an answer, she hung up. "Phew, I'm glad that's over. It was the last thing I needed right now."

Nobody, not even that unpleasant section leader was able to spoil her mood as quickly as her mother did. "So, we're ready, finally." She packed her bag and was surprised how long the sandwich had survived under the greedy eyes of the dragon.

"What do you think of me?" he defended himself. "How can I steal your sandwich while this, this..." he was looking for a suitable word.

"...poor excuse for a mother?" Kaja helped him out, already in a much better mood. Grateful for the suggestion, he agreed with her.

"Yes, I think that's the term you humans use, although I don't know what there is to excuse. But I digress. What I wanted to say was: Of course I won't nick your sandwich while this poor excuse for a mother is having a go at you." The dragon explained, slightly embarrassed.

Kaja went over and gave him a hug: "You know, you can be really sweet when you want to."

"Me? Sweet? Never!" Lance was so shocked at the compliment that he angrily hissed at her: "Can we go now?"

When they reached Lake Tuerler, Kaja released Zorro from his leash and basked in the autumn sun. Now, on a mid-week day in autumn, when very few people were visiting the small lake, her dog could roam freely without disturbing anyone. Kaja was glad she had brought a warm jacket. Despite the sunshine, the wind could be chilly. She watched a few ducks swimming in pairs on the water and asked herself whether Tim would be coming to the meeting with Simon tonight.

'You're a stupid cow. As if you haven't got enough problems already.

Do you really want to get entangled in a romantic affair?' she argued with herself. But apart from that, she was looking forward to hear what Simon had found out. And she was curious which direction her life would take from now on. When the words of the section leader had finally sunk in, just about when she finished clearing her office, she had resolved to start composing job applications immediately. But instead, she had taken the liberty of going on an afternoon trip with her dog.

A smile appeared on her face as she watched Zorro unsuccessfully chase the ducks. "Be careful. Don't drop into the water again." She shouted cheerfully. As a puppy, he had boisterously run out on the frozen lake and had promptly broken through the thin ice into the freezing water. Luckily, he had been small enough for her to grab him by the scruff of his neck and pull him out. But now it was autumn and no dangerous sheaths of ice were covering the water.

Kaja was glad that she wasn't sitting at home, racking her brains over job applications. Perhaps this was an opportunity for her to find out what she really wanted from life. Should she go for a similar job, the same kind of work? Or was it time to try something completely different? She shook her head. It was too soon to tell. Kaja had a vague feeling that going through all this trouble would have been in vain if she was to carry on as if nothing had happened. Her problems would only surface again.

She sighed. Perhaps she should pay Mémé another visit? But even without going there, she knew what her grandmother's advice would be: find out what is important to you and just do it...

"And? What is important to you?" The dragon interrupted her thoughts.

"Perhaps I'll write my memoirs about living with a dragon." she answered keeping a straight face.

"Haha. Very funny."

"I thought I'd wind you up, just for once."

"You'll have to try harder." Lance laughed. "But why don't you ask Miri? Perhaps she can give you some useful advice."

"Miri?"

"Yes, aren't you going to see her tomorrow?"

"Well yes, but I'm not sure if she'll be at all interested in my problems."

"She's your sister, isn't she? Your dragon sister. And that's what sisters are there for."

"Hm. And why do you think it'll be a good idea to talk to her?"

"Let's put it this way: I'm not the right person to talk to. I'd probably give you the same advice as Josephine. But Miri might be able to help you sort out the chaos in your head."

"Chaos, is it?" she grumbled. "OK, you may be right. I'll talk to her tomorrow. And tonight I can fully dedicate myself to putting the world right." she said theatrically.

For no particular reason, she felt nervous. After they had come back in the afternoon, she had treated herself to a nice, long shower, washed and blow-dried her hair, applied new make-up and spent ages deciding which jeans to wear. While doing all this, she was more or less trying to convince herself that an unexpected free afternoon was the perfect opportunity to have a beauty session that had been long overdue and that it had absolutely nothing to do with the prospect of Tim turning up tonight. But despite those efforts, her thoughts were still going astray. It didn't help either that the dragon, lazily sprawled on the sofa, was moping that she was taking Zorro to the meeting but not him. This was why he was butting into her monologues at any possible opportunity with a disgruntled: "Yeah, as if." or similar comments.

At exactly eight o'clock, the door bell rang. This must be Simon and hopefully Tim. She put on her favourite, well-worn leather jacket, grabbed Zorro's leash, put the laptop under her arm and left the flat. She almost bumped into Simon who was already standing outside the door.

"Simon!"

"Kaja! Did you expect to see someone else?" he said amused. "We have an appointment, remember?"

"Er, yes of course we have an appointment." she stammered. "I was just thinking..."

"If you're missing Tim, he sends his apologies. He had to go somewhere else and may join us later." He gave Kaja's outfit an approving look. "But I'm sure he'll be very pleased to see you."

"I... oh, thank you. Do you have space for a second canine monster in your car or shall I follow you in mine?" she tried to change the subject.

Simon smiled about this obvious attempt to change the subject. "No problem. I've got my company car today. It has two dog cages so they won't get in each other's way."

"That's great. Where are we going?"

"Do you have any suggestions? I'm from Bern and don't know Zurich very well." he replied in his broad Bern dialect and with a cheeky grin on his face.

Kaja had a spontaneous idea. "Why don't we go to the Irish Pub? It shouldn't be too noisy at this time of the day and when we're done with our detective work, we could play a round of darts."

"Darts?" he didn't sound convinced.

"You'll see, it's fun. Almost like playing chess, only that I have a chance of winning against you this time." she pulled his leg.

"OK, I'll give it a go. Just show me the way."

They were lucky to find a parking space not too far from the pub. To make things easier, they decided to leave their dogs in the car. The animals seemed quite content with their accommodation and, to compensate for their patience, would be taken to the lakeside for some exercise afterwards.

Simon opened the door for Kaja and they entered a cosy establishment, with the typical layout of a bar in the centre of the back wall of the room, seating corners along the sides, a snooker table at one end and two darts boards at the other. Simon ordered himself a Guinness while Kaja went for a cider.

"Fancy some fish and chips?"

"Do they do it here?"

"Yes, and it's legendary. So?"

"Yes, why not."

Simon was amused about Kaja's choice of venue and asked: "Where do you get all this Anglo-Saxon influence from? I didn't expect that from someone who grew up in the Grande Nation." he commented, hinting at her time in France.

"Oh, there hasn't been that much influence. My grandmother is a rather cosmopolitan person and I have too much liberal Swiss blood in me." Kaja laughed.

After they had finished their meal and tried to clean their greasy fingers with tissues that were rather inadequate for the purpose, Simon touched on the actual subject of their meeting.

"Any new developments your end?" he wanted to know from Kaja.

"Yes, you could say that." She told him how she had repeatedly tried to get hold of Max and gave him a detailed account of her conversations with Thea. Finally, she told him about the unexpected summary dismissal that afternoon. When she had finished, Simon simply nodded. "You don't look like this is news to you?" she was unsure what to make of his reaction.

"Some of it is, some of it isn't. But first of all: How are you coping, now you've lost your job?"

"Well, I don't know. My emotions are all over the place." She straightened the stained tablecloth. "Since the merger, our work climate had got noticeably colder. It was not even a consolation to have an otherwise exciting job. And most recently, I didn't even have that any more."

"What didn't you have?"

"I didn't have any new projects. I was just getting stressed out sitting in an office with nothing to do."

"I can understand that." Simon agreed.

"To cut a long story short, I think my dismissal was absolutely preposterous. There's something very dodgy going on here and I haven't quite worked out what it is. But, and this is a very big 'but', I feel free. I haven't been so free for a long time. Perhaps I realise that everything is possible now, both in a good and a bad sense. I have the freedom to decide what I want to do with my life, at least in the short term. That sounds rather pompous, doesn't it?" she smiled at him, slightly embarrassed.

Simon shook his head. "No, I don't think so. There is some truth in the saying 'Every cloud has a silver lining.' You don't sound like you'll be starving if a pay cheque doesn't arrive at the end of the month. So I don't think I need to be worried about you." he grinned.

"You're right. I'm not swimming in cash, but I'll survive for a month or two." she was pleased to confirm. "But don't keep me in suspense. Come on, tell me what you've found out."

"Well, I don't have any solid proof for what I'm going to tell you, but I think I'm on the right track: As you correctly assumed, the whole story started with the merger of the two companies. For an uninformed outsider, it looked like a logical progression, a friendly agreement between two companies that complemented each other and that had co-operated successfully on various projects in the past."

"But that's not..."

"Please let me finish. I deliberately said this was the picture they wanted to present to the public."

"Exactly. Before the merger, we had virtually no contact with them at all." Kaja could not refrain from commenting.

"Apparently, the original situation was like this: PC Lux Solutions had very talented and highly motivated employees. The company generated enough income to keep it afloat, but not enough to expand its operation. This was why they kept looking for investors and possible partners. Qubus had a lot of money, but serious problems in delivering orders on time. Although their finances were healthy, they were cutting corners on salaries and staff incentives."

"Which makes it difficult to recruit competent people. Take Google as a prime example. They do it right." Kaja mumbled as she realised where Simon's story was going.

"That's right. And it explains the low morale and ruthlessness of some of their staff.."

"Such as Little Freddy."

"Such as Little Freddy. You would've thought this was their chance to clear up their act, but unfortunately their top management is no better than the lower ranks. As they say: Like father like son. After Qubus failed in a take-over bid for PC Lux Solutions..."

"Why did they fail?"

"PC Lux Solutions didn't have any debts, so they were not under any pressure to sell. Their only problem was that they didn't have enough cash to expand without external help. They were determined not to sell. I presume - and now we're really just speculating - that they've entered into some form of contract to determine future co-operation and to establish who will take the lead under which circumstances."

"I'm sorry, now you've lost me. This sounds terribly complicated." Kaja interrupted him.

"OK, let's use an example. Let's say both sides agreed to meet certain deadlines in their work."

"Well, it should go without saying..."

"Yes, but that's not the point. Listen: what if they had agreed that the more deadlines you miss, the bigger the other partner's share in the decision-making process becomes."

"That wouldn't be a bad arrangement. I don't see what you're getting at..." Simon waited for Kaja to catch up with him. "Oh, I see what you meant about low morale. All they needed to do was to make it look as if the former PC Lux employees were delivering bad results for Qubus to become the sole owners of the partnership by the end of the year. And it wouldn't cost them a penny." She shook her head. "That's incredibly clever."

"No, I wouldn't call it clever. If they carry on like this, they will have lost all their good staff by the end of the year and thereby the real value of PC Lux. But our clever managers may well have overlooked this unimportant detail."

Lost in thought, Kaja played with her empty glass. "Or they're just speculating on selling the business. They could do that, once they secured the majority vote, couldn't they?"

"That's true. It hadn't occurred to me. But they'd have to act quickly, before anyone gets wind of the fact that they've messed up so many projects over the year."

Kaja was thinking. "I've just had an idea, but I'd have to check it out first. Damn, I haven't got access to the system any more." She nervously drummed her fingers on the table top.

"What's your idea?" Simon wanted to know.

"I'm not sure, but I seem to remember that all those projects that went wrong were internal ones, which means that an outsider wouldn't necessarily know about them."

"Perhaps they're not so stupid after all."

"It gets even better. If all the faulty programs were manipulated in the same way as mine, the correct code would still be available. Once 'those responsible' - such as me - are sacked, they can quickly replace the faulty sections with the original programming code for a perfect result."

"I knew it was a good idea to meet you." Simon grinned. "I couldn't have come up with this all by myself."

Kaja beamed. "It feels good to finally solve the mystery, if only in small steps. I was just thinking: we may have until Monday to make a copy of some of my code that they've tampered with, and then do it again when they've put it back in order."

"But it won't get us anywhere. If we confront them with the evidence, they'll just claim they've put right what you've done wrong." Simon objected.

"Hm, you're right." Disheartened, Kaja leaned back in her chair.

"Hey, don't give up so easily. As a programmer, you should be used to searching for solutions."

"Thanks for the encouragement."

"I have a feeling the real evidence is in the contract. If my assumptions are correct and we can prove our suspicion that several other PC Lux employees experienced similar problems, we could establish a pattern."

"It could be a start."

"Our problem is that the contract was nowhere to be found on the server."

"On the server? You mean..." she looked at him waiting for an answer.

""Exactly." Simon couldn't help a little, satisfied smile.

"You hacked into the company server?"

"Yes, we did. Not me personally, I don't know enough about these things, but one of my colleagues is an absolute ace when it comes to snooping around other people's networks."

"I'd love to be his apprentice for a day or two." Kaja grinned.

"You're very welcome. I told you: you can come over and see us any time."

"I'll certainly take you up on the offer. Time is not an issue for me any more." Suddenly, her expression turned serious again. "But first things first: how're you planning to get your hands on that contract?"

"I think I'll pay the inner sanctum of your former employer a visit and you can to help me."

"Help you? It'd be my pleasure, but I don't even have access myself any more." she replied perplexed.

"You don't?" Simon raised his eyebrows to give his next revelation more weight before presenting her with a fake ID badge that looked very convincingly like her old original one.

"You made a copy!?!"

"Of course I did. That's what I needed to borrow yours for."

"Now that you mention borrowing: I still don't quite understand how you gained access to my flat." Kaja challenged him.

"It's a trade secret." he replied cheekily. "Let's talk about the badge again..."

"... and quickly change the subject."

"It's been issued for a lady called Calamity Jane, not for you."

"How did you do that?"

"Well, we thought once we'd hacked into the system, we might as well register a new employee for them."

Kaja shook her head in disbelief. "OK, I see you got it sorted. When are you planning to make your move?" she wanted to know.

"First, I want to try and tie up a few loose ends. I'll let you know. Although..."

"Yes?"

"I'd prefer it if you came with us. It's not our normal practice, but you look like you can keep your nerves under pressure. And you've already done it, all by yourself, I understand."

Well, he understood wrong. Kaja thought back to her night-time caper with Lance and how invaluable his help had been. But this was hardly something she could share with Simon. So she let him continue.

"It would make things much easier if we had someone with sufficient local knowledge with us. Of course, we could get hold of the floor plans, but they wouldn't save us from nasty surprises."

"OK, count me in. But I still have one important question waiting for an answer: what happened to Max?"

"If I were you, I would make a mental note of everything you've observed so far. But don't get too worried about him. If I remember correctly, you went AWOL as well when you visited your grandmother for a couple of days, didn't you?"

"Maybe you're right." Kaja agreed but wasn't fully convinced. She had an uneasy feeling in her stomach when she thought of Max. That feeling told her something was terribly wrong. She sighed. For the moment, all she could do was wait for his call and keep her eyes and ears peeled. Then she suddenly had a thought.

"I could ask Thea to check for me if I'm right with my theory about the spoilt projects. And she could also find out what happened to the employees that were assigned to them, without raising too many suspicions."

"Good idea. But try not to communicate by e-mail. You never know who else might be reading them."

She looked at him slightly insulted, as if to say: 'I'm not a complete idiot, you know.'

Simon was quick to apologise: "I know you weren't born yesterday, but sometimes one can forget the most obvious things."

"Look, your lover-boy's finally turned up." she suddenly heard Lance's voice in her head.

"My... who?" It took her so much by surprise that she made the mistake of speaking aloud, earning herself a strange look from Simon. "Don't worry, I was just talking to myself." Luckily, Tim's arrival stopped her from making even more a fool of herself.

"Hey, you two, how's the conspiracy going?" he wanted to know.

"Hi, come over, take a seat." Simon got up and the two men patted each other on the back. Then Tim bent down, gave Kaja a kiss on the cheek and a casual hug. "Hi, long time no see."

"Yes, in the meantime, my life's been turned upside down." she joked to cover her embarrassment.

"You're blushing, you're blushing!" the dragon sang in her head, inaudible to the others.

"That's not true." she hissed, although her burning ears told a different story.

"Is there something wrong with you or are you still talking to yourself?" Simon was starting to get worried.

"Something like that."

"Oh my, your head's all over the place. I'd better leave you in peace." Lance realised.

"Brilliant idea." Kaja replied, this time telepathically. "What're you having?" Kaja asked her two friends and got up to go to the bar.

"I'll have another Guinness."

"Make that two." Tim added. They both watched her walk off. "You got yourself an amazing woman there." Simon finally said when she was out of earshot.

"Hm, I haven't got her yet." Tim replied with a decidedly impatient tone in his voice. "And anyway, I'm sure she'd be delighted if she could hear us talk like that: 'Got myself a woman.' As if I was dragging her to my cave like a Neanderthal." Tim shook his head in frustration. "Perhaps I should try that. At least she'd find it difficult to run away."

"I've never seen you so impatient." Simon watched his friend from the corner of his eye.

Tim tried to rub the stress from his face. "I know, I know. It's because I've never met anyone giving me so many mixed messages. I guess it's got something to do with my profession and me being away so often. She's somewhat traumatised by her family. I'll be around for another three weeks at the most. Then I'm off to Iceland for a photo shoot, standing in for a colleague who's sick. I wasn't sure whether to take it on, but I couldn't resist."

"And now you're wondering whether it's worth making a pass at her?"

"Yeah, I guess..."

At this point, Kaja came back. "I thought the bar staff would take forever. Could one of you two gentlemen give me a hand, please?"

"Of course." Tim jumped up and took the two pints of Guinness from her. In the meantime, Kaja had managed to compose herself and was now simply happy to see Tim. For the first time, she pushed all the 'What ifs' aside and decided to enjoy the evening. "So, and who's going to beat me at darts?"

After three enjoyable rounds of darts, which Kaja was pleased to have won by considerable margins, they left the pub and collected their dogs from Simon's car. Over by the lakeside, they released Zorro and Tsar who quickly disappeared in the undergrowth, apparently looking for scraps of food someone might have thrown away.

"Hey, come back." all three humans shouted in unison, but their four-legged friends were too busy to pay any attention.

"Let's just move on quickly. They'll soon follow us." Kaja suggested, knowing Zorro all too well. "Zurich Lake is great for walks in the autumn. Most people find the weather too chilly, so you have the footpaths all to yourself."

Boisterously, Kaja balanced on a low stone wall running along the shore.

Every so often, rustling noises indicated that the resident rats and mice had been disturbed in their nightly hunt for food. Zorro and Tsar were busy keeping the little rodents on their toes.

"Kaja, do you mind if I let Tim give you a lift home?" Simon asked.

"No, not at all. If Tim doesn't mind?" She looked at him hoping for a positive answer.

"No problem."

"In that case, I'll leave you two to it. Have to be up early in the morning." He gave Kaja a hug.

"I'll be in touch, OK?"

"Of course. See you soon. And many thanks for everything."

"You're welcome." Simon turned round and walked back to his car, followed by Tsar, who had finally decided to obey his master.

"Hey, I need to have a word with you. Why did you have to show me up at darts like that?" Tim said with a twinkle in his eye and tried to playfully ruffle her hair. At least this was his intention but somehow he couldn't let go of her silky dark hair and pulled her head slowly closer instead. For her part, she felt so excited and tense that she could hardly breathe and was mesmerised staring at the beautifully curved lines of his lips. She was all too aware of his hand at the back of her head and her senses were working overtime. She expected a playful kiss - and Tim had nothing more in mind. A little kiss wouldn't hurt. But all good intentions went out of the window as soon as their lips met. A fire was raging in Kaja's stomach and she dug her fingernails into the fabric of his jacket. His stubble tickled her cheek and she started to bite his lower lip, tenderly at first but then with more and more passion, which in turn prompted him to explore her mouth more deeply. Kaja could no longer think rationally and snuggled up to him even closer. Tim pressed her against the rough trunk of an old tree and his mouth felt glowing hot on her skin, starting at her lips, then wandering to her ear and down the side of her neck. Now it was Kaja's turn to take the initiative. She took his face in her hands and searched for his lips again. He smelled so good. She couldn't get enough of him and tried to find the naked skin under his jacket, which wasn't an easy task in this cold weather. Eventually, she gave up the attempt and giggled.

"What's so funny?" Tim wanted to know, his nose still buried in her dark hair.

"Too many clothes."

"Too many clothes?"

"Yes, you're wrapped up in too many layers."

He took her hands in his. They were ice-cold, although the rest of her body was burning hot. He grinned. "Perhaps not a bad idea. Your fingers are too cold."

She dryly replied: "That would've been the least of your problems. -

Phew..." She exhaled audibly.

"Yes, you're right." He straightened his hair. They smiled at each other, embarrassed and unsure what to do next. Zorro used the opportunity to look for Kaja's attention, poking his nose at her. Grateful for the distraction, she bent down and tickled his ears.

"Hey, big boy, are you done chasing all the rats and mice in the area?" Zorro barked as if he wanted to say something. "Alright, we're coming." She apologised to Tim: "He hasn't had his dinner yet. It makes him restless."

Tim took the hint. He nodded and simply said: "Let's go home then." Kaja was glad he seemed to be relaxed. She casually linked her arm with his and desperately tried to sort out her thoughts, which wasn't easy with all those hormones still playing havoc in her body. Eventually, she decided to stick to the original plan and simply enjoy the evening.

They walked back to her flat without saying a word. At the door, Kaja was unsure whether to ask him in or not. Tim relieved her of making a decision. "Are you OK now? I'll have to be off, want to drive back to Bern tonight and it's rather late already." Now it had become clear that they wouldn't continue where they had stopped earlier on, Kaja felt slightly disappointed.

'Don't be silly!' she told herself. 'Just an hour ago, you were not even sure you wanted this to happen.' - "Have a safe journey." she said and gave him a quick, innocent peck on his cheek before hastily getting out of the car.

'What a narrow escape.' she thought when suddenly she heard his voice: "Haven't you forgotten something?"

"Zorro!" she shouted turning red with embarrassment. She opened the back door to release Zorro from the boot. "Take care of yourself." she said to Tim before resolutely closing the door again and walking away.

'Nice try.' Tim was angry with himself. First he had complained to Simon that he didn't know what do to and then he had pounced on Kaja at the very first opportunity. He had no idea whether this was going to benefit or harm his long-term prospects. The choice of words made him smile. He was quite sure she had enjoyed what had happened between them. But perhaps she too felt as if lightning had struck. 'Let's see the positive side of it. Now she can clearly see what she's missing out on.' He couldn't help this typical macho thought. And he didn't even feel ashamed. Instead, he had a satisfied grin on his face all the way back home.

"And, did you have a good evening?" Lance wanted to know with a knowing look in his face.

"Erm, yes I did. I hope you weren't spying on me?"

"Me? Spying on you? I don't have to. Seeing you grinning like a Cheshire cat can only mean one thing..."

"And what would that be?" Kaja snapped at him. She still found it confusing that this dragon could read her like an open book. Where had her right to privacy gone since he had turned up? she asked herself feeling half angry, half amused and dropped on the sofa. She was too happy to get upset.

"I know what a girl looks like when she's been kissed." he said, now in a bad mood himself. Disturbed by the tone in his voice, Kaja looked at him. "Oh, don't look at me like that. I do realise this Tim must be good for you, but that's no reason for me to be happy. Maybe later." he added with a sour face. "Much later."

"Perhaps in about 724 years? time." she pulled his leg.

The corner of his mouth started to twitch. "Perhaps." In the meantime, he had sat down next to her and was seemingly occupied watching his feet dangling in the air. Kaja poked his side. With time, she had learned how to focus her mind in such a way that she didn't reach into thin air when trying to touch him. "Hey, I'm ticklish."

"I know." she said and continued until they were wrangling on the floor laughing hysterically.

He put up his hand in surrender. "OK, OK, I'll be happy again."

Kaja giggled uncontrollably. She helped him to his feet and asked:

"Better now?"

"Much better."

"Good, you'll always be my dragon, I hope."

"Don't worry, you can't get rid of me that easily." he reassured her.

Back to being serious again, she said: "By the way, you sound more convinced than I am."

"Convinced of what? I can't follow you."

"That Tim is good for me. I'm not so sure about that."

"Women..." Lance rolled his eyes.

"What's that supposed to mean?"

"Well, you come home as bright as a button, obviously had a good time with him and all you can do is worry about possible problems that may never come to pass, spoiling all your good mood. Why don't you move your cute butt to bed and stay on cloud nine for a little longer?"

"Oh, if only it was that easy..." Kaja started.

"Yes, it is that easy, I assure you. Problems, especially hypothetical problems, will still be there tomorrow. The only difference is: if you switch back to your happy mode now, you'll be all fresh and relaxed in the morning. And as an added bonus, you may have the memory of some hot dreams stored up for a rainy day."

Kaja opened her mouth to say something but closed it again. This dragon could be very convincing when he put his mind to it. "So I'd better heed your advice." she laughed.

"Good, now we've cheered each other up, let's go to bed and enjoy our happy dreams." he replied with a twinkle in his eye.

23

Something kept ringing in her ears. Annoyed, Miri pulled the duvet over her head and wished for the hundredth time since she had moved in to this flat that the walls were not so thin you could hear your neighbours' telephone ring at the crack of dawn. It really wasn't doing her headache any good. Would somebody answer that damn phone, please? Frustrated, she rubbed her sticky eyelids and sat up. Suddenly she realised that it wasn't a phone, it was the door bell. Bugger! She had agreed to join Kaja for a walk this morning. Somehow, the idea had seemed much better on Thursday evening than it did now. Miri kicked off her duvet, which Chili, who had been waiting patiently on top of it for her to wake up, greeted with an angry hiss. Disgruntled, he jumped off the bed and disappeared into the tiny kitchen.

When the door bell rang again, she mumbled angrily "On my way.", ran to the window, ripped it open and shouted: "Kaja? 's that you?" In the street, she could see Kaja taking a step backward and looking up to her flat.

"Hello? Ready to go?"

"Erm, almost. Wait, I'll drop the key down so you can wait up here for me to get finished." she croaked.

A broad grin appeared on Kaja's face. "You do that." She dropped the key from the window and Kaja caught it skilfully. Miri didn't wait for her to get into the house, but started a hectic search for some clothes and took a shower, hoping this might help her to rise from the dead more quickly.

When she came back from the bathroom, barefoot and in jeans and t-shirt, an aromatic smell of freshly brewed coffee filled her flat and fresh bread rolls were laying on the tiny kitchen table. Miri quickly rubbed her short curls dry and sat down on a folding chair opposite Kaja. "I woke up in hell and the shower must have teleported me to heaven." She tasted the hot coffee. "This certainly is heavenly. I have to remember the trick. Or is it part of the dragon service?"

Kaja laughed. "You can't train a dragon to do that. No, since I realised I'd woken you up and you had to have your shower first, I took my time to get the bread rolls. See them as a peace offering for being woken up so abruptly. And when I saw you had Hawaiian coffee in your cupboard, I couldn't resist making a pot of it."

"I know. It's one of my little sins, this Kona Coffee. Shockingly expensive, but also exceedingly good." She took another sip and closed her eyes enjoying the taste.

"Got home late last night?" Kaja enquired casually.

"You could say that." Miri mumbled into her coffee mug. In fact, she had hoped to meet someone to take her mind off the man she had met on Thursday. Or to bump into him again, although she didn't even know his full name. She had been waiting for one of the two things to happen and realised she must be in a rather sorry state. She had been hanging out at her favourite bar all night and emptied her wallet in return for alcoholic drinks. Luckily, there hadn't been too much money in that wallet, otherwise she would have felt much worse this morning. She sighed and shook off the unpleasant thought. "And you? What did you do yesterday?" she asked Kaja who was waiting patiently for her to finish the coffee.

"It's a long story, believe me. I'd better tell you on the way." Kaja grinned. "My day was extremely eventful."

"Well, let's go then. I'm keen to hear your story."

As soon as they were sitting in the car, Miri fired questions at Kaja who filled her in on the business side of things, adding the conclusions she and Simon had come to as well as a few other details Miri had not heard about yet.

"There's something I don't understand." Miri said when they got out of the car.

"What's that?" Kaja asked, expecting a question about the strange things going on in the company. She released Zorro from the car and the dog joyfully jumped around them barking. Lance gave him a disapproving look, but otherwise kept unusually quiet, pretending to be invisible.

"Aren't you distressed about being sacked? What're you going to do?"

Kaja was still surprised herself that the dismissal didn't cause her any more distress. "To start with, I'm in a lucky position in that I've saved up a little bit of money to tide me over for a month or two, giving me time to decide what I want to do or at least to find another job. On top of that, I hadn't really enjoyed working at the company for the past six months or so. Of course, I had a few friends there, but I can always meet them outside work, if I want to." They turned onto a grassy forest path. The autumn air was refreshingly clear and the fallen leaves rustled under their feet.

"Yes, you can always meet them, especially those particularly important to you. And? Do you have an idea which company you're going to apply to?"

"Hm, not really. I know a few names in the industry I would be interested to work for. But I feel this unexpected dismissal is my chance to do something completely different."

"Hear, hear. The girl has actually discovered her intuition." the dragon

270

teased her in an attempt to finally get involved in the conversation.

"Go on, rub my nose in it." Kaja snapped. Turning back to Miri, she said: "What I wanted to say was: under normal circumstances, I'd never questioned whether the work I did was actually the kind of work I wanted to do. Perhaps I would have woken up one morning in fifteen years time, asking myself if this was it, my whole life."

"But it was your free decision to choose this education and this job. Or wasn't it?" Miri was still not able to follow her.

"Well, yes. And I do enjoy my work. But that doesn't say anything about whether I want to spend my entire life doing programming, whether I even want to be employed in a big company."

"What would be your alternatives?"

"Get further training, get into computer games, work freelance, I don't know..."

"Make scented candles, grow herbs..."

"What?" Kaja stopped walking so abruptly that Miri almost bumped into her.

"Watch out what you're doing." the dragon grumbled. Zorro, who sensed something was wrong, came back from his excursion into the undergrowth and barked excitedly.

From a small path to their side, a slim rider on a small red horse approached them in a fast trot. She reined her horse to a walk, but it did not seem to like it. It did slow down but then nervously pranced on the spot. Kaja grabbed Zorro by his collar and pulled him to the verge by the side of the path. Luckily, he had stopped yapping.

"Sorry, you can't go any further here. This is all private property." The lady barked at the small group in an unfriendly tone. "And I'd appreciate it if you could keep your dragon under control. He makes my horse nervous." With these words, she skilfully turned her horse on its hind legs and sped off. Miri ducked just in time to avoid the pebbles being kicked in her direction.

"Oh my, she was in a foul mood." Kaja was outraged. "Who does she think she is?"

"Erm, Kaja?" Miri interrupted her with a perplexed look on her face.

"What?" Kaja was still in full swing, ranting about the unpleasant encounter.

"I hate to break the news to you, but..."

"What do you want?" she looked at Miri impatiently.

"I think we've just met the other sister."

"My sister? I don't have a sister... Or do you mean...?"

"Exactly, our third dragon sister." For a moment, they were both quiet. Only the jays kept arguing in the trees as if nothing had happened. Finally Kaja composed herself: "I don't believe it. And I had expected the third one to be just as nice and easy-going as you!"

"Maybe she is."

"Hello? Have you just missed something? This one was anything but nice."

"I know, but perhaps she had her reasons. It's not every day you meet a dragon. Perhaps she's confused."

"That's not the impression I had of her." Kaja fretted.

Kaja was in fact not too far off the mark. The woman was so upset about the intruders in "her" forest that she did not realise she had just seen a real dragon. Strictly speaking, it was not her forest, of course, even if she had just claimed it was. It didn't matter. The important point was that nobody would normally stray that far into it.

"Don't you think it's unfair, Foks, that there's no place for us to have some peace?"

The chestnut gelding twitched his left ear in her direction, but in the meantime kept focussed on a dangerous-looking tree stump. The women anticipated the evasive manoeuvre and applied slight pressure with her leg to stop him from baulking and to steady his nerves. Absent-mindedly, she patted his neck. She did not have a clue what those two young women, their neurotic dog and that obnoxious shiny blue dragon were doing in her forest. There was nothing exciting to be seen here. She frowned. Something seemed wrong when she thought back to the group. Suddenly she stopped her horse. Foks snorted indignantly. 'A dragon? Oh my, I think it's time for me to see a shrink. My paranoia seems to be getting out of hand.' The little horse again twitched one of his ears, this time the other one, and reared his head. She shook her head in disbelief and signalled Foks to move on.

What the woman had not noticed was the dragon sitting on that fearsome tree stump in front of them and interrogating her horse. "Hello, I'm Lance, a dragon."

"Ah, thanks for letting me know." the chestnut snorted with contempt. "I'd never have worked that out myself."

Lance decided to ignore the sarcasm. After all, he had a mission to accomplish.

"I was wondering: What's the name of your rider?" he enquired casually.

The horse looked at him suspiciously. "What business is it of yours? She's my rider." he insisted. "And now I'm going to take her home safely, away from you." The chestnut was about to rear but a firm press of his rider's legs and her calming words stopped him from doing so.

"Now that you're still here, you could at least tell me her name. I'll leave you in peace if you do, I promise" - 'At least for now.' he added in his thoughts.

The horse flattened his ears. "Keep your hands off Sierra, or you'll have me to deal with."

"I admire your loyalty." the dragon replied calmly. "And thank you."

Foks reared his head and trotted off. Lance watched horse and rider disappear into the forest. Praise to the Great Dragon that she wasn't called Nicole or any other run-of-the-mill name. Sierra was definitely something for him to go on.

"Lance?" Kaja turned full circle, looking for her dragon. Of course he was notably absent when she needed him most. "That's so typical of him. Just when it gets exciting and we need his advice, he simply disappears."

"What're we going to do?" Miri asked.

"What do you mean?"

"Well, obviously, our lives are somehow intertwined via this dragon story."

"We know that already. What's your point?" Kaja didn't know why she was sounding so edgy.

"Now we've found our third sister, but we don't even know her name or where she lives." Miri explained patiently.

"You're right." Kaja admitted reluctantly. "Somehow, this encounter was just one surprise too many for me in the past 24 hours. I find it hard to cope with change anyway, so I'm sorry if I sounded a bit off just now."

"Has anything else happened that you haven't had the chance to tell me yet?" Miri asked in surprise, deliberately ignoring Kaja's last sentence.

"Well yes, it has." Kaja replied with an awkward smile. "Let's turn back. Perhaps we can take a sandwich stop while trying to figure out how to find this mysterious horse lady."

"OK, I like the sound of food."

"Me too." Lance could be heard coming from nowhere.

"What's that now?" Kaja joked. "Are we having a conference call in dragon fashion?"

Miri had to giggle. In a much better mood, the three of them went back to the car.

They bought some bread rolls in one of the few surviving small bakeries in Zurich and took them home to Kaja's flat, as they were not in the mood to search for another good place to have their lunch. "I didn't realise I was so hungry again." Miri said with her mouth full.

Kaja tried to swallow her food first before replying: "That's because you're not used to outdoor exercise and fresh air."

"That's true." Miri said with a guilty face. "I don't go outside as often as I should."

"As I want to." Kaja corrected her.

"Hey, that's my job." Miri pulled her leg.

"What is?"

"To tell you what to do and what not to do, at least with regards to your intuition."

"And I thought it was his job?" Kaja asked nodding vaguely in the direction where Lance was sitting with a glass of elderberry brandy.

"Well." Miri seemed a bit reluctant to reply. "Perhaps it was but it seems he's passed the task on to me."

"As long as you don't boss me around..." Kaja gave her a friendly tease.

Relieved that Kaja had taken her revelation so lightly, she decided to dig deeper and get some more information out of her. "So come on, tell me what else happened to you yesterday, apart from getting the sack?"

"We took a walk near Lake Türler..." Kaja started.

"That's not what I meant." Miri interrupted her, frowning.

"I know, I just wanted to see how far I can stretch your patience." Kaja grinned. "Later, I met Simon. I've told you already, haven't I?"

"Yes you have. What happened next?"

"Tim had promised to come as well, but he had some other business to attend to first. He finally turned up about ten." Kaja was so slow giving her account that the normally placid Miri felt she wanted to nudge her to speed things up. "Tim. Is that the guy you made the third candle for?"

"Yes, that's him." Kaja's face had taken on a dreamy expression.

Miri looked over to Lance: "Do you think I can make her go any faster if I give her a good shake?" She was almost bursting with curiosity.

"You can give it a try, but I wouldn't bet on it. I had to worm it out of her last night myself. And the result was less than meagre."

"At least now I know she slept in her own bed." Miri stated.

"Can you please stop talking about me as if I wasn't here?"

"You are not really here. You're somewhere in a pink haze of dreams." Miri retorted glibly.

Kaja raised her hands in surrender and had to laugh. "Alright, I'll try to get to the point. First I literally destroyed them at darts." Kaja allowed herself a satisfied grin at this point in her story. "And then we went for a walk with our dogs."

"I haven't heard anything to justify the pink haze yet." Miri interrupted her impatiently.

"If you'd stopped butting in you would've heard the rest already." Kaja teased her. "At some point, Simon discreetly said his goodbyes and Tim and I kept walking on, all by ourselves." Her eyes had taken on that dreamy expression again. "And then he kissed me. - We kissed." she corrected herself.

"And?"

"Nothing. He took me home and that was that."

"OK, but did you enjoy it? Did the angels sing and make your heart skip a beat? Come on, tell me. I want to know it all." Miri was all too aware that her own life wasn't full of romance at the moment.

"The angels didn't sing. It was more like the eruption of a volcano. Practically uncontrollable. Fantastic. Frightening! And as far as my heart was concerned..." Kaja sighed.

"Here we go again: She lets her head do all the work when talking about her heart." Lance commented without being asked.

"Hey, that's not fair. I do listen to my emotions. But I won't easily confuse lust with something more important. Especially if my head knows that my heart might be in danger."

"Oh my, you poor thing. You lucky girl." Miri had to admit that she felt a touch of jealousy. Of course, she didn't begrudge Kaja her romance. But she would have liked to get some for herself.

"I really don't know what to think."

"Exactly, that's the point. Perhaps you shouldn't think at all about it." Lance grumbled.

"Just enjoy what's happening to you. You'll have enough time to worry later, if you ever need to." Lance gave Miri an appreciative look and took another indulgent gulp of his elderberry brandy.

"If you want to become a dragon's apprentice, you're in the right place and seem to have the right qualifications."

Kaja gave him a glowering look but then turned back to Miri "You're right and I'm trying. Last night was the result of just enjoying and thinking as little as possible. It remains to be seen whether that was a wise strategy."

"What's new. She's always doubting herself."

"If you don't have any constructive contributions to make, you might as well go back to your den." Kaja snapped at him getting fed up with his wisecracks at her expense. Offended, Lance instantly curled up and shrank to his cat-sized shape.

"Now you've hurt his feelings." Miri was concerned. "But I know where you're coming from. My dragon girl also used to stretch my patience to the limit. - Did he like his candle?"

"I haven't given it to him yet. I didn't think I was going to see him when Simon turned up on his own."

"I'm sure you're seeing him again soon." Miri tried to cheer her up.

"Hm, sure." Kaja said vaguely. "I'm going to pay Simon's company a visit soon. Once I'm in Bern, I might as well pop round to see Tim, too."

'Hear, hear. Kaja must have given this more thought than she cares to admit.' Miri thought. But she didn't want to keep harping on and changed the subject.

Miri grabbed the last remaining bread roll and gave it a good inspection.

"Are you going to eat it or give it a scientific analysis?"

"I was trying to figure out how best to share it. Unless you don't want any?"

"You're a real glutton, you are. Have it all if you want to. But if you only want half of it, I can lend you a special tool."

"A special tool?"

"Well, you know, the thing that some people call a knife. I'm sure I have one somewhere."

"Oh you..." Miri laughed and threw a cushion at her.

"A pillow fight? Can I join in?" Lance asked and quickly grew back to his normal size.

"No, you can't." Kaja put him in his place. "And don't take it the wrong way. I have something important to discuss with Miri."

"I'm surprised you two never run out of words."

"That's because we're girls." Miri replied in her sweetest voice.

"As if I hadn't noticed." the dragon mumbled, but only very quietly, to be on the safe side.

"What did you want to talk about? Our dragon sister?"

"No." Kaja replied, but then corrected herself. "Or maybe, but later. First, I would like to ask you something. Just before our memorable encounter with that so-called sister, we were talking about my professional future. And you said something I didn't quite understand."

"Yes, I know what you mean. I only added herbs and scented candles to your list. They're also things you know a lot about and enjoy dealing with. At least that was my impression the last time I came to see you."

"Hm." Lost in her thoughts, Kaja got up and went over to the large window, looking out on her patio. "You're right." she eventually said and returned to her place on the sofa. "But what am I going to do with candles?

Do I really want to move to France?"

"Who says you need to move to France? If people buy those things over there, I'm sure they'll do so here as well."

Kaja gave Miri a doubtful look. "And where am I going to grow my herbs?"

"Why not in your garden?"

Now Kaja had to laugh. "As much as I admire your optimism, this garden is definitely too small and too shady for such a project."

"That's a shame." Disappointed, Miri sank back into the cushions. But she wasn't going to give up that easily. "Well, in that case you'll have to move." was her pragmatic advice.

"Move? Now hold your horses. That's definitely one change too many. I love my flat!"

"OK then." Miri gave in. "But promise me to keep it in mind, will you?"

Kaja grimaced. "That's exactly the problem. I'm afraid I won't get the idea out of my mind now. But let's move on to the next issue on our list: our sister. Or more precisely: the woman we think is our sister." Kaja took a deep breath. "I have no idea why this morning's encounter upset me so much. You and I get along so well, why shouldn't the same be possible with her?"

"Oh, yes, sisters are always bound to be best mates!" Lance could be heard saying in a sarcastic voice.

"How many sisters do you have?" Miri was interested to know.

"Seven." the dragon proudly announced. "And we argue every day if we find time for it."

"That's part of your character. You like arguing." Kaja said. "Can we get back to our subject now?"

"If you carry on being so hard with me, I won't tell you what I've found out." Miri had been listening to their banter with fascination, but now it was her turn to interfere. Delighted that at least one of them was prepared to listen, he started to give his account of the conversation with the horse.

"Sierra? What kind of name is that?"

"I don't have a clue." Miri said. "But your dragon is right. We're lucky she's got such a rare name. It'll make her easier to find."

"That's true." Kaja pondered. Curiosity had got the better of her. "I'll try and see what I can find about her on the net."

"Suppose we find out where she lives. What shall we do then?"

Kaja had not got that far in her thoughts yet. It hadn't been more than two minutes ago that she had been simply annoyed about the strange woman. Now she shrugged her shoulders undecidedly. "I don't know. But I'm sure we'll think of something. Perhaps my invaluable dragon can come up with an idea." she said in an affectionate tone and tickled him under his wing.

"It's high time you realise how irreplaceable I am." he grumbled, pouting.

"Are you staying for dinner?" she wanted to know from Miri. "Is it already time for food again?" Miri was shocked.

"No, not yet. I just wanted to know because I need to do some shopping." Relieved, Miri stretched and said. "Thanks for the invitation, but I think it's time for me to go home now. Tidying up and things. Let's talk again next week. Perhaps we'll know more by then."

"OK, in that case, I'll go for a jog. Lance, are you joining me?"

"Oh... well, no, I still haven't recovered from today's exertion." was his lame excuse.

"Lazy bones. I should know you by now."

24

Kaja spent the next few days searching for Sierra with little success. She had been able to compile masses of data about the name, even found 110 entries in the telephone book, but was unable to narrow her search down. In between, she went for long walks, mulled over job ideas in her head or even allowed herself to miss Tim for a few minutes here and there. But before long, she forced herself to abandon those thoughts and to concentrate on her main task.

By Tuesday night, she was so frustrated with her fruitless investigations that she decided to pick up the phone and call Simon. "I was wondering." she said after they had finished their usual small talk. "Do you know how to locate people?"

"Yes, that's what we do for a living. Are you in trouble? Does somebody owe you money?"

"No." she hesitated. "It's rather a private matter."

"Is it about a man?" he asked her straight. After all, he didn't want to help Kaja getting into an affair with anyone else but Tim. It may have been childish, but his loyalty was firmly with his friend.

"No, I've lost touch with a woman I know." Kaja felt the little white lie was justified. After all, she was trying to find her sister. "I used to know her, but I don't have a clue where she's living now or what her surname is."

"But you do have a Christian name?"

"Yes, but that's about all the info I have."

Simon started to take some notes but then had a better idea. "Didn't you say you wanted to visit us and see how we do our work?"

"Yes, I'd love to."

"Why don't you come over and see me tomorrow? I can show you what to do and you can do your own research here. What do you think?"

"That would be great. There's no better way to learn about your job."

"Did you manage to get hold of your boss?"

Kaja was embarrassed to admit she hadn't tried to reach him for the past few days. "No problem. As we said: there's no need to get worried too much. See you tomorrow at ten." Simon said and finished their conversation.

Kaja hung up and, before she lost all courage, dug out her mobile to send Tim a text: "Do you want to take me out for dinner? I'm in Bern tomorrow."

Kaja's heart jumped with excitement. She tried to convince herself that this was only due to the prospect of seeing Simon's workplace and solving the mystery around Sierra. Of course, it had nothing to do with Tim, absolutely nothing.

"You know, if self-deception was an Olympic sport, you'd win a gold medal." Lance teased her. But she was wise enough not to get into an argument with him again.

'What am I going to wear tomorrow?' she panicked.

"That's certainly the most important question, considering that you're having a meeting at a security company, followed by an unimportant dinner with Tim..." Lance commented. He was lying on Kaja's bed watching her stand in front of the wardrobe, undecided what to wear.

"Oh, shut up, you! You're not helping at all." How stupid of her to expect fashion advice from a dragon. She might as well have dressed like a medieval damsel.

"I heard that." Lance seemed rather amused.

"I'll give Miri a call. She'll be more reasonable than you." Kaja decided.

"Would you mind coming round? I have an emergency here." Kaja asked her on the phone.

"OK, I'll come over. Have to go out later anyway."

"You're going out?" Kaja looked at her watch and was confused. It was almost eight o'clock. "You're quite a night owl."

"Mh." was Miri's vague response. "So, do you want me to come round or not?"

"Yes, please. You're a star." Kaja was relieved.

Just fifteen minutes later, Miri was at her door. "That was quick." Kaja said, pleasantly surprised.

"So, what's your emergency?" Miri wanted to know and followed Kaja into the flat.

"Oh, you'd better come through to the bedroom. I'm hoping Tim will take me out for dinner tomorrow."

"What do you mean: 'you're hoping'?"

"Well, I invited myself by text - but I haven't got a reply yet."

"And she's been waiting for ages, at least half an hour..." Lance taunted her, still lying on the bed. Kaja poked her tongue out at him and Miri had to suppress a smile.

"Why are you going to Bern tomorrow?"

"Oh, sorry, I was so excited I forgot to tell you."

"You're excited? I wouldn't have guessed." Lance interrupted her again.

"OK, OK, I am excited and it's all your fault." she claimed and poked her finger into Lance's chest.

"My fault? Why's that?" he protested.

"It was you who told me to simply enjoy the whole thing."

"Yes, I did, but only after you started to have a crush on that Tim. What I did was just damage limitation." he defended himself.

"Can you two perhaps stop squabbling now?" Miri intervened. "It would give us a chance to solve the fashion problem." She pulled a pair of dark blue jeans from the wardrobe as well as a silver grey top with long sleeves and a deep neckline. "Try these." she said to Kaja and handed her the two garments.

Kaja gave them a doubtful look. "I can't even remember if I've ever worn this t-shirt before."

"Well then, it's high time." Miri advised her and resolutely pushed her into the bathroom.

"And? What do you think?" Kaja turned a full circle. The neckline almost stretched from shoulder to shoulder, nicely showing off her neck and collarbone area. The supple fabric fell loosely round her waist and hugged her soft body curves with its shiny colour. The jeans sat low on her waist and accentuated her well-trained bottom without flattening its shape.

"Well, look at that! I'd take you straight to bed if I was a man. Do you have any high heels?"

"I was rather thinking of my high boots. I can walk in them for longer if I really have to."

"I thought you wanted to go out for dinner, not for a walking holiday?"

"I'd like to be prepared for all eventualities." Kaja replied slightly embarrassed. In the meantime, Miri had delved into the depths of Kaja's wardrobe and now re-emerged with a shoulder-long, thin, green-blue scarf which she wound round Kaja's neck. "So, now put on your boots so that we can get the full picture."

She posed in front of her two friends again. "Perfect." Miri commented. "Casual, practical, but also cool and sexy."

"And what does my dragon advisor say?"

"Hm, as long as you keep your jacket on, you'll be alright." He replied in a foul mood.

Kaja had to smile. "If you find it too daring, it's definitely spot on! Thank you, Miri, I'd never have come to a decision without you."

"No problem. That's what sisters are for." Miri said, giving Kaja a hug.

"We're a good team. Can I offer you a cup of tea before you go?"

"Yes, why not? Now you can tell me what you're doing at Simon's."

"Of course," Kaja gave Lance an accusing look, "as we were interrupted earlier on."

"Strange how quickly I've got used to having a dragon around." Miri said as she and Lance held out their cups for Kaja to pour the tea.

"Let's see how quickly our sister gets used to him."

"Do you mean you've found out who she is and where she lives?"

Kaja pulled a face. "No, I tried but I'm stuck. That's why I called Simon earlier on. I know his company can locate people, so I'm going to the capital tomorrow to see him. You can think of Tim as being only my reward for a good day's work." Kaja giggled. "What are we going to do when we know where she lives? I mean, we can hardly ring her up and say: 'Hi, we're three dragon sisters. You're the third one. She'll think we're ripe for the loony bin. For a moment, I thought I was myself." Kaja voiced her concerns.

"I thought it might be better we pay her a visit and take Lance with us, just take her by surprise and confront her with the fact that she can see him. You can hardly miss him, can you? At least we can't."

"True, you found it quite easy to accept him. In fact, it was you who had to convince me to admit to his existence." Kaja remembered.

"Please keep me informed, whatever you do." Miri asked her. She got up and put her empty cup in the kitchen sink. "I'm sorry, but I'll have to leave you now." she said, taking a regretful look at her watch.

Kaja jumped up. "Yes, of course. And thank you for your emergency help." They gave each other a hug and even Zorro received his bit of TLC. Kaja watched her leave from the window. Where was Miri going so late on a Tuesday night? She looked to Lance for an answer. But he put on his most innocent face and was busy studying the bottom of his empty tea cup. By now, she knew her dragon well enough to understand that he had no intention of answering her question. She shrugged her shoulders. When they met again, she would just ask Miri. After all, she had pestered her long enough with her own problems. This was something that had to stop, she resolved.

In the meantime, Miri was on the way to her usual hangout and asked herself for at least the tenth time why she had interrupted yet another enjoyable evening with Kaja, only to look for a bloke to get off with. A psychologist could write a Ph.D. on me, she thought, angry with herself. But it was too late to have any doubts, she had arrived at the bar.

25

Kaja was on her way to Bern and - yet again - stuck in a traffic jam. She was late anyway. And she had not heard anything from Tim yet, which didn't help to improve her mood either. She turned up the volume, this time listening to an old Massive Attack CD. It was just the right music for the mood she was in. And for being stuck in traffic. What kind of relationship was this going to be with him living in Bern and her in Zurich? Sooner or later she'd go mad.

"He isn't that often in Bern anyway." Lance interrupted her thoughts. Obviously, he had been tapping into her mind. "You still don't get it: as long as you don't mark your thoughts clearly as private, I can hear you think just as loud and clear as if you were talking to me." Her shiny passenger defended himself.

"OK, I see. So it's not your fault."

"That's right."

"And how exactly is your statement supposed to cheer me up? Among other things, my biggest problem is that he's away so often. And whenever he's around, he's stuck in Bern."

"While you're chained irrevocably and for all eternity to Zurich." the dragon said pityingly, nodding his head in sympathy.

"Huh, what're you trying to tell me?" Irritated, Kaja turned her head to look at Lance and almost saw too late that the queue of cars in front of her had come to a standstill. She had to brake hard and narrowly avoided hitting the vehicle in front of her.

"Heavens, Girl! I won't get hurt in an accident, but I'd find it rather sad if you got smashed up in a car. Pull yourself together!"

"Then don't distract me with such touchy subjects." Kaja hissed at him, still in shock from the near miss herself.

Lance waited for his protégée to calm down and to gather her concentration before explaining: "All I wanted to say is: nothing and nobody is forcing you to live in Zurich. Now you're between jobs, it's an ideal time to assess where you might want to live. Or if you want to travel. Or Tim might want to move. Or..."

"Alright, I get the picture. I'm behaving as if my current situation was set in stone and I'm failing to realise that it is up to me to change it."

"Well... yes." the dragon replied, lost for words at the fact that Kaja had instantly understood what he was trying to say.

"Don't look at me like that." she snapped, watching him from the corner of her eye. "I do reflect on my future and I do remember some of the things we discuss, whether I like it or not." She had a cheeky smile on her face. "You are right, but my thoughts are going round in circles at the moment, particularly because there are so many changes in my life. Normally, even one tiny change can cause me a massive crisis. So, please cut me some slack. And yes: you are allowed to feel sorry for me."

"You would like that, wouldn't you?" Lance taunted her, although secretly he was immensely proud of her. He had intended to ask whether she had given Miri's suggestion any thought to making and selling candles. But he decided to let the subject of future plans rest for now.

"Do you think our plan will work? Trying to introduce you to our third sister?" she interrupted his thoughts.

"Hm, I don't see why it shouldn't work." he said with a shrug. "More precisely, I don't think she'll have much choice in the matter."

"Are we so convincing, Miri and I? Or are we just horrible?"

Lance laughed out loud. "No, you're not horrible. But try to remember: you weren't able to put up much resistance when you met me, and later Miri wasn't either."

"Yes, you're right." She went all tingly when she reminded herself that she was likely to find out more about Sierra soon. If she made it to Bern before the end of the day, she thought, nervously watching the cars in front of them.

Half an hour later, she finally pulled into the company car park at Cerberus Security Services. She found herself in front of an unassuming, large building somewhere on the industrial outskirts of Bern. She looked around, searching for the main entrance. Shrugging her shoulders, she let Zorro jump out of the car. Lance was still curled up on the back seat. "Aren't you coming with us?"

"Oh no, I'd rather have a little nap. Don't want to distract you on your mission."

"Good idea. Enjoy your time off, then."

She slammed the door and calmed Zorro down with a few reassuring words to stop him from jumping up at her excitedly. She decided to walk round the block to look for the entrance. "Hey big boy, do you know how to get in here?" she said without really expecting an answer. But Zorro instantly raced off. Kaja had no choice but to run after her dog. She turned a corner and found herself in front of a fence which marked a large area that was obviously part of the property. It consisted of a spacious lawn and several sections covered with wood chips, apparently intended for dog training. Adjoining the office block, she could see a few elongated wooden sheds. Zorro was yelping impatiently. He pressed his nose through the wire-mesh fence in an attempt to reach his fellow canines, which were roaming free in a separately fenced-off area. They had noticed the visitors already but only two of them thought the arrivals important enough to bark at. Kaja looked up and down the fence and found a gate with a bell-push which she pressed and waited. In the meantime, she put Zorro on his leash, just to be on the safe side. She didn't want him to get into trouble by being over-enthusiastic. Kaja waited a few more moments and was just about to wander off to look for another entrance, when the door to one of the sheds opened and an elderly man with long white hair tied up into a pony tail stuck his head out. "What're you doing here? This is private property." he grunted at her.

"Isn't this part of Cerberus? I'm looking for the entrance." As a precaution, she added: "I have an appointment with Simon." As soon as she mentioned Simon's name, the old man's grim face lit up.

"Kaja?"

"Yes, that's me."

"You can come through here, but please keep your dog on the leash for now. Later, he can play with the others." He briefly disappeared back into the shed, apparently in order to press the buzzer. Kaja pushed the gate and it opened with an audible click. Before she entered, she had to call Zorro to order, as he was all excited and wanted to storm in. Behind her, the gate closed silently before clicking shut again. With his long white hair, jeans and leather jacket, the old man looked like he had stepped straight out of a Western. He approached her, this time with a friendly smile on his face.

"Simon's told me a lot about you and Tim's mentioned you as well. Some strange things you got yourself into, I say."

Kaja was rather surprised by this sudden transformation after his initial unfriendly welcome, but she didn't have to wait long for an explanation.

"The main entrance is actually on the other side. They have a reception area there, with friendly staff and a coffee vending machine." He described these things as if they were located in another universe.

Perhaps for him they were, Kaja thought as she took a good look at him. "I'm not into customer service. I'm more into dogs. Good to see you've brought yours along." he smiled and, since he was talking to her as if he had known her for a long time, Kaja couldn't help but smile back. She assumed that her new acquaintance must be Simon's partner Josef, and his sudden mood swing was probably down to her mentioning Simon's name. This person was quite a character. She imagined he and Luc would get along like a house on fire.

As they reached the main entrance, Simon was just on his way out. "Hi Kaja, you've finally made it?"

"Yes, finally. I was stuck in traffic for ages."

"No problem, I got your texts and the traffic jam was even mentioned on the radio. There must have been a major hold-up. Listen, I've got to go out now, but I assume you'll be around for a while? It looks like you've successfully managed to make friends with Josef..."

"Why successfully?"

"Normally, he rips people's heads off first and asks questions later." Simon grinned.

"Someone's got to look after the place when you're out and about playing detective." Josef grumbled in return.

Simon turned back to Kaja. "When you and Josef are done, you can report to reception. Rosalind will take you upstairs to Toby. He can give you an introduction into searching for missing persons. I should be back by then."

"OK, see you later."

"Bye."

"So." Josef picked up the conversation. "Do you want to go upstairs straight away or would you like to see the dogs first. If your dog gets along with mine, they could play outside together."

"I'd like to see the dogs first. If Zorro can stay with you for the rest of the day, all the better."

An hour later, Kaja was sitting next to Toby in front of a computer and was amazed how quickly he was able to tap into various local authority networks. She was surprised to observe how easy it was. "Don't they use firewalls?"

"You'd be surprised how little protection our public services have in place to guard their secrets. Especially the smaller parishes are not up to speed. Yes, they often do have a simple firewall, but I'm a specialist and have top-of-the-range technology at my disposal." he proudly explained.

"And how do you become a hacker?" she wanted to know, listening to him with fascination.

"There's mainly two career paths if you want to become a hacker. For you, it wouldn't be a problem getting trained 'on the job'. You're quite computer-literate and can even do programming. That would be the clean solution."

"And the other one?"

He grinned. "Or you can do it my way and teach yourself everything you need. Eventually, you get caught when, in a fit of megalomania, you forget to cover your tracks. Your victim might offer you a job - or take you to court if you don't co-operate."

"I presume Simon offered you a job and you were keen to accept it?"

He put on a cheeky grin and ran his fingers through his unruly dark hair, which stubbornly defied his efforts to straighten it out. "Yes, that's what happened." He pushed his own chair out of the way to make room for Kaja. "So, now it's your turn."

The first thing she did was to call up a map of the area where they had taken their walk. Then she set a more or less arbitrary radius around it. As she didn't have a clue how far an average ride on a horse would take you, she had to try and make a guess, assuming that you wouldn't cover a much further distance than on foot. Then she looked for the nearest towns and villages and their electoral rolls. She was lucky: Just her third search turned up a Sierra Küng living in Stein am Rhein near the border.

Apparently, she had the same address as a certain Markus Widmer who featured in several articles on the net. He was a dealer, both in horses and machinery. "Thanks." Kaja said. "At least I have an address now." She quickly noted it down on a piece of paper, together with the associated phone number. Kaja was just thinking whether she should try her luck and give the number a ring when she noticed that Toby wanted to say something but seemed lost for words. "What's up?"

"Hm." he still hesitated.

"Come on, spit it out."

"Simon said if we finished early enough, could you perhaps have a look at our accounting software? It's been playing up recently."

"Of course I can, please show me what the problem is. I'm not sure if I can fix it here and now but it'll be worth a try." She sat down again and stared at the screen. "That's one of ours! In fact, it's a program I wrote myself recently." She pulled up the source code on the screen in order to edit it. "I hate to admit it, but I've really messed up here."

Kaja found two sections where she deleted part of the code and inserted the correct lines.

"So, now it should be fine." she announced after barely fifteen minutes. "I have a patch at home. You should have received it already. Never mind, I'll send you the update again later. Just copy it to your hard disk and restart the program. It should install itself automatically. Just in case I've overlooked something today." Something was nagging at the back of her mind, but she couldn't quite work out what it was.

The next moment, her mobile phone beeped. At first, Kaja decided to look later who had sent her a text, but then she realised she was still waiting for an answer from Tim about their dinner date. So she dug out the mobile from her jacket on the back of the chair. "Would love to!!! Have to re-schedule something first. Where and when?" It was high time for him to get in touch. She quickly replied: "Pick me up at Simon's. I'll give you a call when we're finished here." She was impressed. He had changed his plans just to see her. In a much better mood, she turned back to Toby. "So, what else can you show me?"

Over the next hour, Toby took her round the whole company. There didn't seem to be many employees, at least none that were permanently present.

"We have a lot of freelancers, the company is just establishing itself. Business espionage, which is my field of expertise, is a much larger section than you might think. There's also quite a demand for alarm systems. But those colleagues usually work from home as they are field staff. It wouldn't make sense for them to come here first, only to be sent out again immediately on their first job. The department for personal security consists completely of freelancers, we simply don't have enough clients yet. One of the biggest events recently was the World Economic Forum in Davos, but even there most delegates had made their own arrangements. That's the problem if you're trying to run a security firm in a safe country such as Switzerland." He finished his explanations with a joke.

"Oh, I personally appreciate the fact that you don't need a bodyguard too often in Switzerland, compared to other countries." She grimaced. Considering how often she had arguments with Lance, how much worse would a relationship be with a complete stranger who was employed just to shadow her? "What is this business espionage section about? Simon's told me before, but I can't remember everything he said."

"In fact, the term is a bit misleading. It's not us doing the spying. Our job is rather to prevent such things from happening, we protect companies, guard buildings, computer and server environments, making it well nigh impossible to spy on them in any way. In some of the rarer cases, we're contacted after a suspicion arises that something has been accessed illegally. Nowadays, that often happens electronically and we're asked to establish who took what by which means."

"And you have a certain amount of experience in that field." Kaja teased him. "What about the dogs?"

"The dogs are Josef's pets." Simon's voice could be heard from behind them. "And mine." he added. "But unfortunately, I don't have as much time to work with them as I would like to."

"It seems you're a victim of your own success."

"Yes, you could say that. Have you had any success?"

"I think so. But I'll only know when I see her again. We found the picture from her driving licence, but it's rather blurry." Kaja had a cheeky grin on her face. "Your equipment and Toby's skills are first class."

Toby grinned as well. "Kaja, you won't believe me when I say I got my best training from Simon."

"I suppose you weren't stretched to your full potential as a student." Kaja taunted him.

Simon laughed but looked embarrassed, which was a nice touch for a man as tall and normally as confident as him. He decided not to answer her remark. "Were you able to fix the accounting software?" he quickly changed the subject. Now it was Kaja's turn to be embarrassed. "Yes, now it finally does what it's supposed to do. Erm, it was me who had developed it in the first place and I must have had a bad day." Again she felt that a certain thought should have come to her mind but still escaped her.

"When was that?"

"When was what?"

"Well, when did you develop the product?"

"I can't remember, perhaps nine months ago. Why?"

"I just noticed: it looks like yet another one of your faulty programs. Either you are sloppy, but that's not the impression I have of you, or even back then someone was tampering with your work."

"Little Freddy! I'll kill him! That would also explain why you never received the update patch. As soon as I received the first complaints, I immediately got down to writing a small program that could fix all the reported problems. We sent it out to all the customers who had bought our product. At least I assumed that was the case. Now I have a feeling that none of our customers has ever received the patch." She was swearing quietly to herself while tapping something into her mobile.

"Who're you texting?"

"I'm just making a note so that I won't forget. When I'm back home, I'll send the patch to all the customers again by e-mail."

"You're not working for that company any more." Simon reminded her.

"I know." she huffed. "But I still feel attached to my old workplace, especially to my old team. If we manage to uncover the murky deal, I'd love PC Lux to be left with at least a few satisfied customers. And besides: I have my reputation as a good software developer to defend. I can't have dodgy versions out there with my name attached to them." Simon nodded. He understood where she was coming from.

"Hungry?" he asked when she had finished her speech. Kaja looked at her watch and was surprised to find that it was already 2pm.

She was also surprised not to be invited to the burger stand she had noticed when driving into the industrial area but be taken to the back of the building where a small door took them straight into the middle shed. "What kept you so long?" a grumpy Josef welcomed them. "Don't complain if it's all cold now."

"Don't listen to him." Simon replied to this outburst. "He knows very well that we all have irregular working hours. But he just wants to be a good housewife."

As he was saying that, a wooden spoon came flying in Simon's direction which he narrowly managed to avoid.

"Hm, that smells delicious." Kaja tried to mediate.

"So says the diplomat's daughter." Simon teased her.

"Now would you please let the girl enjoy her meal?" Josef butted in and served both of them a plateful of steaming hot polenta with lots of cheese and vegetables.

"Did Zorro behave himself?"

"He was quite happy exploring the whole yard together with Tsar. In fact, Zorro did the exploring and Tsar made sure he didn't overstep his visitor's rights." Kaja had to laugh imagining her dog sniffing at every corner while having his very own bodyguard.

"Do you feel like doing some work with the dogs this afternoon?" Simon enquired. "Or would you rather make your way back to avoid the rush hour jams."

"No, I have lots of time. I'm going to see Tim tonight."

"Oh, I see."

"Nothing to get excited about. We're just going out for a meal. But I don't even know whether I'll be hungry again, after being fed so generously here." Enthusiastically, she ate another forkful of her food. "I thought it'd be stupid of me to go to Bern and not say hello to him..." Kaja realised she was talking too much and quickly changed the subject. "Yes, I'd love to do some dog training." Simon quietly grinned to himself. It seemed Tim was on the right track.

While they were having their coffee, Simon suddenly asked her a question. "Are you still unemployed?"

Kaja looked at him in surprise. "Officially, yes, I am. Although I wouldn't describe my status that way. I'm sure I could find a job anywhere if I put my mind to it."

"That's why I thought I'd ask sooner rather than later, before you're unavailable again. I was wondering if you wanted to join our team. We urgently need a developer for security programs and so far I have a very good impression of you."

Kaja was completely taken by surprise. "I don't know. I'm sure I'd enjoy it. But I have to take care of a few things first." It was a gross understatement considering her whole life was currently in turmoil.

"You don't have to make a decision right now."

"Does it mean I'd have to work in Bern?"

"I think you could do most of it from home, but your presence here will certainly be required now and then. My idea is to employ you as a freelancer to start with. It means you'd be free to turn down a project if you're not free or don't feel like doing it."

"In principle, I'd be delighted to work for Cerberus. But can I have some time to think about it, please?"

"Of course, you can." Simon said, only to tease her: "Five minutes enough?"

Kaja laughed. "That may be a bit too short, but I'll let you know by the end of the week Would that be OK?"

"Yes, I can live with that." He offered his hand and they sealed the agreement with a handshake.

"Are you two having an afternoon chat or shall we do some useful work?" Josef wanted to know.

A little later, the sun broke through the clouds and Zorro went about his training with gusto. So much so that Kaja felt a pang of guilt she didn't train him more often.

"Have you forgotten? You're in the enviable position of being able to decide what to do with your life. How much time you want to spend doing which activity and all that." Unnoticed by the others, Lance had joined the group.

"There's some truth in that, but it's not the whole truth. If I try to do my own thing it'll take a lot of time and effort." Lost in her thoughts, she watched the scenery. The sun was already low above the horizon and a few wisps of cirrostratus completed the picture of a pleasant autumn evening.

"Don't forget: if you do things you enjoy, it'll give you the energy you need."

"Maybe." Kaja replied and said to Simon, who was just doing a retrieval exercise with Zorro: "Perhaps I can call Tim now and ask him to pick me up. I suppose we're finished here soon?"

"Of course, give him a call. Didn't you come by car?"

"Yes, I did, but it'll be easier for me to follow Tim. If I try to find my way through Bern on my own, it'll be past midnight before I arrive." she joked.

Simon had been briefly distracted by Kaja's question and had not noticed Zorro quietly snatching the exercise stick. "Hey, bring that back." he shouted.

But Zorro would have none of it and ran in endless circles round the exercise yard with his booty. Kaja simply had to laugh when she saw the proud expression on his face.

"Zorro, come here." she shouted, but with no more success than Simon and his commands.

He turned to her and said: "It's best to ignore him. He'll soon get tired of the game. Have you decided already whether you want to work for us?"

"You don't happen to be the pushy type of boss, do you?"

"Me? Never." he said with a cheeky grin. "Hey, it looks like you can save your phone call."

"What do you mean?" Kaja asked. She had just bent down to grab Zorro and could not see a thing through her long dark hair.

"Look who's here..."

Kaja looked up and a broad smile brightened up her face. "Tim, what're you doing here so early? I was just about to call and tell you we're almost finished."

"I was on my way already and thought I might as well come round to see how you're doing." The two men shook hands.

"Howdy greenhorn, no bears to hunt today?" Josef wanted to know and offered Tim a cup of coffee.

"Thanks. No, not to today, I have a date with a witch instead." he joked with a mischievous glance in Kaja's direction.

"Let me put Zorro in the car." Kaja quickly replied.

She could have done that later, but she was so excited thinking about this evening that she just needed a moment by herself.

"You're not skiving, are you?" the dragon wanted to know.

Kaja blushed. "No, I'm not!" although for a moment, she had toyed with the idea.

"Good." the dragon was satisfied. "And don't forget, I expect a detailed report including all the saucy details. If you promise me that, I'll make myself scarce now and leave you two lovebirds to get on with it. I'll see you at home tomorrow, sometime during the day."

"How kind of you." Kaja scoffed at her bossy dragon, but he could not hear her as he had already disappeared in a glittering cloud of dust and a few puffs of smoke.

After they said their goodbyes, not without a reminder from Simon for her to seriously consider his job offer, they strolled back to their cars. "Is it OK if I just follow you in my car? I don't know my way through Bern city centre at all." Kaja excused herself. Damn, she still didn't have her nerves under control. Take a deep breath, she reminded herself.

"You come here." Tim said in a soft voice and pulled her closer by the sleeve of her jacket. "I haven't had a chance to say hello to you properly." He gave her a tight hug and Kaja expected a stormy kiss like the one on Friday night. But Tim surprised her with a gentle, but determined kiss instead. He held her face in his palms and finished it with a tender bite at her lower lip, which caused a real firestorm in her. Tim let go of her and took a step back to take a better look at her face. "Better?" he wanted to know.

"Hm." Kaja looked at him. "At least that answers one question."

"So? Does it?"

"Yes, it does." she replied resolutely and pressed him firmly against the side of his car to kiss him again. The kiss he had given her before was not enough. It had been a good start but it was nowhere near enough for her liking. This time it was she who let go of him first. "Now that's better." she said with a satisfied grin on her face. "Shall we make a move?"

"Whoa, hang on, I need a moment to catch my breath."

Sitting in the car, Kaja felt the old worries creeping up on her again, nagging her with all sorts of possibilities and impossibilities. "Not now!"

she decided. Without thinking twice, she put her favourite Pink! CD into the hi-fi and turned the volume up full. Distracted by the music, she was somewhat surprised when she had to park her car behind Tim's with no restaurant to be seen.

"I thought you were going to feed me?" she wanted to know when she got out of the car.

"That's what I'm going to do. May I introduce: Tim's Extravagant Dining Experience."

"Experience?" Kaja asked and released Zorro from the boot of her car.

"Yes, meaning you can help me cook." Tim grinned cheekily.

"And it's your job to supervise my cooking, I suppose?"

"Yes, I'm good at that. - Ouch!" he complained when Kaja gave him a playful dig in the ribs. He went to his car and produced two large bags of shopping.

"Is this where you live?" Kaja looked up curiously at the bland façade of the house in front of them.

"Yes, at the moment I do. I haven't had the flat for long." He unlocked the door and let Kaja step into the stairwell first. "To be honest, I don't particularly like my flat. I always feel like I'm living in temporary accommodation. The fact that I was travelling a lot didn't help me feel at home here either. You'll see in a minute what I mean." On the second floor, he stopped in front of the first flat, unlocked the door and held it open for Kaja to enter. Zorro pushed past them impatiently and immediately started to explore the flat.

It took Kaja just one look to understand what he meant. In the hallway and in the first, obviously unused, bedroom, packing cases were still piled up, gathering dust. The hallway led straight past an orange-tiled bathroom into an open-plan kitchen which extended on the right-hand side into the sitting room. A few photographs had been pinned to the walls. The kitchen was small, a 1970s design in avocado and white, but clean and functional. The sitting room was the most homely space in the flat. Two antique leather armchairs invited you to drop down in front of the telly and relax. The floor was covered with a worn Persian rug. In one corner there was a neat pile of National Geographic magazines. "As you can see, the place is not as cosy as it could be, at least not throughout." he raised his hands to apologise.

"Well, I didn't give you much time to get it ship-shape and Bristol fashion. It's only your hallway and that first room that need sorting out. Or is it your bedroom?"

"No, my bedroom is on the other side." he laughed. "Are you ready for your cooking experience?" he challenged her with a grin. "Zorro is all geared up it seems." He pointed to the dog who had made himself comfortable in a corner of the kitchen after finishing his tour of the flat.

"It depends." she said suspiciously. "And you can beg until the cows come home." she added with a glance towards her four-legged friend. "Do you really think I didn't see Josef feed you this afternoon?" Zorro responded to this statement with an extra innocent look, resting his head on his paws.

"Are you better with tomato sauce or do you prefer to do the salad dressing?"

"Can I do the dressing, please?" She didn't wait for an answer and bent down to a cupboard where she expected to find oil and vinegar. Good. Extra virgin olive oil from an organic source and delicious balsamic were available. She got up and inspected the spice rack. Italian herbs and herb salt. It couldn't get any better. "Do you have any ketchup? And milk?"

"Yep." she heard him say somewhere from the depths of the shopping bags.

"Perfect. You'll have a special balsamic salad dressing à la Kaja." she informed him. In the meantime, Tim had unpacked the bags and held up a bottle of red wine. "In case you're getting bored or are running out of words." he said with a conspiratorial twinkle in his eyes.

"I can think of a few other things we could do if we run out of words." Kaja mumbled.

"What did you say?"

"Nothing. Can I have a glass of that merlot, please?"

While Tim was chopping the onions for the tomato sauce, Kaja quickly prepared the salad dressing. Three spoons of balsamic vinegar, one spoon of olive oil, a dash of ketchup and a generous measure of milk, some spices - ready.

"It looks like you chose the easier job." Tim concluded, when he saw her sitting relaxed by a side table.

"But I still have to prepare the lettuce." she re-assured him.

Tim sprinkled a teaspoon of sugar over the sweated onions and waited for them to caramelise. Then he deglazed them with some white wine and waited for it to be completely absorbed. In the meantime, Kaja had opened a tin of tomatoes and emptied it into the frying pan. Tim added a cup of vegetable stock. "So, now this needs to simmer for half an hour. I know that you like tuna, but do you also like sweetcorn?"

"In the sauce?"

"Exactly."

"No idea. I like sweetcorn in general, but I've never tried it in tomato sauce."

""It works a treat." Tim explained enthusiastically. "If you carry on with the salad, I'll look after the pudding."

"Good, we have a deal." She peeled a pepper, half an apple and the cucumber and chopped them all into small pieces. Then she added a spring onion and of course the lettuce. When she had finished, she turned round and peeped over Tim's shoulder just as he was stirring melted chocolate into something that looked like sugar and egg yolk. "Looks delicious, smells delicious."

"And tastes delicious." he confirmed. She bent closer to his face and licked a speck of chocolate from the corner of his mouth."

"Stop, stop, stop. If you get me in trouble like you did earlier on by the car, we'll never get anything to eat today."

She laughed and raised her hands, stepping back from him. "OK, I'll stop. Where did you learn to cook so well?"

"If you have to live on instant soup and porridge as often as I do, you learn to appreciate a good meal. And since I can hardly go back to mummy all the time, I taught myself how to do it. As a bonus, I can score points with the girls." he teased Kaja. He opened the fridge and put the dessert inside.

"I'm sure you can." she grumbled.

"So, just need to boil some water for the spaghetti and we'll be all set in about fifteen minutes."

Kaja sat down on one of the leather armchairs and started to rummage through a box of photographs. Tim glanced over to her. She looked really cute today. He wanted to be close to her, preferably naked, in his bed... But he also just enjoyed her company. The only thing that worried him was that he had not told her yet he would be going away again soon, in two weeks time, for a full four weeks. He sighed. Perhaps she could come with him? He would ask her. Soon. After the meal, or whenever.

"What's that in this photo? It looks funny." Relieved to get distracted from his sombre musings and erotic fantasies, he went over to Kaja and glanced at the picture. It showed a huge elk bull which was trying to push its massive antlers into a comparatively small, bright yellow tent. He had to laugh as he recalled the incident.

"This is Paul."

"Paul?"

"Yes, Paul. It happened during a photo shoot in Sweden."

"I thought elks were rather shy animals?"

"Normally, they are. But this one was a young and exceptionally nosy specimen. We had pitched up in his territory for quite a while and he must have decided it was time to take a closer look at that yellow nest where people crawled in and out at various times of the day."

"But none of you were at home at the time, or were you?" Kaja asked, fascinated, while secretly looking for clues whether the second member of the team had been male or female. She knew it was a stupid thing to do.

After all, she had not been leading a completely celibate life for the past ten years either. Nevertheless, he would be going on another trip soon. Up to now, she had assumed he was on his own most of the time.

"No, Sven, my guide and employer had got up at the crack of dawn to buy provisions and I was just returning from my usual morning reconnaissance tour. You can imagine how shocked I was, but I still had the presence of mind to press the trigger. It wasn't a very professional shot, though, and the picture is a bit blurry."

"So, what happened next?" Kaja wanted to know, captivated by the story (and, yes, relieved that his partner was called Sven, clearly a man. All those absurdly jealous thoughts quickly evaporated from her mind.)

"Apparently, I was not the only one in shock." They were interrupted by the noise of the boiling water. "Hang on, I'll finish my story in a second, just putting some spaghetti in the water."

He got up and went over to the cooker. He skilfully opened the pack, judged how much pasta they would need and stirred it into the water. Kaja watched him work in the kitchen.

She liked the fact that he was able to concentrate fully on whatever he was doing. She asked herself if he was the same in bed and felt butterflies in her stomach.

Tim turned back to Kaja and casually leaned against the breakfast bar. "Where was I?"

"You had just frightened a nosy elk." she reminded him cheerfully.

"Ah yes. So he jumped up and wanted to run away. Eventually he did, but he took our tent with him, one of his antlers got caught up in a guy rope.

"And so he made off with your tent and all that was in it?" Kaja couldn't stop laughing as she imagined the picture.

"Luckily, the rope gave way after a few metres and all I saw of him was a cloud of dust. I wouldn't have forgiven him if he had taken my sleeping bag. It was bad enough already. The place looked like a bomb site. I had to spend the rest of the day restoring our camp."

"Did he come back?"

"It was most surprising. Despite his nasty experience, he turned up again. But this time, we were better prepared."

"What did you do?"

"We put an electric fence around the camp. It's standard procedure if you are in bear country. However, there weren't many bears in the area so we had initially thought we could do without. It didn't stop Paul, as we had named him, from coming close to us. When I first met him, he had a taste of our porridge and seemed to like it. Talking of food: I think our pasta is al dente now."

He fished some spaghetti out of the water and took it to Kaja for her to try.

"Mh, it's just right. And high time, too. The smell of your delicious tomato sauce makes my mouth water."

Over the meal, Kaja told Tim about Simon's offer to work for him freelance.

"And? Are you going to accept?"

Kaja played with her fork. "I'm not sure yet." she admitted. "So much is happening in my life at the moment, I don't know whether I'm coming or going. I just don't want to make any rash decisions and miss out on other opportunities. By the way, this meal is delicious." she added, speaking with her mouth full.

"Thanks, glad you like it." He was pleased to see her enjoying the food. "I can understand your reservations about the job offer. But on the other hand, wouldn't Simon's suggestion be ideal in your situation? If you're working freelance for him, you can always reject projects if they don't suit you. Or you could quit at any time."

"That's all well and good, but he wouldn't have made such an offer if he expected me to turn him down every so often. He obviously needs someone to do the work."

"Oh, he certainly needs someone or he wouldn't have asked you. But at the moment, you can't tell whether you'll have enough time and motivation to take on all of his projects. If you don't, it'll be his problem, not yours. If he doesn't like the risk, he needs to employ someone full-time."

"Hm, looking at it that way, you may be right."

"Of course I'm right. And if I decide I want you to come with me on one of my photo shoots, Simon and his projects will have to wait." Tim said boldly and pushed his empty plate aside.

Amused, Kaja glanced at Tim. "What makes you so certain that I would come with you?"

Tim leaned over the table and looked intensely into her eyes. "I'm not certain. But I'll do everything I can to convince you. And believe me, I can be very convincing."

Kaja believed every word he said. She could barely take her eyes off his. In the dim light of the sitting room, his eyes looked nearly black. Almost out of nowhere, an electrifying tension had built up between them. Kaja suddenly felt very insecure and wanted to look away as Tim reached across the table to put his hand at the back of her head.

"We still have some unfinished business to see to." He whispered and kissed her passionately.

The blood was rushing through Kaja's body. Only when a fork fell to the floor with a loud clang, did they let go of each other. Both of them were breathing heavily. Kaja tried to clear her head but everything seemed to be in a haze.

Tim got up and took her hand. "Come this way." he simply said and led her into his bedroom.

Some time later, seconds, minutes, light years - for the life of her, Kaja was unable to tell - she was huddled up under his duvet while Tim had gone to the kitchen to take care of the pudding. She was so relaxed that she had to be careful not to fall asleep in the meantime. The events that had just happened ran through her head again like a film. She was stretching like a happy cat, when Tim came back from the kitchen. He was wearing just his boxers and carrying a white plate with a small chocolate cake on it.

"You both look so delicious, I can't make up my mind what to nibble first." she said in mock despair.

"I'd go for the cake. It's nice and hot and full of surprises, but perhaps not the only surprising beauty in this room." he admitted when Kaja sat up in bed.

In a sudden moment of bashfulness, she pulled up the duvet to escape his look. "OK then, let's have the cake. I'm as starving again as anything."

"I did notice." Tim joked. Kaja was about to give him a glib reply when she noticed the soft, almost runny filling of the small cake. "That tastes marvellous." she sighed indulgently.

"By the way, when I got the cake, I let Zorro pop out for a minute. Now he's sleeping contentedly in the sitting room."

"Thanks." she said with her mouth full. When the cake had completely gone, Kaja meant to get up and take the empty plate back to the kitchen.

But Tim smoothly took it out of her hand and shoved it under the bed. With a powerful movement, he swept on top of Kaja and lowered his head to give her a hot chocolatey kiss while his hand caressed her naked body from her ribs down to her hips. "Where were we earlier on?"

26

Kaja woke up. Apparently, it was early in the morning. She could see the first light of dawn outside and cuddled deeper into the sheets and into Tim. Normally, she didn't jump into bed with her lovers on their first night. She had always found it difficult to deal with the inevitable morning routines at such an early stage in a relationship. But strangely, it didn't bother her now. Perhaps that wasn't so strange after all. When they were younger, she had often stayed over with his family during their long summer holidays. She smiled, thinking back to the adventures they had lived through together. Despite the cosy warmth of the bed, she had to get up to go to the loo. Carefully, so as not to wake Tim, she got out of bed. 'I'll give him his wake-up call later.' she thought and smiled in anticipation.

Back from the bathroom, her eyes fell on something on his desk. In the meantime, dawn had got brighter and more daylight fell into the room. She found a travel guide to Iceland. Curious, she stepped closer and picked the book up. Something slipped out and slowly tumbled to the floor. She bent down to pick it up: a flight ticket. Strange. Hadn't he told her that his next project would take him to Brazil? But Iceland seemed to be more in line with his work. He had spent a lot of time in the icy north. She looked for the date. His flight was due next week! Paralysed, she stared at the ticket as if her gaze could somehow change the figures. But it was beyond doubt: Tim would be gone again by the end of next week. The thought got her all choked up. It seemed reality hadn't taken long to catch up with her.

'You'll better get used to it.' she thought cynically. But did she really want to, was she able to get used to it? Kaja had no idea. All she knew was that she wanted to get out of here and be on her own. As quickly as possible. Quietly, she collected her clothes and got dressed. She was almost out of the door when she hesitated. Shouldn't she leave at least a message? On the one hand, he deserved to be kept in the dark - on the other hand she had been as happy yesterday as she hadn't been for a long time. Torn between the desire to take revenge for being abandoned again and regret at destroying a brand-new, wonderful relationship, she tiptoed back to leave a brief message on his desk.

Just as she had finished writing the post-it note and sticking it to his flight ticket, Tim woke up. Bad timing. "You're up early." he mumbled, half asleep and rubbed his eyes. He sat up in bed and took a closer look at her. "You're dressed already?"

She avoided looking into his eyes and murmured. "I have to go. Thanks for everything."

"You want to go? But... I don't believe it. You can't just disappear as if nothing had happened." His voice sounded genuinely annoyed, which made Kaja angry. If someone had the right to be annoyed it was her.

"So?" she said in a sharp tone. "Perhaps you should have thought about that when you decided to keep it a secret you're going to disappear yourself at the end of next week." To underline her words, she held the flight ticket in his face.

"Oh, dammit! I meant to tell you."

"Oh did you? When was that going to happen? The day before you're off?"

"No, certainly not. And anyway, it's completely different. I don't just disappear, as you call it. This is my job."

"That may be so. But I would still have preferred to know before..." she stopped, not knowing what to say. "Well, before all this happened." She made a sweeping gesture with her right arm.

"Would it have changed anything?"

"Yes... no... maybe. What do I know? But it's too late to find out now." Kaja stormed out of the room, called Zorro, who had listened to the verbal exchange with suspicion, and was gone from the flat seconds later.

Tim slumped back onto the pillows. 'Well, done.' he thought. 'Really well done. Couldn't have done it any better.' He sighed. Then he pushed back the duvet and discovered Kaja's scarf that had been hidden underneath. He took it in his hands and buried his nose in the soft fabric. The scarf smelled of Kaja and of her perfume. Damn!

Kaja drove all the way to Simon's company feeling totally numb. She thanked Josef for looking after Zorro the day before and asked him to tell Simon she'd be happy to work for him.

"Don't you want to tell him yourself?" He looked at his watch. "He should be here any minute. We normally have a cup of coffee together at eight."

"Thanks, that's very kind of you. But I'm very busy today and traffic to Zurich is always unpredictable." It was the last thing she wanted right now: a coffee break with Tim's best friend!

"I see. Well then, hope to see you soon. And have a safe journey." Josef replied. He scratched his head and thought that these young people could be rather awkward. 'Luckily, I'm well past it.' he thought shaking his head and started making the coffee.

When she finally reached the A1 to Zurich, she took a deep breath. With any luck, she could be home in an hour and hide in her bed. It was the best cure, always and for everything. At least as long as she was actually asleep.

"It's an escape mechanism." her helpful dragon explained when she reached home and wanted to disappear in bed without saying a word.

"I don't care. Call it escapism or whatever. The fact is: I didn't sleep much last night and need a couple of hours to catch up. I'm sure you can wait that long."

"Oookay." Lance said slowly. "Looks like somebody is on edge here."

"Congratulations. The penny has dropped." Kaja retorted sarcastically.

"It didn't take much to notice. If you were a dragon, you'd be spouting flames from your nostrils while speaking."

"Can you do that?" Kaja was briefly distracted from her sombre thoughts, trying to imagine the picture. Against her will, she had to laugh. "You'll have to show me sometime. But I'm really tired now. Do come and wake me up if I don't come out of the room by myself."

Satisfied that at least the despair had disappeared from the face of his protégée, he left her in peace and put up with the prospect of having to wait a few more hours for her report on the past day. Miri might call later on and do the waking up for him. He had already prepared a telepathic message to her. Strictly speaking, this did not comply with the dragon rules of engagement because he was only responsible for Kaja. But he decided that the boundaries became blurred if the other two sisters could see him as well.

The telephone rang at eleven, slightly later than requested, but then that was better than nothing. After the fifth ring, he finally decided to answer himself: "Hello." he had to clear his throat. ""Hello, who's there?"

"Erm, Lance? Is that you? Or have I got the wrong number?"

"No no." he replied stroppily. "It's me. I'll just get Kaja for you."

As Miri was waiting, she wondered if Lance always answered the phone. It would be a rather useful task for him to do.

"No, I only do that in exceptional circumstances." She could hear his voice in the receiver. "I'm not her damn secretary." he steamed.

"Go steady with the pleasantries." Kaja's voice came from the background. She took the receiver from his paw. "Hi Miri. What's up?"

"That's what I wanted to ask you. But I don't have much time, just taking my ten minute morning break. My uncle's going to have a fit if I'm not back on time."

"He's a slave driver." Kaja caught her breath. Obviously, she wasn't quite awake yet. "Sorry, I didn't mean to say that."

Miri laughed. "No problem. You hit the nail on the head. Shall I pop round after work? I finish at four today."

"That would be great. I've got lots to tell you." Kaja promised.

After she'd hung up, she made herself a large pot of coffee. She reminded herself to ask Miri where she got that delicious Hawaiian coffee from. Her own brand didn't taste half as good since she had tried hers. After her belated morning routine, she got dressed to take Zorro for a walk. Lance was still waiting for his report and she informed him he would have to join them if he wanted to have the news now. Bad-tempered, he agreed and at the same time felt heroic pride for his sacrifice.

Kaja who, for a change, was able to read his thoughts, shook her head with amusement. "You're not heroic, you're just curious." she corrected him.

He grimaced. After they had walked for a while, Lance said: "OK, I admit it, I'm curious. So how did it go yesterday?"

"Badly." Kaja replied with sadness.

As she didn't add anything to explain, he enquired impatiently: "Would you mind divulging a little bit more detail?"

With a sigh, Kaja pulled herself together and told him how the day had gone. When she had finished, Lance said: "Let me summarise: You liked what you saw at Simon's company." She nodded and he continued: "And you're quite certain where to find that Sierra?" Another nod. "You successfully solved a computer problem, were offered a job, had a relaxed evening and later a hot night with Tim?" A third nod followed. "The only disappointment was that he's going back to work earlier than expected? And that's all that makes you say the past 24 hours went badly?"

"Well, yes, that's it... but if I look at it through your eyes, I feel that I... How shall I put it? May have exaggerated a bit?"

"Phew, am I glad that you noticed that, too."

"No need to have a go at me." she defended herself.

"Oh, no, I do need to have a go at you, just to give you the right perspective. You have to..."

"OK, I got it, I will do my best." she laughed.

"Right. That sounds better." Lance didn't seem fully convinced. "And when are you going to call him?"

"I'm not."

"You're not? But I thought we agreed."

"Yes, we did. And even though I'm happy to admit that yesterday wasn't all that bad." she corrected herself. "...was actually quite good, I'm still upset that he'll be gone next week. And that he'll be gone again soon after that. And that he didn't bother to tell me. It wasn't helpful in building up my confidence."

"And now you think giving Tim the silent treatment will solve your problem?"

Kaja gave him an enervated look. "No, of course not. But I want to get my life back on track first. I feel once I know where I'm going, I'll be much better able to deal with my feelings for Tim. Perhaps then I can be more relaxed about him being away so often. And in the meantime, if he's a bit worried or annoyed about not hearing from me, well, it serves him right." she said with a mischievous twinkle in her eyes. Deep down, Lance had to agree with her.

When Miri arrived about 4 o'clock, Kaja immediately blurted out: "Guess what: I'm pretty certain where our dragon sister lives. Shall we try our luck and pay her a visit?"

Miri found her enthusiasm infectious and picked up the idea: "Yes, let's go."

"I was hoping you'd say that. I already prepared some rolls and filled the water bottles. We're ready to rock."

"How far are you going to take me?" Miri was surprised to see the size of the food packs.

Kaja laughed. "It's not all that far. The address is close to the forest where we first met her. It made sense anyway as she was out riding her horse. But I haven't eaten all day. I can hardly sit next to you in the car munching away and not offer you any food. So I made two large packs."

It didn't take long for them to be on their way. Miri was excited and bombarded Kaja with questions, until she laughed and said: "I can't tell you any more. All I have is this address. And who knows? Perhaps she doesn't live here or she's moved away or we have the wrong Sierra. Nothing's certain."

After an hour's drive, they stopped in front of an unassuming timber frame house. Kaja switched off the engine. They looked at each other. "So, what's the plan?" They went into a silly giggle to cover their nervousness and anticipation.

"Look there." Miri pointed to a sign attached to the barn next to the house. "Riding Lessons."

"Since when did you want to learn how to ride a horse?"

"Not me, but you do." Miri grinned. "We could register for lessons as an excuse to start a conversation. We don't want to look like travelling sales people or Jehovah's Witnesses when we knock on the door."

"You're right. But why is it me who wants the lessons and not you?"

"Because you have more experience with large animals. Look at Zorro."

"Zorro?"

"He's much bigger than Chili." Miri defended herself.

Kaja rolled her eyes. "OK then. Let's try our luck. Lance, you stay in the background until I signal you to appear."

"What kind of signal? Sign language? Smoke signals? Morse code?" he counted with the help of his clawed fingers.

"I'll just call you, silly."

"Ah yes."

"Come on, let's go before I change my mind." Miri urged them on.

"As long as it's not you who's got to do the riding." Kaja mumbled. They got out of the car and rang the door bell. At first, nothing happened. After a few moments, Miri asked with a nervous look on her face: "Shall I try again?" Instead of an answer, Kaja pressed the bell again herself.

"Sierra, can you answer that damn door?" somebody shouted. Judging by the voice, it was a man. Then the door swung open. "Yes?" he said in an unfriendly tone.

"Er, we were looking for..."

Miri nudged Kaja with her elbow and interrupted her. "My friend here would like to have some riding lessons."

"Yes, I'd love to learn how to ride a horse." Kaja bubbled along. "I've always been fascinated by those big animals."

But the man was not listening. "She's back there, behind the first barn door." Without waiting for an answer, he disappeared back into the house.

"That's customer service for you." Miri stated. "Never mind. Let's go." They jumped down the three steps leading to the door and went to the barn door at the back of the building.

With some effort, they managed to open it. As they couldn't find a light switch, they had to feel their way through the barn in the dark, only to encounter a second door that proved to be even more stubborn. Kaja swore quietly. Finally they reached the courtyard. It was swept clean and on both sides, several horses stood in groups in enclosures and watched with interest as Sierra lunged a white pony in the small central arena.

The woman noticed their arrival, looked briefly over to them and said: "Hi, I'll be with you in a sec." Then she fully concentrated on her work with the small white horse again. Miri and Kaja went over to the other horses and watched Sierra as they stroked the inquisitive muzzles pushing at them.

"You're not even afraid of horses." Kaja realised.

"No, I'm not afraid, but I'm not keen to ride them either." Miri grinned. "Although, given a small one such as this," she pointed to the pony in the arena. "I might change my mind."

"Aren't you done yet? We need to be off soon." The man's voice bellowed from a window in the house. Sierra stoically ignored the interruption and continued her work. The window was shut with an angry slam.

Five minutes later, Sierra lowered her whip to the floor and took two small steps backwards, a signal that made the white horse turn on the spot and trot up her. She put a well-earned treat in its mouth and caressed the nape of its neck. Finally, she led the pony out of the arena into one of the enclosures. There, she took off the bridle, opened the gate and released it with a friendly slap on its croup to join its colleagues. As she came over to the two women, she bent down to pick up the lunging whip that she had dropped earlier on. As her fiery red curls covered her face, she pushed them back with a smooth gesture and straightened up.

"Hello, you two. I'm Sierra." She offered her hand to welcome each of them with a hearty shake. Something made her suspicious. Hadn't she seen these two women before? And why had she received an electric shock when their fingers met? The other two must have felt it as well, judging by the way they looked at each other.

Kaja took the initiative. "Hi, I'm Kaja and this here is Miri. I'm looking for some riding lessons and as we were just passing by..."

Sierra was irritated. She regularly had such enquiries, but something didn't seem to match up here. Was it the tone and the message? Or the message and the body language? She blinked. Did she really see that? Was there a dragon sitting on Kaja's shoulder? She shook her head in disbelief. She had already seen one recently. In the forest. A big one. And now she remembered where she knew the two women from!

"Can we start again, please. Why are you here?"

"Because..." Kaja was just about to start her story about the riding lessons again when she realised that Sierra was staring mesmerised at her left shoulder. She turned her head a little. "Lance! I told you to wait! Do you always have to go like a bull at a gate?"

"So you can talk to him?" Sierra sounded relieved.

"Uhm, yes, I can." Kaja was embarrassed to admit.

"And you find this reassuring?" Miri was surprised.

"Well, it means either I'm not going bonkers after all or at least I'm not the only one doing so. So, what's the real purpose of your visit?"

Kaja and Miri looked at each other. "We would like to have a chat with you about the dragon. Only if you have time for us, of course. Otherwise, we can come back later."

"It seems to be really important to you." Sierra was amused. The male voice interrupted them again. "That's Markus, my partner." she hastened to explain. "He's rather busy right now. Normally he doesn't shout that much. - Markus, can you come down for a minute?" she shouted back.

The man appeared surprisingly quickly. He just briefly looked at the two women. "Are we ready now?"

"I'm sorry, but you'll have to go on your own. These two ladies may want to write an article about my work."

"About your work? Tell them it'd be better if they wrote about my company. Your riding is a fruitless business anyway."

"Don't you notice anything about these two?" Sierra wanted to know, casually ignoring everything he had said.

"What am I supposed to notice? Perhaps I should take part in the interview and give them our key data."

Sierra waved at him. "No no, I'll take care of that."

"Yes, we would like to talk to Sierra on her own first." Miri came to the rescue.

Dissatisfied, Markus left them.

"Thank you." she said to Miri. "So, since Markus will be gone in a minute, we're free to stay here. Come with me, please, I'll make you a cup of tea." She led them to a small door.

"See." Miri whispered to Kaja. "Perhaps she's a really nice person after all." They didn't have the chance to discuss any more details in private.

"This is my tack room. It's not very warm in here, but we can talk in peace." She immediately went to boil the kettle, put three chipped cups and a selection of herbal teas on the table.

"Would you mind getting something stronger for me, please?" Lance wanted to know. He had grown back to his normal size and gave her his most innocent look.

Sierra hadn't had the chance to take a closer look at him before and was now much too busy taking in his full appearance to notice any change of expression in his face. "Good God, you're huge. And you can talk! I don't believe it." Suddenly, she wasn't so sure any more of what she had let herself in for. Her tack room seemed to shrink with every passing minute. Overwhelmed, she sank on one of the chairs.

"I promised you last Saturday I'd have a word with my dragon." Kaja said, a bit confused by Sierra's strong reaction. But then her first reaction back in the forest had been somewhat too calm, she realised.

"Yes, you did." she grumbled. "I talk to my horses, too. But they don't talk back, definitely not by resonating a voice in my head." She shook the appropriate part of her body and tried to steady herself by playing hostess. "Tea anyone? And no, before you ask again. Tea is all I have." she informed Lance, not without shaking her head again in disbelief. "I don't believe it. Now I'm already having an argument with that beast." she mumbled to herself.

"Hey, I did hear that."

Now she couldn't help but grin. "We're a bit touchy, aren't we? A typical male. Provided you are a male?"

Lance puffed out his chest.

"OK, definitely a male."

The other two laughed.

"What's so funny?"

"You are. On the one hand, you are in shock and on the other, you're having an argument with him. Which, admittedly, is an easy thing to do with Lance."

"The fellow seems a bit temperamental."

"Exactly, that's what he is."

"Hey, I'll make myself scarce if you don't stop it."

"No, you'd better stay here. Otherwise we'll have to fill you in afterwards anyway. Allow me to introduce Lance, my dragon." Kaja introduced her companion. "Lance, this is Sierra, apparently our third member."

"Wohoo, are we the founding members of the Swiss Confederation?" Sierra joked, but then reluctantly stretched out her hand to shake Lance's paw. The other two looked at each other.

Finally Kaja plucked up the courage to ask: "Are you ready for a fantastic fairytale?"

Sierra leaned back in her chair. "It can't get more fantastic than this. We have a dragon in our midst already."

"Just wait."

"Well, I don't even know where to start." Kaja was lost.

"Perhaps I should give it a try? You explained it to me already." Miri took the initiative.

"I didn't have to explain anything to you. You knew everything about dragons already. Go on then, tell Sierra how it is all linked together."

So Miri briefly summarised how they had met and what they had experienced together. And despite keeping the story brief, it took her almost an hour to tell it. Sierra just listened quietly and didn't interrupt her with any questions.

Only at the end did she ask with a blank look: "And what's that all got to do with me? Don't get me wrong, I find your story exciting and I'm glad I've met you." Which, as she was surprised to admit to herself, was true. Normally, she didn't readily take to strangers. "It's only that... I definitely don't keep a dragon for company, at least not one of the interesting type."

Here, they were interrupted by Markus again, who shouted from the courtyard: "Sierra, don't forget to prepare the invitations."

Enervated, she rolled her eyes. The two others gave each other a meaningful look. "Yes, I will." She picked up their conversation: "As I said, no magic dragons in my life, but otherwise enough trouble."

"We do understand." Miri was quick to say. "And we won't stay long. To be honest, we're not sure ourselves how you fit in with all this. I don't have a dragon either. Lance is definitely Kaja's. But for some reason, you and I can see him as well. We're convinced it's not a coincidence."

"Perhaps all women can see him and you're just not aware." Sierra said with hope in her voice. They shook their heads, but Sierra ignored them. "I know what we'll do. You heard that I have to write invitations. We're hosting a small party for our customers. Why don't you come as well? That way I can see for myself if the dragon is visible to others."

Kaja was about to decline. She felt Lance was not a circus attraction to be put on display. But the dragon was quicker: "Of course, we'll be delighted to come. Thanks for the inviting us." Kaja looked at him in surprise.

"Do her the favour. She looks like she can do with some distraction. And so can you." he whispered to his protégée.

"Ouch, that was below the belt. But unfortunately, you're right. Yet again."

"No offence." he said and tickled her. She just managed to suppress a fit of laughter. Their little discussion had taken place unnoticed by the others. 'Perhaps having Lance as my very own dragon has its advantages.' she thought with childish satisfaction. Miri had agreed to come as well in the meantime and wrote both their telephone numbers on a piece of paper which Sierra took and said, apologising: "Unfortunately, I'm running out of time. But I'm looking forward to seeing you the weekend after next."

"Likewise. And do get in touch if you happen to be in Zurich. Promise?"

"OK." Sierra replied, thinking that she rarely got away from the stables, never mind as far as Zurich.

"She's nice, isn't she?" said Miri when they were back in the car.

"Hm, yes, she is." Kaja had to admit reluctantly. "Lets herself be pushed around by her partner. Or is it her husband?"

"That's true."

"I'd be out of it as fast as I could." Kaja claimed.

"I don't know. Aren't you being a bit harsh? We don't know anything about them or what kind of relationship they have."

"I've seen enough. It's horrible."

Miri glanced at Kaja from the corner of her eye. "You can be quite arrogant. You know that?"

Kaja wanted to protest, but then resigned herself, admitting: "You may be right. Perhaps I'm the last person entitled to comment on other people's relationships." For a moment, they both kept quiet.

Finally, Miri asked quietly: "Did everything go alright with Tim yesterday?"

"Hm, you could say that." Kaja said melancholy voice.

"Was the sex so bad?" Miri asked with her eyes wide open.

Kaja had to laugh. "No, on the contrary."

"So, what's the problem?"

"Well, in order to keep the light-hearted tone of our conversation, let me just say my problem is that in the near future, for the next few weeks to be precise, I won't have the pleasure of enjoying good sex."

"Why's that?"

"Because the hero of my story is swanning off to Iceland next week."

"How come? I thought he was due in Brazil in two months time?"

"It looks like his plans have changed." Kaja said moodily.

"And what now?"

"I don't know. This morning I was angry and stormed out of his flat. Now I'm simply at a loss." She sighed. "I think I'll just forget about him and deal with it when he's back. I can't change anything at the moment anyway."

"Don't you want to go with him?"

"To be honest, no, I don't. I'm much too angry. He neither told me of his plans nor did he invite me to accompany him. On top of that, I'm just turning my whole life upside down or it is turning upside down by itself... I don't even know which expression describes my situation better." she added. "I can't just make off to Iceland in all of this."

She stopped and concentrated on her driving. It had just started to rain and most other drivers on the road were acting as if they had suddenly forgotten how to drive. She skilfully overtook one particularly anxious driver and pulled back into lane in front of him.

"If you two want to have a future together, you can't just adapt your life to his. It's got to be give and take."

"That's my feeling exactly." Glad that Miri understood, she smiled at her.

Kaja had just dropped off Miri at her flat, when her mobile rang. The agitated voice at the other end was Sierra's. "Listen, were you serious about your invitation? I think I'll be in Zurich tomorrow night..." She didn't finish the sentence.

"Erm, yes, of course. Shall I text you my address?"

"Thanks, that'd be great."

"Good, why don't you come over at seven? I'll cook a meal and let Miri know. Perhaps she can come as well."

"You don't know how much this means to me." Sierra said and hung up.

Not sure what to make of the conversation, Kaja looked at her mobile. What was all this about? As soon as she reached home, she got in touch with Miri. "Yes, I'm free - at least until ten." she quickly added. "Shall I bring something?"

"I don't know. Haven't made any plans yet. I'll give you a call tomorrow, if I think of something."

"Good, see you then."

Kaja hung up and went to take a shower.

27

Refreshed and snuggled up cosily in her favourite tracksuit, Kaja was sitting cross-legged on the sofa, a notepad and a pencil in her hands. Next to her, on the coffee table, she had a bar of dark chocolate and a glass of milk.

"Is that what you call a healthy dinner?" Lance scoffed as he came strolling from the bedroom.

Without looking up from her papers, she said: "The elderberry brandy is next to the cooker. Help yourself."

The dragon looked at her in surprise. "In that case, your dinner is perfectly fine." he was quick to approve and grabbed the bottle before Kaja could change her mind. "What are you doing there anyway?" he was interested to know. "It's rather unusual to see you without a laptop."

"I wanted to do some paper-based brainstorming first. That's easier and more direct. But I'll need my laptop later to research a few things." Finally, she raised her head and noticed the questioning look on his face. "I'm jotting down a few ideas what to do with my professional future before assessing their feasibility."

"So I'd better leave you in peace." Kaja nodded absent-mindedly, her thoughts already occupied with her notes again.

Lance had finished the bottle of elderberry brandy and cuddled up to Zorro. "Do you really have to?" the dog snarled. But when he realised that Kaja wasn't giving him any attention and Lance was ignoring him as he always did, he resigned himself to his fate, rested his head on the pillow and went back to sleep with the tiny dragon rolled up next to him.

Two hours later, Kaja got up and stretched her stiff limbs.

"Whichever way I look at it, if I want to do more than just programming, to be more precise: if I want to deal with plants and candles, I need a new home." she said aloud and listened to her words echoing in the room. "A new home. Somehow it sounds better than it did a few weeks ago. But what good is the idea if I don't have a solution to match?"

"At least now you know what you're looking for." was Lance's pragmatic advice as he started from his nap. He stretched and grew back to his normal size. Unfortunately, he had forgotten about the dog being in close vicinity and Zorro promptly yowled as he found the dragon sitting on his tail. Angrily, he barked at him.

"What's up with you two?" Kaja asked, barely paying attention.

"He caught my tail!"

"Lance, you've got to be more careful." she told her dragon off.

Zorro looked at Kaja in surprise and then said to Lance: "She understood me, I mean she really understood me and didn't just guess what I was trying to say."

"Yes, our little girl is learning." Lance agreed, sounding rather satisfied, but only after he had made sure of leaving sufficient space between himself and the dog.

Finally, Kaja looked over to them. "Hey you two, have you lost it completely now?"

They looked at each other in shock and then started to laugh and bark respectively.

"I'm pleased to see you agree with each other for once, but I'm seriously trying to work here." she said sternly, or at least she tried to give that impression. But her effort was wasted. Neither of them paid any attention. Shaking her head, she turned back to the papers. A property with a large garden and no immediate neighbours would be ideal, she mused.

Over the following day, she searched various property ad web sites. It was a tiring and fruitless effort. Either the properties were too bland (No terraced houses, please!) or they were way beyond her financial means. So she was relieved when her phone rang around midday.

It was Simon. "Listen. We said it seemed impossible to find electronic versions of the contracts between PC Lux Solutions and Qubus. All the more surprising since I've found out that there's a legal department in the same building and it is linked into the same server network."

"Do you have any idea where the original document could be?"

"It may be far-fetched, but I think they might keep it in an executive safe."

"Really?" Kaja wasn't very convinced.

"I have a gut feeling that tells me it's worth a try."

"OK." That argument was hard to refute, with a grandmother called Mémé and a shiny blue dragon sitting next to her. "Do you need any help?"

"To be honest, if you have the nerves for it, I'd prefer you to come with me. Of course, I have the floor plans of the building, but it's always helpful to have someone with local knowledge at hand, especially if something goes wrong. But it's also illegal..."

"Hm, I went in there in the middle of the night and everything went well."

"Yes, but you were an employee back then and could have talked your way out of any trouble, claiming you were doing overtime."

"That's true, but I'm happy to take the risk." Kaja said, shrugging her shoulders.

"Good. Are you free tonight? I'm already in Zurich."

"Tonight?" she looked at Lance for confirmation and he nodded. "Yes,why not? Perhaps it's best if I don't have too much time to think about your plan. Are you coming to pick me up?"

"I'll be there at eight so we can go through the details."

"Perfect." she hung up and asked Lance: "Can you watch my back again, please?"

"Yes, of course I can." he was quick to respond. He liked nothing better than a bit of excitement.

As Simon's call had reminded her of her old company, she decided to try her luck again phoning Max but, as before, she ended up straight in his mailbox. Slowly but surely, she was getting seriously worried. She dialled Thea's number. Perhaps her friend had some news for her.

"Hello stranger." she was greeted. "I thought you'd disappeared from the face of the earth."

"I know." Kaja replied meekly. "I needed some time to digest everything that's happened."

"Of course you did. Only pulling your leg." Thea laughed. "And? What's new?" she wanted to know, straight to the point as always.

"You mean apart from me showing an interest in you again?" Kaja joked.

"Exactly. Come on, spill."

"Even at the risk of boring you: Have you heard anything from Max? Or do you have any idea where he might be?"

"No, sorry, not a sausage. He's really disappeared from the face of the earth. And senior management, now almost completely consisting of Qubus staff plus two rather unpleasant former PC Lux colleagues, insist on their version that he's just on an extended training course." By now, she was talking in a hushed voice. "They're sacking one competent employee after another. I'm really surprised that I'm still around."

"It only proves how irreplaceable you are." Kaja tried to cheer her up.

"Yeah, yeah." Thea said dismissively. "I'm already writing piles of job applications in order to escape the bad atmosphere here."

"Is it that bad?"

"Worse." came the dry answer.

"I was wondering," Kaja changed the subject. "do they have a special meeting on tonight or anything else?"

"Let me have a look. No, not today. Why're you asking?"

"Oh, believe me, you don't want to know. I'll tell you another time when the walls and phones don't have ears." Thea took the hint and soon ended the conversation.

That evening, she waited impatiently for the clock to turn eight. She was keen to get started. Apparently, the planned mission had made her more nervous than expected. Miri had called her in the afternoon. Kaja had used the opportunity to tell her that she was seriously considering the suggestion of going self-employed with scented candles and was already looking for a suitable property. Miri had been happy for her and promised to keep her eyes open. She was going to meet Sierra later. Perhaps she could come up with an idea.

When Simon arrived at eight sharp, Kaja was all set to go. "Hold your horses. We need to do some planning first." he dampened her enthusiasm. "Can I come in for a minute?"

"Uhm, yes, of course." she said slightly embarrassed and let him enter the flat. "Sorry, I'm more excited than expected. Can I offer you a drink?"

"Oh yes, please. And if you have a sandwich or some sort of snack...?"

"Does he think we're a service station here?" Lance complained, eyeing up Simon suspiciously.

"Shush. He's not so different from a certain dragon, only that he wouldn't demand an alcoholic beverage." she put him in his place.

Simon, who had been looking out at her little patio, turned round. "Did you say something?"

Damn. Had she been talking aloud again? She quickly turned to Simon and said casually: "No, sometimes I just mumble to myself."

He looked at her in disbelief. In order to distract him, she offered him the ham sandwich she had just made. It worked. "Is a glass of water OK or do you prefer something else?"

As he had his mouth full already, he just gestured that water would be fine. Kaja was relieved. She wouldn't have known what else to offer. Tea perhaps, but it was hardly a drink for a man. She had to smile.

"Exactly. And why do I always get it then?" the complaint sounded in her head.

This time she made sure to transmit her words by thought only. "Because your preferred alternatives are whiskey or brandy. Or are you serious about wanting water instead of tea next time?"

When Lance kept quiet and turned away, offended, she had to smile again. "Don't be such a diva. You'd better listen to our discussion so that you know how to protect me later on."

These seemed to be the right words to get him out of his sulky mood. He sat down in a corner of the room, fully alert so as not to miss any detail of the conversation.

They ran through their arrangements one last time. On the floor plans Simon had brought along, Kaja pointed out the characteristics of the building and possible obstacles. "Good, we know how to get in, at least in theory. At this entrance here" she pointed to a particular spot on the plan, "they don't have a porter. It's only a small side entrance. We can use the staircase to get to the second floor."

"Using the side entrance is a good idea. I wasn't sure if it was only an emergency exit." Simon was happy.

"Once we're on the second floor, we'll reach the only critical point."

"Why is it critical?"

"Because there are many employees who often stay late, doing work or other things."

"Other things?" Simon raised his eyebrows.

"Well, on my last late night visit, I learned that our offices can be used for various purposes." she grinned.

"OK, I understand. Let's hope they've all flown the nest tonight."

"Exactly. Once we've cleared that level without incident, we'll reach the staircase and can go up one more floor to the executive suite." She pointed her finger to the location on the floor plan. "From then on, I'll leave everything to you. I neither have a clue what we're looking for nor how we should go about finding it."

"We're looking for a contract dated around the time your company merged with Qubus."

"Not the exact date?" Kaja was surprised.

"Maybe. But on the other hand, the document we're looking for may have been drafted at a later point."

"Oh, OK then. But what if it's kept in a safe?"

"Trust me, I can deal with that."

"Have you become a safe-cracker recently?" Kaja joked.

"Sort of. We're lucky that the safe is linked to the rest of the network..."

"Seriously? But then - anyone with your talents could..."

"...re-program it. Exactly."

Kaja could only shake her head at so much stupidity or so much luck, depending which way you looked at it. "How come they don't know? You'd have thought a computer company took such possibilities into consideration!"

"You'd have thought so, yes. Their only excuse could be that electronic business espionage is still rather rare in Switzerland, compared to other countries. And your average safe-cracker doesn't have the skills and technology that I have at my disposal. Not yet. And that makes people complacent and lazy."

"So it seems. Shall we make a move?"

Simon checked his watch. "It's just after nine. Let's wait another half an hour so we'll be there about ten. I haven't had a chance to thank you for accepting my offer." he tried to take her mind off the adventure.

She laughed. "No, I have to thank you. At least I won't have to starve if my other plans don't pay off quickly enough."

"What other plans do you have?"

She told him and realised how her idea was coming more and more to life. As she spoke, details emerged that she had not thought of before.

"Can I see one of those candles? Have you got one here tonight?"

"Oh yes, I have." She went over to the display cupboard. Tim's candle stood in front. "Here you are." She gave it to Simon.

"It's huge. And it smells lovely."

"Well, I won't make all of them that big. This one is a present for..." she stopped.

"Sorry I didn't catch that. Who for?" Simon was still distracted, admiring the candle.

"This one is for Tim. I haven't had a chance to give it to him yet." Her expression became withdrawn. "If you want to, you can take it along. It'll be easier for him to collect it from you." she said casually.

Something had gone wrong. Simon was quite sure of that. He looked at her inquisitively, but then decided to let the matter rest. At least for now. "I'd rather not." he said. "I'd be worried I might break it. In any case, I can imagine there's a market for such products. But first of all, you'll need a place to make them."

"You hit the nail on the head. I'm already searching for one. But it may take a while."

After checking his watch again, Simon got up. "Come on, let's go. The waiting's over."

Just twenty minutes later, they parked the car in a side street not far from the company. "Ready?"

Kaja looked at Simon doubtfully. "Maybe... I think so. And if not, we'll find out soon enough."

"It's still not too late for you to stay behind. You've already helped me tremendously by explaining the floor plans."

"No, I'll come with you. Two pairs of eyes are better than one."

"Good." They got out of the car and left Tsar behind. Simon strapped a slim bag round his waist. They both wore ordinary clothes, jeans and dark pullovers in order to blend in with the darkness.

"I'll go ahead. See you later." Lance said and disappeared.

They passed the badge-controlled gate without any problems, even though getting through it together on one ID was a bit of a squeeze. Kaja suppressed a hysterical giggle and led Simon up the stairs to the first floor. "Two people coming down." the dragon warned her in good time. In a quick decision, she pulled Simon into the ladies room.

"What..."

"Shush!" she pressed a finger to her lips. Now Simon could hear the steps, too. She quickly pushed Simon into one of the cubicles, just in case one of the passers-by was a woman who needed the loo. But they were in luck. The walking sound quickly moved away, down the stairs.

"Your ears are quite keen." Simon was impressed.

"I'm doing my best." Kaja mumbled, more to herself. "Let's get on with it." Without further interruption, they reached the first floor and found the next stairwell. Before they went up, Kaja stopped for a moment.

"Lance, everything clear up there? We're coming now."

"Nobody here."

To Simon, she said: "We're almost there." They ran upstairs two steps at a time and soon arrived at the top floor. "Quite cosy they have it here." Kaja stated when she found her feet almost disappearing in the long pile carpet.

"And the views are not too bad either." Simon agreed.

"Aren't you here on a mission?" Lance could be heard from one of the offices.

"Come on, let's start our search." Simon said, as if he had heard him.

Kaja secretly rolled her eyes at the two men. Lance had found a bottle of Jack Daniels on a desk and settled down, helping himself to the drink unashamedly. Kaja only hoped that Simon wouldn't notice the contents of the bottle disappearing bit by bit.

"It'll be best if you check the ring binders and any other papers you can find. I'll take care of the safe. Just make sure you put everything back in place exactly as you found it."

"No problem. By the way, what did you do to the safe?" she wanted to know as she leafed through one pile of paper after another.

"I simply changed the password between today 10pm and tomorrow 3am. I thought that'd give us ample time."

"Clever move."

"I think I need to get my eyes tested. Or go to bed earlier." Simon commented.

"Why's that?" Kaja looked at him in surprise.

"I could have sworn that whiskey bottle was three quarters full when we entered, now barely half is left." He shook his head.

"Maybe the lighting played a trick on you." she said casually.

In the meantime, she hissed at Lance in her thoughts: "Hands off that bottle or we'll get found out."

"Spoilsport."

"You'd better give me a hand."

"There's nothing in the safe." Simon sounded disappointed.

"Maybe I have something here." Kaja handed Simon a file packed with papers. He quickly flicked through it.

"Is it what we're looking for?"

"Maybe. I'll make some copies, just in case." He pulled a slim digital camera from his hip pouch and quickly took a photo of each page. Then they carried on searching for a little longer but eventually gave up.

"I think that's it. We've had a look in every folder and only found the one document looking promising. Let's get out of here before our luck runs out."

"Fine by me."

She straightened the last pile of papers and cast a final, scrutinising look round the office. As it was almost identical to the section leader's office in which she had been given the sack, her mind wandered back to that surreal scene. She started. Now she knew what she had wanted to tell Simon but always kept forgetting. By now, he was on his way out of the room and she hurried to catch up with him. She grabbed him by his sleeve and made him stop. "I finally remember." it bubbled out of her.

"Whatever it is, good for you, but be quiet now. We don't want to be caught in the last few yards."

Shocked and slightly offended, Kaja followed Simon's instructions. It didn't help that Lance was on Simon's side for a change. "Stop sulking. He's right. I think I heard something just now, but everything's quiet again."

Five minutes later, they were back in the car. They had narrowly missed a Securitas man on patrol. Simon had noticed him when they were about to leave the building. So they had waited nervously for him to turn the next corner before they could move on. When Lance had given them the all clear, which for Simon came from Kaja, of course, they had walked as quickly as they dared without raising any suspicion from chance observers back to the side street where their car was parked.

"Phew, I don't think I could make a career of this. I'd be a nervous wreck in next to no time." Kaja moaned.

"Nevertheless, you did pretty well." Simon praised her. "Now come on, tell me what you suddenly remembered earlier on."

"My dismissal was based on the accusation that I was sexually harassing my boss, Max, which in itself is complete nonsense."

"OK, what else?"

"I was supposed to have upset Max's wife."

"So far, so plausible." Simon commented, earning himself a frown from Kaja. "I was only referring to the story. A jealous wife makes sense."

"But that's the whole point."

"He's not married?" Simon tried to confirm with raised eyebrows.

"Not only that, he's not into women at all."

"Oh, in that case, the story's plausibility takes a hit." Simon agreed. "Are there any other inconsistencies?"

"Certainly some details that only raised my suspicion when seen in context. For instance, the section leader knew that I had been trying to contact Max for several days. He claimed Max had complained about me, but that doesn't make sense in connection with the rest of his claims, which he had obviously invented."

"Hm." Simon was thinking. "Which would mean" he finally said, "that your section leader knows where Max is and also that he has access to his phone. It doesn't look good." He shook his head. "Let's get back to your place. I need some more details from you."

"You mean..."

"At the moment, I don't mean anything. But it looks like the whole thing is more serious than I thought." he answered grimly. In subdued silence, he drove them back to Kaja's flat. "I need his home address and, most of all, his mobile phone number, the one that you tried to call all that time."

"What're you going to do with it?"

"We'll try to establish his last location and then we'll take it from there." When he saw the worried look on her face, he briefly squeezed her arm. "We'll find him, somehow. Don't get too upset."

After he had gone, Kaja did exactly that: "'Don't get too upset.' What else am I supposed to do?" She paced up and down the sitting room, gesticulating.

"Don't you have anything to say?" she hissed at Lance.

"Erm, I thought I'd better keep quiet since my advice wouldn't be that much different from his. There's nothing you can do at the moment. So you'd better concentrate on finding a new home and on all your other plans. In short: get your mind distracted!"

Kaja was about to give him a belligerent reply, but somehow all her energy had drained away. Tired, she sat down on the sofa and hugged a large cushion.

"Come to bed, before you're falling asleep here." the dragon reminded her. She followed him to bed and pushed him off her pillow. Surprisingly, she fell asleep straight away.

28

The next day, Kaja decided to pay Miri a surprise visit in her bookshop. Out on her run with Zorro in the morning (Lance had excused himself claiming that he had had a really bad night because of her.), she had mulled over the plans in her head and had come to the conclusion that, if she was to start her own enterprise, she needed to accept the offer Mémé had made on her last visit, meaning another short visit to France was due soon. She didn't want to discuss the issue over the phone. But she wasn't keen on travelling on her own either.

"I'll come with you. You don't need anyone else for company." Lance had protested.

"I rather thought of asking Miri if she wanted to come with me."

"That's a completely different matter." he replied enthusiastically. He had already been worried that she might ask Tim.

"So I was right in thinking that the prospect of having two girls for company would change your mind." she laughed. "You're so predictable."

Lance preferred to keep a dignified silence.

At the bookshop, Miri was nowhere to be found. Kaja decided to browse through the books and wait for her to turn up. But instead, a grumpy man appeared, keeping a jealous watch over her, apparently just waiting for a book to be dropped or a page to be bent. The interior of the shop was lacking any personal touch. 'That's strange.' Kaja thought. She had expected Miri to have turned it into a little fantasy land, using her artistic skills. In principle, the old, wooden, well-aged bookshelves gave the shop some character. But the carelessly arranged books and the dark, unsightly carpet rather gave you the impression of not being welcome.

"Lance, why don't you go and find out where Miri is and whether she's got time to come to the front. I'd rather not ask this disguised prison warder and get her into trouble." Lance signalled her he had understood and went off on his search, unnoticed by the man.

He was back in next to no time. "She's in the store room and can't come to the front right now. But her lunch break is due in half an hour. If you can wait that long, she'll meet us by the fountain."

Kaja looked at her watch. She could buy some food in the meantime. "Good, let's get out of here, before this watchdog decides he doesn't like us."

Half an hour later, they met in front of the big fountain. Kaja had bought some pasta salad and an olive baguette. Miri gave her a long-winded apology: "I'm so sorry. I would have loved to come out and say hello. But I had an argument with my uncle earlier on and he usually consigns me to the store room after that."

"No problem. I suspected something like that. That's why I sent Lance to look for you."

"Another practical use for a dragon." Miri grinned. "Is he for hire?"

"Hey, stop it right there, I'm not your full-time errand boy!" Lance rebelled and spouted little flames from his mouth. "That'll be the day..." he ranted on.

Amused, the two women watched the dragon get in a huff and a puff. Finally, Kaja turned back to Miri.

"What was your argument about?"

"Oh, nothing special. I'd just made another attempt at convincing him that the bookshop could do with a makeover. It's so uninspiring at the moment."

"That's exactly what I thought when I saw the shop earlier on." Kaja agreed with her. "And I asked myself why your creative talent hadn't left its mark anywhere."

Miri sighed. "Books are a serious matter. They don't mix well with my ungodly creations." she perfectly imitated the reproachful voice of her uncle.

"Ungodly? Was he serious?"

"Oh, he was very serious. I should add that both my uncle and my aunt are very religious."

"But still... You could have done something completely different for the bookshop."

"Of course I would have. But enough about me. How come I'm honoured with your visit?" Miri skilfully diverted the conversation away from her relatives.

"I wanted to see you, give you an update and invite you for a holiday."

"Hang on. That's a bit much in one go. A holiday?"

"Well, just a weekend away, to be more precise. I want to visit my grandmother."

"The one in France? The one who knows Lance as well?"

"That's her. Do you want to come with me?"

"When?"

"This weekend. I know it's a bit short notice. But you're at work during the week and the weekend after we're invited to Sierra's party."

"Oh, I almost forgot. Hm."

"You're not up for it?"

"Oh, yes, I am. Certainly. It's only that I'm supposed to work this Saturday and I don't think I'll get a day off in the current climate." Miri replied sounding disappointed.

"Even if you fall sick, rather unfortunately?" Lance suggested with an innocent face.

"Lance!" Kaja protested, even though she had briefly pondered the idea herself. "Miri could get into even more trouble."

"Why not? It's a brilliant idea. Count me in." Miri jumped at the suggestion. "Friday lunch time, I'll have to go home as I am close to dying."

"Are you absolutely sure?"

"As sure as I've been for a long time. It's ages since I last managed to get away."

"Good, in that case, I'll pick you up at one and we can set off straight from your place. Take a warm jumper and a raincoat. You can never be sure about the weather."

"I will. But now it's time for me to go or the slave driver will send out a search party."

"The way I see it, Miri is in desperate need of another job." Kaja mumbled, as she and Lance watched her hurry across the road.

"All in due course." was Lance's cryptic reply. "Don't you want to invite Sierra as well?"

"To be honest, I don't think she'll be able to drop everything at such short notice."

"You may be right." Lance agreed.

"And then it'll get rather crowded in my Peugeot, considering the back seat is occupied by a dragon and a large dog."

"I could make myself really, really small and sit on someone's lap." he was keen to suggest.

"Yes, you could." Kaja imagined the picture vividly and rolled her eyes with amusement.

Back at home, she noticed her mobile phone flashing. Two missed calls. Both from Tim. But he hadn't left a message. Perhaps it was better that way, she decided. She was determined not to return his calls. Let him go to Iceland first and postpone any decisions until after. Resolutely, she banished all those memories of her night with Tim welling up in her and desperately tried to control the longing tension in her stomach. She had a life to organise.

She decided to make her visit to Mémé a surprise and refrained from calling her. Instead, she had to endure a call from her parents, resulting in a fifteen-minute monologue on how to find a proper job. Freelancing for a security company obviously didn't fit their idea of serious work, she commented to Lance afterwards with an ironic smile on her lips.

"I'm sure they think I work as a bouncer now."

But even if it hadn't been a pleasant conversation, it didn't stress Kaja out as much as it used to. Lance was pleased to see that she quickly found her composure again and continued to work on her plans.

Just before dinner, she had a brief call from Simon: "It looks like we are in luck. The document you found is indeed a contract between the two companies."

"And? Did you find any clues to explain the strange things going on in the joint venture?" Kaja was keen to know.

"Maybe. I haven't had the time to go through all the legal gobbledegook yet. But it looks like the more successful shareholder will indeed hold 51%

after one year, giving him a free hand in management decisions."

"OK, but what has it got to do with Max?"

"I don't know yet, but I hope we'll be able to ask him soon, in person."

"You mean you found him?"

"Not yet, but we were able to establish that his mobile phone searches for a network signal at irregular intervals. I suppose he or someone else is switching it on and off occasionally."

"And what can we do about it?"

"We wait and hope he'll switch it on again soon so that we can locate it."

"It could be an endless waiting game. I only hope there was no need for us to get worried." Kaja said.

"That's what I hope, too." Simon replied, but it didn't give Kaja much encouragement.

Friday lunchtime came very quickly. Miri was already waiting in the street outside her flat.

"Glad you could make it." Kaja welcomed her.

"I'm looking forward to our trip. I was lucky that I could persuade the old lady living next to me to look after Chili."

"Of course, he needs taking care of as well. I almost forgot about your cat."

"Yes, I can hardly take him with me like you take Zorro. But I begged Mrs. Weber and she eventually agreed to take him."

"Aren't you worried that she'll be half-hearted about looking after him?"

"Oh, it's all pretence. She actually loves it and spoils him rotten. Then it's up to me to put him back on his usual diet. She only moans a little in the beginning to make it look as if she's got a busy life."

"That's OK then. Make yourself comfortable. We'll be on the road for a few hours."

Miri turned round on her passenger seat and said hello to Lance and Zorro before kicking her shoes off and finding a relaxed sitting position. "I have some travelling provisions here." She bent forward and produced various items from her rucksack. "Matchmakers and chocolate rice crackers, juice, hot Kona coffee, some apples and, to keep us nicely filled, a selection of cheese and ham rolls."

Kaja laughed.

"You don't like them?"

"Oh yes, I do. But please have a look in the bag behind my seat." Miri reached for it and looked inside. It contained exactly the same things, minus the coffee, but with the addition of a few energy cereal bars and some bottles of water.

"I can't match your coffee." Kaja admitted openly. "And to be honest, I had hoped you would bring some."

"So it looks like mission accomplished. Would you like a cup now?"

"I'd love to."

"Does your grandma like coffee?"

"I'm sure she'll like this one."

"Oh, in that case I'm relieved. I have a bag for her, as a thank-you."

"Really?" Kaja was slightly jealous. "You shouldn't have."

"Of course, I had to. It's only thanks to you and Mémé that I can have a long overdue holiday."

After a moment of silence, Kaja commented innocently: "Perhaps I can share it with her."

Miri grinned. "No worries, I've got some for you as well."

Kaja grinned back, embarrassed. "You know me so well. I'm hooked on your coffee and it brings out the worst in me. You don't need to give it to me. Just tell me where I can buy it and I will get some myself."

"OK, I'll give you the supplier's address when we're back. But you can keep the pack I bought for you."

"That's so typical. Nobody thinks of me in the back here." Lance complained.

"Or me!" Zorro whimpered with him, for once agreeing with the dragon.

Kaja rolled her eyes. "Miri, can you please give Lance an apple and shut Zorro up with one of those giant dog biscuits?"

"I will." She bent forward to search her bag again and then Kaja's, before offering the suggested items to their back-seat passengers. Zorro was over the moon with his biscuit, but the same could not be said for Lance.

"An apple? Are you serious?"

"You always nick them from me, don't you? I thought you might be pleased."

Irritated, Lance inspected the fruit before resigning himself to his fate and biting into it.

"What's wrong with you?" A satisfied Zorro asked him, munching at his biscuit. "I can't complain about the food." Now it was Lance's turn to roll his eyes.

Eight hours later, with most of the rolls and sweets gone, they crawled out of the tiny Peugeot, feeling rather stiff. Lance disappeared in a starry blue cloud while Zorro set about exploring the area.

"We can leave the luggage in the car and fetch it later." Together, they approached the small house.

"It's so beautiful here." Miri stopped and admired the landscape.

Kaja took a deep breath of the cool autumn air. "Yes, it is. I have to come back at least once a year to re-charge my batteries." She went quiet. "Unfortunately, I haven't had time to come more often recently. Come on, let's see if Mémé is home."

"Didn't you announce our visit?"

"No, I wanted it to be a surprise. Although, come to think of it, it was meant to the same last time. But she was already waiting for me." She frowned.

"Intuition." Miri guessed. "Whatever. We'll find out soon enough. There's light in the kitchen, it looks like she's in."

Kaja pushed the old, wooden door open. Her entrance made the two old people inside jump with guilt. Mémé was first to gather herself, got up from the kitchen table and rushed over to Kaja to welcome her and give her a hug. "Oh, there's someone else." she noticed. "Do come in."

Miri, who was not used to such a warm welcome, entered the kitchen hesitantly. Mémé turned straight to her and gave her the same tight hug as she had welcomed Kaja with. "I'm Josephine and you must be a friend of Kaja's."

"Yes I am, my name's Miri."

"Come on, sit down. Kaja, as you can see, I have a visitor." "This is Luc." she said to Miri.

"And you really didn't know I was coming?" Her granddaughter asked surprised. Mémé looked slightly embarrassed.

"It looks like it."

Kaja looked at her in disbelief.

"I've been rather busy recently." she defended herself.

Kaja smiled and looked straight over to Luc, who in turn kept staring at his hands. "Yes, I'm sure."

"Can I offer you a nice cup of tea?" Mémé tried to distract her visitors.

"Oh, that'd be lovely." Miri, who had stayed in the background, joined the conversation.

"I'd better be off now." Luc grumbled.

"No, please stay." Kaja took his hand. "I have a candle for you in my car."

"Oh, you remembered?" He seemed happy.

"Of course I did."

"And what about that young fellow. What was his name?"

"Tim." Kaja helped him, desperately trying to sound casual. "No, I haven't given one to him yet. I'll do that when I see him."

"And I thought you'd bring him along the next time you came" Mémé intervened. To Miri, she said apologising: "I didn't mean you're not welcome here, of course."

Miri smiled at her: "I know what you meant."

Kaja mumbled almost unintelligibly: "I'd better get the candle now."

Luc got up and gave Josephine a peck on the cheek. "I'll go with her to the car and then straight home. I'm sure you have a lot to talk about."

"Mais bien sûr." She returned the kiss and, with obvious affection, pushed a stubborn strand of white hair out of his face.

"How long has this been going on between the two of you?" Kaja wanted to know as they went to the car together.

"Uhm, you'd better put that question to your grandmother." he mumbled into his beard.

"Oh yes, I will, don't worry." she replied impatiently. "But I've got hold of you on your own first."

"I can't remember the exact date." He was looking straight in her face now. "I've admired Josephine for ages. You can't imagine how happy I am right now. But... how do you feel about it?"

Kaja listened to her own emotions and thoughts in turmoil for a moment. But then she grinned at him. "It's wonderful. I just didn't expect this to happen. You two can be so secretive!"

Luc blushed. But it didn't stop him from retorting. "You're no better. What's up with your Tim?"

She sighed. "You're like a dog with a bone. Can't let go, can you?"

Luc didn't let her avoid the issue and just looked at her in anticipation. She finally gave in.

"I'm really fond of Tim. But that's no good if he's always on the move, is it?"

Luc frowned. "On the move?"

"Yes, right now, he's on his way to Iceland. And then he plans to go to Brazil and who knows what comes next."

"I see."

Kaja was relieved not having to explain any more. She opened the car door and reached inside to get Luc's candle. She had wrapped it in a soft cloth to protect it on the journey. "Here, I hope you'll like it."

He opened the cloth and tested the aroma. "Mh, peppermint... and a hint of lemon grass, just in the background."

"Exactly. Do you like it?"

"Very much. I'll light it tonight, straight away."

"Alright then. I'll go back inside. Perhaps I'll see you tomorrow." Kaja suggested.

"Yes, and don't forget to bring your pretty friend."

Kaja laughed. "Don't let Mémé hear you say that."

"Your grandmother is way above such things."

"You may be right."

When she came back, Miri and Josephine were engaged in an animated conversation. Ria, the white cat, had curled up on Miri's lap. Obviously, Miri was truly a cat-person, Kaja thought smiling. Lance had also made himself comfortable at the kitchen table, with a bottle of his beloved elderberry brandy in front of him and a game of patience under way. Her head brushed against a bundle of dried herbs pinned up on one of the thick beams and a rain of small lavender blossom fell on her. Mémé looked up asking: "And? Was he impressed?"

"Impressed? With what?" Kaja was confused.

"The candle, of course. I know he's impressed with Miri." she replied cheekily. Miri looked from one to the other and didn't know what to make of the conversation.

"I'm glad you can see through that sly fox. And I like it even better that he knows that you know." Kaja said with a meaningful grin. To Miri, she said: "Don't worry. It was just a joke at Luc's expense, not yours." Miri relaxed and laughed with them. "To answer your question: yes, he liked the candle very much."

"What did you put in it?"

"Peppermint and lemon grass." She pointed at her friend. "Miri was a great help in making it. She also gave me advice on the selection of herbs."

"So, she's the second one in your trio. The number three has always been a very powerful one." Mémé stated, lost in thought. "Who's your third sister? Have you found her yet?"

"Yes, we have, recently." Miri answered. She told Mémé of their accidental encounter and how they had tracked Sierra down after a long search.

"Long? It seems to me you've found her relatively quickly." Josephine objected.

"Hm, with hindsight, you may be right. But we were so keen and impatient that it seemed like an eternity to us."

"I'm curious, too, where you three are heading." Mémé admitted.

"I still don't have a clue what the purpose of all this is. It's not as if we were the three musketeers or something like that."

"Perhaps we are." Miri giggled. "No,seriously. We're not living in a fantasy novel or are destined to save the world. Of course I'm happy to have met you and that we've made friends. I don't know enough about Sierra yet, but she seems to be alright, too. But where do we go from here?"

"Sierra is a really nice person. But you're right: what's the purpose? And why do we have a dragon?"

Josephine had been listening to the two young women for some time without saying a word. She also watched the dragon who seemed to have dozed off at the table. Only the tip of his tail twitched occasionally and belied the impression that he was fast asleep. "What does Lance have to say about it?" she interjected. The dragon secretly winked at her. Kaja and Miri looked at each other. And then they looked at the dragon.

He stopped playing the game and opened his eyes. "I've told them all I know. The dragon council hasn't been any more specific."

Mémé thought for a moment before suggesting: "I don't think you're expected to be great heroines. Instead, the magic of your bond is becoming apparent in smaller things."

Hearing this, Miri went strangely silent, while Kaja, in her usual manner, tried to dig deeper and asked Mémé for a more detailed explanation.

But finally, she gave up and said to Miri: "Come on, time to go to bed. You can sleep in my room, if you like."

"That's fine by me." Miri was quick to accept, glad to find a bed soon. The journey had been more exhausting than anticipated.

"And where does that leave me?" Lance wanted to know.

"Sorry, you'll have to fend for yourself." Kaja told him boldly. "I'm fully booked up." Zorro was about to give the dragon a gloating bark but stopped when she added: "Perhaps Zorro can make some room for you in his basket." The dog was relieved to hear that the dragon found the offer too insulting to accept. It would have been a nightmare.

The next morning, Kaja woke up to the delicious smell of Hawaiian coffee. She sat up and saw Miri lying next to her, still asleep with Ria rolled up by her neck. It looked like Mémé had already received her present yesterday. Quietly, so as not to wake her friend, she tip-toed out of the room, only watched by the sleepy gaze of the cat. She put on some woollen socks, changed her pyjama bottoms for jogging ones, took a warm fleece and made her way down the steep wooden stairs to the kitchen.

There, she found Mémé and Lance having coffee together. "That coffee is lovely." Mémé praised the brew. "Your friend is very welcome here." she grinned.

"I'm hooked on it as well." Kaja admitted laughing.

"Considering the time of day, you seem to be exceptionally bright." Lance grumbled and gave Kaja a sour look.

"Yes, I am. And how was your night, my dearest dragon?" she replied in an exaggerated friendly tone.

"As if you wanted to know. But I'll tell you anyway: it was horrible."

"That's not true. He took over my bedroom." Josephine revealed what really happened.

"That's so typical! Why do you women always have to stick together?" the dragon exclaimed and stormed off in anger.

"He seems rather touchy today." Kaja commented, watching him leave. "He didn't even make the effort to disappear in his usual way."

"Don't worry. He's angry because I didn't put any elderberry brandy in his coffee. But there's a limit, even for dragons."

"That's what I've been trying to tell him all the time. Perhaps he thought he'd have an easier ride with you, for old times' sake."

"Perhaps." It looked like she was going to have Mémé to herself for some time as Miri was likely to have a long lie-in. So she decided to grab the opportunity and discuss the reason for their visit.

"I already told you on the phone that I've lost my job."

"Yes, you did. How're you coping?"

"That's the strange thing: I'm doing very well. Admittedly, I find the circumstances a bit odd and I'm keen to find out what's really happening in the company. But apart from that, I'm actually quite happy. It feels like it was the kick in the backside I needed to seriously question my life and my future."

Mémé smiled at Kaja's choice of words. The girl had summed it up nicely. And it was high time, too. She nodded at Kaja to signal she was listening but didn't want to interrupt.

"It made me realise two things: on the one hand, I don't want to give up the computer work completely. At first I thought I would, but then Simon, a friend of Tim's who's running a security firm, made me an offer to work for him freelance. That took me by surprise and I hesitated as I had and still have other ideas. But when I discussed it with Tim, I realised that being a freelancer allows me to decide how much work I want to do in this area."

"That sounds ideal. Almost as if you were your own boss." Mémé commented. "And what about your other plans?"

"Well, those other plans are the reason why I'm here. When I was still searching for solutions, Miri gave me the idea of starting my own business, similar to yours."

"You mean dealing in candles and scents?"

"Exactly." Kaja carefully watched her grandmother, worried how she would take the news. But there was no need to be concerned.

"But that's wonderful! After all, it was your idea in the first place."

"Don't talk nonsense. You had been doing it in your little workshop for years." her granddaughter objected.

"I had. But you were the one with the business sense." Mémé insisted. "There's no reason to suggest you won't have the same success in Switzerland as I have here. How are you planning to do it? Do you want to come back here to live and manufacture and just go to Switzerland to sell? Or are you looking to start your own production line there?"

Kaja hummed and hawed. "Hm, well... that's the problem. I'd love to stay in Switzerland. It's not that I wouldn't like to live here, but..."

"It was only a question, not an expectation on my part." Mémé calmed her down.

Kaja looked at her, relieved. "But I need a place where I can make the candles and grow some of the herbs, the ones that can cope with less sunlight. I might even use some local varieties that you don't have here. It's only that my flat is not suitable for such a venture."

"That's true."

"That's why I started to look for an old farmhouse or something similar. I don't mind it being a bit shabby. But it is difficult to find such a place to rent, even more than to buy." She took a deep breath. "And that's why I meant to ask you whether you were serious about the ten percent that you've saved up for me, whether I could possibly have it?"

"Of course you can. That way, the money stays in the same line of business." Mémé was happy to confirm.

Kaja felt a load being taken off her mind. She rushed over to her grandmother and gave her a hug. Tears were welling in her eyes as she said: "Thank you for always believing in me."

"Now now, no need to get sentimental so early in the morning." Mémé replied, patting her back, just as she used to when she was a little girl. "It's rather a reason to celebrate."

Kaja sat down and blew her nose. "You're right." she grinned. "Perhaps even Lance will have a chance to get the drink he missed earlier on."

They spent some more time discussing various aspects of their future co-operation. Some time later, Miri joined them and went all bubbly with excitement until Kaja exclaimed: "Stop, my head is spinning from all those figures, lists of herbs, wax mixtures and emulsions. I can see myself coming back here regularly and watching you work. There are still so many things I need to learn."

"Only do what you like doing. With time, you'll develop your own ideas anyway and soon I may be the one learning from you." Mémé joked.

"You're right. First things first. I need a base to work from."

"I mentioned it to Sierra and she said she'd ask around." Miri stopped for a moment. "I even had the impression she already knew a suitable property."

"You hadn't told me. That would be marvellous."

"I just remembered. You can give her a call later on."

"I will. So, now that's done, who's coming to the village with me?"

"By the way, what's up with Tim?" Mémé suddenly asked.

"He's, uhm, well... He's in Iceland at the moment. That's all I know." was Kaja's pert answer. "And what's up with Luc?" she retorted.

Mémé looked out of the window, lost in thought. "I found real love, by chance. At least on my part. For him it was hard work. I didn't use to have time or space for anyone else in my life."

Kaja looked down, feeling guilty.

"Oh, don't. It had nothing to do with you. You weren't here that often anyway. If that had been the only reason, we would have got together ages ago." Mémé was quick to clarify.

"Yes, you're right." Kaja agreed. "My relationship with Tim is more complicated." she explained. "Perhaps I'm complicated. I can't deny it. But just like you did back then, I feel I need to finish other things first, such as this project, before I'm willing and able to deal with more complex issues."

The other two women nodded in understanding, although Miri's romantic nature would have preferred an immediate happy end. The only question was: what would a happy end have to look like for Kaja to accept it?

29

On Sunday night they arrived back in Zurich, tired but in high spirits.

Kaja had called Sierra from France to find out more about the house she had mentioned to Miri. Her description was rather vague. An old farm house in need of updating, lots of land and some outbuildings. Kaja had no idea what to make of those buildings. They could be anything from a tatty kennel to a pigsty. Sierra had promised to arrange a viewing and to find out whether the property was for rent or for sale. She hoped she would hear from Sierra soon, but she had sounded rather stressed on the phone. Kaja frowned. She wished she could find the time soon to get to know Sierra better. The friendship between her and Miri had been almost instantaneous. It felt as if they had been friends for ages and had only lost track of each other for a while.

All was well between them, apart from the occasional fits of jealousy concerning her dragon, Kaja thought with amusement. With Sierra, it was different. She liked her, but somehow she couldn't make sense of her. Not yet.

"You're no longer jealous because of me, but because of Miri." Lance's voice insisted in her head. She stopped mid-movement, her hands holding a pile of dirty clothes from her weekend trip, destined for the washing machine, and was about to give him a sharp reply when she realised there was some truth in it, whether she liked it or not. "I didn't know I was the jealous type." Kaja admitted.

"What are you afraid of?"

"Afraid?"

"Yes, jealousy is often based on fear or insecurity, to put it differently."

"I see. Hm, I don't know." She tried to work it out. "Perhaps I'm not sure what a new person in my life will do to my relationship with Miri, who's become a very close friend." She hesitated. "I'm also afraid that Tim will become addicted to his adventures."

"So he'll go away on his regular trips. What's the problem? He'll be back. You've survived very well without his permanent presence so far."

"I don't even expect his permanent presence. It would drive me mad."

"Ah yes, but it would be nice to have him close by and on call when you need him." Lance teased her.

"Yes, that would be nice." she admitted and had to laugh. Now that he had put it in words, it sounded rather selfish. She looked for the washing powder.

"Will you like Miri less, once you've got to know Sierra?"

"That's completely different." Kaja protested.

"Exactly..."

"You're right. I should have a little more trust in people."

"I think so. Not only in others, but in yourself, too."

"So, now you've practised your psychiatrist skills long enough at my expense." She put a few more clothes in the machine, slammed the door and started the programme. "Anyway, where are you?" She curiously looked round the laundry room, but couldn't find him anywhere.

"Let's play hide and seek." His voice challenged in her head. Silly.

But she still went on searching for him. "You could at least speak loudly so that I can hear you." She was getting annoyed.

"That would be too easy."

On top of the washing machine, there was a tumble dryer and for a split-second, she saw something blueish moving behind it.

'Gotcha.' she thought, carefully sneaked up on the appliance and quietly extended her arm to grab the scaly tail.

"Hey, that's not fair!"

Kaja laughed and rolled her eyes.

"What would have been? Having me search forever and a day?"

"Yes, at least."

Sierra gave her a surprise phone call on Tuesday afternoon. She still sounded stressed, but insisted on joining Kaja for the viewing on Thursday.

"Aren't you busy with your party preparations?"

"I have to get out of the house, otherwise I'll go mad." she explained.

"If you want, I can come back to your place afterwards and help with whatever needs doing."

"Have you ever mucked out a stable?" Sierra taunted her.

"Erm, no." Kaja replied, irritated. "But I'm sure I can learn." After all, it wasn't rocket science.

"We'll see. Pick me up at two." And so she hung up without a further word.

"What the heck..." Kaja was staring at the receiver in her hand.

"She's a bit brusque, your new friend." Lance commented.

"I think she's just stressed at the moment." Kaja defended Sierra, although she wasn't sure why. She hadn't been very friendly, but at least she had arranged the viewing.

In the meantime, she was keeping busy sorting out finances and collecting ideas. Miri had found several cheap books about growing local and exotic herbs in her uncle's bookshop. Kaja worked her way through them with great enthusiasm, in addition to regularly consulting her own reference books about essential oils. There was no point in planting herbs that had no practical use. In her initial euphoria, she had even considered creating a range of perfumes but later, as she gathered more information, decided against it. Better to start her venture with products she knew and was comfortable with. She could always branch out later.

"I'm really proud of you." Lance said as they sat together over a glass of elderberry brandy. In all fairness, Kaja was only sipping hers while Lance was having his usual generous helping.

"I'm honoured, but why do I deserve it?" Surprised, she glanced at Lance, past her feet which were resting on the coffee table.

"To start with, I'm impressed with your ideas and secondly, I admire you for considering and even embracing change. That's a big step for a woman who fought tooth and nail against even the tiniest of changes only a few weeks ago."

"But I didn't have a choice, did I?" she replied, slightly embarrassed.

"On the contrary, there could have been a thousand other ways of dealing with your situation. And most of them would have involved a degree of passive suffering. But you decided to accept the hand that was dealt to you and played the cards your way." Lance's voice was starting to sound melancholy.

"Hey." Kaja was alarmed. "Don't even think about disappearing from my life."

He laughed. "That's another change in you. Not so long ago, you took every opportunity to point out that there wasn't any room for me in your life."

"Well..."

"What about a game of cards?" Lance changed the subject and produced a pack out of nowhere.

On Thursday afternoon, she arrived at Sierra's house at exactly two o'clock. She had just parked the car when Sierra came through the barn door, followed by a medium-sized, black and grey dog with brown spots on his face and paws and a white breast.

Sierra opened the passenger door and asked Kaja, who was still sitting behind the wheel: "Thanks for picking me up. Can I bring Joker along?"

"Does he get on with other dogs? I have Zorro with me. And he'd have to sit on your lap." She made an apologetic gesture towards the back seat which was fully taken up by Zorro and Lance. "Sorry my car isn't very big."

"She's alright with other dogs. I don't know about dragons, but I can take her on my lap. She loves that."

"You're lucky she's not as big as Zorro." Kaja commented.

Sierra smiled. "That's true. Let's go then. Just follow the road."

Kaja looked at Sierra and noticed that she was nervously looking back to the house. "Something wrong?" she asked as she started the engine and skilfully reversed out onto the main road.

"No." Sierra said evasively. "I just had a disagreement with Marcus about the urgency of this viewing."

"Well, that's understandable. I haven't been searching for very long and you're so busy with your party the day after tomorrow..." Kaja said, feeling guilty.

"That's not the point. I wanted you to see the property as soon as possible. I have my reasons." Sierra's face looked withdrawn and she seemed to be concentrating on the scenery passing by outside.

Kaja wasn't sure how to react, so she kept quiet. It wasn't an unpleasant silence between them and it was only interrupted by Sierra's occasional directions.

About fifteen minutes later, Sierra started to talk again: "We're almost there. I won't blame you for thinking it's in the middle of nowhere, but I really like it out here. I've always been the 'lone wolf' type." They passed through a small village. "At least they have a railway station here with an hourly service and a small grocery shop. But nobody knows how long that'll survive." She admitted openly. "Let's move on. We still have a little forest drive in front of us."

As she drove, Kaja took the landscape in. The forest consisted mainly of deciduous trees. The sun was sending a few rays through the thinning autumn leaves. Some branches were almost bare already. The road went slightly uphill. Suddenly the forest opened up and revealed views into the valley. A few cattle were grazing and some isolated farms were dotted around in the countryside. So far, she liked what she saw. "Before you reach the next house, take a sharp right turn onto the gravel track."

Kaja reduced her speed and turned onto the unmetalled road which took them through another wooded area before they finally reached their destination.

"You can park here, on the right-hand side. We won't obstruct anyone."

"Isn't the owner coming?"

"No, he's given me the keys and asked me to show you around." Sierra replied. They got out of the car and released their dogs. It took them no more than two seconds to sniff each other out before starting to explore the property together.

Only now did Kaja have the chance to take a closer look at the surroundings.

"This location is amazing, it's like a high plateau." All around them, there were overgrown pastures, marked by a ramshackle wire-mesh fence.

"Come on, let's look at the rest. I'm afraid the views are almost the only positive aspect." Sierra commented and pulled a sour face. She removed the two weathered bars that formed a makeshift gate and went in. Kaja admired the views for another moment but then followed her friend.

"By the way, what kind of name is Sierra?" Kaja wanted to know.

She smiled, embarrassed. "My parents spent their honeymoon in the States and must have had a memorable night in the Sierra Nevada or thereabouts." She looked at Kaja. "That was the start of me, or so legend has it."

"How romantic." Kaja laughed.

Sierra sighed, but her eyes went all soft. "My parents are the greatest romantics on earth. Still, after more than thirty years." She said this with some sadness in her voice, but quickly collected herself and concentrated on her role as a property guide. Kaja and Sierra stood in front of a small brick building that was missing half its roof and had a few broken windows. Wild vine had climbed up the outside walls and apparently found its way inside.

"That's part of it. I don't know what the original purpose of the building was, but with a little bit of work you could convert it into a cosy holiday home."

Curious, Kaja peeped through one of the broken windows. "Can we have a look inside? I love exploring old buildings."

"Of course you can..." Sierra selected a large key from the ring in her hand and struggled to open the old wooden door. Inside, it was rather dark as the vine stopped the sunlight from coming through the windows. They both went inside. Kaja slowly wandered through the small building with its peeling plaster. Two minutes later, she was back by the entrance. "It's bigger than it seems from the outside." she commented.

"You're right. I'd almost forgotten that it has three rooms."

"You've been here before?" She asked surprised.

"Yes, otherwise I couldn't show you around." was Sierra's tight-lipped answer. "Let's move on. There's lots more to see." After locking the door again, they went over to the main building. The gravelled footpath, now covered with weeds, led them in a slight bend past a small orchard and what Kaja assumed must have been the original stables. The main house could be seen in the background. As they passed the apple trees, Kaja picked up a worm-eaten apple. "They're probably best for making juice. Can be rather sour." Sierra warned her.

"I don't think this one is." Kaja replied, carefully biting into it to see where the worm was hiding.

"Do you want to have a look at the barn or are you more interested in the house?"

"You said the barn might be ideal for my candle production?"

"Exactly. It would be perfect for your plans. At least from what Miri told me." She pushed the door open. "The animals were kept in the stable next to this barn. Here they used to park their machinery."

"This is huge! I could store tons of material." Kaja was surprised. "And there's much more light in here than I thought."

"Wait till you've seen the hayloft." She pulled down an extendable ladder. "I hope you're not afraid of heights." she grinned and began to climb up. The dust made Kaja cough and Sierra apologised. "Sorry, it's been a while since this was cleaned." Kaja followed Sierra up the steep ladder. "This would need a proper staircase." She shouted to Kaja over her shoulder. When they reached the loft, Kaja looked around. On the right-hand side, there was a solid wall, the full height of the room. Sierra saw Kaja inspecting it and explained. "It's a firewall. The rest of the original hayloft, still functioning as one, is located behind it. As you can see, there are five large roof lights on each side. That's why there's so much light in this part of the barn."

Kaja just couldn't stop wondering. "What did they have planned here? I mean, that's easily a thousand square feet."

"Your estimate is almost correct. This was meant to be an artist's studio. That's why this part of the barn has been insulated and the firewall was put in place to meet the regulations." She thought for a moment. "You could even put a second floor in here. There would be enough headroom. But the lighting then needs a different solution."

"Windows?" Kaja suggested light-heartedly.

"Yes, you could put some in. But you'd have to disguise them, because this is a conservation area." was Sierra's serious explanation.

"You seem to know a lot about this property." Kaja was impressed.

"Just a bit." again the answer was rather brief. It made Kaja suspicious. But she didn't have much time to think about it as Sierra asked her to climb down the ladder. "A staircase would indeed be a brilliant idea." she mumbled as she reversed down the rungs. "Just a word of warning." Sierra said as she waited for her on the ground. "This was the most up-to-date part of the whole property. It doesn't get any better."

"And the small house we saw earlier, was that the oldest part?"

"Well, yes. Let's inspect the rest. We can skip the stables. You're not planning on keeping animals, are you?"

"Not yet, but who knows? Ideas like that come with the location. They don't seem very real in a city apartment with a tiny patio."

Sierra laughed with her. "Yes, I suppose."

They left the barn and closed its large door with joint efforts. Then they continued to the main house that immediately adjoined the barn. It was an old timber-framed house. Just as with the first building, it was covered with wild vine. At least the windows were all still in place. They were old-fashioned secondary glazed windows similar to the ones Kaja knew and loved in Mémé's home. The heavy oak door was relatively easy to open and they both entered. Behind the door, a tiled floor area led immediately into the kitchen, which was dominated by an old wood stove. Next to it, a more recent gas heater had been installed and a ghastly kitchen unit fitted.

"Who's been let loose on this one?" Kaja was amused.

Sierra snorted. "My thoughts exactly. Cheap and cheerful must have been their attitude. It had been rented out for some time and the last tenants apparently decided to 'update' the kitchen. If I was living here, this would be the first to go, even if I had to live on bread and water for a few months."

Kaja looked outside through one of the dirty windows. She could see their two dogs running around. "I'm glad they didn't get lost." she murmured. They were just chasing each other through an area that looked like an overgrown garden. "Did they grow their own vegetables down here?"

"Yes, it used to be a vegetable patch, this part of the house faces south west. I'm sure herbs would grow there as well, especially along the wall."

Kaja nodded in approval and followed her friend into the living room. "A tiled stove!" she shouted with delight.

"It's lovely!" she heard Lance say and discovered him already sitting on the stove bench.

Sierra raised her eyebrows. "So you do show some interest in the place?"

The dragon waved at her dismissively. "I prefer to do my own exploration in such houses."

Sierra turned to Kaja again. "This tiled stove is a real asset in the winter. The chimney runs through the bedroom upstairs, giving it some heat as well."

"How's the rest of the house heated?"

"I don't know. I would have to ask them. Electric heaters, I suppose."

"Ouch!"

"Exactly. But the logs are free. The woodland behind the house is part of the property."

Kaja looked at the edge of the forest a few hundred yards away and was impressed. Upstairs, there were three bedrooms, one double and two singles, as well as a bathroom which was in a state similar to the kitchen.

The bedrooms were nothing out of the ordinary. Only a few exposed beams revealed some of the charm the neglected house must once have had.

Sierra closed the bathroom door abruptly and said. "Let's go back. Perhaps we'll have time for a cup of coffee together."

Kaja had to rush to catch up with Sierra, who was downstairs by the front door already. "Is anything wrong?"

"Nothing important. Let's go now. I have to be back by six to feed the horses." Kaja was somewhat surprised, but didn't say anything. Instead, she hurried to get the dogs and the dragon back into her car. Sierra hesitated for a moment and cast one last look over the yard and past the willows into the valley. Then she got into her seat as well and signalled Kaja to set off.

30

"Did she really say you could live there almost rent-free if you were prepared to refurbish it? At least in part? That's unbelievable. Is she sure she understood the landlord correctly?"

"The farm belongs to her parents."

"Her parents? But why..."

"Why doesn't she use it herself? I've been wondering about that, too"

"Perhaps you should have asked her." Miri joked, sitting on the sofa with crossed legs.

Kaja, who had settled down opposite her on the floor, poked her tongue out. "I did, but Sierra is very good at ignoring unwanted questions."

"Yes, I noticed that as well. Especially when they concern her personal life. Did you get the impression she's fallen out with her parents? That could make matters difficult."

"No, I don't think that's the case. Mind you, she didn't say much about that or anything else. But I thought the tone in which she spoke about her family was a rather loving one. And that's something you and I would find difficult with ours."

Miri nodded in approval. "OK, let's recap the details. Living there rent-free sounds great. But the refurbishment will cost money, won't it?"

"As far as I understood it, the plan is this: We agree on a notional amount of rent, but instead of paying it to the landlord, I can use it to bring the property up-to-date. For example: if we agree on 3000 Francs and my initial investment is 30,000 Francs, I need to live there for 10 months before I break even. If I move out earlier, he will pay me the difference."

"And what if you decide to stay longer?"

"I'd start paying the agreed rent, unless I decide to assign further funds to the refurbishment, which would take us back to our initial agreement allowing me to balance it against the rent. I can do that at any time."

"And do you think it's a realistic plan? The way you describe it, it sounds like a fairy-tale castle, albeit a rather draughty one..."

"I think I should give it a go. I don't have to buy it but can still use it exactly the way I want. That in itself is a rare opportunity. And secondly, the actual house needs updating but the studio is insulated and heated so I can start my candle production straight away. I had expected it to be the other way round, but this is much better. I have no problem cooking in an ugly kitchen so long as my business ideas don't have to wait."

"What does Lance have to say to all this?"

"The moment he saw the tiled stove, he disqualified himself as an unbiased advisor." Kaja grinned.

"No, I didn't." the dragon protested, having materialised out of nowhere. "In any case, my dragon sense tells me that this house is perfect for you two."

"For us two?" Miri was irritated. "It's meant to be Kaja's house."

"It is, but you're going to visit me, aren't you?" Kaja asked as she hadn't even noticed Lance's strange choice of words.

Miri hadn't taken it too seriously either and picked up on Kaja's comment instead. "It looks like I need to put my poor old car back into service."

"You'd better. You wouldn't make it up here on your bike."

Miri shrugged her shoulders. "I do have a car and I do like driving. It's just that I rarely need it in the city."

"I'm pleased to hear that you're thinking of coming." Kaja was relieved. "I wouldn't like being holed up in the middle of nowhere with no one to visit me. But I can come and visit you, too." She got up to boil the kettle. "Do you want a cuppa as well?" she asked looking over her shoulder.

"Yes, please."

Kaja turned round, surprised. "Really? You don't have to leave me yet?" she asked, checking the kitchen clock. It was almost 10pm.

Miri avoided looking at her. "Tonight, I'd rather be with you."

Kaja smiled. "I'm honoured. But I don't want to be the reason for you becoming a couch potato."

"Oh, I won't. After all, we have Sierra's party to look forward to on Saturday. And two weeks later, I'm invited to an early Halloween party.

Do you want to come along?"

"Erm, I'd rather not. I'm not into fancy dress parties. Masked people scare me."

"What are you going as?" she was eventually curious to know.

"You nosy parker!" Miri teased her. "Refusing to come but wanting to know all my secrets? Tut, tut."

"That's right. You can't do that." the dragon interfered as well.

"I think my impertinent dragon needs shutting up." Kaja said in her sweetest voice and handed him a glass of elderberry brandy. "You're so lucky that we paid Mémé an extra visit or you'd be missing out on your treat."

She offered a second glass to Miri and poured one for herself. "Let's propose a toast."

"To your new home."

"To my new home, although I haven't got it yet. I can't believe my luck. I definitely have to thank Sierra on Saturday."

"Have you made up your mind to take it?"

Kaja put on a strained smile. "I'd never thought I'd be this quick. Even at the risk of being laughed at by a certain dragon: the decision has long been made. Not in a rational way, but a gut feeling told me instantly that this was going to be my new home. It's as if it had been waiting for me. And since it looks like I can afford it, even the logical thinking part of me is satisfied. But that's irrelevant. I just know I do want to live there." She glanced at Lance who seemed to be studying the business pages of a newspaper that was three days old. He could be quite considerate, if he wanted to.

On the other hand, Miri was so touched by Kaja's emotional outburst that she had to fight back her tears. Kaja got up and gave her a hug. "Don't cry, little elf, this is a reason to celebrate."

Miri blew her nose and had to laugh. "Ha, little elf. More like an elephant elf. Has anybody ever told you that elves are supposed to cute and delicate?"

"Oh, you're certainly delicate, just a bit curvy. But I don't think anyone's ever complained about your curves, or have they?" Kaja challenged her. This time, it was Miri who poked out her tongue. Then they both broke into a laugh and dropped onto the sofa.

"We can be so childish."

"That's the understatement of the century." Lance scoffed, only to be hit around the ears by two cushions.

Kaja spent the whole of Friday compiling lists of items she would need for the refurbishment. The night before, she had spent hours looking at the floor plans with Miri, redesigning and furnishing them in their thoughts. They were not even real floor plans, as Sierra did not have any. Kaja had simply drawn them up from memory. Miri had turned out to be a talented interior designer. What in the world was she doing in her grumpy uncle's bookshop? Kaja could not think of a single reason.

"So you haven't asked her yet?"

She shook her head with guilt. "Unfortunately, no, I haven't. There has just been too much going on recently, so I kept forgetting. I know it's a lame excuse."

Lance patted her shoulder. "I'm sure she knows she can count on you if she's got any problems." Kaja got up from her desk and stretched to ease the tension in her back. "Hm, I'm not sure about that. She might know, but it doesn't mean she would actually ask me for help. I think she's used to dealing with everything on her own."

"I think I know someone else who's just the same." the dragon mused, rolling his eyes in mock desperation.

"Yes, I know, I have the same habit. But you have to give it to me: I'm improving."

"That's true. So I guess all's not lost with Miri either."

Kaja looked at him, not fully convinced. "Hm, maybe. At least she stayed with me last night and didn't run off again at 10."

"I think she could do with a dragon, too." she added.

"Hear, hear. So you finally acknowledge that I'm useful to have around?" Lance was delighted.

"Don't let it go to your head." Kaja was quick to put a damper on him.

"Have you spoken to Tim yet?" he suddenly changed the subject.

She turned to give him a stern look. "I don't think that's any of your business. And if I understood you correctly, you're not too unhappy about the radio silence between him and me."

"Yeah, I know, you need to deal with the rest of your problems first and so on and so forth... and of course I'm happy. But it's just so unlike you to let somebody stew."

"Perhaps that was something I needed to learn, too." she retorted and turned back to her lists.

Lance retreated to the roof, sulking. In one aspect, he had to agree with Kaja. As far as he was concerned, Tim might as well freeze up in Iceland. But that was no use to him if it made his protégée unhappy. On the other hand, she wasn't really unhappy at the moment. Perhaps he just needed to trust her to do the right thing. "Thank you, I'm honoured." he heard Kaja's sarcastic voice in his head.

"Hey, since when can you get into my head?" he asked aghast.

"Since I've just tried." he heard her cheerful reply. OK... this was getting interesting.

He decided to relax and wait for her next move. But then the telephone rang downstairs and their telepathic connection was interrupted.

It was Simon. "No luck with Max's mobile so far. It's still switched off. But we're ready to trace it. If either of us is lucky enough to catch Max or at least his mobile while it's switched on, we'll spring into action."

"That's good to hear. I'll try to ring him more often from now on. I'm embarrassed to admit that I've almost forgotten about it for the past few days."

"Don't worry. That's what you have me for. You're not likely to be any luckier than we are."

"It looks like it. Have you got anything useful out of the contract document?"

"Yes, we were right in suspecting that it regulates the shareholder majority."

"And how can we use this knowledge?" Kaja got excited.

"To be honest, at the moment, we won't do anything. My immediate priority is your line manager Max. He may be able to help us when we go to court."

"Right." After a moment of silence, she asked: "So you think he's still alive?"

"Presumably, as long as we don't hear otherwise. Let's not assume the worst. He could even be playing cat-and-mouse himself and not being held captive at all."

"Oh, but that doesn't sound very realistic to me."

"Neither does it to me." he admitted. "But you should never give up hope."

"OK, I'll be in touch if I hear anything."

All those worries about Max somewhat spoiled Kaja's high spirits about the house. Neither Miri nor Mémé were available to speak to on the phone. So she tried to distract herself going for a jog with her Flashdance music on full blast. Unfortunately, she couldn't enjoy the music for long as she had to call Zorro to heel repeatedly. The ground had been soaked by recent showers, driving mice and other rodents to the surface and giving him plenty of prey to chase.

Back home, she ripped off her clothes and was about to take a shower, when the phone rang. For a moment, she was in two minds whether to answer, but then the prospect of a hot spray of water was more tempting.

After the shower, she went to the kitchen to re-heat a plate of spaghetti left over from last night's meal with Miri. As she passed her desk, she saw the red light blinking on the answer machine. She casually pushed the play button. "Hello Kaja... It looks like you don't want to talk to me." Tim! "That's understandable." He hesitated. "But only partially. Anyway, I don't intend to confide my thoughts to this machine here." His voice was starting to sound annoyed. "My flight to Iceland leaves in an hour. I don't know when I'll be back." Now his mood had reached the defiant stage. A few seconds later he had hung up.

Suddenly, the phone rang again. Hoping Tim would be trying again, she answered without looking at the caller display.

"Kaja, darling." Her mother's voice came chirping down the line. "How are you?"

Slightly thrown off her track, she answered: "I'm fine, and you?"

"Oh, we are completely stressed. We're in Paris this weekend and had planned to go south to see Josephine. But you know what it's like. All those commitments..." She didn't finish her sentence. 'Exactly.' Kaja thought bitterly. 'I know what it's like. You've never had time for your daughter either.'

"Have you found a new job yet?" her mother changed the subject when she realised Kaja wasn't going to ask any further questions about her own exciting life.

"No, Maman, I haven't. In fact, I've decided to become self-employed and move to the country."

"Don't be so silly." Her mother was shocked. "And may I ask: What kind of self-employed business do you want to get into? Anything to do with IT?"

"Partly. But most importantly, I want to become the Swiss subsidiary of Mémé's operations in France." Damn, she had already said more than she wanted to.

"Oh, there's no future in that. You may be better off becoming a simple market trader. Or even better yet: why not become a proper farming girl?"

"You know what, Maman? I had really hoped you would show some interest in what's important to me, your daughter, and what's important in my life. And I thought you might be happy for me. But obviously, that's asking too much."

"You make it sound as if it was your life's ambition. But we both know it's just one of your pie-in-the-sky ideas. I do hope you'll come to your senses soon."

Kaja gave up. At least it sounded as if their conversation was coming to an end. And for her, it couldn't have come soon enough. Her instinct was right. Her mother finished the call rather briefly.

Kaja leaned back in her chair. "Phew, that was the last thing I needed today." She shook her head in disbelief. Promptly, the radio playing in the kitchen started to make scratchy sounds. She bit her tongue to suppress a laugh. But she had good reasons to laugh. Her mother spent her whole life trying to keep afloat in a sea of artificial priorities and rules and struggled to understand anyone outside her social circle. 'And that's her problem, not mine.' Kaja realised. 'Although we're both losing out in the process.' Slowly, she got up and walked over to Zorro who was lying in his basket. She hunched down next to him and ruffled his ears. "We're much better off, aren't we? Do you realise what kind of good life you'll have? There's that large garden to roam around in and chase armies of mice..." She sat there for a while longer and told her faithful companion about their new life.

In the meantime, Lance sat at the kitchen table not daring to make a noise, so as not to disturb the two of them. He was proud of his protégée. "Oh Josephine. I think your granddaughter is slowly growing up." he whispered with a tinge of sadness.

"I know." the prompt answer echoed in his head.

31

The next day, she went out shopping. When she came home in the afternoon, she was surprised to find Simon waiting for her. In her flat. Kaja was not sure whether to be angry or impressed at the ease with which he was able to gain access. Lance felt uneasy as well as someone had invaded his territory. But Simon got straight to the point. "Last night, I was able to narrow down Max's location. He's somewhere within a 30 mile radius north east of Zurich."

Kaja frowned. "Zurich, Schaffhausen, Thurgau, maybe St.Gallen" she listed the possible cantons. "You couldn't pinpoint his location any better?" she looked at him for a positive answer.

"Sorry, that's all I have. I had hoped it would remind you of something in connection with the company."

Kaja thought feverishly. "No, really, it doesn't mean anything at the moment. Didn't you search Max's flat? Did you find any clues there?"

"No, he didn't leave any papers behind and apparently took his laptop with him."

"That's unfortunate. So we're none the wiser."

"I wouldn't say that." he replied. "At least we narrowed his location down to about one fifth of the area of Switzerland."

"Well, that's still like trying to find a needle in a haystack. I'll ring him again. Right now." Resolutely, she reached for her mobile, dialled the number and waited for the ringing tone. Secretly, she was praying to all gods known to her that she wouldn't get to hear the dreaded "The person you are calling is currently unavailable."

"That's an illustrious collection of deities you're calling upon." Lance commented silently.

"I can't afford to be choosy at the moment." she explained telepathically. "It's ringing. Now do your magic." she hissed at Simon.

He did something on his laptop that had been sitting on the table, ready to be used. "Bingo." he exclaimed after a few minutes that seemed to Kaja like hours.

"And? What are we going to do now?" Kaja was a bit lost.

"I'll go there and inspect the area."

"You haven't told me yet where 'there' actually is."

"Ah, yes. Look, I've got a map here." He turned the laptop so that she could see the screen. It showed a location just outside of Schaffhausen.

"And once you're there, you're storming in, all guns blazing?"

"First, I should try to establish whether he is there of his own free will or if he's being held captive." he grinned. "I prefer people to be happy when I turn up. However, if it happens to be his secret little hideout, for whatever reason, his happiness may be limited."

"But that's not very likely, or is it?"

Immediately, he turned serious again. "No, it isn't. With everything you told me and what we know about the events in your company, it's not very likely. That makes it all the more important that I get more info and assess the situation."

"Tonight, I'm in the area anyway. Can I come with you?" Kaja asked him, excited.

"Where are you going?" he asked back without answering her question.

"I'm invited to a friend's. They're having a party."

"In that case, I suggest you visit your friend and I'll pop round once I know more. Then we can discuss our next steps." He added assertively when he realised she wasn't satisfied with his answer.

"OK." she replied hesitantly. She wasn't happy being excluded, but she had to accept that she couldn't be much help on this occasion. She quickly jotted down Sierra's name and address and handed the paper to Simon.

He looked at it. "Your friend?" he tried to confirm with raised eyebrows. "You were rather quick finding her." he grinned.

"It's complicated..." she started to explain, but then stopped.

Simon put the paper in his back pocket. "Don't expect me before nine."

"OK."

When Miri came an hour later to pick her up, Kaja was beside herself with excitement and worry about Max. Lance welcomed her at the door.

"Miri, you've got to do something. Cheer her up. Apparently, Simon was able to locate Max and Kaja is having kittens."

"That's understandable. Now the story is getting real." She put her handbag on the kitchen worktop and followed the sound of Kaja's mumbling coming from the bedroom. "Hey, what are you up to?" Miri was watching wide-eyed, as Kaja emptied her wardrobe.

"I'm looking for my black trousers." the muffled answer came from inside the piece of furniture.

Irritated, Miri looked at herself. She had chosen some washed-out jeans and a fluffy pink pullover that accentuated her curves. "Do they have a dress code tonight?"

"No, but all being well, we'll rescue Max later on and I need to be dressed appropriately." Kaja emerged from the wardrobe.

"Erm... we? Are you sure you don't want to leave that to the professionals? I mean, the idea he might need rescuing would be proof that the whole story is much more serious than we thought." Miri voiced her concerns.

"Yes, you're right. And I will try to keep out of harm's way. But I would like to play a part in it."

"I see. And what does Simon say?"

Kaja frowned. "He hasn't said anything yet. He'll drop in at the party later tonight. Apparently, Max is somewhere quite close to Sierra's home. So he'll be able to discuss his next steps with us."

Miri decided to let the matter rest for now and hoped that Simon would make her see sense. "Is this what you're looking for?" she said instead and showed Kaja a pair of dark blue jeans.

Kaja looked at it. "No, not really. But they're dark. They'll have to do." She quickly slipped them on and completed her outfit with a black polo-neck sweater. "So, ready to go. All I need is a little present. Although, I'm not even sure if one is expected." She took a warm leather jacket and sat down on the sofa to put on her well-worn cowboy boots.

"I have one. Perhaps we can say it's from both of us." Miri suggested half-heartedly.

"What is it?" Kaja was curious to know.

"Here, have a look." She nervously fidgeted with a small parcel.

Kaja peeped inside. "Oh, it looks like the small white pony she was training when we went to see her. Is it one of your own works of art?" She reached in the box and took it out. It was about three inches high and two inches long, made of hardened modelling material, painted white and decorated with a fluffy, dishevelled mane. Its defiant head showed the unmistakeable expression of that very pony they saw on the day.

"Well, not really a work of art..." Miri looked at her creation, doubting. "I did make it myself, last night. Initially, I wanted to do a red horse, like the one she was riding when she first met us. But somehow it kept escaping me and I wasn't able to catch it. Instead, I always saw this white one in front of me. So that's the one she's getting." She carefully wrapped the small figurine up again.

"I'm sure she'll be very pleased." Kaja reassured her. She jumped up to give Zorro one of his large chewing bones. But the dog had suspected all afternoon that he was supposed to stay home and didn't fall for the red herring. Instead, he got up and blocked the door, wagging his tail excitedly.

Enervated, Lance rolled his eyes. "As soon as one family member's been made happy, another one plays havoc."

"Leave Zorro alone." Kaja told the dragon off and led her stubborn dog to his blanket where the bone was already waiting for him. "I won't be long, alright?" she promised Zorro, who watched her leave with his sad doggy eyes.

Once they sat in the car, Miri said: "Am I glad that Chili doesn't look at me like that when I have to leave him home. I couldn't bear that."

Kaja sighed. "That's one of the reasons why he's with me most of the time. But today he'd have to stay in the car for the whole evening. And it is your car. He'll be much more comfortable at home."

"But you didn't leave him there just in order to save my car, did you?"

"No, of course not. I would have asked if that was the case."

"Pleased to hear that. He couldn't have done much damage anyway." Kaja cast her eye over the dusty interior of the old vehicle and concluded that Miri was right.

When they arrived, the party was already in full swing. Lance was so excited about being allowed to join them, that he boisterously started to pinch canapés off people's plates and swap their glasses round as they made their way through the crowd. "Lance, will you stop it?" Kaja hissed at him in shock. When they finally reached Sierra, she had had the opportunity to follow the small group with her eyes for some time. Kaja wished the earth could swallow her up. "I'm so sorry." she apologised. "My dragon is really bad-mannered, but I can't change him."

Sierra's mouth twitched with amusement. "That's the proof I needed. It seems to be true that nobody else can see him." She inspected the shiny figure from top to bottom. "That's quite amazing considering his size. Lance, please feel free to pull any trick on anyone you like."

Perplexed, Kaja looked at Sierra. "So you're effectively giving him carte blanche? Are you sure that's what you want?"

"Let's just say: all these people here are friends and clients of Marcus'. I had all the hard work with the preparations, so I deserve to play a little joke on them." Her eyes flashed mischievously.

"Respect, madam." Lance gave her the hint of a bow and disappeared among the crowd.

Sierra reached to a small table behind her and handed her two friends a glass of champagne each, before taking one for herself. "Now we're here together, let's drink to our health. It doesn't look like we can get rid of each other easily anyway." she joked. "To us!"

"To the dragon sisters!" Kaja took a sip from her drink and added: "The dragon sisters. Yes, I do like the sound of it."

"I have a little present for you." Miri remembered and searched in her bag for the small parcel.

"For me?" Sierra stared at her.

"Yes, go on, open it." Kaja encouraged her. She carefully untied the ribbon that was holding it together and found the little horse inside. "That's Bounty. You've made Bounty for me!" She blinked a few times to suppress the tears in her eyes.

"Is that the name of the little white pony you were exercising when we visited you?"

"What? No, that was one of her granddaughters. Bounty was my very first pony and died a few years ago. But you're right, they look very much alike. Spontaneously, she gave Miri a hug and then Kaja as well. She stashed the little horse in a pocket of her cardigan. "So, now let's join the party and watch our guest of honour play his pranks." she said and looked at the two women with a beaming smile.

As promised, Simon arrived at nine at the address Kaja had given him. He got out of his car and hesitated in the dark. From an open window, he could hear music and distant voices. It looked like he had found the right place. So he went up the few steps to the entrance and rang the door bell. It took a moment for the door to open. He had actually intended to enquire straight after Kaja, but when his eyes fell on Sierra, he forgot about the purpose of his visit. All he could do was stare at her. In order to disguise the turmoil in him, he couldn't think of anything better than to give her a deprecatory look from top to bottom. She was tall and slim, with a well-trained body and a head of red curls, tumbling over her shoulders. At the moment, however, she seemed to be rather apprehensive towards him. In other circumstances, he might have tried to defuse the situation with a casual remark, but tonight, he just didn't have the time for such niceties. Which was really a shame, he thought when he looked into her amber eyes, reminding him of a tigress.

"Listen, I don't care if they're employing you as a bouncer tonight, I just need to have a quick word with Kaja." he said in a tired voice. Nevertheless, his tone was sharp enough to reveal that he was used to having his orders obeyed. It was something that had caused Sierra allergic reactions recently.

She looked suspiciously at the tall man. Admittedly, he was quite good looking and had piercing blue eyes that were currently fixed on her. But his over-confident manner got right up her nose. How dare he call her a bouncer!

"Who wants to know? And most importantly: why?"

Irritated, he looked at Sierra. "Is she here or isn't she?" Resolutely, she wanted to slam the door in his face, but found he was quicker, putting his foot forward to block it. With the same determination that she had just shown, he grabbed her rudely by her upper arm and pushed her aside. Luckily, as Sierra was still considering whether it was better to give him a kick in his shin or ram an elbow in his side, Kaja and Miri suddenly turned up.

"Sierra, are you OK?" Confused, Kaja let her eyes wander between Sierra and Simon. Simon instantly let go of her, as if she had burned his fingers. She wasn't the bouncer, she was the lady of the house!

"This bloke's looking for you."

In his thoughts, Simon quickly erased the word 'lady'. "Your friend here seems to be a right dragon." he growled, whereupon the three women broke into a hysterical giggle. Irritated, Simon looked at the three of them one by one. Somehow, his mission to pick up Kaja had turned out to be more complicated than he had thought. And with regards to Sierra, first impressions could be rather deceptive.

"He didn't want to tell me why he needs to see you. And anyway, how did he know you were here?"

"Because I told him. Sorry I didn't warn you, I completely forgot. Sierra, may I introduce: this is Simon. He's helping me with a problem I have at work. Simon, this is my friend Sierra." Stiffly, they shook hands.

Then Sierra turned to Kaja again. "Is this work problem so urgent that you need to discuss it with him on a Saturday night?"

"It's rather complicated. I'll explain it another time. Miri, do you want to come with us?"

"Hey, this isn't a Sunday afternoon stroll." Simon interfered.

"I think I'd better stay here. I'm not made of the same superhero stuff as you, Kaja. I'll happily leave the action to you. Is it OK if I don't join you?"

Taken by surprise at this sudden turn of events and by the memory of the electric shock she had felt when Simon had tried to push her aside, Sierra could only nod. "But you must explain to me what our sister is involved in." she added a second later. 'Good. Apparently, my brain is back online.' Sierra thought in self-mockery.

Kaja was relieved and took a deep breath. "That settles it then. You'll hear from me tomorrow. I'll let you know how we get on tonight."

"I do hope so. Good luck!" Miri gave her a brief hug.

"Are we done with all the girlie talk? It's time to go." Simon asked impatiently.

"Yeah, I'm coming." Kaja rolled her eyes and said goodbye to Sierra. "Thank you for the invitation. Your guests are safe now, Lance is coming with me." She only whispered the last sentence because she didn't want Simon to hear. He frowned but refrained from making any further comment, for which Kaja was grateful. The atmosphere had already become so tense that you could almost touch it with your hands.

"What kind of Neanderthal was that?" Sierra, still angry, wanted to know from Miri as they made their way back to the party.

"Neanderthal?" Miri grinned. "You must have been quite annoyed with him if you didn't notice anything else."

"What else was I supposed to notice?" Sierra steamed angrily.

"For instance that he's quite a handsome Neanderthal..."

"What good is that if he doesn't know how to behave?" Sierra replied grumpily. She linked her arm with Miri's and guided her towards the kitchen." Anyway, what was all that about?" she asked, changing the subject and Miri was all too happy to fill her in.

"And it was me who helped you find that one." Simon was steaming as well, as they drove towards Schaffhausen.

"I have no idea what went on between the two of you. I do think she's a very nice person."

"That's exactly the problem. Nothing went on between us. It was as if we were from two completely different planets."

Kaja decided to let the subject rest.

"You'd better." Lance agreed with her quietly.

"So, what's up with Max? Have you really found him?"

"Yes, I have."

Kaja exhaled audibly. "Thank goodness. Is he OK?"

"As far as I could make out peeping through a window: yes, he seems alright."

"But?" Kaja asked after a moment of silence as Simon made no effort to give her further explanations.

"He's being kept in a building that's difficult to get into unnoticed. It looks like an old storage depot. And he wasn't alone, otherwise I would have got him out already."

"That would have been my next question..."

"It sounds as if the people holding him are not sure what to do next. But listen for yourself." He dug out his mobile and pressed a few buttons without even looking at the display while he was still driving.

After some crackling, the sound quality improved and Kaja could hear voices:

"...high time we took care of the problem."

"That's exactly what we're doing. We've taken him out of circulation."

The first voice sounded unnaturally calm and very cold. In contrast, the second one was more defensive and a bit insecure. "And what do you think will happen if you let him go?" the calm, but thereby ever more threatening voice wanted to know.

"Nothing will happen. He doesn't have a clue who kidnapped him. I took care of that. And by then, the deal will be done and dusted. Nobody will give a damn about his suspicions any more. Especially if we make it known that he embezzled company funds."

"Those are exactly the points that make me nervous. He's heard your voice. I think you're making a mistake by underestimating him." For a moment, there was silence. Then the calm one could be heard again. "I don't like loose ends. Don't forget whose fault it was that he was able to find out so much in the first place. Think about it, think very carefully. I'll have to go now." Then the recording stopped.

"A quarrel amongst crooks." Simon stated. "It may be helpful or it may increase our risk. Did you recognise any of the voices?"

Kaja nodded, in shock. So far, it had been all exciting and of course a bit worrying, but this recording had brought home to her how serious the situation was and how grave the consequences could be.

"Are you OK?" Simon asked, having noticed, despite the dim light in the car, how she had turned pale.

She perked up. "Yes, at least I'm not the one being held captive." She went quiet for a moment. "And yes, I did recognise one of the voices."

Simon glanced at her. "Which one?"

"The one that sounded as if he wanted to defend himself. It was my section leader. I don't know the other one. But why did you leave Max to his fate in order to pick me up? What if they've killed him in the meantime?"

"Do you really think I'm that reckless?" Simon replied, slightly amused.

Kaja looked out of the window, where the landscape rushed past in the darkness. "No, of course I don't. I'm just worried, that's all."

"I called in some of my colleagues and also informed the local police. I waited for one of my people to arrive before I made off. He's watching the situation and waiting for everyone else to arrive. If anything unforeseen happens, we can react immediately." Kaja was somewhat relieved to hear that.

"So, here we are." Simon parked the car by the kerbside. 'Listen.

Your job is to stay here and wait." He gave her a walkie talkie and briefly explained how to operate it. "Only use it in an emergency. As soon as we get Max out, we'll bring him to you so that he can see a familiar face until the ambulance arrives. - In case he needs one." he added when he saw the terror in her face.

"Isn't there anything else I can do?"

His face turned hard. "No. This is not a game, Kaja. We're trained to deal with such situations, you're not. Do you understand?"

Reluctantly, she replied: "Yes. OK."

"And besides, Tim would rip my head off if anything happened to you." He mumbled as he quietly left the car and softly closed the door.

"What's Tim got to do with this?" she asked angrily, but Simon could not hear her as he had already disappeared into the night.

Since their last date that had gone so disastrously wrong, she had tried to avoid any thought of Tim. It had been easier than anticipated. But now she realised that the main reason was that she had just been too occupied with other things. Or, more precisely, she had occupied herself in order to nip any unwanted thoughts of Tim in the bud...

Frustrated, she ran her fingers through her hair. She couldn't believe it! Here she was, in the middle of a detective story and all she could think of was a past one-night stand. In a quick decision, she reached for the door handle to get out.

"You'd better stop it right there." Lance reminded her in a strict voice. "I won't allow my protégée to end up in the crossfire."

She ignored him and tried to open the door. But it wouldn't move. "Lance! You're supposed to help me."

"But I won't help you get into trouble. Even less so if it's just an excuse for not dealing with your feelings for Tim. You know very well that it isn't just a one-night stand that binds you and Tim together."

"But not much more either." She growled between clenched teeth. "For most of the time, he's not here anyway."

Bored, Lance chewed the gum he had nicked from Simon. "So, have we reached that point in our discussion again? Honestly, Kaja, I'm disappointed in you. I'd thought you were a step further on by now."

Kaja started to whistle and demonstratively inspected her finger nails.

Lance rolled his eyes and tried to blow bubbles with his gum. Suddenly, something caught his attention. He looked through the back window and hissed at Kaja: "Get out of here, quickly."

"I would, but I can't, thanks to you."

"Go, go!"

Kaja sensed the urgency in his voice and tried the door handle again which responded with ease this time. As she slipped out on the pavement, she complained. "Can you ever make up your mind?" She had barely finished thinking the sentence, when a running figure approached the car from the other side.

"Keep down." The dragon promptly ordered her when she tried to straighten up to get a better view. In a reflex, she hunched down. The driver's door was opened from the other side, somebody jumped in, started the engine and drove off with squealing tyres. Why had Simon left his key in the ignition?

Kaja got up. "That was the section leader. We can't let him get away just like that."

"He won't." Lance said with a satisfied smile. "Look..."

Just 200 yards up the road, the engine in Simon's car started to splutter and the vehicle eventually came to a halt. In the bright spot of a street light, they could see the driver trying to re-start the car until he obviously decided it was easier to make his escape on foot. He desperately pulled at the door handle, but with no effect.

"You're a genius." Kaja praised her dragon. ""Now he's trapped, just like I was." She was satisfied. "I only hope Max's rescue goes to plan." Anxiously, she looked towards the old storage depot. Suddenly, she heard a gunshot. It made her jump. Her heart was pounding. Although she knew it was stupid to run over there in response to a shot, she couldn't help it. Lance had no choice but to follow her on his wings.

"Women." he grumbled. But deep down, he was quite proud of his protégée. He overtook her so he would be able to give a warning if the situation became hairy. They approached the property which was surrounded by a high thuja hedge. "Wait here." Lance ordered her as he could see from his elevated position that someone was leaving the building. However, he could not yet establish who it was. When she made no attempt at obeying him, his only option was to use a magic spell. It wouldn't keep her for long, but it was better than nothing.

"What the..." Kaja was lost for words. That devious dragon had glued her feet to the ground. Without thinking twice, she used her fingers to draw the protective sign in the air that Mémé had taught her as a child. Her feet immediately answered her brain's commands again. Apparently, she had taken in more of the advice than she thought. She wanted to start running again but then hesitated. It seemed the enforced break had helped her brain catch up with events. Lance must have had good reasons to root her feet to the ground, she reluctantly admitted to herself. From then on, she approached the high hedge slowly and carefully, trying not to make any unnecessary noise. She sneaked up to a gap where workers must have pushed through in search for a short cut to the nearest hot dog stand which now stood lonely and deserted in the darkness. Now that the blood was no longer singing in her ears, she could hear somebody running towards her. But she couldn't make out if it was friend or foe. She feverishly tried to decide what to do as the steps came ever closer.

At that moment, Lance warned her: "Kaja, be careful. It's the nasty stranger. If you want to stop him, now's your chance."

'Great advice.' Kaja thought angrily. 'What am I supposed to do?' Now the shadow had almost reached her. In an impulse, she decided to hide behind the edge of the hedge and wait until the man was only two steps away. Then she summoned all her courage, or whatever was left of it, and stretched out a leg. The man dropped like a felled tree and slammed face down into the stone pavement. When finally two men from

Simon's team arrived, she was still standing frozen in the same spot. It didn't take them much effort to restrain the man on the ground and put him in handcuffs. Relieved, Kaja noticed that the man was bleeding from a cut on his head but was otherwise very much alive. At least the colourful swear words that came from his mouth with every breath seemed to imply that he was.

Her legs trembling, she sat down on the pavement. Slowly, she felt the shock setting in, realising that she had just brought down a criminal in the truest sense of the word. Someone put a blanket round her shoulders.

"Normally, I should arrest you for not following my orders." she heard Simon's voice next to her. She had not heard him coming. "I'm serious, Kaja. From now on, you'll only get office work to do. Still, good job." He added reluctantly.

"You know what? I've just come to the same conclusion." She turned to her left to look at him. "Oh, you're bleeding!" she screamed in horror when she saw him pressing a blood-stained tissue to his left upper arm.

"It's only a graze." he said dismissively. "And it was my fault. I didn't expect that scumbag to start a shoot-out. Joseph won't be happy with me. And Tim neither." he added grumbling. "At least we got hold of one of them and Max is free now."

"Is he OK?"

Simon pointed to the ambulance that had parked a short distance down the road. "They're just checking him over. But as far as I could tell, there's nothing wrong with him that a bit of rest and tender loving care couldn't fix."

"Oh, I'm so relieved. By the way, we got the other one as well."

"You what?" Simon jerked up.

Kaja quickly told him how the section leader had stolen his car - and how it had suddenly stopped.

"You were lucky to get out in time."

"Hm." Kaja replied vaguely. She could hardly tell him about her dragon-based early warning system.

"But what I don't understand: Why didn't he just run off? And why did my car stop so suddenly? That vehicle is as good as new and I've never had any problems with it."

Kaja hummed and hawed. "Erm, it may sound a bit strange to you, but electronic devices often play up if I get upset in their vicinity..."

Simon registered her explanation with scepticism. But he couldn't come up with a better reason himself. He took his walkie talkie and gave some brief orders. "My team is taking care of him. Do you need a lift home?"

Kaja briefly thought about it. "I'd like to quickly say hello to Max. If he needs to go to hospital, I'll go with him. And you should show them your gunshot wound, too." She pointed to his arm.

He squirmed. "I'd rather not. Joseph can take care of it."

She shrugged her shoulders. "It's your call." She was about to leave him but then turned round again. "Thanks and - I'm sorry about your car."

Kaja went with Max to the hospital from where they called his partner André, who had been sick with worry since he hadn't been able to get hold of Max. But as he had not known whom he could trust, he had been too scared to call anyone for help. When he finally arrived at the hospital, Kaja left and made her way to the railway station. She would have liked to get to know André, but tonight, she was simply too tired.

'Luckily, there's a direct train from Schaffhausen to Zurich.' she thought exhausted. Now that her adrenaline had reached normal levels again, she felt drained. She would even make an exception and get a taxi from the railway station to her flat, she decided. She was definitely not in the mood to join some late night partygoers in the cold, waiting for a tram or a bus.

At one in the morning, she finally made it home. Zorro welcomed her frenetically. The poor creature must have felt that she'd been through a lot and was desperate that he hadn't been there to help her. She just about managed to take a hot shower before tumbling into bed, allowing Zorro to join her for a change. She patted the empty space on the mattress next to her and he didn't need much encouragement. She wrapped her arms around him, rested her head on his thick fur and was gone in an instant.

32

Kaja spent the next few days in bed. She had caught a nasty cold and couldn't stop sneezing. Her itchy nose was glowing like Rudolph's and her voice had become hoarse from coughing. So she stayed in bed most of the time (she had little choice anyway, with a dragon as her guard) and was much too tired to get into any arguments. When she was asleep, she was haunted by wild dreams of manhunts, mafia dealings, parties and people abandoning her. But as her dreams kept changing, she assumed her brain was processing her recent experiences and learned to live with them. Miri paid her a daily visit to bring food and make endless cups of tea.

"You don't have to, really." Kaja had fended her off at first.

"Why not? Aren't you hungry?" had been Miri's concerned reply.

"Well, yes, I am."

"You see, popcorn and tins of tuna certainly won't get you any better." she had implored with a worried look on her face.

And as Miri provided her with a constant diet of delicious food and entertaining reading material, Kaja had eventually given up resisting her. She spent hours on the phone to Mémé discussing her plans. On the other hand, she ignored a phone call from her parents. She also managed to cancel her contract on the flat, find a follow-up tenant and even arranged a viewing. On the fourth day, she decided she had enough of lazying around. Full of energy, she got up early and gave both her flat and herself a spring clean. She changed the bedding, loaded the washing machine with dirty linen, chased Zorro from room to room with the vacuum cleaner and opened all the windows to air the place. It was a good day's work and she felt exhausted afterwards. That flu must have drained her body more than she cared to admit. But she was satisfied with the result. On the other hand, the cleaning didn't provide her with the distraction she needed. Uninvited, Tim managed to sneak into her thoughts repeatedly. Defiantly, she gave the taps in the bathroom another polish. When there was no spot left untouched, she finally sat down in the living room with a cup of tea, hoping to enjoy the rest of the day. For a brief moment, she wondered what Lance had got up to. He had made himself scarce for the past few days. Only at night time, he had faithfully kept her company. And yesterday, when she had been still too exhausted to do anything more than take Zorro to his usual patch, but was already fit enough to sit up in bed, feeling miserable about her laziness, he had distracted her with a game of poker. And, if her memory served her right, he had fleeced her for all she'd got! Her debts amounted to one bottle of whiskey and three bottles of elderberry brandy. Ah, it had been well worth the entertainment. Otherwise she'd have gone mad, for sure. And she would have kept on wasting her energy thinking about Tim.

Kaja decided to return Miri's favours and cook a meal for her. She sent a text asking her not to bring any food tonight and grinned at Miri's prompt reply: "So you're back from the dead? :-)"

"You could say that." she said to herself and fetched Zorro's leash. "Come on, my favourite monster. Time to give your paws a workout." Zorro couldn't believe his luck. Excited, he jumped about with an ear-splitting howl. "Alright, I'm on my way." Shaking her head, she watched him rush to the door in big leaps.

After the walk, Kaja painfully realised that she had not fully recovered yet. It had been a wise decision not to go for a jog. That would definitely have been too much for her. But the fresh air had done her good. On the way, she had called Sierra to arrange the handover. They had signed the tenancy contract at the party last Saturday. Kaja was still surprised that Sierra didn't want to live in the house herself, but had only received vague answers to her repeated questions. So she had finally given up on the subject. Now she just shrugged. It was none of her business. For her, it was a lucky co-incidence that Sierra didn't want to use the property herself, for whatever reasons.

She had also done some shopping and was now ready to work on her lists again. Tomorrow was the scheduled viewing of the flat and there had been a number of enquiries in her e-mail inbox. There was no doubt she would find a suitable tenant. This wasn't a game any longer, it was real. In about ten days' time, she wouldn't be living here anymore. She was surprised how little all these imminent changes upset her. Maybe she just didn't have time to worry, she concluded. Or she had indeed become more laid-back. Whatever the reason, it would help her to survive the next few weeks even better.

She decided to wait for Miri to arrive before starting to cook the meal and instead fetched some packing cases from the cellar, started to dismantle her office furniture and packed some books. She was still busy when Miri arrived at six. "I didn't expect you to be in the middle of packing already. You're beginning to scare me." she laughed as she came in.

"I'm sure Zorro would agree with you. Since I've started, he's been watching me suspiciously and even tried to get himself in that box over there." she pointed to the opposite side of the room.

"Haven't you told him that there's no way you'll leave him behind?" Miri wanted to know.

"Of course I have, at least a dozen times. I described our new home to him, he was even with me when I went to view it. But apparently, he doesn't believe me." She looked down at Zorro who was resting on her feet making every effort to look as pathetic as possible, flattening his ears and returning her look with worried eyes. "It's not fair of him. I've never left him behind, anywhere." But unfazed, Zorro continued to play the poor dog being hard done by.

Kaja closed the box she had just finished packing and pushed it over to the others she had filled earlier. "I haven't started preparing our meal yet. It's more fun doing it in company." she grinned.

"You seem to be much better now." Miri was pleased to observe. "What are we having?"

"To be honest, only spaghetti with some salad and one of Mémé's pre-cooked sauces."

"Sounds alright to me. Can I help? Wash the lettuce or something?"

"No no, just sit down and let me get on with it. It's the least I can do after all the tender loving care you've given me."

"I couldn't allow you to starve yourself to death, could I?" Miri replied, amused.

Kaja deliberately ignored that comment, got the large spaghetti pot from the cupboard and filled it with water to boil. In the meantime, she prepared her favourite salad dressing, chopped some avocados, bell peppers, gherkins, an apple and a spring onion and washed the lettuce.

When the spaghetti was almost al dente, she poured Mémé's sauce into a small pan and heated it up. In the meantime, Miri had laid the small table next to the sofa, providing a comfortable setting for their meal. As they sat together, they discussed Kaja's move and refurbishment plans for the house. "First, I think I'll be looking for a nice kitchen. Perhaps I can start at IKEA."

"Yes, they're less expensive there." Miri agreed.

"I do hope so. And then I want to paint the rooms. Can you help me select the colour schemes?"

"With pleasure." she was happy to get involved. "Sierra told me that you can ask her brother if you have any joinery work to be done. Apparently, he'll be back from a round-the-world trip next week and does not have any jobs lined up yet. That means he's available and can do it for a good price."

Kaja reached for the salad bowl and used her fork to pick out the leftovers. "Sounds good. Anything that makes my life easier is very welcome. After all, I already want to start on my candle and fragrance stuff while still doing the refurbishment."

"Stuff?" Miri teased her. "Don't you have a proper name for your business?"

"To be honest, no, I don't. I didn't want to choose a name that limits my area too much. If I called it 'Candles of Delight' and also offered soaps and lotions, as Mémé does, it just wouldn't get the message across."

Miri nodded in approval. "Take your time. I'm sure you'll come up with something appropriate."

"Certainly, but suggestions are always welcome." she replied, giving Miri a deliberately challenging look.

Her friend laughed. "OK, message received." For a moment, they sat quietly, each immersed in her own thoughts while Amy McDonald softly sang her latest hit in the background.

"And how are you these days?" Kaja suddenly wanted to know.

"Me?" Miri looked at her, surprised.

"Yes, you. Ever since we met, you've been there for me, helping me with ideas and in practical ways. And I barely had an opportunity to ask about you. I must seem terribly selfish and wouldn't blame you if you started looking for a new best friend."

Miri laughed. "I'm fine. And don't worry, you can't just go looking for another dragon sister." she said with a twinkle in her eye.

"No, come on, seriously." Kaja insisted.

Miri thought for a moment. "I am serious. The time since I met you, Lance and - most recently - Sierra, has been one of the most exciting periods in my life. The fact that I've got to know a new dragon, even if he's not my own, is a big bonus."

"But what else is happening in your life?" Kaja kept on, feeling that Miri was trying to hide something from her.

"Well, the only thing that bothers me at the moment is that I'm lacking direction. I'm doing a half-hearted job for my uncle, have my own flat and get plastered every couple of weeks... Not quite my idea of a fulfilled life. On the other hand, I don't have any solid ideas what I could, should or would want to change..." She threw her hands in the air. "There's no point being unhappy about it since I don't have an alternative plan."

Kaja thought she could come up with a dozen or more plans for Miri to put into action, but she only said: "You'll see. One day you'll wake up and find your dream's right in front of you."

Miri cocked her head. "Even if I need a dragon to open my eyes?"

"Even if you need a dragon, yes." Kaja confirmed with a smile.

"Can you ask Lance if he's for hire? I'll pay him by the hour as I don't think Maxi will ever turn up again. Where is he anyway?" she asked, trying to change the subject.

"No idea. He's made himself scarce recently." She shrugged her shoulders.

"That's strange."

"Yes, but I can hardly put him on a leash. At the moment, I'm so busy that I simply don't have time to argue with him."

"Let me know if you need a hand with your packing, OK?" Miri said when it was time for her to go.

"Thanks, I might take you up on it." They gave each other a hug.

"Safe journey home." Kaja said and watched her walk off to her car.

33

Miri stood in front of her wardrobe. She was looking forward to the early Halloween party in a few hours time. She didn't know much about the people who had invited her, but who cared? She shrugged. At least they had said everyone could stay the night, which she found pretty generous. Over the past few weeks, she had been so busy helping Kaja with her move, that she had hardly found the time to go out. So she decided tonight was going to be a well-earned reward. In anticipation, she rubbed her short, blond curls dry with a towel and applied one of Josephine's scented body lotions. That weekend, when she had gone to France with Kaja, she hadn't been able to resist buying various things from Josephine's product range. Interestingly enough, they included a crème with orange blossom oil. She smiled. It seemed Kaja had not been too far off with her choice of candle ingredients. She applied some glitter to her arms and cleavage. Now she was all creamed and powdered, she rolled a pair of black opaque tights up her legs and put on a tiny pinafore dress made of a greyish-green, crumpled material. It had a low-cut front and barely covered her bottom. Hoping it wouldn't be too cold, she complemented her outfit with a tiny pink bolero jacket. Finally, she slipped into her pink ballerina shoes and went over to the bed where she had kept a pair of delicate elf wings safe from accidental damage. She would take them along and only attach them once she was at the party. Otherwise they wouldn't survive the journey. She decided to leave her handbag at home and only put enough money for a taxi in a small holdall that also contained her comfortable sneakers, a t-shirt and a pair of loosely fitting jogging bottoms, to be worn the next morning. All she had to do now was to apply some make-up. She quickly brushed on greenish golden eye shadow and skilfully applied silver-grey eye liner. Finally, she added several layers of mascara which accentuated her smoky grey eyes. Satisfied, she turned in front of the mirror. Perhaps she would meet someone exciting tonight. Perhaps even a half-decent man. It would make a change from all those losers she usually attracted and fell for. She poked her tongue out at her mirror image and left, elf wings in hand.

Two hours and several glasses of champagne later, she was leaning against a wall, feeling tiddly and slightly sad. So far, the evening had not been worth the effort. The other guests' costumes showed little inspiration. Most of them had limited themselves to a tiny crown (the women) or a plastic set of vampire teeth (the men). How original! Everyone was trying to appear as cool and mellow as possible. Heaven forbid they might exchange a few words with a complete stranger. The hosts had not even recognised her, but admittedly, Miri did not remember where she knew them from either. Perhaps her e-mail address had simply found its way onto some obscure mailing list. She sighed. At least she could look forward to having her own private room and a bed to sleep in. The estate was of an impressive size. However, Miri wondered whether it was better to go straight home tonight. She couldn't imagine the party picking up.

"Hey, you're squashing your elf wings." a male voice with a hint of an accent she wasn't able to identify could be heard from behind.

Surprised that somebody had made the effort to speak to her, she turned round and looked into a pair of bright blue eyes, framed by ash blond strands of hair that fell casually across his forehead under an Australian leather hat with its chinstrap dangling on his chest. In an instant, her eyes registered every detail, but happened to rest a bit longer on his chest that emerged from a faded shirt. The rolled-up sleeves revealed muscular forearms and made her wonder if the rest of the man was just as strong and well-defined. To match his hat, he was wearing a leather vest over his shirt and a knife under the belt of his tight jeans that promisingly hugged his slim hips and muscle-packed thighs.

Unconsciously, she licked her full lips.

"And? Have you seen enough?" the stranger asked, amused. But in the meantime, he himself had taken the opportunity to explore her from top to bottom. Her fair blond locks fell closely round a heart-shaped face and contrasted well with her black eyelashes that framed a pair of nearly dark blue eyes. She wasn't very tall and of a delicate figure, but padded out in just the right places. She definitely fitted his picture of an elf. Through her thick eyelashes, she gave him a teasing look.

"You forgot your crocodile."

"My crocodile?"

"Well, as in 'Crocodile Dundee'. I suppose that was the idea, wasn't it?"

He looked at his outfit and had to admit she had a point.

"One of the best costumes I've seen tonight. My compliments."

'Costumes?' he asked himself, irritated. This was his work gear! Only that he had dug out a clean set of clothes on this occasion. He briefly looked at the other guests. Of course, now he remembered. An old friend had picked him up from the airport and brought him straight here, saying something about a fancy dress party. That would explain the elf wings, too. Thinking, he rubbed his unshaven chin. It seemed the long flight had exhausted him more than he allowed himself to admit. "I'm Matt." he introduced himself, took a step towards her and rested his hand on the wall, just above her head. Now that they were almost touching each other, he noticed she had a wonderful fragrance about her. Miri felt a tingle in her stomach. "And who are you, my butterfly lady?"

"I'm simply a butterfly lady." she whispered before wrapping her arms around his neck and kissing him. The intensity of that kiss took them both by surprise. He took a step back to break the body contact.

"Whoa." he said, slightly out of breath, and added in that soft accent she had by now recognised as being Australian: "I didn't know butterflies were like dynamite."

Miri, who had managed to get her raging emotions under control for a moment, asked casually: "Shall we find somewhere less crowded? Or are you still looking for your crocodile...?" She left the challenge hanging in the air between them. Finally, he gave in to temptation and pulled her close for another fiery kiss. "A lady's wish should be my command. That's what they told me." he whispered in her ear. With a cheeky glint in her eyes, she replied: "I love men with good manners." Then she took his hand and led him away from the party to a quieter part of the large house.

The next morning, she woke up disorientated between rumpled sheets. When the memory of the night before came slowly back to her sleepy mind, she broke into a smile and stretched like a satisfied cat. She had been right. Spot on. Her chance encounter last night was a direct import from Australia, although his roots were in Switzerland. But that was all she knew about him. Miri grinned to herself. They hadn't wasted too much time talking. Where was he anyway? She looked around. His clothes were gone. The only sign that last night had not been a dream was a single pink rose and a sheet of paper on the bedside table. She reached over to take the two items. Dreaming, she closed her eyes and smelled the rose. She knew it had been part of the party decoration. But obviously, he had made the effort of finding one and coming back to leave it here. She took the sheet of paper and scanned the text.

"Good morning, butterfly lady. - Thank you for an unforgettable night. Sorry I had to leave so early. You look cute when you're asleep..."

He had added a telephone number with an area code she did not recognise and signed "Matt". How sweet. She turned the note over in her hand, not knowing what to do with it. So far, her adventures had mostly involved guys who made sure not to leave a phone number the next morning. On the one hand, she found such an attitude annoying, but on the other, it had served her well so far, as she had to admit. Whatever. Now she would have breakfast and then go home. In an exuberant mood, she jumped out of bed and put on her casual clothes. She just stuffed last night's outfit into the holdall and, without her noticing, left his note between the sheets. Miri grabbed her battered elf wings and left the room without looking back.

34

"Phew, finally." Kaja got up and stretched. She looked round the storage room. Yes, she had been busy these past few weeks. There had been lots of interest in her old flat and she had eventually found a young couple her landlord was happy to accept as new tenants. With the certainty that they would appreciate her old home just as much as she did, leaving it behind had been easier than anticipated. Then she had paid Mémé another visit to collect the basic set of equipment she needed to get started. Soon, she would have to keep her own stock and source her own supplies of wax and all those other things she needed, but for the time being she was well sorted. She didn't even know yet how many candles and fragrance sets she would be able to sell, but she was optimistic. As a special treat, Mémé had given her a prime selection of dried herbs and hand distilled essential oils, which Kaja had just placed on the storage shelves. Everything was clean and clearly labelled. Luc had also given her a surprise, in the form of a complete candle drawer, manufactured to Mémé's exact specifications. She wiped her hands on the stained but incredibly comfortable, loose-fitting trousers and looked to the ceiling, trying to find a spot for the drawer to be installed, ideally as close as possible to the old-fashioned wood-burning stove.

She had to grin as she thought back to the varied reactions she had received when her friends saw the stove for the first time. The more romantically inclined Miri had been instantly inspired to create enthusiastic advertising slogans, such as "indulge in grandma's secret fragrances, hand-crafted over an eternal flame" or "treasures to tease your senses, manufactured the traditional way", whereas Sierra had turned up her nose and asked quite pragmatically if she had ever heard of a fabulous invention called electricity which was supposed to save you the wood-chopping. Kaja had just shrugged her shoulders. Perhaps they both had a point. But in fact, the stove was well suited to her needs, at least for now. It had to be moved from its original place in the kitchen, where Mathias, Sierra's brother, had taken next to no time to replace the unsightly unit with a brand-new modern one. And all that for an unbeatable price. Mathias had made himself indispensable over the past few weeks and carried out various renovations. Not only was she the proud owner of a replacement kitchen now, but also of a new bathroom. She had even learned how to brighten up old parquet flooring using an electric sander. All she had left to do now was to paint the walls. This was planned for the afternoon and Miri and Sierra had promised to come and help.

"Whatever they meant by 'afternoon'. Here they are already." Lance informed her. He had been hanging around in the studio and seen them coming from one of the roof lights. "It looks like you've lost track of time and forgotten your lunch." he complained.

"Really?" Kaja replied unfazed and wiped the fifteen foot worktop just one more time with a wet cloth, despite it being spotless already. The workbench occupied almost the full length of the storage room and was Kaja's pride and joy. It wouldn't stay so clean and immaculate for long, she thought with a tinge of sadness. But that couldn't be helped if she was going to work with molten wax.

"Yes, really. You must look after yourself." Lance woke her from her thoughts.

"Don't worry, Lance." Miri greeted him, brandishing a bag which obviously contained food.

"Just in time to feed the beasts." Sierra confirmed.

"Is there something for me as well? I'm starving." he said with a meaningful glance at Kaja.

"Why don't you go and find yourself a virgin to cook for you instead of getting on my nerves." Kaja complained, but gratefully accepted one of the obligatory tuna rolls offered to her.

Sierra giggled. "You remind me of the goat in 'The Wishing-Table'." she said to the dragon.

"The goat?" he asked irritated. "I'm not a goat. In fact, dragons have goats for dinner." he explained offended.

Kaja waved at him. "Don't take it too seriously, Lance. It was a reference to a fairytale. I'll tell you later." Still suspicious, but somewhat calmed down, Lance accepted her explanation.

Later, Sierra made the ultimate peace offering by throwing him a miniature bottle of Jägermeister. "Now look at that! I could get used to it." He mumbled as he skilfully caught it in his claws.

"Be quiet." Sierra grumbled. "Or it'll be the last one you get." Kaja and Miri gave each other a knowing grin, pointedly ignored by Sierra. The two of them had noticed before that Sierra often tried to appear much feistier than she actually was. "Can we get on with our paint job? I'll have to be home soon to muck out the stables." Sierra asked impatiently and threw her screwed-up sandwich paper straight into the waste bin that stood in the middle of the room.

"Slave driver." Miri mumbled, but nevertheless got up and pulled Kaja to her feet as well.

Kaja had spent most of the previous evening protecting all important areas in the living room with masking tape and spreading a large dust sheet on the floor. This meant they were ready to go now. She had chosen an ivory white emulsion for this room. All three of them working, they made good progress, even with Kaja stopping from time to time to look out of the window, dreaming. The other two watched her and gave each other meaningful looks. After they had finished the first coat, Miri went to the kitchen to make tea. While she was waiting for the kettle to boil, Sierra pestered Kaja with questions about the other rooms. "Which one do you want to do next?"

"Maybe the bedroom." Kaja answered, absent-mindedly.

"And what's your choice of colour?"

"I had a very pale yellow in mind, almost white... wait, I'll show you the sample." She got a bundle of colour charts and fanned it out.

"Have you bought the paint already?"

"Erm, yes, the pots are over there." She pointed to a small room that adjoined the kitchen and was normally used as a larder. Then she looked at Sierra suspiciously and asked: "Why do you want to know all this? Are you worried I'm being too extravagant with my expenses?"

"Oh, goodness, no, I didn't mean it like that." Sierra seemed honestly shocked.

At that point, Miri came back to the room with the tea. "We have a surprise for you." she explained. "That's why she's asking all these questions."

"A surprise?" Now Kaja was completely lost.

"Yes, exactly, a surprise." Miri confirmed.

Not knowing what to make of it, Kaja looked at her dragon sisters who stood either side of her. "Now put away that paint brush and sit down here." Sierra ordered her.

Confused, Kaja put down the tool and wiped her paint-covered hands on the trousers. "OK, I'm all ears. What are you two up to?"

"How's Tim?" Miri skilfully ignored the question.

"I don't know and I don't care." Kaja answered evasively.

"She's lying." Lance, who had just joined them, butted in. "Just ask her what's been on her mind all afternoon." the dragon prompted Miri.

And Miri, duly following his advice, asked: "And what were you thinking of when we were painting and you were staring into space?"

Kaja blushed. "I was thinking... about my candles and stuff." she answered lamely. "But this is ridiculous. It's none of your business!" she suddenly rebelled.

"Now keep calm. That's where you're wrong. We're your sisters and we're here to talk. About everything. You can't just bottle it up and be unhappy on your own." Sierra put the record straight.

"How am I supposed to know? I've never had a sister. And I'm not unhappy!"

"Oh, that's my department. I do have a brother and I can tell you all what it's like having a sibling." Sierra joked in order to lighten the mood.

"OK, you may not be too unhappy. At the moment, it's all going well for you." Miri agreed. "But we think it may be much easier for you to concentrate on starting up the business once you have cleared the air with Tim."

Defiantly, Kaja looked out of the window.

"Hey, Kaja, just consider for a moment if your sisters are right." Lance implored her and gave her a gentle shake.

"And how am I supposed to do that? It's a great idea, but Tim's not here. He could be anywhere in the world right now. And that's the root of the problem." She pulled at her hair in frustration.

"What if you paid him a visit? Just one last holiday before getting fully engrossed in your candle business?"

"You can have a good heart-to-heart and then come back, totally relaxed."

"And they lived happily ever after... You don't even know if it's going to work. I may come back even more frustrated than I already am."

Miri shook her head. "I don't think so. The outcome may not be great, but at least you can tell him your concerns and deal with the situation. At the moment, you're just wasting too much energy with all those what-ifs. Burying your head in the sand is never going to work."

For a while, neither of them said a word until Kaja broke the silence. "And how do you think this is going to work? You sound as if you have a plan already?"

Miri looked at Sierra. "Hm, well, almost. Sierra and I could carry on decorating for you. We'll finish as much as we can so that you're on schedule when you get back. We weren't able to find Tim, but Simon should be able to advise. What do you think, Sierra?"

"Are you serious?" Kaja was in two minds. On the one hand, she wanted to be angry with the other two for interfering with her life. On the other hand, it was a very generous offer.

"Of course they are serious." Lance nudged her. "Now go on and give Simon a call."

Kaja trundled off into the Kitchen to phone Simon.

"Do you think we're doing the right thing?" Miri whispered to Sierra.

"I don't know. But we're not forcing her. It's her own free decision."

Lance cleared his throat.

"What's the matter? Something wrong?"

"Well, her decision is not free if she's being pushed into it by three friends."

"Hang on, I thought you were on our side?"

"I am. And I agree she should go. In fact, I think she must go. But it's not her free decision. We're partly responsible for it."

"Oh well, so be it then. She's got to go. I can't bear the drama any longer." Sierra insisted.

"I heard that." Kaja was just coming back from the kitchen to the living room.

"So when are you going to Iceland?"

"Going to Iceland would be nice." Kaja moaned. "But he was only there for two weeks."

"And where's he now?" the other two asked in unison.

"In the Pantanal."

"Panta-what?"

"The Pantanal, a huge wetland area, mainly located in Brazil."

"I thought that trip was planned for much later." Miri commented, confused.

"Apparently he had mixed up his dates for the dry and wet seasons and" she looked away, "was quite happy that the trip had to be brought forward. He must have been seriously hurt that I broke off all contact with him..." she went silent.

"Well done." Sierra patted her shoulder.

"You think so? I'm not sure..."

"Of course you did the right thing." Miri now joined in as well. "It can never be wrong to listen to your feelings. And if your feeling said you needed some distance, that's what you had to do. But now it's time for a change in direction." she concluded resolutely.

"You're right, both of you. I must stop giving my feelings second priority. Now let's finish this room and then I have a trip to Brazil to organise, before the rainy season sets in."

35

How had she managed to end up in the the middle of nowhere again? Kaja asked herself for the fifty-seventh time in the past ten minutes and, enervated, rested her head on the dusty steering wheel. The car's croaky old horn must have thought this was an emergency and did its best to give her an audible shock. A few birds flew off, squawking disapprovingly. Despite her exhaustion, she had to smile. They were bright blue hyacinth macaws. It had been a miracle she had made it this far. Yesterday, she had arrived in Poconé, the northern gateway to the Pantanal. From there, she had to take a long, partially maintained road into the centre of the wetlands. 'Partially maintained' was a fairly appropriate way to describe the state of the road, she thought. The annual floods made it nearly impossible to keep it in a satisfactory condition. And this was Brazil, where people speak Portuguese and not Spanish as she quickly discovered. But it turned out that the language wasn't her biggest problem. She had met Raoul, her local guide, at the agreed location. Simon had booked him through a travel agent to take her to the camp. So far so good. She had instantly got on well with the local expert, even though they often had to communicate using sign language. He had introduced her to the eight members of his family and invited her to a party last night. Of course she had been happy to accept the invitation. Although tired from the long journey, she had very much enjoyed the social gathering with all its laughing, dancing, eating and drinking. It had helped take her mind off the imminent reunion with Tim. Kaja didn't even know if he would be pleased to see her. She had not announced her visit which, with hindsight, she should have. She sighed. It was too late now. There was definitely no mobile signal out here, never mind a European one.

She took a sip from the lukewarm contents of the water bottle and used the hem of her t-shirt to wipe the sweat off her forehead. Raoul had obviously had one drink too many last night. This morning, he hadn't turned up as agreed. She had even gone to his home, but all she could get out of his wife was that he was still asleep. What a great start! So she had gone to a car dealer and hired a dilapidated old banger to make an attempt at continuing the journey on her own. It hadn't gone very smoothly, though. Too often, she had to swerve and avoid animals or potholes. Only a few miles earlier she had to stop all together as Mama Capybara and her family had decided to roll in the dust in front of her and couldn't be persuaded to move on, neither through good words nor by angry tooting or desperate swearing.

At least the landscape was breathtakingly beautiful, Kaja had to admit. Now, at the end of October, plants flowering in bright yellow and deep red livened up the scenery that was normally dominated by green and sandy colours. She tried to ease the tension in her shoulders and got out of the car. This was where she had to take a turn. She had reached kilometre 63 of the Transpantaneira, the route that was originally intended to link the north with the south of the Pantanal. But it had never been completed. Up to this point, the road was fairly serviceable, but further on, it was said to become very patchy which, as she was told, was due to the annual floods. Unsure what to do, she inspected the narrow road ahead which looked more like a dirt trail. She didn't dare take the car down there for fear the axles of the decrepit vehicle might give way at any time. They had been making funny noises already. From the branches of nearby trees, she could hear the aras calling. They had come back as soon as they realised they were not in danger. But she wasn't in the mood to admire all these natural wonders. Not before she got hold of Tim. She was also worried about the impending rainy season, which was due to start in a few days time.

'What on earth possessed me?' she thought enervated. Tim was likely to come home in a few weeks anyway. She couldn't imagine him carrying on with his photographs once the floods started. Having come to a decision, she went back to the car and got her backpack. She took another sip from the water bottle before stashing it away in the luggage and putting on her brand-new baseball cap for sun protection. At the junction, there was a weathered sign pointing in the direction of the last fazenda on the way. As far as she was aware, this was where Tim had his base camp. "Let's get moving." she encouraged herself and started walking. After all, she still had a fair number of miles to cover.

Three hours later, she was still walking and in a foul mood. At the fazenda, which she had reached about 4 miles down the road, there had only been a single local man, who spoke a language Kaja didn't recognise and which she assumed to be a strong local dialect of Portuguese. The few phrases she had managed to learn on the flight didn't get her very far in that conversation. At least, she had been able to make it clear she was looking for Tim, the quiet photographer, and he had scribbled down a rudimentary map to point out where he was most likely to be found. What that map did not show were all the small creeks that now, at the start of the rainy season, only carried little water and the roots of huge trees that often forced her into detours. Presumably, he had explained all this in a barrage of words. But now she was not even sure she was anywhere near the route marked out on that tiny piece of paper.

"Just pretend you are on the right track." a shiny blue figure suddenly said, hanging from a branch of a tree.

"Are you going monkeys? What're you doing here?" she wanted to know gloomily.

"There's no way I'd allow you to get lost in the swamps." Lance protested.

"But you took your time to turn up here." she snorted indignantly.

"Hey, and I thought you needed time on your own to think.'

She sighed. "Yes, you're right. Otherwise we would have carried on bickering."

"You see." he said triumphantly. "And now you'd better keep moving or we won't make it before the sun goes down." She followed him through the varied scenery hoping the dragon knew where he was taking her.

As suddenly as Lance had turned up, he disappeared again. She was standing on top of a small hill, only a few feet high, looking down on a narrow peninsula with a small structure on it, not dissimilar to a hunting hide. The sun was reflecting in the water, dazzling her eyes. Somebody, hopefully Tim, was crawling along the shore and - well, what was he doing there? Curious and also a bit apprehensive, she sneaked closer to get a better look of the situation.

"Yes, darling, you're doing fine." he laughed. "Give me all you've got. Don't dive too soon..." his pleasant voice sounded both caring and amused. "Perfect, now show me your belly..."

What in the world was he taking photographs off? Kaja asked herself and hoped she hadn't come all the way to catch him taking shots of Miss Brazil 2012. She squinted.

"Do you want to take root here or what?" Lance, who had turned up again, whispered to her. "Go on, run to him." he encouraged her and gave her a gentle push before disappearing into thin air.

Hesitantly, she made her way down the small hill. A twig broke under her step, followed by a splashing sound in the water. Irritated, Tim turned round. She froze, and so did he.

'What if he isn't pleased to see me?'

"Kaja?" he asked in disbelief, a broad grin slowly spreading across his face.

"That's the name in my passport." she tried to cover her insecurity and smiled at him shyly.

He carefully put down his camera and walked towards her. Slowly at first, but then with increasing speed. Kaja started running as well, until she almost tumbled down the embankment and landed in his arms. 'Finally!' she thought. 'I've been missing this homely feeling so much.' After they had hugged each other for a minute, he held her at arm's length. "And I thought I'd messed up for good. I'm so sorry, Kaja."

"I sincerely hope you are." she gave him a playful punch on the nose. "You know me. You knew what my greatest fear was. That's what hurt me most."

He avoided looking into her eyes. "I know, that's what I'm so sorry about. But..." he paused for a moment. "I was even more afraid you'd never agree to see me in the first place if you knew I was due on a trip so soon."

"So, mission accomplished." she commented and couldn't help putting a tiny hint of sarcasm in her remark.

"But I do hope you haven't come all this way to throw that in my face?" he asked, desperate to salvage the situation.

Despite still being angry, she had to laugh. "I thought I'd pop round to have a little chat about how the two of us can become more compatible."

"Become compatible..." he grinned and brushed her hair with his lips."That's a good start." He closed his eyes and rested his forehead against hers. "You don't know how much it means to me you've come halfway round the world to find me." And then he finally kissed her.

"Don't you want to introduce your friends to me?" she asked when they finally managed to let go of each other.

"Hm, let me think." he said and gave her a long look.

She followed the direction of his eyes. Her outfit had become quite rough and dusty. She knew what he was thinking. "Don't you dare call me Ragamuffin again or I'll be gone in a flash."

The corners of his mouth started to twitch and they both broke into a liberating laugh. "Come on, then. Perhaps they've got over the shock and are ready to resurface."

Two days later, they were enjoying the evening sun for one last time, watching the giant otter family play. These beautiful, entertaining animals, which only live in the wetlands of South America, had been the main focus of Tim's trip.

"Their habitat has been more and more reduced in the past few decades, which now makes them an endangered species. They live in groups and enjoy each other's company playing. Once you find them, which in itself is rather difficult, they're easy to watch. In contrast to their European cousins, giant otters are diurnal animals." Tim had explained to her on their first day. For him, it was important to use his photo reports to document the disappearing wonders of the world and to sensitise people to them. Kaja was already looking forward to his next exhibition.

It had been raining for much of the past two days, which the otters apparently enjoyed. Tomorrow, she and Tim would fly back to Switzerland. But now, they were watching in silence as the small animals tried to outdo each other in their daring antics. It was almost as if they sensed there was an audience. Unnoticed by Tim, Lance came and sat down next to Kaja.

"Hi, my dearest dragon."

"Hi, Kaja" For a moment there was silence between them.

"Is it time to say goodbye?" Kaja guessed.

"Yes, but not forever. I'll come and visit you whenever I can."

"Well, I do hope that'll be more often than you're seen at Mémé's." she joked, although she felt a tinge of sadness.

He hesitated. "You've arrived now. You've found yourself. And it'll be the beginning of new adventures. I'm sure you'll do very well. And you're not alone. You've found your sisters."

"So I'm no longer your protégée?"

"No, you're my friend. And should you ever need me, just call."

Despite the tears filling up her eyes, she had to smile. "Thank you so much!" she said to him telepathically as she watched him, for one last time, disappear in a puff of blue sparkle.

"Shall we go back to the fazenda?" Tim interrupted her thoughts.

She turned towards him and smiled. "Yes, let's go."

*

A word from the author

As you may have noticed, I feel very passionate about the fauna of our beautiful planet. You can find a list of endangered species on the Internet under http://www.iucnredlist.org/details/18711

If you want to know more about spirit bears, I can recommend "Der Regenwald der weißen Bären", a German book published by Haupt Verlag, Bern. Klaus Pommerenke, a psychologist, has been watching and photographing white bears for years and has written this book about them and their habitat. In the August 2011 issue of National Geographic you can find an interesting article by Bruce Barcott about the Great Bear Rainforest, including several amazing pictures of the Spirit Bears taken by Paul Nicklen.

I would like to thank team sabìa brazilinfo whose detailed description of the Pantanal has been very helpful. Unfortunately, I have never been there myself, but numerous documentaries about the region have fuelled my fascination with the Pantanal and I hope to have an opportunity to go there soon and explore it myself.

Thanks

I would like to thank my parents who have roused and nurtured my interest in language, particularly in the written word, by providing me with a constant supply of reading material. My gratitude is also due to all my friends, who supported and encouraged me, from the outset, on my journey into the world of authorship.

I tried to keep geographical and zoological descriptions as close to reality as possible. The same cannot be said about locations and buildings, which often only exist in my imagination. So please, do not try to find a Zoological and Botanical Institute of the University of Bern. As far as I am aware, it does not exist.

Preview *The Dragon Child* - coming soon

I hope you have enjoyed reading this book and are eagerly anticipating the second volume of my trilogy. On the following pages, you can find the first chapter of "The Dragon Child". In the course of this book, the dragon sisters become ever closer. Miri in particular is faced with some difficult decisions and is grateful for the support she gets from her friends.

Have fun reading the preview.

Translator's note

At this point, I would like to step out of the shadows and add a few personal words, too. First of all, I need to thank Virginia for entrusting me with the translation of her debut novel. It has been an inspiring, sometimes challenging, but always enjoyable task that I could not have accomplished without her input, as well as the patient and supportive help from my wife Zora and my good friend and colleague Niall Hoskin. We do hope that we have managed to capture Virginia's enthusiasm for her story and would love to see many more of our English readers join the ever-growing dragon community at https://www.facebook.com/authorvirginiafox

Preview – The Dragon Child (Book 2 of the Dragon Sisters Trilogy)

Holger Laux
Dundry, UK
August 2013

1

Already out of breath, Miri rushed up the stairs to her flat, two steps at a time. With shaking hands, she unlocked the door, pushed it open and promptly fell over Chili, her red-striped Maine Coon tom who had obviously been waiting for her. "Heavens, Chili, not now! I don't have time for you." Offended, the cat turned and strutted off, his tail held high. Of course, not without giving her a disapproving look. 'Have it your way.' he thought grumpily. If she didn't want to know his news, it was her fault. Let her find the visitor herself.

But Miri didn't notice anything. Right now, her mind was on other things. She was searching frantically for something in the chemist's carrier bag she had dropped when she bumped into Chili. Where was that stupid thing? Now her mobile phone started ringing. She looked at it. No wonder, it was her uncle. She put it on silent. Apparently, he had finally noticed she wasn't in her usual workplace, the store room at the back of his bookshop. She had left without signing out. After all, she could hardly do what she had to do in the toilet of the shop. Ah, there it was. She took the shrink-wrapped box and went into the bathroom. 'Who in their right mind invented such awkward packaging?' she moaned to herself as she was struggling to break the plastic open. Finally, she got the contents out. She quickly scanned the enclosed leaflet and followed the usage instructions. So, all she could do now was wait. Even after just a few seconds, the prescribed five minutes seemed to become an eternity. Enervated, she left the bathroom and started pottering around in the living room. Not that moving things from A to B and back made any difference. When she realised, she stopped her fruitless attempt at clearing up. Hoping enough time had passed, she looked at the clock on the living room table. Still two minutes to go. Perhaps she should give Kaja a ring? But she immediately dismissed the thought. She didn't want to be engaged in a conversation when the result was due. In a last-ditch attempt to find some distraction, she went over to the window and looked down at the street four floors below. While her life might be changing forever within the next two minutes, the lives of those pedestrians, cyclists and motorists would go on as usual. Again, the mobile interrupted her thoughts. This time, its vibration signalled that the five minutes were over. Now the moment of truth had come, she was suddenly no longer in a hurry to get back to the bathroom. 'Pull yourself together.' she cursed herself. Usually, she wasn't the dithering type. With desperate determination, she marched back into the small cubicle. Carefully, as if the item resting on that ceramic rim could bite, she approached the washbasin and picked up the plastic stick. But without looking at it, she put it down again and nervously read through the leaflet one more time. One visible line means a negative result, two lines mean a positive one. 'Negative, positive, it all depends on which way you look at it.' she thought dismissively. Then she looked across again at the test strip on the washbasin. She gathered all her courage and read the result. Two lines! For a moment, she stood as if lightning had struck. Sweat appeared on her skin and her eyes filled with tears. She slumped against the wall behind her and slowly slid down until she sat on the floor. 'Why? Why me? I'm pregnant!' She sobbed quietly as she tried to take in the news. How did it happen? She had always been so careful. And why had it happened now, just as she had promised herself she would stop chasing useless men and get a grip on her life? Empty-eyed, she stared at the bathroom cupboard. And who was the father? She'd been a good girl recently, hadn't been out. She pressed her hands to her burning cheeks and suddenly remembered the Halloween party almost six weeks ago. She was so immersed in her pain that she didn't hear Chili scratching frantically at the door to get in, nor did she notice the nursery rhyme somebody hummed close by. Desperately, she was trying to gather her recollections. 'Matt' had been the name of her chance encounter, she remembered. At least, he had seemed a decent man. And a handsome one. And rather talented in bed. Alarmed, she realised that the memory of that fateful night made the heat in her stomach radiate out to other parts of her body. Oh no, lustful thoughts were the last thing she needed right now. One could clearly see where this was leading to. A gloomy premonition told her that the fun part of her life was over now. At least it seemed to be with what she had just found out. 'Oh damn, what am I going to do?' She sniffled and pushed herself up in order to dampen her face with cold water. She looked in the mirror and was surprised to still find her familiar face with its short white curls and dark blue eyes looking back at her. Admittedly, her skin was blotchy and her eyes bloodshot from crying. She put a wet flannel on her forehead and enjoyed the pleasant coolness. What was that? Had she put on some music in the confused state of mind she was in while waiting for the five minutes to pass? Not that she could remember. Irritated, she removed the flannel from her face and tried to listen. The song was called Bayushki Bayu and was a nursery rhyme her mother used to sing when she was little. Was she hallucinating? She looked into the mirror again. Behind her, a pink and purple mist was wafting through the room. Abruptly, she turned round. "Lance?" she whispered nervously.

"No, I'm not Lance." a voice said in her head. "Don't you remember me?"

"Maxi?" she stammered in disbelief. "But how..." She couldn't finish the sentence as she broke into tears again. 'It must be those stupid pregnancy hormones already.' she thought and realised her mood was hovering dangerously between wanting to cry and wanting to laugh hysterically.

"Shush..." the huge dragoness comforted her and took her in her arms, which were covered in shiny scales. Miri immediately felt herself transported back to childhood. Back then, Maxi had always been there to ease the pain. Now, it made the lump in her throat grow even bigger.

Just like Lance, the dragon who had been with Kaja recently, Maxi was an astral being. You could describe dragons as some sort of guardian angels. However, these creatures had very much a mind of their own and were not afraid to voice their opinion whether you wanted to hear it or not, as well as the ability to appear and disappear at any convenient or inconvenient opportunity. Maxi had been with Miri throughout her childhood, but then had suddenly disappeared after a traumatic experience. So she had been all the more happy to meet Kaja and Lance. Seeing Lance on Kaja's passenger seat had been so fascinating that she had promptly crashed her bicycle into Kaja's car. Luckily, no harm was done. Lance had been seriously shocked that she could see him. This ability was normally restricted to his protégée and perhaps a close relative. He went to get advice from the dragon council and as it turned out, every few centuries three women form a close relationship and can see each other's dragons. They were called dragon sisters. That's how Kaja came to be her best friend, together with Sierra, the third one in their circle. Sierra had never seen a dragon before, but as she was a pragmatic person, she had quickly accepted Lance's existence. Perhaps it had been helpful that she was an avid animal lover, too, and liked nothing better than to look after and protect anything on four legs.

"But what are you doing here?" Miri eventually wanted to know when she had calmed down, helped by the hummed tune of the nursery rhyme.

"You needed me." Maxi replied, somewhat evasively, it seemed to Miri.

"I've needed you all those years. Why did you disappear from my life so suddenly?" she enquired without even trying to make it sound less like an accusation.

"I can explain it to you later. At the moment, you just need some looking after."

"Erm, no, sorry, it can't wait. I can look after myself very well, just as I have done all my life, thank you very much. But I do need to know why you turn up at this very moment after going AWOL for so many years."

"I can see how well you can look after yourself." Maxi commented, pointing to the pregnancy test in the washbasin.

Miri ignored the dig and looked straight at the dragoness.

Maxi threw her clawed paws in the air and burst out: "OK, if you must know: I'm a mother-and-child dragon."

"What's that supposed to mean? I don't get it..." Now it was Miri's turn to look at the washbasin and its contents. "Is that..."

"Exactly, that's why I'm here."

"Does that mean you've never really been my dragon but Mama's?" Miri tried to make sense.

"You can't say it like that. In theory, I'm there for the mother, but as soon as the child is born, I have an additional protégée and give it more and more attention."

"But if I was your protégée, why did you leave me when my parents died?" Miri stared at the purple creature, completely lost.

"Oh, darling, it wasn't my decision, or only partially. MandC dragons are bound by the link between mother and child. That link was broken when your mother died. Maybe the dragon council would have allowed an exception, but I decided not to apply for one."

"Why not?" Miri was rather shocked. And disappointed. And sad.

"I knew from the few visits we paid to your uncle and aunt that they are rather narrow-minded. I didn't want you to get into trouble. If you had started telling stories of dragons, they would have been quite annoyed, perhaps even given you a good hiding."

"I got those in any case. I regularly managed to upset them all on my own." Miri felt sick.

"I'm so sorry, Miri. Even dragons are not perfect. I tried my best."

She reached over to the door to open it and finally let Chili in. He gave Maxi a gracious nod and started to nuzzle at Miri's legs. She picked him up, held him against her chest and buried her nose in his silky fur. Chili started a loud purr. Miri's head was spinning. It was all too much in one go. Somehow, her well-established life had just come crashing down. She noticed her asthma coming back, opened the bathroom cupboard and was relieved to find a spare inhaler. It had been a long time since she had last needed one. She used it and was relieved to feel her lungs fill with air again. Phew, too much stress was definitely not healthy.

"I need to be alone now." Miri said to her re-emerged dragon. "There's a lot of things I have to sort out."

With that, she turned and left Maxi in the bathroom. Although she was tempted to slam the door, she resisted. She still treasured her childhood memories of Maxi too much. Especially since she had come back now. Slightly dizzy from the emotional roller-coaster of the past hour, she shook her head. With Chili happily resting in her arms, obviously enjoying his special treatment, she went to her bedroom.

*

www.ingramcontent.com/pod-product-compliance
Lightning Source LLC
Chambersburg PA
CBHW031415240626
47154CB00001B/51